PERCHED
^{ON}_{THE} PERIPHERY

PERCHED
^{ON}_{THE} PERIPHERY

JHARNA BANERJI

PARTRIDGE

To order additional copies of this book, contact
Partridge India
000 800 10062 62
orders.india@partridgepublishing.com

www.partridgepublishing.com/india

CONTENTS

To my late husband, Ogo,
who believed I could and would write

ACKNOWLEDGEMENTS

A very big thank you to my late father, Wing Commander Sachindra Nath Chuckerbutty MBE, for having passed some of his fabulous sense of humour on to me. And to my late mother, Mrs Sushama Chuckerbutty, for having generously gifted me some of her creative genes. A still bigger one to my late husband Air Commodore Ajit Kumar Banerji for having bought me a typewriter, believing that I could and would write, though at that point in time all I'd ever written were love letters to him during the separations that a serviceman's career enforced upon us. And last but not the least, to my two sons, Monu (Sujit) and Shonu (Shumeet), and their respective wives Shoto and Della, my eldest grandson Indro and his darling wife Katie for having taken *Perched on the Periphery* out of my laptop and placing it where it is today.

1 BEING NEEDED IS SUCH HEADY WINE

Her heart taking a couple of somersaults then settling down to a series of thudding beats had floundered along with her faltering feet. Peering into the gloom, she had looked intensely in the direction from where the sound of his coming had fallen upon her ears. She knew he was there, but where? And then joy flooding through her entire being, she had spied his familiar figure standing across the chasm of their separating rooftops. But why, she wondered, was he looking at her with such an enquiring, mischief-laden look?

What was he up to, she thought, as eyes a-twinkle below a set of eyebrows quirking upwards, he asked, 'Where are your props today?'

Eyes flying wide open with consternation, she exclaimed, 'Props! Which? What props?'

'Your book of poems and . . . all those . . . all those other tomes that you carry around, what else?' Before she could so much as open her mouth to give a fitting rejoinder, he had veered away from her so-called props and abruptly stated, 'I'm coming over.'

Alarmed, she had croaked, 'But you can't.'

'How you prattle on, of course I—'

'No, you can't, because this roof is not mine and *they* may not allow you on *their* roof.'

'Now let me ask, however have you managed to get us into such a ridiculous spot? Do you really want me to believe that *we* have to get permission, from some sundry creatures that you vaguely call "they"?'

'It happened because of you.'

'Because of me? 'I can see that you are living in a house and the house has a roof. So . . .'

'The house is not mine, so how can the roof be mine? Tell me.' 'That's logical enough.' And as if losing interest in the exchange, he had turned around and started walking away.

Seeing him leave, bereft, she had stretched out a hand to hold him back. And then out of a cloudless sky, water had come cascading down upon her. Oh! How piercing the raindrops were, invasive and icy-cold, and she had cried out a strangled 'Please don't go, Dipto . . . it's raining . . . you'll get wet.'

A rivulet of cold water running along her thighs had forced her to open her eyes. She must have fallen asleep in the chair where she had sat down, a book in hand. Her back was aching and her mouth had gone dry. What was Prodipto doing here with her today? Yes, what was Pilot Officer Prodipto Kumar Roy doing here today? A tremor of something like apprehension had coursed through the pit of her stomach and moved into her heart.

She had risen, picked up the fallen glass, and gone in search of some water. Thirst quenched, she had purposefully moved to a chest of drawers placed directly across the room. Bringing out a photograph nestling there within the folds of her clothing, she had passed a questioning look upon it, then, holding it close to her heart, had moved to a window that overlooked the yard.

The moon was up in a sparkling clean sky! She had stood there and looked down upon the white of the yard now turned to silver. Squat somnolent shadows of the snow-shrouded trees dotted the terrain. Each blob of darkness staining the silvered surrounding was like a negative of the imprint of some ghost out of her past. It had given her an eerie feeling, and turning away from the window, she had quickly drawn the curtain across the windowpane. Even so, piercing the frail armour of the curtaining, a voice calling out persistently had fallen upon her ears. She heard the voice call out, 'Nandita, Nandita, Nandita.'

It was the quiet and subdued yet unforgettable voice of a very dominant mainstay of her young days. She recognised it instantly. The voice was that of Dadu. Startled, she stood transfixed; the voice of her grandfather, how could that be? She had heard that voice all through her childhood and growing years. It was an intrinsic part of her, not separable from that which made up her whole.

And once again, she had sensed rather than heard her name being called. Placing the photograph atop the dresser, she had pushed the drapes aside and peered out. How ridiculous, how could Dadu be out there in the cold? It was just not possible, yet defying reason and logic, she wanted to believe that the surrounding was imbued with his warming presence. She stood enthralled, captivated! It was such a long time since anyone had called out to her by her given name! So long that the unfamiliar sounds that made up her name reverberated within the confines of her brain like a long-forgotten tune that had been brought alive by the alchemy of aloneness and the magic of the moon's rays. And the tune, once wrought, escaping from her head, where it had been born, now ricocheted around like an echo within the four walls of her room. Catching hold of that echo, latching on to the trailing *anchal* of that tune, she had travelled ageless and unfettered through time and space. Inveigled by the magical illusory dimensions that had been created by her mind, once again a child, she had murmured, 'Dadu.'

But if fantasies are to hold sway, then no mirrors should come in their way. Nandita's eyes, alas, had proven far too restless. While ranging across the spheres, they had inadvertently flown open and stumbled upon as mundane a thing as the mirror that hung above the dresser in the room that was now her earthbound domain. One glance at the image reflected therein had shattered all her dreams and brought her tumbling down to earth. She had raised a tentative finger to her face and passed it across her forehead where a not so freshly ploughed furrow ran for the world at large to see. Her eyes, at one time large and luminous and alive, had looked back at her with a lacklustre stare. There was a time when those eyes alone had been enough to ensnare the one who had stood staring at her mischievously from across the next-door terrace at Bhabanipore. Time and tragedy had taken their toll and left their mark upon that pair of enticing eyes. And seated atop the dresser, his photograph, endowed with eternal youth, smiled on!

Shaking herself out of the past, she was drawn towards the compelling presence of the small clock by which she measured her life these days. Lost to the world, she had not realised that the world had moved on towards another day since she had last paid attention to it. She did not remember when, but it was somewhere along the way, in the not-too-distant past of this the journey of her life, that she had ceded her right to decision-making. She did not have the option open to her today to make a random telephone call of inquiry. She had stood a long while at a window fronting the tree-lined drive and had stared out into the hostile blackness that shrouded the entrance.

Her past had called out to her today but where was her present? Out somewhere on those frosty roads, but where? Eyes squeezed tight, palms folded together, she had faced the congregation of all her gods and goddesses.

She had no yardstick by which she could gauge whether her long-distance prayers from Saisborough, this township in faraway Illinois, had wings sturdy enough to fly across the vast tracts of land and endless stretches of turbulent waters that separated the two locations. Did they indeed arrive at the revered feet and reach into the ears of the one whose favours she sought?

Only when she had heard a mixed babble of muffled voices followed by the recognisable footsteps of her grandchildren charging past her door had she let her tensed-up body uncoil. Sagging from the released hold of anxiety, she had lain back as one drained of a soaring, searing fever. She had wanted to run out of her room to see them in the flesh, ask them how they were, but had not done so. Had she emerged from her room, she believed it would have been construed as fussing and interfering on her part. She remembered a jumble of past dialogues that had stayed her feet and sealed her lips forever. They took a near-fixed pattern.

'Thank God, you are home at last,' or something close enough to that, would have surely come spilling from her lips.

And her son facing her, wearing an indecipherable expression, a frown creasing his brow, would just as predictably ask, 'You're still awake, Ma . . . but why?'

'I was too worried to—'

'Worried? What was there to worry about?'

His reply so terse, so cut and dried, had hurt.

And a reluctant dialogue would have petered out into a dead end!

But the unsaid words 'You were never like this, my son, were you?' had sat as heavy as a stone upon her heart.

She had learned from many such failed encounters that for the sake of peace, a charade of sound sleep had best be kept up. The pretence had soon turned to reality, for genuine sleep had thankfully come in and blotted out all the dialogues, all the debates, and all the disputes that lay seething, surging, suffocating, within her mind.

And while she slept, on the prowl up in the skies, a warm, living, growling dark cloud had turned itself into a noiseless sheet of rain and had come down upon the earth. So soft and sibilant and secretive was its advent that she had not heard it arrive, and having marked the territory, soft-pawed it had gone away again without so much as a whisper having been heard. To her dismay, when Nandita awoke, she found that its short and unannounced stay had mauled the unblemished beauty of the landscape and left it looking unkempt, bedraggled, and wounded. The sparkling whiteness of yesterday had turned into a dull and drab, unlaundered and unbleached white, a mere apology of the colour that was. The huge Christmas card that the yard had been just a few hours ago had turned into an abject Cinderella back from the ball.

With the sudden passing away of her young and personable husband, Nandita had been cashiered and all her colours had been snatched away from her. And it was then that Nandita had understood the real meaning of the colour white.

Thakuma, her paternal grandmother, showing an immense degree of leniency, considering the rigidity of her outlook in matters of societal observances, overlooking the dress code for widows of pure white, had ordered one of the reluctant male members of the family to go and buy *ak dojon inchi paad* saris for Nandita. Nandita had looked upon her new wardrobe of a dozen saris with inch-wide black borders with a surge of overwhelming rage. Sorrow and anguish set aside, eyes burning bright with anger and unshed tears, she had bundled together the lot and thrust them back into the hands of the courier of this bounty.

'*Pherot neeye jaao,*' she said firmly, 'and bring back just half a dozen of the starkest of white *thaan* saris for me.' With a short laugh bordering on hysteria, she had whirled around and left the room. And from thereon, having attired herself in a swath of white as a mark of protest against the pernicious ways of society, she had gone her own way. And today, she, the selfsame person, had not had courage enough to pick up a phone to ask her son where he and his family were. She was getting very tired of this timorous Nandita, but what was she to do? 'Something, anything,' she told herself as she walked into the bathroom, clothes in hand. She was running late, she knew, but . . .

Nandita knew that she had woken at much the same time as she normally did, yet here she was, looking around for the shortfall in time as if it was a householder's bunch of keys. With a grimace, she conceded that once lost, time, unlike misplaced keys, was not retrievable.

An individual as time-bound as she had made herself was none too pleased with her tardiness, for among the few luxuries she allowed herself was her first cup of perfectly brewed tea. But this tea was very severely time-linked as it had to be made at a location that was as yet bereft of other unwelcome overwhelming aromas. And to meet that end, she had to make sure that come morning she was the first to make use of the kitchen. The clock told her that either Meeta or Tukun would have already come and gone from there. She would now have to confront the all-encompassing smell of coffee, which would surely be found percolating in a pot on the counter, a smell that her nostrils put on par with an alien takeover of a cultural unit whose mainstay for several centuries had been tied to the drinking of tea. She believed that a Bengali family's early hours of waking should be imbued in the fragrant aroma of Darjeeling, Nilgiri, or Lopchu tea. Any change in this habit was tantamount to an act of treason! But then, the younger generation . . . She had shrugged, crinkling her nose.

And as to how she felt regarding this matter of tea versus coffee that, over a period of time, had come to be one of the better-kept open secrets of the family, to be taken out, mulled over, laughed at, and to be put away out of sight once again.

'How finicky your mom has become, Tukun,' Meeta had laughingly commented one day.

'Mom?'

'*Theek aachey, theek aachey baba!* Fine! Mother, Ma, or whatever, happy?'

'She doesn't like coffee, that's all.'

'Big deal, tea is Bangali, and coffee is . . .'

'You and your assumptions.'

But, an assumption or whatever her son thought it was, it definitely was a fixation with Nandita. On descending to the lower floor, she had entered the kitchen. Though she found the place empty, there were yet sights and signs and smells everywhere that someone had visited the place ahead of her: the dishwasher stood door-ajar, gap-toothed from where a pair of mugs had been removed, news by the kilos spilled out of the heavyweight presence of the day's newspaper that lay in disarray alongside the remains of coffee making. The smell of freshly made coffee hung heavily in the air, and the aroma overwhelmed her senses. It would be a waste of effort on her part to go through the ordained ritual of tea making today. She could tread the entire path, but brewed heaven had gone out of her grasp this morning. Against all civilised norms of tea drinking, she made herself a cup with a teabag dipped in water on the boil for who knows how long.

As she sat sipping the tasteless turbid brew, spewing words, the little transistor seated atop the dishwasher fussily informed, warned, and advised. A splash of rainwater, it said, arriving in tandem with a sudden warm front had caused a thaw to set in sometime in the very small hours of the morning. The big voice within the little radio, continuing ponderously, stated that the vehicles out upon the streets were now skittering around like novice skaters out for the first time upon an ice rink. The populace was being warned of the treacherous intent of the snow that had, on being touched, turned to ice upon the roads. Like the snow, she too had turned to ice; frozen in time, she was trapped within this cold and eerie and lonesome zone from which she could not perceive any possibility of escape. What was the catalyst that had brought about this major change within her that had put her into this quandary? And she had remembered the genesis of this change: a letter.

How could she forget that afternoon when that life-changing missive had arrived? It was a gusty, feisty, grumbling, rumbling, thundering, blundering pre-monsoon day tearing its hair out in its haste to grow into a full-blown monsoon day. Tripping upon its own feet, it had lunged into a sari she had put out to dry in her little balcony. Buffeted around by the gusting moisture-laden wind, it had ballooned out in readiness for taking to its wings.

Faced with the spectacle of all her doors and windows banging their heads out frenetically, the sheets of the day's newspaper chasing one another around the ceiling, the curtains frenziedly flapping around and tying themselves into knots, Nandita had come out on the run onto the balcony and had grabbed the sari all set for flight with not a moment to spare, as her little *tulsi* plant in its tiny plastic planter accompanied by a palm-leaf *haath-pakha* and sundry other small objects had flown past her head and soon gone out of sight. She had tried to see where they had disappeared and had instead seen the postman struggling along the long and narrow strip of land pretending to be a garden that fronted the little set of lower-income-group flats where she had a place of her own. An uprooted tree just about missed him as he ploughed his way across, hanging onto his khaki cap with one hand and the precious cargo of mail in a canvas bag with the other. And while he was still a good distance away from a sheltered spot, the rain had come.

A smattering of small drops had been followed by huge plopping ones, which had soon turned into a deluge. And on coming in contact with the dry earth, the drops of rainwater had released the beautiful scent that the earth holds within its bosom to let go of when the rains first come. Nandita took in a lungful and then another and then another of the perfumed air as she contemplated upon the advent of *kal boishakhi*. How pretentious, how over-reaching was its arrival; even so, how one looked forward to coming face to face with it over and over again each year. A bolt of lightning ran zigzag across the darkened sky as the doorbell rang in consonance with the peal of thunder that had inevitably followed after.

A damp letter in hand, soaked from head to toe, stood Ponkoj the postman, wearing a querulous look upon his face. 'Here you are, *Boudi*, a letter from America for you. Must be from your son, but see how wet I've got bringing it to you.'

'Come in, Ponkoj, I'll get a towel, and while you dry yourself, I'll make a nice hot cup of tea for you.'

'*Na, na, thaak*, let it be, there's no need.'

'Who said so? A hot cup will do you a lot of good.' A peeved postman when you had your one and only child connected to you via the letters he regularly brought home to you? That would never do. 'Let me put on the fan, it will help dry you out.' And she had left the room, leaving him no space for any further protest. Niceties over the young postman had left and Nandita had at last been able to turn her attention towards the letter reading that she had been compelled to keep in abeyance.

Please, Ma, Tukun had written, *why don't you come and join us here? I think it's time you made some changes. Tomal is a handful at one and Meeta is getting very tired chasing him all over the place, you see, she is expecting our second baby in some six months from now. I'm sure you'll be pleased to get this good news!*

She had been none too pleased to hear about the forthcoming baby. Having two babies in such quick succession wasn't good for either of the infants or for the parents, she felt. And how old was Tukun himself that he was getting so embroiled? However, she had expressed none of this and had congratulated them prettily but had not committed herself on the matter of making a move to join them in the US.

Her son knew her better than she realised and, reading between the lines, had written back to tell her: *Ma, it's the done thing these days! Have all the babies you want in quick succession and bring them up together.* And then after having written on sundry irrelevant matters, he had come back to his original request once again. *Won't you please help out? I know you will.* She was being manipulated, she knew, but it felt so good to be manipulated! And then in total sincerity, he had added, *Besides, I don't like to think of you being there all alone so far away in Kolkata, working as hard as you do. I have already begun processing the necessary papers, just say yes, and as soon as they are done, I'll mail them to you. Please, Ma, please say yes!*

How can I, Tukun? After years of hard work, I have just become headmistress, she had wanted to protest but had not written back to say so. Being needed so desperately was indeed heady wine, and the fumes had risen to her head and robbed her of reason. Letting go of her hard-won position at her workplace had been perhaps the most painful part of her uprooting, and having resigned with regret, she had numbly stumbled on with the closure of the rest of the life that she had put together little by little, bit by bit. The flat had been sold, and fitting her life into a couple of suitcases, she had caught a flight to Chicago.

But Tukun, when she emerged from the clutches of the Customs at O'Hare, had so clearly expressed his pleasure at seeing her that all her doubts had been immediately wiped away from her mind. Bodily lifting her off the ground, he had twirled her around and set her down only when she had pleaded for mercy. Looking down with love upon her, breathing hard from the exertion, he had said, 'Oh, Ma, how glad I am to see you here.' And her heart had filled up with light.

Reluctantly at first and then with enthusiasm, she had stepped into the breach. Without any element of doubt in those early years, she had become the centre point of that little universe that Tukun and Meeta were building up together.

'Oh, Ma, how the babies love you,' Meeta would chortle. And Tukun, not to be outdone in the popularity stakes, would add, 'Not more than I do.' And a very pleased Nandita went husky. 'Grow up. Tukun, your father went and named you Tukun . . .'

'And so he wants to remain a little guy forever.'

'Meeta my girl, he had no idea then that I'd grow to be so large.' And they had laughed together.

'Ma, stop cooking all this delish grub, I'm growing a paunch.'

And Meeta would add, 'Please, Ma, don't stop cooking nice things. We'll make Tukun run around the block instead.' And then, almost making her blush, 'Ma, you really are a superb cook.'

She was feted and fawned upon, and slowly she had allowed herself to let go of that part of her that spelt Nandita the individual. The kids still loved her and so did her son, perhaps, but they did not need her as they had at one time. She still cooked as she did earlier, but . . .

Time, alas, has a way of making the most valuable of persons, places, and commodities redundant. And so she too had become redundant. Ten years was a long time, and she had ceded her position in the hierarchy of this household, little by little by little. In little bits and pieces, in little shreds and tatters, till today she did not know who she really was! So much so that in her dream today, she had gone to the extent of telling her Dipto that she had no roof of her own!

She was tired of being a mere bystander; today she would make some decisions, however unimportant or obscure they might be. She would cook the young family a hot meal. Cornflakes and cold milk, what a start to a cold and wintry day! She fried some eggs, buttered some hot toast, and made a steaming hot cup of cocoa each for all three of them. Placing the food upon the table, she stepped back.

Her granddaughter Tanmayee was the first to make an entry. 'Hi, Thamma,' she said in passing, going to the rear glass door of the kitchen. Then face falling, 'Oh, no! Where has all that lovely whitey, whitey fluffy snow gone? We had such a groovy time playing in the snow yesterday,' she added wistfully. 'It was real cool out there. You should have come with us,' She was cut short in midsentence by an admonishing voice. Meeta had made her entry onto the scene.

'Stop wasting your time, Tammy, have your breakfast. Want to be late for school?'

'Tammy?' Nandita had winced at the Americanisation of a perfectly beautiful Indian name.

'I was telling Thamma what fun we had yesterday.'

'You should have better sense than to do *that* now.' The tone ominous, giving a pause between each word, she had spelt out 'Have . . . your . . . breakfast . . . immediately.' The eyes of her mother-in-law trained upon her always made her edgy. And that never did bode well for the children.

'I don't want all this egg 'n stuff.'

'Who's asking you to have *that*? Get yourself some cereal and get on with it.' Looking at her watch, she fumed. 'Where has that boy gone? He should've been down and done with eating.' Looking upwards, she shouted in a voice gone harsh with annoyance, 'Tom . . . Tom, come down *immediately*.' And from the corner of her eye, she had seen her mother-in-law standing there stiff-lipped. She rarely said anything these days but those silences spoke volumes, for the look in her eyes as she stood brooding on the sidelines was so sharp and critical that it managed to make her stomach curl with resentment. Why had she changed so much, she asked of herself, as turning her attention back to her daughter, the flustered mother snapped, 'Not done yet?'

'Aw, Mom, I'm eating as fast as I can.'

Oh, how she nags, Nandita thought. And 'Tom'? She resented the name Tom. Why and how had his given name Tomal become Tom? To please whom had it become Tom? This great rush towards effacing the children's identity, she hated *that* with a fierce intensity. She *knew* they would come face to face with a major identity crisis one day. Only *then* would the parents understand how they had engineered this hurt upon their own children.

'OK, OK, but I'm going to leave that boy behind some day. I refuse to be late at work because of his lazy ways,' she said between gritted teeth, as she bit down into an apple. Her breakfast!

An apple to sustain a full-grown woman, Nandita looked at the cooked meal lying untouched upon the table, and then looked her daughter-in-law up and down from the corners of her eyes. She was certainly thinner now than she had been a few months from today, but the loss of weight, she assessed critically, had brought a certain gauntness to her face that was making her look haggard. Scrutiny over, she concluded that all this dieting was doing her no good, just as this constant nagging was doing no good to either of her children.

Having stepped out of her limits, breaking away from her self-imposed vow of silence, Nandita spoke softly yet firmly in defence of her tardy grandson. 'Young people need a lot of sleep Meeta, it was very late when—'

Breaking in midway into her observation, Meeta had stated in an ominously soft tone, 'I know when we came in. If the rest of us can get dressed in time, so can Tom. He's getting very spoilt and irresponsible with all this mollycoddling.' The snow might have melted in the yard but there was frost in the air. 'Please don't encourage him to be lazy as well, Ma.' The little girl Tammy, though young, could sense the build-up of tension between the two women and looked fearfully from one face to the other. Her grandmother's face had gone chalk white, while her mother's had in contrast become flushed with heightened colour. And it was at this crucial juncture that young Tomal, renamed Tom, had entered, all smiles, upon the scene.

'There you are at last,' said the young mother, turning to the cause of all her immediate frustration.

'Wow, Ma, that's a nice breakfast you've cooked us.'

'Oh, *that*? Are you planning to eat *that* now? Pass the cereal, Tammy.'

Heart afire, Nandita had stood on the sidelines and watched the early morning drama unwind, and the three breakfasts she had cooked had gone from hot to cool, and from cool, on to cold.

'Get the car keys. Where on earth are your jackets?'

'Only weaklings wear jackets on a warm day like this.'

'I won't wear a jacket if Tom doesn't.'

'Yes, you will and so will your brother. Come on, we are getting late, stop dawdling.'

'I'm not dawdling.'

'Yes, you are,' this from the brother.

'Aw, shut up, Tom. No one asked you.'

'Just shut up.'

Poking her tongue at her brother, she had emphatically added, 'No, you shut up.'

'Stop fighting and, that too, immediately, or I'm leaving. Where's your bag, Tammy?'

The bickering of the children and the nagging efforts of the mother to discipline them continued to be heard by Nandita as they walked out of the kitchen and out of the front door, and even till they had got into the car. The voices were stilled only when the car had been driven away. Their departure was like the exiting of a tornado. The silenced kitchen lay reeling under its assault. Nandita sighed deeply, wondering about the upbringing of her grandchildren.

So much! So much of difference had come about in this world! She had harked back to the days of her childhood when the word of her grandmother had been absolute law. Would anyone among them have dared spurn a plate of food placed before them by her?

Dadu and Thakuma had only one son, and he had fathered but a single child and that was their granddaughter Nandita. Nandita, who now lived in distant Saisborough, Illinois, in faraway America! They had three daughters as well with several children each. Dadu had a brother, and several sisters. But sisters and daughters did not count seriously, as they no longer belonged to the family after they had married and moved away. And of course Dadu had many, many cousins, Gangulys all, who lived in different nooks and crannies of the same home.

The joints that kept the joint family together had been showing signs of giving way. And, Nandita recalled how, over this barely held-together empire, battened by the hierarchical powers vested in her by her positioning in the family and by the force of her personality, her grandmother had ruled supreme!

And what to speak of an empire, she herself was hard-pressed to have even a modicum of any kind of control over this little family in which she was ensconced!

She stood wondering what made her so pallid and powerless in comparison to her grandmother. Was it the fact that she had been widowed so soon after her marriage or was it something that she had inherited from her mother? For though her mother had been awarded colour aplenty by her mother-in-law, she was yet a drab and colourless person with no individual will of her own.

But Nandita just could not accept that she was anything like her. Though devoid of colour by custom and her own choice, she had never been a colourless person. Had she not dared to fall in love while living within a milieu where falling in love was a cognisable offence to be dealt with in the harshest of terms? Had she not dared to walk out from within the stays of restraining authority to make a life of her own? Had not power flown from her as she had walked through the corridors of the school where she had taught?

By the rules of the game she had seen being played in her young days, she was the matriarch now. Why then had she come to this powerless, positionless position? Was there some fatal flaw in her, or was it the changing times that had brought her to this positionless position where she stood, not quite in the inner circle, yet not quite out of it. Perched precariously on the periphery of her son and his family's bustling, jostling, full-of-life lives.

She had obstinately moved towards the gas range.

Positioning the cooked food upon the table, she had turned expectantly towards the door as her son entered. When he was growing, people used to say that he was the spitting image of his father. She looked closely as he entered, and wondered why so many had said so. His hair waved as did hers, black and unruly at times. And he was of a different build, more like his grandfather the major general had been, rather than what his father was. And then he had turned swiftly towards her and she had seen her husband Prodipto in that one little movement, in that angle of the face, as he asked, 'Where's the paper, Ma?'

With a catch rising to her throat, she had picked up the pile of sheets of newsprint in disarray and handed them without a word to him.

With a short 'Thanks,' he had taken the dishevelled sheaf of papers from her. 'Look what a mess this lot's in, why must Meeta . . .' he grumbled as he grabbed a bowl. Having shaken some cereal into it, he had splashed some milk onto it and, plucking a spoon out of the dishwasher, had sat down to eat, paper in hand. Eyes upon the day's headlines, he had not even cast a glance towards the plate of food that was waiting expectantly for him upon the table. The mother had looked on in silence.

She sighed softly as she heard the front door shut. She and this house, her companion, were back together again in their aloneness. The sky had gone darker still; was it going to rain again?

Leaving everything exactly where it was, putting aside the devastation wrought upon her heart, she had gone back up to her room and turned back her gaze upon the devastation that had been wrought upon the yard by the storm. It was indeed a bleak sight, saddening beyond compare. Why did she feel so alone, so abjectly alone? She had never felt that she was alone in that little flat of hers in Kolkata even after Tukun had left home. But there were other times hidden away in her memory when she had felt much the same way. Along the path of life's long journey, she had somewhere along the way taken a turn that had brought her back full circle to a familiar well-known spot, a site where she stood alone, hovering unnoticed upon the periphery of other people's preoccupations.

Nandita had been a child who had felt forever marginalised. But then, she had been burdened with the questionable greatness of her father, and her own doubtful usefulness in being a link to posterity for that (questionable albeit) greatness of her progenitor. Had Nandita been a son, matters might have been different. But then, she was a daughter, and not a son.

It was Mejo Thakuma, Nandita's grand-aunt, who always managed to leave a hollow and empty space within the little girl Nandita's heart. Montu, Jhontu, and Rintu, the three sons of her son were the trio upon whose shoulders the future continuance of this segment of the Ganguly lineage now rested. *They were her grandsons!* Her trump cards three while her imperious sister-in-law had none, so should she not be the one with the upper hand? Thakuma did have grandsons, but as they were the sons of her daughters, they, to her chagrin, did not show up in the credit column of her personal bank account!

And while giving battle, the grandmother of these three lads used a high-pitched voice that carried through the corridors of that mansion built by Nandita's forefathers. 'My son may not be barrister . . .'

She was cut short with a dignified and subdued 'Mejo Bou, you know very well no one denied anyone the opportunity.'

Poor lady, she was no match for her superior adversary! But one day, having lost innumerable rounds in this verbal dual, Mejo Thakuma had pulled out the ultimate ace of her pack and thrown it open for the entire world to see. 'You talk of greatness as if it were synonymous with the name of your son. In truth, it is *my son* who has saved this prestigious family from being written off from the face of this earth. He has three sons; each one of them will carry on the illustrious name of the Gangulys into posterity. Your Nandita, your son's only child, is nothing but the living proof of the dead end of your husband's line. Daughters, as everyone knows, are born to help carry on the line of other people's families.'

'Great men do not need sons to commemorate their passage through this earth.' Imperious she was, and majestically she had closed the subject. But for the little girl who had been used as ammunition in this battle royal, it was quite another matter, for her great-aunt's final salvo aimed at Thakuma's door had come hurtling at her instead and had left Nandita wounded. Lacerated by the cutting edge of the brutal words, she had looked down upon herself with disgust and wondered with tears in her eyes how she, a living creature, could be so cursed as to be the dead end of all hopes.

But with courage culled from who knows where, she had slowly shaken off all her inherited encumbrances and had urged herself to stand tall. She had not been willing to accept that she, a living, breathing full-of-life creature, could possibly be the dead end of anyone's hopes, and her faith had been further cemented once she had fallen into the magnetic field of a magical entity, her Dipto, who had dared to, cared to love her!

Travelling between time zones, she had returned, back from her one-time lonely days, into her yet lonelier present. Like the sea at low tide, the clamouring voices from Nandita's childhood home had crept away from the shore of her life, leaving behind only the debris of her memories. She would have to tread carefully or the shards would make her bleed.

Her legs were aching. She had no idea how long she had been standing at that bedroom window. She turned her gaze inwards and went and sat down in a chair. Her unmade, unkempt bed sprawled untidily in a slouch in the middle of the room testimony to the disarray in which the entire home now lay. The tedium of the repetitive and boring tasks lying ahead of her made her hold back awhile.

The rhythm of her daily rounds had been disrupted by the unscheduled visit of her dead and distanced relatives. This was America where she lived; one did not call on people without prior intimation. Did they not know it disrupted the flow of one's life? But how were they to? The time and emotional zone from where they came, a guest walked in when his heart so desired.

The turmoil and upheaval of the long and arduous journey she had just undertaken had fatigued her. Disheartened at the recollection of the morning's events, she had dispiritedly gone towards the rooms the children occupied. Very often she reminded herself of Damini. Damini marooned by circumstances in the household of the Gangulys of Bhabanipore, Damini, devoid of all will or volition of her own.

Yes, Damini, who had arrived at the door of the Ganguly family when she had just turned eighteen. A widow with no prospects other than the worst, she had been positioned as maid of all menial jobs in the Ganguly household by her maternal uncle who had no desire to feed and clothe her for the rest of his life.

Clutching onto her mother's sari and peering out from behind her, Nandita had looked on with interest at the advent of Damini. Like a *jatra* being staged, the entire episode had come to pass in the centre of their courtyard.

The duo of uncle and niece had been waiting long hours for an audience. The uncle, an emaciated unpleasant-looking individual, stood a few steps ahead of the dark-as-ebony, buxom lass who trailed behind, clutching a small bundle.

And then she had heard her say, 'She looks quite old to me.'

No, she does not look old to me, the little Nandita had thought. But why is she so big in the front, she had asked herself, looking at the full-breasted form of Damini with care. And then, what a pretty face she has, I think I would like to have her as a friend.

Falling upon Thakuma's feet, the uncle had wailed, 'She is quite young, Ma, she really is.' Then, afraid of doing damage to his own prospects of getting rid of a burden, he had added a corrigendum. 'But she is old enough to work very hard.' Turning to his niece, he had threatened, 'Let me not hear any complaints about you, my girl, or . . .'

And that was how Damini had come to be installed forever in the household of the Gangulys, *a part of the whole, yet never quite a part of anything.*

Picking up the empty coffee mugs, Nandita had hesitated a moment before negotiating the stairs. Instead of stepping downwards, she slumped down instead upon the topmost step of the staircase. Why did she feel as if she was fast becoming Damini herself? She was fast becoming a Damini, but certainly not Thakuma! She would have to do something about that, but what?

Today, her heart was not in the mundane, moribund tasks she performed every single day.

Never would she abdicate her independence, she had told herself in a spurt of anger that had been born out of the total insensitivity of her near and dear ones. And when she was not yet twenty, she had declared her very own war of independence. But caught in the snare of emotions, she, at a much later date, had gone and succumbed to circumstances and ceded ground.

What was she doing here, why was she killing herself, what was her future? For the first time perhaps, she clearly asked herself what reason she had to have made herself into a Damini. She walked down the stairs without picking up the cups from where she had put them. An unfamiliar strain of resentment surged through her heart as she entered the kitchen and encountered the sight of the table loaded with stale, shrivelled-up food.

The transistor was still at its task of terrifying the humans holed up at home. It spoke with relish of the accidents, the near accidents, and the possible accidents that the iced-up roads had conjured up. The voice within the small radio was insistent, persistent, and very frightening to have as a sole companion in a home void of the people out of her past and of her present. Nandita quickly stepped across the room and stilled that voice of doom.

She moved towards the centre of the kitchen and her nose curled with distaste. The dining table lay cluttered up with an array of plates, glasses, bowls, cups, mugs, spoons, still more spoons, forks and paper napkins, four differently decorated cartons of cereals, a gallon can of milk, a carton of orange juice, and a bowl full of fruits. And adding to the clutter sat four incongruous plates of cooked food.

She picked up the plates one at a time and scraped the contents into the garbage bin, then she poured the glass of cocoa with its thin skin of cream into the sink and moved to the next plate and its accompanying glass. She had become American enough to be able to throw away good wholesome fresh food into a dustbin. In her other incarnation, she would have been tied up in knots with guilt, had she but thought of performing any such deed. The last plate was the one she had placed in readiness for her son. Picking up the plate deliberately from the table, she had furiously scraped off the congealing mess into the garbage can. And it was then that she had heard the distinct thud of the arrival of the day's mail.

2 A LETTER THAT DID NOT QUITE GET WRITTEN

The garbage bin had soon swallowed up the physical evidence of Nandita's disappointing debacle. But the foetid after-smell of failure, frustration, and leaking egg-yolks had lingered on, somewhere deep down within her psyche. Standing at the threshold of the kitchen, she had wondered a moment what next to do. The recently arrived mail was still sitting upon their doorstep! There was a time when it would not have lain thus neglected, for then a gem in the form of a letter from home had nearly always emerged out of its bulky bosom. And what a celebration they had made of those arrivals.

Like trophies, the letters would sit atop their newly acquired sideboard for a couple of days at least. 'How many for me?' Without fail, Tukun would ask on seeing the display as he returned home from work.

'Expecting some letters, dear husband?' asked his young wife mischievously. 'Who will write to you?'

'My mum-in-law perhaps, she loves me a little bit more than she loves you.'

'More than she loves *me!* Not possible.' A trifle perturbed 'Don't be silly . . .'

'Have you written a single letter to her, Tukun?' his mother had asked with a smile.

'Must one write to expect a reply, Ma, what of her love for her one and only son-in-law?'

'*Bandor,*' what a monkey he was, she had affectionately admonished.

'Look, Ma, has received a pile of them.' Turning to her mother-in-law, Meeta said, 'How lucky you are, Ma, to have so many people who love you so much.'

'Don't even try to compete with her, Meetu, like a film star, Ma has a regular fan following back there in Cal.'

Yes, she thought, a star status conferred upon her by the aura that hung around that little piquant something about being in that unattainable far-off land of milk and honey called the United States of America, to which so many hankered to be linked, but for how long would it last?

Letters had never littered her life with the abandoned abundance of fan mail, for she had never been a star. No, that would be an untruth, for she had been a star to someone, though it was for just a fleeting moment in time. The one for whom she had been a star, a prima donna, and the prime moving force of his life had written but a handful of letters to her. The letters he had carried around in the pocket of his winter uniform before posting them carried a whiff of the scent of naphthalene balls in which they had been stored through the summer months, embroiled with the distinctive perfume of the aftershave he always used!

And the starched stiff summertime khakis with their mixed set of inputs of starch and sweat and steam, from the hot and heavy iron that had passed over its surface. A potpourri of all these scents had been left upon one of the last letters he had written her. In that, he had exhorted her to come and join him: *Must you go on trying to please my parents?* he had asked of her. *If you don't come back immediately to me with that little rascal of ours, I will resign my commission and come and stay beside you at home. And may God help us if Daddy drives us out of his regal government lodgings.* She had not taken his threat any too seriously; it just did not do to displease one's seniors, she had told herself, and had laughed it off. It was a pity that letter writing was fast becoming a thing of the past. How delightfully alluring was the telltale perfume each of those missives carried, if only you would expend a few moments in trying to guess from whence it came. She should have heeded that call. For only a few letters later he had cut short his sojourn upon this earth and gone out of the reach of pen and paper.

That short-lived stardom, alas, had indeed been short-lived, and her recently acquired star status had soon begun to change as well; you have to remain centre stage to hold on to the allegiance of your fan club. As for Meeta, she had promoted herself from letter writing to the joys of telephoning. Her brothers had moved America-wards and her parents had also joined the bandwagon soon after. The grandbabies needed some caring hands! Tukun had continued to remain letter unfriendly. So the only recipient of letters was Nandita now. On very rare occasions, a letter did stray her way but those missives conveyed nothing more than some random words written down in ink. The heartbeats underlying those words were no longer audible. The nourishing kernel of caring that had linked those earlier communications had slowly but steadily dried up, and now only the chaff of near-forgotten relationships had remained. And so, over the years, the arrival of the mail had ceased to excite her curiosity. She had tried to turn her back upon its boring repetitive inroad, but it had such a big and bulky and boisterously invasive persona that if you were a trapped-at-home individual, it managed craftily to draw you into its orbit.

'Had we been in Kolkata, we could have made a lot of money selling *raddi*,' Meeta had opined in one of those early days.

'A brilliant idea, we can carry the lot back when we manage to go home some day. Do you think it would cover the cost of our tickets, Ma?'

And Nandita, moving away from the banter, had asked, 'Why do they waste so much paper?'

Emerging from the kitchen, she had stood uncertain of her next move. Then she had moved forward and opened the front entrance door that led into their home. Grudgingly she had bent and picked up the lot to place it upon a small table. *The days of plenty have come to us,* Nandita thought as she looked down upon an array of fliers brandishing an array of enticing offers, *we don't have time for you now.*

It was from Meeta that she had learnt that there were treasures aplenty hidden away within these voluminous sheaves of printed matter. 'Ma,' her daughter-in-law had warned, 'you must keep a close watch on the coupons and offers that . . .'

'Coupons and what?'

'They have these wonderful little colourful coupons placed here and there within the papers. I have to go to work,' she had grimaced, 'otherwise we could have done it together.'

'Done what together, Meeta?'

'Collected the coupons and kept them aside. It's unbelievable, Ma, really the discounts one can get . . .' she had paused as if overwhelmed and then concluded, 'are really unbelievable.'

'Show me what to do.' And the just-retired teacher Nandita, becoming a gifted student in the hands of an able teacher, had learnt the art of wading through the stacks of papers that arrived each day in search of those tantalising little coupons. Coupons that promised perhaps an extra hundred pack of plastic party-spoons, or an additional packet full of paper table-napkins or a twelve-pack of rose-hued toilet paper! What if they, as a family, were as yet washers rather than wipers and never used them!

Tukun, being a male, had wanted to know why they were running after a bunch of items that they really did not need. 'Do we really need so much of—' And he had been cut short.

'Need indeed! Is that the only reason why one buys things? Oh, Tukun, why must you be so boring?' Meeta had demanded of her husband. 'You buy things because, because they are . . .'

'Come on, Tukun,' Nandita had remonstrated, 'the poor child never buys a single thing for herself.'

'I wish she would. Would be more interesting than toilet paper and plastic spoons, don't you agree?' He had chuckled while ducking to avoid a flying missile directed his way.

In those early years, Meeta and she were comrades-in-arms out in search of hidden treasures secreted away within those bounteous coupons. And then, there were those magic moments when a dozen or so mismatched plates fell into your lap, all for a few cents plus some minuscule percentage of tax. *It only happens in America*, she had gleefully written and told a friend of hers. *Where else can you get a dozen unchipped plates for almost nothing?*

'Ma, those are saucers,' Tukun had objected. 'Saucers without cups, what on earth are you going to do with them?' But they had been bought all the same. After all, a twelve-cent outlay on a dozen plates, how long could that be debated?

It had been fun being poor; with the arrival of the dollars, the tenor of their existence had somehow changed.

'Come on, Tukun,' the young wife would coax, 'Ma is dying to go out, and so am I.' Meeta had a soft and cajoling way with her those days and would craftily augment the argument she had put forth with a persuasive pout. Having pre-empted all objections on her young husband's part, she would scurry around, readying the two little ones for the day's outing.

The mother in Nandita had felt a twinge of sympathy for the son in search of a little respite on a hard-earned weekend.

'Meeta, Tukun looks tired, doesn't he?'

'No, he doesn't.' And giggling like a schoolgirl bright-eyed with excitement, she would come and give Nandita a hug. 'I know you want to go shopping as much as I do.'

'But—'

'There are no buts, Ma, we are going shopping.'

The whispery voice of the sympathetic mother masterfully quelled, she had put together the precious loot she had culled; the offers were there, but never there dangling before your eyes forever. A small delay and all those twofers, all those delicious discounts, all those promised amounts of redemption made on purchases would just float right out of their grasp. The very thought of wasting away such 'God-given' opportunities was agonising to these new initiates to the art of American life and living.

The next week would assuredly bring its very own crop of allurements, the young man had tried to reason, but it was to no avail. For this week's offer on sardines in oil could well veer course and turn into mackerels in tomato sauce the next. What a calamity that would be, Meeta had heatedly pointed out.

And a weakened Tukun had given in grudgingly and then gone on to enjoy the shopping spree ordained and orchestrated by his wife. A look at his mother's face at this point of the weekly negotiations had amused Tukun each time it came to pass. He was still acutely sensitive to her feelings, the mother thought, looking back upon those days in the not-so-distant past. For, sensing her discomfort, he would reassure her with a hug and a near-set dialogue. 'Ma, as you can see, both of us are being manipulated by this outsider; shall we let her get away with it?' Strangely enough, the more he stressed the closeness of the bonds that tied them together as mother and son, the stronger her ties with this so-called outsider to their family had become.

And so, purse bulging with those coupons, they had ridden off in state, in search of a bargain or two and some reprieve away from the daily grind of housework and home. Seated sandwiched between the two grandchildren, each strapped into their child seats, with Tukun at the wheel and Meeta beside him, they had as a team gone off on these hunting missions come Sunday.

The drive had been long as they lived a long distance away from the shopping malls they usually frequented. Nandita loved these little family outings so much that she had never let out a squeak even though each little jolt, each turn that the car took would invariably deliver a painful dig to some part or the other of the middle parts of her anatomy. Cars of the size that

Tukun had acquired were not designed to accommodate any add-ons such as a grandmother. As they were breaking the norms of the society in which they now lived, a little bit of discomfort accruing to the add-on in the family group could well be expected! The car, with its windows rolled up, would become a little India along with the music that played within its carapace. And the music with its links to their roots had a calming, soothing, lulling presence that enveloped them all and made them into a happy unit safely packaged away from the otherworldliness that just lay outside their carefully rolled-up windows.

Those were fun days, fulfilling days! Two grubby babies, a happy young couple, and an 'impaired' Nandita—what a strange procession they made as they wandered from store to store in that sprawling shopping mall. There was so much there to hold one's attention in that world full of wonders that their day out had sped along on oiled wheels. It would culminate at a little eatery of their choice.

'What will you have, Ma?' was a question to which her son already had an answer! He knew it would be a baked potato in its jacket, swimming in molten butter. Yet he asked!

'Must you ask?' she would ask with a smile. 'And no—'

'Cheese, please.' He would end for her. The taste of those baked potatoes soaked in molten butter that she invariably ended up eating had always lingered on in her mind as the symbol of unmitigated happiness.

But those days had long since ceased to be! The young family had adapted to the new land and life that they had adopted. And so, Nandita too had long since ceased to be a new immigrant, yet she had never gone beyond being a newcomer to this land where she now lived. Those bonding outings were now a thing of the past. And with it, the chase after the coupons had ceased to have any significance.

For quite a while, she had continued with enthusiasm with her task of collecting those colourful promissory notes, but more often than not, those collections she had put together had to be thrown away, as neither Tukun nor Meetu, she realised in a while, had time now to waste upon such frivolous pursuits as running after cheap goods. They as a family did venture out together occasionally, but those trips were so forced and hurried that it no longer was a fun thing to do.

The flow of letters from India had also almost dried up and turned into a mere dribble. So this daily arrival had long since failed to speed up Nandita's heartbeat, but it had managed somehow to hold on to her in its compelling magnetic field, as it managed even now, to hold out a nebulous promise of a missive that perhaps lay in its bosom like the hidden *taal* within a *tabla*.

On the verge of leaving the living room, she had tidied up the bundle into a neater stack, and as she did so, an all-too-familiar cream-coloured envelope, with its dull brown imprint of the Ashoka Lions had fallen onto the floor. She picked it up and looked down upon it.

The letter she now held in her hand had but a trace of a lingering aroma of a Bangali's *ranna ghor*. It carried with it the scent of fish fried in mustard oil, of *paanch phoron*, the seasoning for all seasons in Bengali cuisine. It was perhaps the circular postmark with a semicircular Kolkata sitting within its confines: stamped upon the Indian Post and Telegraph Department envelope that had conjured up the flavours of a kitchen in West Bengal for her.

She had accepted long ago that the sources and the wellsprings from which all her personal communication had once risen had nearly all dried up. Yet a faint hope of receiving a word from someone who cared to remember her had continued to hold her in its sway. Her love-hate relationship with letters stretched way back into her past, back to the time when she had just been ten and a cream-coloured envelope postmarked from Varanasi had been handed to her. She had run in and handed it to her grandfather.

Thrusting it towards her grandfather, she had suggested, 'See how sweet scented it is.'

'Doesn't it smell just like the *thakurghor* where all our gods and goddesses live?' He had taken the letter from her and looked around for his glasses.

From the fast, fleeting changing expressions upon his face as he read through the not-so-long letter, she had known that this was a missive that carried within it a message of far-reaching consequence. Her grandfather had beckoned to her and, holding her close, had shed a few silent tears. Though so young, she had sensed his need for privacy and had never alluded to this momentary show of weakness on his part. From that day on, she had recognised that each missive of significance exuded a scent and a presence and a personality of its own. That letter from that holy city clinging onto the banks of the River Ganga had carried with it the scent of turmeric and sandalwood and incense and camphor and crushed marigolds, flowers sacrificed at the altar of intense devotion.

And this letter she now held in her hands had its antecedents linked to a less rarefied domain, the kitchen rather than a prayer room. Having failed to pin down the writer of the letter, she had pulled it out from its housing. This was Rekha's hand, a hand she knew very well, a hand that had refused to grow up despite all the coaxing and cajoling she had at one time expended upon it. She just could not visualise a grown-up Rekha, nor did the handwriting help. She could remember a leggy ten- or eleven-year-old struggling to pull down the hem of her skirts as they kept steadily moving upwards upon her person as she had rapidly kept shooting up and up and up. In no time at all, the hem had travelled most immodestly up from just above the upper edge of her knees and come to rest somewhere around her mid thighs. Those spindly legs then were totally bereft of any sensuality and should have posed no threat to anyone. And yet, Thakuma, forever out in search of omissions and commissions, had been none too pleased with *that* innocent leg-show. Or so she had thought!

Out of the blue, it had suddenly occurred to Nandita, letter in hand, that it was perhaps not the imagined seductiveness of Rekha's bare and skinny legs that had disturbed Thakuma's heart so replete with the prudery of that era. It must have been the sight of the fabric of Rekha's outgrown dress, stretching and straining so tightly across the newly changing terrain of her chest with its just-emergent, barely visible twin bumps. Breasts were unseemly giveaways of an impending state of womanhood, best kept under wraps, well out of sight of inquisitive eyes. No wonder she herself had been bundled into a sari, no sooner than she had shown the first signs of burgeoning puberty.

Pushing all else aside, she had gone back to reading the letter. And she had discovered to her utter astonishment that this Rekha, the little girl of her imagination whose handwriting had refused to grow up, was a grandmother today! How strange it was that you yourself and the people around you kept growing older along with you! And all those people dead or alive who had moved away out of your sight and from your horizon remained frozen in time, in a state of fixity. You knew, at a particular level of *knowing*, that they too must have moved onwards along the path of ageing, yet there was a sense of disbelief when one actually met up with the reality of the ravages of the universal reach of time. And today Rekha too was planning for her old age. An eleven-year-old walks out of your life because her family chooses to move away from your neighbourhood, and next when you hear from her, she is a widow, a mother, a mother-in-law, and a grandmother.

It took a little while for all this to sink in.

Rekha was reaching out to her through the barriers of time and space in search of a sustaining source with which she could connect in this, her journey into the unknown. Had she, Nandita wondered, gone back after a long drawn-out absence of so many long years to the now-dilapidated mansion of the Gangulys? She must have. Kakima was the last among the earlier generation that, cursed by the boon of longevity, had still lingered on! There was a time when a constant flow of written words like a far-reaching hand had reached out to her across the oceans. But time had taken its toll! Arthritis had grown from strength to strength within the joints of Kakima's fingers and left her without the power to write. The written words had fallen along the way, and the isolation of Nandita had taken on a new dimension.

Taking up the letter, she took the steps down and, moving to the living room, took a seat facing the street running down the front of the house. And only then did she really get down to taking in what the letter really had to say.

It was not as if this letter carried with it any message of gloom, but the undercurrent lay deep down in the history of the life that kept peeping out from between the lines. This letter in itself was a joyous outburst coming from the heart of a person looking out towards a bright horizon where loneliness was to be forever banished. She was wanted, she was needed, she was the most important person in the whole world; her son, and his wife, were beckoning out to her.

The most important thing that Rekha had wanted to know was as to how many cotton *saris* she should bring along with her when she came. So many minuscule concerns and finally the last query: *Nanditadi, I have no other woollens except for two shawls, one black and the other white. Now that the winter months are almost over, I can surely wait for the next winter to come round before buying any woollens.* Poor Rekha, exulting in the warmth of her dreams, could not possibly imagine the bleakness that could very well catch up with this warmth that was enveloping her heart now, and leave it suddenly uncovered and cold one day.

What was she to tell her? *Rekha, it is not the type of coldness that can be banished with the help of a few woollens that you should fear; it is the freezing cold of isolation, a cold akin to what one would possibly feel while floating about absolutely alone in outer space, with all the familiar signposts drifting away and with not a single friendly outpost appearing to take its place within sight!* She had seen a movie not so long ago where a man accidentally loses his mooring from his spaceship and floats away, away, away into the eternal whirling of outer space. For nightmare-filled nights on end, that image of the man drifting away lazily, effortlessly into oblivion had kept coming back to haunt her.

With urgency marking her every movement, Nandita had gone in search of pen and some paper. This was a letter that could not wait till tomorrow to be answered. And surrounded by the clutter of a home left untended, she had sat down to write a reply. She had to be warned!

Resist, she wrote to her young friend out of the distant past, then pausing a moment, went on to add, *with all your might and main!* Pen poised in mid-air, she contemplated a while upon the written words and wondered why they appeared to be so hysterical and melodramatic on paper. There was no hysteria whatsoever hidden in her considered statement. Each word she had put down was based upon her felt experience and upon a set of totally rational feelings that she had analysed at length!

Would Rekha be shocked to receive such a missive? Perhaps! But let her be shocked, let her be startled, and let her wonder at this sudden outburst, thought an unrelenting Nandita. She wanted somehow to make her friend look afresh at all the pros and cons of this decision of hers to join her son and his family in the United States. Alas, it was such a long time since she had expressed herself either in speech or in writing that she found her competence sorely lacking to convey all the subtle shades of her tormented inner feelings. With disuse, she had forgotten the art of bringing about a match between the speed of her thoughts and the sluggishness of her pen. The years fraught with loneliness had taught her to live within the web of her own thoughts and made her forget how to unravel and communicate them to others. And here she was presumptuously trying to unload her heart and her soul onto paper! What she wanted to share with Rekha needed a far more competent pen than hers had become. It was like going to war with a rusted sword!

But, however blunted the tip of her pen might have become, she would wield it yet with passion, if not perfection, today. For she had to make Rekha understand that this one step she was about to take would have far-reaching consequences upon the tenor and texture of the remaining years of her life.

Having trod along the same path herself, Nandita wanted somehow to alert her of the terrible wrenching pain that she would have to suffer during her initial uprooting. And then the latter-day anguish which would follow upon the belated realisation that she had in truth no space she could call her own, no patch of earth in which she could throw down those roots anew.

She remembered one stormy day tucked away within the folds of her memory somewhere in her very distant past when a full-blown monsoon storm had come gusting and torn up an oleander tree in full bloom. Panchu *goyla* and Manik *dhopa* were fortunately at hand; one had come to deliver some extra milk and the other was there to collect the week's wash.

They were strong men with strong backs and arms and the fulsome oleander covered with large bunches of blood-red blossoms had soon been brought back onto its feet and replanted where a new pit had been dug by them in accordance with Thakuma's instructions. It was at the other end of the courtyard, where a more controlled and disciplined wind blew! But in spite of all this ministration, the flowers had all withered away, as had the buds that were to have come into bloom in their footsteps! And sad to say, though apparently in good health, that lithe and lovely tree never again had borne a single bud or blossom.

Rekha was hankering to be uprooted today as she herself had once hankered after. Having allowed her heart and her emotions to overrule her reasoning self, she had taken the plunge and packed her bags. From the queen of her universe (very modest albeit) she had allowed herself to be reduced to being nothing more than a mere appendage to a unit. She had been a very important appendage to that unit at one point of time, but today, she knew, that vital need for her presence was already well past.

A whispery word of caution emerging from her brain had tried to raise its voice, but the temptations that had been laid out before her had swamped that thread of disquiet. Her inner voice quelled, she had let go of her hard-earned career and the one-bedroom flat that she had acquired instalment by painful instalment. And having put paid to her autonomous state of life, she had moved into her son's very pokey little condominium said to be located in Chicago. It was neither a safe nor a smart place to live in, but there was a great deal of happiness and togetherness in that little home then. Both success and affluence were as yet a very long way off from the lives of the inhabitants that lived in that happy home. The children were mere babies in need of constant care, and Nandita had happily taken over this task of caring. Their mother had to perforce go out to work to rake in those few extra dollars to augment the income of her husband.

Nandita, left at the helm of affairs at home, had been content to the extent a free bird with newly clipped wings can be. Enmeshed by her never-ending duties, she had never had the time or the option to carve out a niche of her very own. The children had grown up faster than she could have ever imagined while Tukun had moved on from success to success. They now had no need to hang on with a fingernail hold to Chicago. The affluent lived away from Chicago but not quite. Those lovely little towns with their share of the pricey Lake Shore, with their prestigious universities and their glamorous stores, with Illinois added on at the end of its name, was the place to be in. And so, Mr Sudipto Roy, the newly become US citizen, had moved there, but not into a condominium. A two-car garage home was the least that could now accommodate them!

Emerging out of her swift little journey into the past, she picked up the pen once again. *Rekha*, she wrote, and came to a rapid halt there. Her letter was progressing like a passenger train upon a narrow-gauge track in India. It stopped at every imaginable station, and it stopped at every imaginable non-station! Her scattered thoughts had alighted at one such stop and gone off. One of those wandering thoughts had landed up beside her and pondered a while along with her upon her own life. 'Here you are,' the thought said, 'comfortably seated in a comfortable warm home, yet there is such a lack of warmth within you. Why?' Yes, why was it that she felt there was something terribly wrong with this life of hers? Where was the joy, where was the contentment of life and living? *With the passage of each succeeding year, she seemed to have moved further and further away from the mainstream of this her existence here with her son and his family.*

A ray of weak early springtime sunshine, having escaped from the clutches of the clouds, had come and fallen across her face. Averting her eyes from the sudden onslaught of brilliance, she rose guiltily to make amends and the letter from Rekha, sitting on her lap till then, fell to the ground. And then she remembered Rekha's letter and her failed attempts at writing a simple straightforward reply had mocked her.

Too late by far for a proper meal, she had toasted a couple of slices of bread and buttered them and brewed herself a cup of tea. Plate and cup in hand, she had gone up and into her room; having pulled up a chair alongside the window, she had sat looking out as she ate the simple fare she had brought up with her. Not a soul stirred anywhere! And all around her lay the house as empty and hollow as a false promise! The trees stood bare-limbed and unmoving, though a crisp breeze was blowing out there. A wayward wrapping of some little titbit, having made its way out of the garbage bin, was being buffeted around mercilessly; she watched as its punishment went on. Not a sound was to be heard from anywhere, and the sky, a dull grey, overlooked this silent world.

It was as if she was one solitary shipwrecked soul who had been washed up upon an inclement uninhabited desert island.

How she wished today that she had a pen powerful enough to create images in words, images that would be powerful enough to stand up on their own and speak for themselves. She had neither the skills nor the ability to get across to Rekha the absolute quality of aloneness that could engulf the life of a goal-less person here. Would Rekha be able to understand what Nandita meant if she were to tell her that the world lying outside the perimeters of the home in which you lived never crept up and lapped against the shores of your existence? That no wedding *shehnais*, no noisy bands, no *puja* or *mela* loudspeakers, no persistent vendors cajoling you endlessly with their myriad wares bothered you. No beggars nor ascetics calling out to you with their outstretched bowls, no cawing of crows at dawn intermingled with the acrid smell of smouldering coals in their freshly lit *chulas* ever assailed or irritated your senses! No gas shortages, no load shedding, no taps running dry, no delayed monsoons harbouring the seeds of the fear of drought with its terrible aftermath of water and food shortages ever disturbed the even tenor of your existence so as to fill your heart with anger and frustration. But at the root of this ever-recurrent feeling of irritation, anger, and frustration lay some happening, some interaction: the leavening to keep reminding you that you were still alive.

Lost in thought, she kept sitting where she was in the chair where she had sat down to have her simple meal; the gloom outside had lightened a shade, she observed. And then through her peripheral vision, she glimpsed a quicksilver movement somewhere to her left out in the yard in the direction where the maple tree stood. The wind had died down, she could see as she came and stood by the window. The colourful wrapper, having been let off the cat and mouse game, now lay exhausted under the garden seat. The yard lay before her as still as death, and then through the double-glazed windowpanes, she spotted a bushy tail; a squirrel was out there on the barren branch of the naked maple tree. As she bent to pick up the empty cup and the plate, she saw the neighbour's tawny cat make a stealthy entrance. It was stalking the squirrel as it came scampering down. She gave out a very big sigh of relief as she saw the squirrel come to a sudden halt and go scampering up out of the reach of the big fat cat.

This was the only neighbourly visit that they ever got, and she wasn't quite sure from where exactly this visitor came. Was it from the next home or the one beyond it, or perhaps even from beyond that? The only time one got to get a glimpse of the neighbours who lived to their left was during the summer months; the ones who lived on the other end she had never seen at all. An inflatable pool would be hauled out come summer by the visible-from-the-top-floor-neighbours and placed in the centre of the lawn. Filled to the brim, it would become the centre point of the existence of the family from then on. On lean days in terms of people at the plastic poolside, a lean young woman would shed all her clothes and lie face down upon a sheet spread out upon the grass. Her well-oiled body would be left to cook in the sun all day long. Nandita wondered sometimes whether she was a bicoloured being, one shade in the front and another in the rear! The woman lying prone out there perhaps had no idea that she could be observed from the western wing of the Roy homestead; or it was possible that even if she did know she did not really care? *It was her body, to do as she willed with it, was it not?*

Neighbours as an entity, as she had once known, were quite another species of human beings! By nature she was an insular person, but the nature of neighbourly relationships being what they were, she had been drawn slowly but steadily into the mainstream of the collective lives that the residents of that cluster of flats liked to live. They knew everything worth knowing about her and she in turn knew all there was to know about them. And an ever-growing network of relationships had developed rapidly and had pulled her slowly yet steadily into its vortex.

There were those moments when she had resented not having a life that she could call her own. But she had recognised later that in that particular style of life and living invaded by the needs and the demands of the many, the empty crevices of your heart were never allowed for long to remain empty.

And today in her life here in America, her heart was beleaguered by empty spaces that were as large as potholes, not just mere crevices!

With the passage of each single day, her longing for the life she had left behind had grown from strength to strength. Burnished and placed upon a pedestal, all the trials and tribulations of that life she had led back there in Kolkata had emerged adorned with a halo. Unravelling the tangled skeins of her thoughts, Nandita had slowly realised that the reason why it was impossible to get over the longing for India lay in the obtuseness of India! Even if that country with its countless problems angered, teased, and troubled you ten times a day, in return it did not allow you to languish away, isolated with boredom and loneliness.

Nandita looked out and saw the cat was still there looking longingly up at the tree where the squirrel could be seen going about with its tasks. Perhaps it was a lonely cat, out in search of some companionship even if it was from a moving ball of fur that it would have liked to devour. She thought perhaps they were kindred souls, for there he was whiling his time away, concentrating upon a squirrel that was really and truly out of his reach while she, standing on the sidelines, was whiling away her time watching the cat contemplate the squirrel. She thought that perhaps it was time she got to like *this cat*; after all, he was *the only neighbour* who cared to pay her home a visit. With a sudden spurt of activity for some unknown reason, both the cat and the squirrel had whisked their individual tails and gone out of her sight.

She had risen, picked up the empty cup and the plate, and gone down slowly back to where she had left the letter she had begun writing to Rekha. A frown creasing her brow, she had looked down with distaste upon the hysterical screaming words she had penned just a few hours back. It did not look right. Rekha had not asked for her advice or her opinion upon anything more important than what clothes she should carry with her when she moved here!

Tearing the page off, she had crumpled it into a ball and thrown it into the wastepaper basket. Then drawing the letter writing pad to her, she had picked up the ballpoint pen. After putting down a few niceties, she had suggested that the fewer the cotton saris she brought along with her, the better it would be. Washing, starching, and then ironing six yards of material was no easy matter in this environment. She had then disabused Rekha of her false notion that the hot winds would begin to blow in New Jersey where she was moving, with the arrival of spring. *Please be adequately clothed in woollens when you arrive. It won't do for you to fall ill as soon as you get here.* Asking her to call up as soon as she was able, she had ended the letter with her good wishes. Propping up the letter against some books, Nandita had gone back to the kitchen and from there out into the yard.

It was bitterly cold out there; pulling the loose flowing end of the sari close to her, she told herself that she would stay but a moment, for all she wanted to do was to take in a breath of fresh air. But it had taken her a while, for her eyes had fallen upon the squirrel that she had been observing moving around out on the branches from up above. She had watched fascinated as the squirrel scampered upwards. And her eyes giving chase to that beautiful little animal had clambered up and up along with it upon the dead branches of the tree! And it was then that with a sudden surge of inexplicable joy, she had spotted an infinitely beautiful sight!

At first she saw just a small spot of green and then another and then another where she thought nothing but barrenness still reigned. No wonder the squirrel was up and about. The signs were there that the dead world of nature was coming back to life again. A sudden surge of joy had run through her heart like a silvery ball of mercury and left it light and buoyant! For one fleeting moment, she was glad that she was here; she could never have seen this tableau that nature staged each year of the fading away of life and its rebirth come spring had she stayed on in Kolkata. It was signs such as these that kept reminding humanity that there really was no final thing called either life or death; it was an immensely reassuring thought. As she turned to re-enter the warmth of the home, she wished that like the dead trees, she too should somehow be able to bring herself back to life once again.

Leaving behind the company of the squirrel, the big fat cat, and the tender burgeoning leaves, she had gone back into the warm but lonely interior of the home but there was an imperceptible spring back in her steps as she walked around the house, tidying as she went. The children would be back soon; freshening up, she had come down to receive them. They had entered in a rush strewing school bags, water bottles, jackets, shoes, socks, sundry sticks and stones, and even a live frog.

'Go and put that frog out in the yard.'

'Why?' Seeing his grandmother's stern looks, he had obeyed without any further questions. 'I'm hungry,' he said, retrieving the frog and moving outwards. He was back in a moment. 'What have you made for us today, *malpoas*?'

'You love bagels, have some with cream cheese.'

'But I want *malpoas*, Thamma.'

'I'll make them for you tomorrow, I was busy today.'

'Doing what, Ma?' Having let herself in, Meeta asked from behind.

'A friend of mine is moving to the US, she wanted to know about so many things. So I wrote back.'

'So what did you tell her?'

'I told her not to bring too many cotton saris with her when she comes.'

3 ALL FOR THE WANT OF A PALTRY POSTAGE STAMP

Sudipto was a puzzled man! The change that had come about in his mother's personality had him totally intrigued. He had practically lived his entire lifetime with her, yet today, she was tending to become a total stranger to him. So slow and insidious had been the process of change that he had not noticed its coming till it had grown into a full-grown entity. A state of near total breakdown in communication between the two of them had come about and taken the place of the comfortable relationship that they had once enjoyed. He had no idea how or why this had come to pass, but that it had come to be he could not help but be uncomfortably aware of.

The tight and drawn expression she now wore like a mask upon her face angered and irritated him beyond measure. It was as if she was pointing an accusing finger towards him whenever he chanced to look her way. What exactly was he to be held guilty of? True, she had brought him up a fatherless child with care when he was young: had he ever denied that single-handed, single-minded contribution on her part? But was he not in turn taking care of her now that she was getting on? Why was she then receding into some hidden-away recess within her where none could reach? She was never a garrulous person but he had observed though quite recently, that she spoke very few words to anyone these days. A gamut of indecipherable expressions that were beyond his comprehension had moved in to take the place of the spoken words she had earlier used. When she did speak, it appeared to him that the real thoughts and feelings that she wanted to express had been hidden out of sight, beneath a thin sheath made up of meaningless words that she had created for just this purpose. And therefore when on rare occasions they chanced to exchange a few words, he was hard pressed to understand what in truth she was trying to convey to him. It was as if he was interacting with a foreigner who had strayed into his domain, each endowed with a tongue which was, alas, largely unintelligible to the other.

This morning's exchange over the purchase of a few postal stamps had left him nonplussed. Having shrugged himself into his suit jacket, he was about to let himself out when she had suddenly handed him a letter. Looking down upon the letter, he had directed his gaze enquiringly towards her.

'Will you please . . . would you please . . . post this letter for me?' The tone, apologetic and halting, had fallen false and jarring upon his ears.

He pointed to his wristwatch. 'I'm running late, Ma.' She had said nothing but had continued to stand rooted to the spot, looking at him. With a barely disguised look of impatience upon his face, he suggested, 'Why don't you post it yourself?'

'I have no stamps,' was all she said, as he held out the letter to her!

'If you go out into the yard, you'll see . . . winter is almost over. Why don't you walk down to the post office?' She still stood impassive. Irritation mounting at the delay this meaningless exchange was causing, he continued with 'And once there, you can get the stamps and post the letter as well.'

'Post it when you can.'

'Really, Ma, why don't you make a little effort to go out and do a few tasks yourself?' Wearing an inscrutable expression upon her face, she had looked up right into his eyes. He could not hold her gaze. Perturbed by the shortness of his own tone, he had tried to make amends. Awkwardly placing a hand upon her back, he said persuasively, 'Besides, stepping out will do you a world of good.'

'I'll go for a walk, *but . . . you* get the stamps for me.'

'But why, Ma?'

'Where's the post office? I don't know the way.'

'Come on, Ma; how can that be possible?' he had asked in incredulous tones.

'I go out alone so seldom that . . .' she mumbled. 'And I'm not used to mixing with the people of this country.'

'What kind of mixing with people does one need to buy stamps, Ma?'

'I can hardly understand a word of what is being said around me, Sudipto, so . . .'

Strange, so many years in America and she said she knew neither the tongue nor the people of the country. And 'Sudipto'? Why had she taken to calling him Sudipto all of a sudden? His brows had creased together at this formal address. When he was a schoolboy, he knew he was in deep trouble whenever she chose to address him so. 'Sudipto,' she would call out to him in bone-chilling tones, to ask him about some minor misdemeanour or to enquire about a scholastic grade that had chosen to take a slippery path downwards. And today she had addressed him as 'Sudipto' all because he had asked her to go out and get herself some postage. Hiding his hurt, he had stretched out his hand, '*Theek aachey*, if you insist, I'll post it.' Without a word, she had handed him the letter, and without another word, he had taken it from her. And he was gone.

Throwing his briefcase over his shoulder into the rear of his car, he had reversed out of the garage in a sharp arc onto the road and, tyres throwing up gravel, had taken off at an injudicious speed. Though he had not let it be seen, he was inordinately hurt. Why was his mother behaving in such a strange and unreasonable manner? Why?

Normally an even-tempered man, he had felt a surging torrent of resentment and anger course through him. He had been perplexed by the changed nuances of her tone of voice as she had requested him to post her letter. Why had she chosen to speak to him as if he was some outsider? And why had she placed their relationship upon a formal plane by addressing him as 'Sudipto'? Coming to a screeching halt at a red light, he had sat drumming impatiently upon the steering wheel while his mind, unhampered by any change in the traffic light, had kept going round and round in circles working out the mystique of his many names.

The light changed and he took off just as he realised with a jolt that he could not remember when last his mother had addressed him as 'Khoka', that special little appellation that was used for a beloved little boy in Bengal. He had ceased to be a little boy years ago but he had continued to remain the beloved son whom the mother had continued to call Khoka even when he was a grown man. He had rebelled at times but it was no more than a face-saving device, for how could he deny how good it felt to know that he was so very special to her!

Immediately after his marriage, his mother had decided that a name such as Khoka was not quite suitable for a married man. He had always been Tukun to the rest of the family and to his close friends, and from that day, he had become Tukun to her as well. But it was not as if the name Khoka had been completely expunged from the records. On those special moments when she wanted to express how much she cherished and loved him, she had brought the name back out of the closet and wrapped it around him like a warm and soft as silk *pashmina* shawl. And today, Nandita his mother had once again become the stern and forbidding senior teacher of the school where he had been one of her pupils at one time. She had addressed him with the formality with which she would have called out to any one of her myriad students.

Smarting from the pain she had inflicted upon him, he drove on. Even after being at the wheel of his beloved car for ten long minutes, his ruffled nerves had continued to remain in a state of disarray. The lulling cadence of the car skimming over the road had worked its wonder eventually. And having shelved the strange behaviour of his mother away from his mind, he had entered his place of work, if not with exuberance then with equanimity.

Back at home out of sheer force of habit, Nandita had gone around from room to room, straightening, tidying, and cleaning up as she went along. That letter, the bone of all recent contentions was lying open upon her bedside table; as she had picked it up to put it away, her eyes had strayed to the date scrawled upon the right-hand top corner. And 'Mother mine, what is this?' had escaped from her lips. That letter she was in such a hurry to reply to was almost three weeks old. Rekha was perhaps already in the US by now! How strange it was that she had not paid any attention to the date when she had read and reread it the previous day. Had she been but a bit more observant, she would not have brewed such a storm in a teacup. A whole day wasted on agonising over what she should write to Rekha, ending in a non-letter and then that unpleasant altercation with Tukun!

None too pleased with her own self, weighed down with a sense of abject failure, she had picked up from where she had left off. She stopped for a moment in front of the dresser in her room where a cluster of photographs serving as keys to her memory bank stood in serried ranks. The smiling face of a boy with shining bright eyes had looked back at her out of a couple of them. The one to the right she remembered having snapped when that boy had returned home triumphant with his first public examination result.

And just next to that snap was placed one in which her Khoka stood wearing an exultant look upon his face. He was standing squinting into the sun, holding on to a kite: the very first kite he had hunted and brought down from the skies. After all, he was a kite-flying flyer's son! So this was a trophy he could not help but cherish. Montu had dropped in one day, and in a sudden upsurge of nostalgia, she had wanted that her son too should learn to fly a kite. She had urged her cousin to teach her son the art of taking off into the skies. 'Teach him, Montu.' And then in a more cajoling tone, 'Please!'

'Why? You were always chasing us away from the roof when we came up with our kites, I remember.'

While thinking, *the happy days of my life are all a tangle with kites and so I owe it to Dipto's memory*, she had said aloud, 'It is a useful expertise.'

'Is it?' Montu had laughingly asked. 'It hasn't got me very far, has it?' But he had taken his young nephew under his wing and initiated him into the fine art of kite flying!

And that very first kite he had downed had come as a *nazrana* to Nandita his mother! She knew no relationship could possibly remain at the same plane forever. Even so, need the change be so hurtful and distancing? Today, though she and her son lived under the same roof, they had drifted so far apart that when they met, it was as if they were strangers.

Did the growing up of a child demand such a heavy price from a parent? And while removing some invisible dust with the *anchal* of her sari from the photographs of her son, she had remembered the dramatic entrance that his father had made into her life one day.

One bright and beautiful day, riding upon a colourful kite, Prodipto Kumar Roy had come and landed up into her life. She was sitting on the rooftop of the only home she had ever known, that of her ancestors, the Gangulys of Bhabanipore. At the precise moment the kite had landed upon her, she was making painful efforts towards mastering some English poetry. From the kite, her eyes had travelled to the thread that trailed from the offending missile, and from the thread onto the next-door household's roof, from there to a hand that held a bobbin from where the thread had started out on its journey of assault. At the end of this voyage of inquiry, behind the offending hand, stood a young man grinning happily from ear to ear as he looked towards her. 'Hello there,' he had called out in English, with a friendly wave of his unoccupied hand.

Nandita, heart pounding with fear, had looked back towards the door that brought one onto the roof. And chatty as ever, he had continued, 'You were so

terribly engrossed in your studies, so I had to . . .' And he had shrugged towards
the kite. 'There, wasn't that a wonderful bit of flying? It's all in the training,
you know,' he informed her. 'Had to find means to warn you . . . that studying
too hard could damage your brain.'

Mad, absolutely mad—training, what training? she had thought. And
then cocky as ever, 'I forgot to ask, but . . . tell me are you deaf . . . or
dumb . . . or something?' A lovely rejoinder had come rushing to her brain, but
her tongue had refused to transform it into spoken English. And cutting into
her speechlessness, the offender spoke up. 'May I have my kite back, please.'

Face flaming, she realised that she was still holding on to that offending
piece of flying frippery, and promptly let go of it. And as he manoeuvred that
colourful emissary, Nandita had scrutinised him from under hooded eyes. She
had seen very few films but she knew all about films and film stars, so she
could see that he looked very much like a hero out of a Hindi movie. But what
on earth was a hero from Bombay doing on the rooftop of the Mukherjees?

Having landed the kite expertly back at his feet, in a voice laden with
mischief he had provoked her with '*Am I pleased* that God has spared you
your hearing though, alas, he has robbed you of your tongue.' Peeved at his
behaviour, she had decided then and there to bring him several notches down
from the pedestal of stardom where she had placed him in haste and had
docketed him as a Punjabi youth instead. In the meanwhile, having rolled up
all the trailing thread, the young invader had teased, 'What's your name, or
don't you have one?' And like a startled pigeon, she had flown from the roof,
realising the enormity of her trespasses.

A kite had brought romance and love into her life; no wonder she had
wanted her cousin Montu to impart some training to her son in the fine art of
kite flying. It was time Tukun took his own son in hand and introduced him
to the joy of connecting with the blue of the skies. Some family traditions had
a need to be maintained. Maybe one of these days she would drop a hint to
Tukun. Perhaps not, she had sighed.

And then the telephone trilled, cutting into her roseate reminiscences.

'Is that you, Nanditadi?' asked an unfamiliar, hesitant voice.

'Rekha?' She sensed that it must be Rekha; even so, she asked.

'You did not recognise my voice? Of course you didn't, how stupid of me.'

'Yes, it has been a long time . . .'

'Did you get my letter?'

'Yes. I did, but it came only yesterday.' And the unspoken words *And I spent an entire day replying to it* made her smile to herself.

'What were you doing? I hope I didn't disturb you?'

'*Kee jey bolo bhai*, I was doing nothing important.'

'I'm glad you phoned,' she said instead.

'Oh, Nanditadi, I've been dying to speak to you, but I didn't know how to get an interstate number.'

'Hope you're liking America.'

'Yes.' Was there perhaps a shade of hesitancy there? 'I love being here, my little granddaughter just dotes on me . . . but I miss my Kolkata.'

'*So do I,*' she wanted to say but, changing tracks asked, 'Remember those good old days, when I was trying to teach you?'

'Of course I do. If we had not moved away, perhaps it would have been different. You know I gave up studies after my tenth, and my handwriting,' she said with an apologetic laugh, 'you must have seen, is just as horrible as ever.'

'It doesn't matter, Rekha,' she soothed and the crazy words of caution against excessive erudition that Prodipto had implanted in her brain had come hovering on her tongue. What if it had spilled over?

But Rekha was not as circumspect and wanted to know, 'How could you marry a man you did not know at all, Nanditadi? We all did, but then . . . they did not live in far-off Delhi. And they did nothing as strange as flying planes and things as your husband did. Weren't you afraid to go away like that, Nanditadi?' So Rekha had been keeping tabs upon her life!

'I'll tell you someday.'

Still holding on to the telephone, Nandita wondered what she would tell Rekha if ever she did. Tell her that she had married no stranger? Tell her how he had landed a kite upon her? Tell her how angered she had been by this boorish intrusion into her privacy? Tell her that despite her initial reaction, she had gone up onto the roof in search of him the very next day! She remembered once again how she had fled from the terrace on being asked her name, and from there, she drifted along the stream of her reminiscences.

The next day when she climbed, books in hand, up to the roof, all resolves of hatred and acute dislike forgotten, she had not found the Punjabi youth there. She had felt a terrible pang of disappointment while looking across at that empty terrace that lay across from her. At the end of the third day, she had assured herself that she had never really seen him at all. On the fourth day, she had decided that the distillation of some Mughal history into her brain was the need of the moment. And just when she had managed to push the stranger out of her head to make room for some history, she had heard someone call out softly to her by name and ask in Bangla how she was. Somehow the Punjabi youth had learnt to speak Bangla, but he did have a funny accent!

'Where had you gone away?' she had demanded of him as if he were duty bound to tell her about his movements.

'Why? Did you miss me?'

'Don't be silly, why should I miss you?'

'Then why did you ask?'

Just like that and she had gone on to ask, 'Where did you learn to speak our language?'

'Your language?' he threw back at her, laughing out loud.

'Ssh!' she had cautioned, putting a finger to her lips. And he had laughed louder still. Fearing for her life, she had gathered her books and her wits together and fled without so much as looking back. But the very next day, she had gone back again onto the roof, to continue with her studies, of course!

Damini, getting curious, had asked why she was spending so many hours on the roof these days. And Nandita had replied part truthfully that in this house of perpetual turmoil, the roof was the best place to study for an examination as exalted as the one she was about to take. Damini knew nothing about exalted exams but knew a great deal about the marriage market and had warned Nandita to take care.

'Make sure, Didi, that you don't turn as black as charcoal. No one will marry you if you turn as dark as your Daminidi.'

'Who said I want to get married? See what happened to Boroma, to my ma and to Kakima and to you. Men have made too many rules, and I don't like them and will never follow them.'

And she had ended up telling Damini that she herself would never marry.

And Damini, ignoring her outburst, had said, 'Go now and study. But mind you stay in the shade, no one wants to marry a dark girl, so . . .'

And laughing at Damini's obtuse refusal to accept anything of what she had said, Nandita had escaped to the roof with books enough to open up a sizeable library! But just as she was settling down in her niche on the terrace,

Montu and Jhontu had invaded her privacy. They were both armed with kites. But no sooner than their kites had attained an enviable height and had started dancing around among the clouds, a warring kite had erupted from the Mukherjee terrace and gone off zooming up and up in hot pursuit after them.

'Ah! So he is still here,' Nandita had told herself with an unaccountable sense of relief and joy. His sudden disappearance after their very first encounter had rendered her strangely vulnerable. Her books forgotten, she had watched with bated breath each manoeuvre, each strategic move of the war that had been waged up there in the sky. Poor Montu and Jhontu were no match for the ace flyer who was their opponent. Their kites downed, they had gone away despondent at their defeat. And Nandita had turned wrathfully upon the victor of the uneven contest.

'You should be ashamed of yourself,' she had thrown across the gap at the stranger who was not quite a stranger to her now.

'Why?' He had grinned back.

'They are just boys, and see what you did to their poor kites.'

'All's fair in love and war, Nandita.'

Nandita, opening a book, had decided to turn her back upon his provocative reasoning.

'Still pretending to study, I see . . .'

Her eyes were moist as, brushing a finger affectionately across the framed photograph of her young son, she had moved away with a sigh back to the window. Neither the cat nor the squirrel was to be seen anywhere, but there was another interesting visitor out there that held her attention immediately. A far less hesitant and insecure sun than the one that was to be seen of late was out at long last. A welcoming sweep of golden sunshine emanating from it had reinvented the dull and dreary world and turned it into a place of wonder once again. Tentatively she opened the window of her room and stretched out her cupped hands to rake in some of the gold. But no sooner than she would bring her laden hands back into the room, the gold held cradled there would instantly fade away. It was still bitterly cold outside but the gold rush on show had inveigled her with its bounty. She remembered as she stood hesitant that she had promised her son that she would go out and take a look at the world lying outside the four walls of their own home today. The son who was there, a physical proof that his father had not been just a figment of her overheated imagination.

She wanted to run off somewhere very far away where she would be able to shake off the troublesome threads of her tormenting thoughts. She would try out today whether or not going out of the confines of the home would help. But so many fears had assailed her senses, and so many doubts had come crowding into her mind at the very thought of going out alone. So intimidating had been the prospect of going out unescorted onto the streets that lay beyond the periphery of their own home, that she had almost abandoned the idea of indulging in this incredibly daring bit of adventure. Time had indeed brought about a major change in the personality of Nandita. For a woman as independent as she had been at one time, fear and trepidation were indeed strange reactions to a simple act of stepping out. She had been angered beyond measure on coming face to face with her transformed, hesitant, fearful self. She had decided then and there that there would be no backing away from *this walk* that she had been shying away from.

She had gone in search of appropriate clothing and footwear; going out was not as simple a matter as Tukun going off to work in his well-heated BMW had made it out to be! A jumble of space-age garments fit for a walk on the moon hung at all times from the hooks on the closet in the entrée, but where was the parka she normally wore? One of the children seemed to have graduated into it. So unused was she to going out on her own that her hands shook as she selected one that looked nearest to her size, for she felt as if she in truth was about to venture out on a moonwalk!

Placing the garment upon a chair close to the front door, she delved deep into the interior of the closet where countless pairs of footwear lay huddled together. Pulling out the only pair of closed shoes she owned, she had passed a tentative hand across its surface; they felt none too inviting. Even so, she had pulled on a pair of borrowed socks, forced her feet into the pair, and hobbled around for a while trying to accustom her feet to the bondage of closed footwear. Then going up to her room, she had washed her face and passed a comb through her hair, and she was all set for the day's outing. When she pulled the door shut behind her, she presented a strange sight. She had hitched up her white sari two to three inches above her ankles to save the hem of her draped garment from the springtime slush. So her white socks with 'Adidas' written in red across its top, sandwiched between her shoes and the heightened hem of her sari, looked like a giant hoarding placed there for the benefit of the legions that lived and loved and procreated at ground level. The parka was too large and came down somewhere to her knees and the sleeves had to be rolled up to allow her hands to peep out. A pair of mittens that had fortuitously been lying around in a crumpled state at the bottom of one of its capacious pockets had given much-needed protection to her bare hands.

It was a good thing that she had not taken a look at herself dressed in her full cold-cheating regalia. She was a woman with as near a perfect figure as was possible at her age. The oversized parka had managed to obliterate her bodily lines and the fringes of the sari peeping out from below looked like a ballerina's tutu that had slipped down and fixed itself on to the wrong place. It was not a very elegant image that the elegant and dignified Nandita projected that day. On the other hand, the crisp cold air had touched her perfect skin and brought colour rushing to her makeup-free face. Her large eyes had moistened with the sting in the air and looked luminous and large upon her face. The cold breeze had played about with the tendrils of hair sprinkled with white that had escaped out of the strict tutelage into which she had put them and made her look younger by far than her years merited.

She had some idea about the layout of the town and decided to walk down towards the post office even though she had so obtusely refused to go there to fulfil the errand of buying some stamps. With what would she have bought those stamps? she had thought, with deep resentment welling up inside her. Did Tukun expect that she would stretch out her hand and ask him for money? Had he forgotten what kind of a person his mother was? How many times had he asked her to repeat the story of her life to him? He knew how she had walked out from the home of her ancestors one day, with him in her arms! How old was she then: not even twenty. Rebelling against their antiquated ways, she had gone away to Delhi. But even there, she had been met with nothing but disappointment. For the very modern Roys who spoke more often than not in English, went ballroom dancing, and ate at table with knife and fork had suddenly become stereotypical Hindu parents left with a widowed daughter-in-law. Nandita's father-in-law, stunned by the sudden death of his only son, had been left immobilised by grief, while his wife had gone in search of a scapegoat upon whom she could heap all her anguish to keep a hold on to her sanity. It was not as if she ever let a single word of recrimination fall from her lips, but her silences spoke volumes. And picking up her son, turning her back upon them, Nandita had walked out of their lives as well!

Yes, in her mindlessness, she had walked out on those grieving parents!

She had realised much later that she should perhaps not have taken the listless reactions of her broken-hearted mother-in-law so much to heart. What right had she, in a childish act of petulant retaliation, to take away their grandson from them, the only living proof they had that their son had once lived upon this earth? Anger past, she had realised that she should not have dealt them such a cruel blow. But by then, it was far too late for her to undo her mistakes, for within the year, she had lost both of them.

A letter had arrived soon after stating that in his last will and testament Major General T. K. Roy had left all his movable and immovable properties in the name of his daughter-in-law, Mrs Nandita Roy! So ashamed was Nandita of her own actions that she had never been able to bring herself to make use of that legacy. Much later, much later when Tukun was a grown man, she had told him about the legacy. And together they had decided that with it they must commemorate the memories of the father, the mother, and their son. Prodipto's mother having died of cancer, they had bequeathed the amount to the cancer hospital where she had breathed her last.

Yes, so ashamed was Nandita of her own actions that she had never been able to bring herself to make use of that legacy, and so had had to continue with her life of eking out a living on a schoolteacher's salary. She had done her B.Ed. much later but that had certainly not made her affluent! The journey thus begun in a spurt of anger had been strewn with obstacles. But crossing all hurdles, she had taught herself to stand up alone upon her own two feet. What she had earned had barely met their needs, but they had more than just survived. But at a later date, the selfsame woman who had so jealously guarded her economic independence, succumbing to emotional pressure, had thrown it all away. Since leaving her job in Kolkata and moving to Chicago, she had never earned and therefore never had any money to her name.

Money was far more than just legal tender. Money spelt freedom and independence and the right to make an independent choice, an independent decision. When all decision-making slowly percolates away out of your hands, then even the simple making of a choice between the purchasing of a pound of nectarines versus a pound of apricots becomes a matter of earth-shaking importance to the person who has slowly drifted away from the mainstream.

Her little flat in Kolkata had been bought with her own earnings from the housing board. She had sold that flat and auctioned away her independence by leaving her job when she had just become headmistress of her school. Today she hankered after that slim and semi-starved pay packet that she had let go of without a murmur. And she had thought for a moment that she could persuade Rekha away from her resolve to come and make her life here with her son.

It was not as if she wanted for anything. In the melee of shopping that Tukun and Meeta had to perforce perform each week, her needs had been thought out and always been met. Whenever required, a stack of white saris would arrive from the haven of Indian condiments and spices: Devon. The blouses and petticoats she stitched herself. Tukun had never put any money in her hands; but then, when did she ever go out to shop alone? For that matter, shopping since the advent of affluence into their lives had become such a rushed affair that it was fitted in somehow between times. The children and Nandita rarely if ever joined them these days on these expeditions. Even her feet were the same size as Meeta's so there had been no need to go specifically to get herself a pair. So in a manner of speaking, what was she to do with money, when she had no outlet where she could spend it?

She had always felt the post office was much nearer to home than it really was. Goodness, it was far; car rides were so misleading! She wanted to turn round and go back home for she could not perceive how this tripping along aimlessly down an empty chill road could be considered a pastime designed to alleviate the boredom and feeling of solitude that now lay within her like a heavy stone.

But before turning back, she had paused a moment and looked around and up into the trees while resting her feet. It was an awesome, breathtaking sight that met her eyes. The apparently dead trees had all come alive just like the sprinkling of trees sitting in their own backyard had come back to life again. These trees lining the street were so tall that she had not noticed this magnificent show of life resurgent that they had on display. She had stood mesmerised by the magnitude of this awe-inspiring proof that in death lay life and in life lay death. The proof of the magic of spring was everywhere on show; the trees had sprouted leaves that were as delicate and fuzzy as the first appearance of a beard upon a young lad's face. The tree-lined boulevard with its tender and touching growth had held her back from retracing her steps homewards.

She started walking slowly onwards, all discomforts forgotten. A young woman with a baby in a pram trundled past; like ships upon a vast ocean, they had crossed one another and moved on and away from one another. They would perhaps never meet again but a smile had tied them momentarily together and created some magic. A cluster of crocuses had fallen to her eyes, as had a solitary daffodil that was on show in a garden across the street. She was wondering whether she should cross the street to feast upon that lovely splash of colour when she had sighted a wilful and beautiful cocker spaniel. The cocker was wearing a coat of burnished caramel fit for a queen, and it was hauling along a lovely windblown woman upon a leash as if in truth she really was a queen. The spaniel's coat and the woman's hair were a perfect match, but who the owner was and who the pet was not all that clear on viewing them together as an ensemble. It was a strange but endearing sight of bonding between that little dog and the tall young woman that had brought a smile to Nandita's lips. And as they rushed past, the girl had raised her hand in a wave and thrown 'Have a good day' over her shoulder. Nandita's right arm had automatically risen in response to this greeting. But though her waving hand had managed to only fall upon the disappearing backs of the duo tied together by a leash, she had felt for a fleeting moment that she too was somehow a part of that entourage.

The sight of this twosome had brought back many memories of happier days to her mind. Nandita had recognised a bond here that existed only between two creatures that truly cared for the other. She had savoured many such ties but today, alas, they were but mere fading memories that she had even forgotten to place among rose petals! And with a sense of acute loss, she had looked back upon the indistinct images of happier days left behind somewhere in the murky past. The smile that had earlier wreathed her face had soon been chased away by a look of thoughtfulness, and that in turn had been replaced by a wistful expression.

From a short distance away, a very large man, back upright, a pair of sad blue eyes crinkling in the corners had watched the ever-changing expressions upon the face of the woman who was walking towards him. But it was her eyes that had caught his attention! For the sadness lying within his soul had found a matching resonance in the shades of sorrow that lay within the woman's eyes. The incongruity of her attire had fallen to his eyes in the passing, as they were in total variance to the personality of the person who was carrying them around. But it was the face and the eyes placed upon that face that he saw. It was a mobile, readable face that gave away the volatility of her thought processes. She was not a particularly young person, yet there was a vulnerability about her that endowed her grey-haired persona with a patina of youth. For a fleeting moment, he had felt there was something strangely familiar about her, but he had let it pass, for he could not perceive how he could possibly have known her. He had loomed large over her as they had crossed, but lost in thought, she had not looked up at him.

It was later, much later that the face of the woman had come drifting across the big man's mind once again, and this time round, the smiling face of Meg had been juxtaposed with that of hers within the same frame. A trickle of memory had brought a day out of the past in front of him. His wife Meg and he were guests at a function in the New Jersey home of an Indian family, and this woman had sat beside Meg and explained the proceedings to the two of them. He was sad that he had not been able to place her immediately. He would have liked to know how she was doing.

Nandita's journey to the post office was progressing very slowly. But then, getting to the post office was but a mere setting of an aimless goal. To her surprise at this point, a small twinge of hunger had come from nowhere and given her a little nudge. She never ate before two in the afternoon, and here she was feeling hungry at just a few minutes past midday. She wished she had brought along something with her; an apple or a sandwich would have gone down very well at this point. The avowed objective forgotten, the intimations of hunger quashed, she had meandered on, savouring every little delight that this journeying had in store for her.

But her legs were tiring, and a little garden with not a bloom to its name had beckoned to her with its inviting array of empty benches. She had gone up the few steps that had to be taken to get there, had thrown herself down upon the seating that was nearest to the entrance, and had looked around. A very large building towered over the park on its western periphery. From where she sat, she could see the near-naked trees of the park reflected upon the surface of the frontage made up of glass that the building seemed to have. She had gone past by car on this road many a time, yet she had never once noticed either the garden or the large building that stood companionably beside it. Her curiosity aroused, she had risen and walked up to the end of the garden where the building was located. She stood at a slight elevation in comparison to the grounds facing the massive structure. A discreet board placed on the right-hand end of the gate proclaimed that it was 'The Home'.

The Home? Whose home, what home? Nandita wondered as she looked on from where she stood. And then with a slight shift in the position of the sun or the repositioning of the clouds in the sky, what had been till then an inscrutable impenetrable façade had become a transparent partition. Through this transparent wall, she could clearly look down and into the Home. The breath had been squeezed out of her chest, and she had been left gasping. Spread out before her was an array of human beings all into a state of acute debility and advanced old age. She could not clearly make out what they were doing but it appeared as if some of them were partaking of a meal. The wheelchairs were easily distinguishable both by their bulk and their contour. And a large number of them were in use, she could see. It was a depressing and frightening sight to chance upon on a beautiful and resurgent springtime day! Old age was an absolute reality that was linked with a long life. What if she were to live on and on and on?

Nandita had been brought up in a joint family, where people who were old and very old were very important components of that which made up the whole. Somehow the face of ageing was neither frightening nor grotesque in that milieu. The newborn baby, the growing child, the young, the middle-aged, the old, and the very old all coexisted together side by side like the many disparate threads that go into the making of a many-hued piece of tapestry work. But here, segregated, separated, and herded together, the ageing and aged took on a nightmare-inducing awesome persona.

Averting her eyes, she had fled from the distressing scene that lay spread out right before her. She had run across the length of the garden and stumbled down the few steps that were to bring her to road level. A gentle, supportive hand had steadied her unsteady descent. She had looked into the kind eyes of an elderly person. With a smile, he had moved on but not before saying, 'Take care,' with total sincerity. It was only after he had walked away from her that she noticed he needed the support of a three-pronged walking stick to get about independently. It sent a surge of shame coursing through her, yet so disturbed was she that she had allowed herself to slow down only after she had been able to put a considerable distance between herself and the Home.

Breathless from the speed at which she had walked, she had let herself in and had looked around with changed eyes upon the all-embracing comfort of her familiar surroundings. A little bit of thankfulness at what she had: a few blisters, a bowed-down shoulder, and a mixed bag of experiences had all been credited to her account that Friday morning.

Organising a dinner party on a Friday night was to Sudipto's mind one of the most inconsiderate acts that anyone could possibly indulge in. At the end of a long and arduous five days at work, a man needed some time to get into the mood for socialising.

'Why didn't you make some excuse?' he had growled, eyeing his bed longingly. 'I'm dead tired. I just want to laze around and then crash . . .'

'Into your bed of course.'

'Any other suggestions?' She had glowered, and he had grinned. 'OK. Just, just, just give a rub down to my back, please, Meetu and I'll see if I can . . .' he said, squirming.

'Who asked you to play so much tennis?

'Mahadevan's paunch.'

'Mahadevan? Who is Mahadevan?'

'A chap I bumped into in the office lift one day. He is quite a big shot.'

'Is that why you play tennis with him?' she had asked with a mischievous smile.

'Don't be silly. We met again on the tennis courts and since then he has adopted me as his tennis playing buddy.'

'But who is this Mahadevan?' He had shrugged and picked up the remote.

Zapping channels, Tukun said, 'You want to know who Mahadevan is?'

'No, I don't. Not now certainly! Come on, Tukun,' she pleaded, 'take a quick shower, please, it is quite a drive away to Patkar's place.'

'I'll bring him over one day and then you can see for yourself who he is!'

'Come on, Tukun, we are getting terribly late. And I can do without knowing all about this Mahadevan of yours.'

But can we? Was he an archetypal Indian? No, not quite! So who was Mahadevan?

Mahadevan was a man who had made some positive moves while still very young and earned himself a place in the sun! A place in the oh-so salubrious sun that blazed down upon the United States of America.

When he was just fifteen years old, Mahadevan had met his maternal uncle's wife's sister's sister-in-law's son-in-law at a wedding. The guy was visiting India for the first time in six years. Not only had he forgotten to speak Tamil, he had also forgotten to eat with his fingers. But that had taken nothing away from his shine; in truth it had enhanced the gloss of his persona in the eyes of those youngsters who had looked upon him in wonderment.

He was quite a showstopper, dressed as he was in a blazing red Chicago Bulls T-shirt and a pair of Wrangler jeans. Those young and admiring eyes could see nothing amiss in the baseball cap he wore so rakishly upon his head, nor in the incongruous pair of Nike sneakers that he was sporting on his feet, at this Tamil Brahmin wedding. The tales he had told that gaggle of youth about *the life fantastic* he now led in that far-off land had left them so full of a yearning that not a single one among them had been able to do any justice to the wedding feast that day. As for Mahadevan, who had been among those who had sat at the feet of the great preceptor, life had taken on a new direction for him thenceforth. He had decided then and there that El Dorado would be his!

The very next day onwards, he had gone ferreting around in search of a means to his end and had come up with just the right answer. He would just have to get himself a seat in the IIT. The Indian Institutes of Technology had been tailor-made to fulfil a need of the great nation called the United States of America. He would have to somehow earn himself a seat there.

From that day onwards, Mahadevan had begun putting in ten hours a day on mathematics, another ten on physics, and another score of hours on chemistry. How he managed to find thirty hours to spare in a day made up of just twenty-four segments of an hour each, no one could really explain. However, with these hours and hours of extra work backed by his bristling-with-cleverness Tam-Brahm genes, at age eighteen years two months and a few days, he had made it to the IIT.

The day Mahadevan had entered the portals of the Indian Institute of Technology at Powai in Bombay he was a made man. For no sooner than he had completed his four-year course of studies in electronic engineering, and the results had been declared, he had been swooped down upon and been borne away to the land of his dreams. Barely past his twenty-second year, he had flown off and landed upon a branch loaded with flavoursome fruit in that far-off land across the seven seas. The successful son had gone back to India but once: that to marry Sumathi, the young woman his parents had chosen for him. It was quite a number of years after his arrival in the US that he had thought of bringing his parents over to stay with him and his family.

And that is how Mahadevan at first and then his entire family had moved in and taken up a tiny but meaningful fraction of the vast, variegated, and verdant land that made up the United States of America.

And while we were ruminating upon the success story of Mahadevan, son of Neelakanthan, the remote had been snatched away from Tukun's hand and he had found himself being manhandled into the bathroom.

Emerging from the bath and pulling a Gap T-shirt over his head, still wet from the shower, he had reiterated, 'You should have made some excuse, a weekend should begin reasonably after a whole days lazing around. This Patkar and his—'

'Patkar is your friend, not mine, his idea of a weekend happens to be somewhat different from yours and you very well know that.'

'When will this fellow understand that Saturday nights have been specially created for partying?'

'And Friday evening till Saturday afternoon for sleeping.'

'Whose side are you on, Patkar's or mine?'

'Patkar's, who else's?'

'It certainly looks like that. Come on, let's get going if we must; we have a long way to go.'

'I thought I'd wear a sari but not a single blouse fits. Do you think I am putting on weight?'

'I'll tell you later, I can never tell by merely looking at you.'

'Tukun, you are incorrigible.'

'Thanks for the compliment.'

'Tukun, you really are incorrigible,' she giggled as she kept sifting through a pile of saris she had placed upon the bed.

'Forget about the sari, wear something comfortable and let's go. Is Ma coming with us?'

'No.'

'I hope you've told her that we're going out and that we'll be late.'

'You tell her.'

'Hey, tell me, Meeta, is there something wrong with Ma?'

'Wrong with Ma?' she said while scrutinising a T-shirt with *Welcome to Pattaya* written across it, and another with *UCLA* emblazoned upon the chest.

She had never been to Thailand or to the University of California, so the choice was to depend more on the conviviality of the upper garment with the trousers she had chosen to wear that evening than upon any other consideration.

'Yeah, that's what I said, didn't I?'

'That's nothing new, is it? She seems to have changed over time. I don't have the time to sit and entertain her, or to find out what's going on inside her head.' The velvet trousers she had chosen to wear were causing her somewhat the same problem as her blouses had been giving. But eventually, holding her breath she had been able to zip it up. She would have to eat sparingly this evening, she thought wryly as she let out her sucked-in tummy.

'Is that the problem?'

What problem?'

'Aren't you listening to me?'

'Of course I am, but what is all this talk about Ma in honour of all of a sudden? We must remember to pick up a bottle of wine and some flowers on our way,' she had reminded as she fished around for a clean handkerchief in her cupboard.

'I asked her to go to the post office and she refused outright. She agreed to go for a walk, but she just wouldn't agree to buy those stamps that she needed.'

'Which one of these T-shirts do you like?'

'Didn't you hear me? I said Ma refused to go and buy herself some stamps.'

'Maybe she didn't have the money to buy the stamps. And you know how fussy she is about "this is mine, that is yours" business.'

'No money to buy a few stamps, did you say?'

'Does she have any money with her?'

'She doesn't?'

'I don't think she does, after all, she has never gone shopping on her own, has she?'

'You mean to say we never leave any money with her when we go out; what if she was to need some money when we are out?'

'Come on, Tukun, we are getting late.' Stuffing some dollar bills into her handbag, she turned to him and said, 'How do I look, not a day more than twenty-five, what do you say?'

'Yeah, but does she have any money at hand when we go out?'

'There's enough money lying around on top of the dining room sideboard. She can make use of that, can't she?'

'Why don't you give her some money to spend?'

'Why don't you? After all she's your mother, not mine. And, Tukun, if we keep delaying any more, it just won't be worth motoring all that way!'

'Are the kids coming?'

'Yeah, they must be already seated in the car, come on, let's get going.'

Before going out, Tukun had walked across to his mother's room, sat down upon her bed, and told her that they were going to the Patkars' and would be back very late. What has come over Tukun today? she had thought as she had heard them drive away. She savoured the notion of being alone, for she needed some space where she could ruminate upon the day with no tensions, no arguments, no silent recriminations coming in the way of her thought processes. The unaccustomed walk Nandita had taken, compounded with the jumble of variegated emotions that her encounters of the morning had brought to her, had left her totally drained and fatigued. She had eaten early, checked all doors and windows, switched off most of the lights, and gone upstairs. She had changed and washed and said a short prayer and gone straight to bed.

As she changed the position of her pillow to make herself more comfortable, her right hand had encountered a bundle of papers there. She had not put anything under her pillow, so where could they have come from? Switching on her bedside lamp, she was totally taken aback. For there, sitting under her pillow, was a wad of notes! She could roughly gauge that there were at least two to three hundred dollars there. She never cried, but today, tears sprang to her eyes. The vision of those people living out the last years of their lives herded together had come crowding in her mind's eye, and shame, utter and absolute shame, had washed over her entire being. Suddenly the litany of 'my home, my life, my money' that had been playing on within her for ever so long all appeared to be so meaningless and shallow.

Sleep washed away from her eyes as if by a deluge, she had lain long hours with her eyes wide open. When at last she was on the verge of falling asleep, she had heard the comfortable sounds of the young people letting themselves in. Reassured, she had soon fallen fast asleep but in her hand, like a child's new toy, was clutched the wad of notes, the symbol of a belated recognition on the part of her son that she was an entity on her own rights.

4 WHERE NANDITA MEETS GRACE, BILL, AND HERSELF

Those dollars had been sitting waiting for her to go out and do something, anything with them. But for that, she would have to go out. Go out? Nandita had remembered that laborious walk she had taken that cold and blustery early-spring day. In terms of her aching feet and her aching back, it had been an uncomfortable experience.

While on the other hand, though she had not exchanged a single word with anyone as she had trudged along, those communicating smiles, those good wishes thrown her way in the passing, those hands raised to wave out to her had all reached in somewhere within her and warmed her heart. Strangely enough, though she herself had made little or no effort, that single foray taken for the first time all by herself had managed to create an invisible bond between her and the world outside. And giving greater importance to her weighed-down shoulders and the few blisters she had acquired that day, she had run back and bolted herself into the safety of her home. It was almost a month since she had taken that walk up to the rose garden. She would go out again to breathe in large deep breaths of that soft sweet scent of freedom that she had inhaled after a very, very long time that day. She had a sudden urge to take off then and there, but she could not perceive how she could get dressed and take off for a walk that led to no particular destination, leaving the home in the state it was in. It would have to be another day.

She woke the next day to a bright and beautiful day smiling down upon her and decided this was the day. She dressed with greater care than she had lavished on her own toilette in a very long time. A light cardigan with not a hint of colour to its name had taken the place of the cumbersome parka she had worn on that first outing. Her body unburdened and her spirits strangely light and buoyant, she had felt as if she was a different person altogether, a person who could even perhaps make the daring decision to carry a sandwich with her that she could munch as her lunch, seated upon an unknown bench in an unknown location. Fixing herself a couple of sandwiches, she had wrapped them and put them into a sling bag; a can of Coke and an apple had joined them as well. This was going to be a regular picnic, she thought as, scooping up a knife and dropping it into the bag, she had checked her key and her purse, now no longer empty, three times over and had let herself out of the house.

Less than a month ago, she had trod on a near empty sidewalk; the trees had appeared to be bald if not scrutinised with care, and the grass was yet to make its appearance then. Nandita looked on in wonder. Out on foot, one saw the world through different eyes; never did one see change so marked in the land from where she hailed! The trees now proudly wore a head cover of resplendent emerald and the swathes of dun-coloured earth assigned for lawns and grassy verges had become a soft and silky green. The pavements had come alive with perambulators; babies were out on jaunts, with their mothers in attendance. So busy was she smiling down at the little ones that before she knew what was happening, she had arrived at the rose garden.

The empty garden of the other day was no longer empty. Old men and women apparently residents of the Home now dotted the benches. Out in the open away from the confines of their glass-walled home, there was no grotesquery or strangeness that could be attached to them. Nandita had almost fled from there, ashamed at her earlier reaction at the sight of the elderly people. But her legs were tired and she knew the next set of benches she would encounter would be downtown. All the *sunny seats* she could see were occupied. She had sat down upon a bench that was right under a tree. But away from the sun's rays, the springtime chill was still lingering there.

She had felt as if she was being observed and had raised her head sharply up, only to encounter a vague figure beckoning to her from a distance. That the woman seated at a distance was old did show through; but as her body was effaced by a camel-coloured coat and her face was shadowed by the brim of the hat she wore, what she really looked like was none too clear to Nandita. The beckoning figure was patting a vacant space lying beside her upon the bench where she was seated. She was bathed in gold for a splash of sunshine lay lolling beside her upon the bench where she sat.

Never having interacted directly with the people of America, Nandita had felt somewhat hesitant and shy to make the move towards accepting the generous offer of a seat in the sun, so to speak. A shackling bout of shyness had held her back for a moment, but pulling herself together, she had gathered up her satchel and moved towards the beckoning hand. As she came and stood beside the elderly woman, her eyes had fallen upon the pins sticking out from the hat that she had moored onto her hair. The facets of the crystal flowers sitting atop those pins had caught a ray of passing sunshine and had come alive. It had reminded her of something warm and comforting. As warm and comforting as the flickering light of that *diya* she had placed each evenfall at the foot of her *tulsi* shrub, back there in her flat in Kolkata.

Remembering her grandfather's need in his latter years to be spoken to in higher decibels, she had raised her voice while smiling down self-consciously upon the occupant of the bench and loudly said, 'Thank you' to her. With a twinkle in her watery blue eyes and a slow chuckle in her throat, the old lady had pointed to her hearing aid. And a girlish giggle emanating from God knows whence had escaped from Nandita's staid and self-contained self as she had taken the offered place in the sun upon the bench.

'New to our town, honey?'

A timid no and a shake of the head was all she could bring out of herself; it was as cryptic a response as one could possibly give.

'Ah, there I go prying again.'

'*Na, na,* I mean, no, you were not . . .'

'I guess when you get this old you forget all that your old mama taught you about not being inquisitive,' she had chuckled.

'You weren't, you weren't, I don't know why I've become so stupid, can't give a . . .'

'No need to upset yourself, honey.'

'Please . . . forgive me! But I . . . come out so seldom . . . that I've almost . . . forgotten to give . . . a proper answer.' With that, Nandita had looked towards her benefactor with a little smile of apology, and the old lady had smiled widely back with teeth more even and white than the Creator had ever supplied anyone with.

The face unalloyed by the kindness that distance and the shading by the hat bestowed was a study in baroque art. The woman's ageing countenance wore a veritable mask created by layers of make-up. The attempts made to cling on to a youth that she had long since left behind would have been hilarious had these not been so pathetic. The pancake foundation had been laid on with a heavy hand and then further reinforced with a heavy coating of peach-coloured facial powder. The mascara and eyeliner had been carefully matched to the colour of the irises of her eyes. The colour had fled and created a halo of fine blue lines that had sprung outwards from the corners of her eyes. She had painted her mouth a screaming scarlet, and the colour had seeped out of its borders and flown out in little rivulets along the tributaries that had been carved out by time around her lips. Her cheeks had been rouged a lively roseate hue, and the rouge too had settled down within the folds of the sagging flow of her facial skin. Seeing through the wrinkles and the creases, the little rivulets of lines that radiated away and out from her lips and from her eyes, she had been able to perceive the real beauty that underlay the face that was what it was today. She must have been a real beauty at one time, she had thought.

Nandita was at a loss as to what she was to make of all this. With a face totally bereft of make-up, she felt almost naked seated beside this woman with her multihued visage.

Her ruminations had been broken into as the old lady had stretched out her hand towards her, and Nandita responding had put out her right hand in her direction. Taking the outstretched hand into her own, she had smiled at Nandita and said, 'I'm Grace, I live in that home there,' pointing towards the glasshouse called the Home. Allowing Nandita a breather, she had asked, 'What's yours?'

'Oh, I'm sorry. I should have told you. Nandita—I'm called Nandita.'

'Live far, honey?'

Yes, very far, she had wanted to say, *I live in my past most of the time,* but had said no. The elderly woman had looked enquiringly and Nandita had added, 'On South Woodford.'

'Good, that's not far, or is it?'

'No.' And then realising that she was back to her monosyllabic responses, Nandita reiterated, 'No, it's not that far from here.'

'What did you say your name was?'

'Nandita.'

'Pretty name, but would you mind if I shortened it? May I call you Nan? That there whole name of yours is kinda long and tricky.'

'Please. Please call me as you wish. Do call me Nan if that's what suits you.' Nandita, who had such strong reservations against the Americanisation of Indian names, had slipped into the same format without so much as a murmur of dissent passing her lips. It was possible that she had not even perceived the coming about of this transition wherein she had so painlessly traded away her name Nandita for a shorter version that was far better suited to the American palate.

Having checked to see that her dainty little hat had not veered away from its anchorage, Grace had informed her, 'I'm off now.' However, she had cautioned 'Take care,' as she rose painfully upon her creaking limbs, limbs that were unwilling to obey her commands but were coerced into doing her bidding. And Nandita had looked on in admiration at this battle being waged between a weakened body and a strong-as-steel mind. Feeling a sudden outflow of affinity for this elderly stranger, she had wanted to give a little hand of help but had held back. Her childhood experience had taught her to tread with caution here! The elderly did not care to have their infirmities paraded in front of the world at large.

Seeing Grace getting ready to leave, a sense of forlornness had swept through Nandita, and she had asked with a surge of unaccountable anxiety, 'Will I see you again?'

'Sure you will, honey. If the sun is out, then so is Grace. On a bright and warm day, if you happen to come this way again, my child, you'll be sure to find me here. Come soon . . . people like us are kinda starved for young company,' and with that, she had wobbled off with the help of her three-pronged walking stick.

Nandita, wanting to put the record straight, had wanted to remonstrate that she was not really young, that she was the grandmother of two fast-growing children. But the moment was lost to her and she was left with the residue of that statement made by Grace. She had sat awhile with a gentle smile radiating from her face that in truth made her look young. To be called young, even though on a mistaken assumption, was indeed a warming experience. But to be called young at that point of her life when she had accepted without any reservations that she had reached the veritable end of all hope and aspirations had made those words very special.

Unaccountably out of the blue, she had felt the presence of that little ray of hope that she had so carelessly let go of that had sustained her through all those years of hardship when she was bringing up Tukun all alone. She could not recall when or where or in what moment of insouciance she had allowed it to slip out of her grasp. And here it was, though without a physical presence, peeping over her shoulder once again. Just a handful of simple words lay between them, yet they had created a bond such as Nandita had not experienced in a very long time. She had somehow reminded her of her Boroma, though two such disparate creatures one could rarely find. Boroma, colourless by societal decree, juxtaposed to Grace, replete with colour—what a strange pairing it was, yet the feeling had persisted.

But Boroma, 'robbed of all colour' Boroma, was such a colourful person to be with. What a fund of lovely tales she had, and with what vim and verve she told them! As gentle and toothless as a newly born babe, her gummy smile lit up that little universe where Nandita's origins lay. *Paan* chewing with a dash of *zarda* was an acceptable vice on the part of a widow, and so she had taken to that little bit of sinning without restraint and, in consequence, had lost all her teeth long before Nandita had become conscious of her presence in her life. And no orthodontist had given her a set to replace what she had lost.

On first coming close to Grace, all she had seen was the makeup on her face. But she felt now as she sat thinking that it was some kind of a statement that she was making, which went way beyond just the putting on of some colour upon an aged face! She was totally confused, for a strange thought had suddenly floated in and taken up a commanding position within her mind. A question had arisen out of it: was this woman's excessive use of make-up and her own absolute eschewal of it just the opposing faces of the same coin? Were they both making an unspoken statement of defiance to a world forever dictating terms to the likes of them?

One little encounter with an individual called Grace and how strange it was that through her she had been reminded of her beloved Boroma. Bathed in the weak springtime sunshine in a faraway land, she had sat reminiscing upon little snippets out of her life where Boroma had played some part.

She was lying with her head upon her Boroma's lap when the old lady gently passing her fingers over her face asked, 'Why has my fragment of the moon got these dark circles under her eyes? Is it too much of studies that is doing this?'

'Boroma,' chipped in one of her cousins, 'she only pretends to study. I saw her holding her book the wrong way round yesterday.'

Nandita had risen and given chase and the tormenting voice had been quietened. But another voice that kept buzzing around in her head had refused to be stilled.

And out of the blue, that voice had spoken up. 'Still pretending to study, I see . . .' it said.

'I'm not pretending . . .'

'Yes, you are. When do your exams get over? I can't hang around in Calcutta forever.'

'What do my exams have to do with your being in Calcutta?'

'Everything! I can't propose to you across the yawning chasm that . . .' And he had indicated the divide between the two roofs. 'As soon as your exams get over, I can take you out and—'

'You are mad,' she had squeaked in a tremulous voice.

Overlooking the interruption, he had gone on: 'hold your hands or even come down on my knee, if you so desire, and then propose.'

'You are absolutely mad. No one will allow me to go out with you.'

'Why?'

'Because . . . because . . . I don't know. But they won't.'

'Then I suppose you'll have to come up to the roof after dark tomorrow and I'll see what can be done about this horrible little pathway that is keeping us apart.'

'I will not come.'

'Yes, you will.' And he had grinned at her. 'And I think it's time I introduced myself: my name is Pilot Officer Prodipto Kumar Roy. I am a fighter pilot, and I have a permanent commission in the Indian Air Force, given to me by as exalted a person as the president of India. My father, Major General T. K. Roy AMC, and my mother, Mrs Sujata Roy, live in a big government bungalow very close to India Gate, in New Delhi. Genetically, I am a Bengali so I speak Bangla, I speak Punjabi because I like to, but in truth Hindi in all its nuances is closer to my heart and my tongue, and of course I speak English, as you already know! But whatever be the language I may speak, at heart I am an Indian, and nothing but an Indian.' He had looked at her and smiled and said, 'I am indeed a rare commodity, grab me while you can; there are not too many Indians in India.' And then mischievously, 'Want to know more about the man you're about to marry?'

'Who said anything about my marrying you?' she demanded spiritedly of him.

'I did; who else?'

'You are absolutely mad.'

'There you go again; tell me, are you always so repetitive?' She had glowered, and with a matter-of-fact 'See you tomorrow evening,' he was gone.

The next day had dawned and a restless Nandita had tried to hold herself back from going to meet Prodipto Roy but had succumbed eventually. For how could she ever live out her life without knowing what it was that he had planned for her that evening!

Stealthily she had crept up and gone and stood in the shadow of the water tank that sat atop the terrace. And then she had seen him in an indistinct blur. And then he had called out, 'Nandita,' softly at first, and then a little louder, and then again louder still.

Frightened at the possible outcome of his raised voice, she had stepped out from the shadows and shown herself.

And then she had heard something like 'I'm coming over,' and she had then seen him running towards her, and before she could understand what was really happening, he was riding in an arch over the gap and a pole had clattered at her feet.

In a terrible surge of panic, she had choked out, 'Why did you do that? You could have died.'

'No, not before my time! Besides, when you believe in reincarnation, dying young is one of the nicest things that can happen to a person. So I look upon death with no fear at all. You die young, get born again, then you contrive to die young again, what better recipe can one have for eternal youth. But believe me, right this moment when I have come to propose marriage to you, I have no desire to die.' And then taking both her hands into his own, he had asked her simply, 'Will you marry me, please, Nandita?'

'You want to marry me? But why?'

'Because I think life would be more fun if you were to walk along with me for the rest of the way. I happen to have fallen for the frown that you always wear on your face while looking disapprovingly at me.'

'What? You have fallen for my frown?'

'And your smile and your deep erudition and the twinkle in your eyes.'

'You are making fun of me.'

'Perhaps a little bit, but I still think I wouldn't like to go away from Calcutta without you.'

'*Why don't you, why can't you understand* that I do not have any control over the destiny of my life.'

'Good, so the answer is yes.' And with these words, he had put a seal upon his assumption that they now had a covenant between them. Placing both his hands upon her shoulders, he had drawn her to himself and planted a long-drawn-out kiss upon her lips then vaulted back across the chasm. Nandita had stood transfixed at the spot where he had left her, more frightened by the responses given out by her own body to this hug and a kiss than by the act itself.

For a long while, she had lingered on the terrace facing the fear of the unknown. She had crept down only when she had felt the cooling down of her face upon her palms and had gone to bed directly without partaking of a single morsel. The headache she had planned to feign as an excuse had soon been converted into a reality. Head reeking with the smell of Little's Oriental Balm, she had kept all prying eyes at bay. But quite naturally, the emotional upheaval had left a feathery shadowing under her eyes the next morning that the sharp eyes of Boroma had detected!

And cutting into her ruminations upon the hard-to-believe happenings of the previous evening, Boroma had called out to her and asked, 'Come here, Nandita, tell me when are your examinations getting over?'

And Nandita remembered having almost blurted out '*You want to marry me?*' but had voiced a sage and sane 'Very soon, Boroma.'

'I don't like these dark circles under your eyes. What need is there for girls to imitate boys? All this sitting around with their faces buried behind books is not meant for them.' And then a worried 'If you look like this, who will want to marry you, tell me?'

But someone really, really handsome does, Nandita had wanted to boast. But 'Oh, Boroma!' was all she had said as she had buried her face upon the comforting bosom of her beloved great-grandmother-designate that day!

The next day, Nandita had heard from Kakima that Mukherjee Didima had come over to pay a courtesy call that morning. The word was soon out and Boroma was all a-flutter! A handsome prince had come to take her little princess away! And she had sent for Damini, for Damini always got to the bottom of all that went on in that home! And the two women had put their heads together and had woven myriad colourful dreams! Both Boroma and

Daminidi had each been dealt such foul hands by fate yet had the generosity in them to rejoice in the happiness of others. They were indeed individuals beyond compare. Was it possible that in Grace she had today found yet another gem?

Almost all the benches around her had emptied out as she sat brooding over those days long left behind by her. Where had they all gone? From Grace, her mind had raced away out of the park onto Boroma and onto the saga of her romance-filled tryst with Prodipto. And when she had returned from the journey back in time, the sight of all those benches devoid of all life had taken her by surprise and left her feeling terribly forlorn. Gathering together her wits and her luncheon bag, she had moved slowly on. Going past the glass-fronted façade of the Home, she had taken a glimpse that way and had sighted many a vaguely familiar face within. It was lunchtime in there and they were all at table. Having placed the disappearance of all those humans within a safe context, relieved, she had plodded on far happier than she had been when she had begun her march forward.

Nandita had been tempted to turn back, but today she could not bring herself to go back to a lonely meal within doors. With human beings seated within sight, one could fool oneself into believing that one was not alone and companionless at mealtime. It was really not so far, and her ever-constant companion, her thoughts, keeping her company, she had conquered the distance far sooner than she had thought she would. The cluster of benches shadowed beneath the circle of towering buildings downtown was all occupied. The weather was too wonderful by far to be wasted away, and so countless persons escaping from their burrows in search of a piece of sunshine had thronged wherever it was possible outdoors. Her aching limbs and her gnawing stomach had quavered in tandem at the very sight of this invasion. The prospect of a reprieve-less trek back home was beyond contemplation! What was she to do, turn back? Wait it out? But she had had to do neither. It was fortunately getting to be close to the end of the time allocated for a midday bite, and in a very short while, the people crowding the benches could be seen leaving in ones and twos to go back to work again. A much-relieved Nandita had thankfully found herself a place next to an elderly woman who sat reading a book in total self-absorption. She had looked up for a moment as Nandita sat down; exchanging a smile, she had gone back to the engrossing company of her book once again.

Nandita had wondered should she perhaps have also brought a book along. What a ridiculous idea, she scolded herself.

Her persuasive, insistent hunger had urged her to pull out her sandwiches immediately, but to eat seated within a throng of unknown persons had not come easily to Nandita. Except at picnics, within a familiar group made up of family and friends, she had never eaten outdoors. This al fresco meal would be an experience that she would have to face embarrassingly alone. Though she had stepped out in search of company today, she could have done with a little less of it just now. The social norms that ruled this society were unknown to her; a host of questions had crossed her mind as she dipped into the satchel, pulled out the sandwiches, and began to unwrap them. Should she or should she not offer to share her simple meal with her neighbour before boorishly sinking her teeth into its inviting softness? All questions and their answers were propitiously taken care of, for her neighbour had risen to leave. With a friendly nod cast Nandita's way, she had moved on, leaving the bench to her and her alone.

Just two days out alone in the all-pervasive environment of this all-enveloping, all-embracing country, Nandita (just renamed Nan), preparing to munch upon a meal made up of cheese sandwiches and a can of Coke was fast imbibing the spirit of America. It was insidiously making inroads into her personality but she herself, and the world around, had no idea that a change as startling as this was coming about in a person who had so rigidly held out against this absorption into America for so many long years.

Readying herself to sink her teeth in for the first bite, she had heard a very American, very male voice ask from somewhere above, 'What a pleasant surprise. Mrs Roy, isn't it?'

From her seated position, whisking the sandwich away and clamping her mouth shut, she had looked up and into a smiling face that was looking down upon her. A pair of very blue eyes twinkled from under a pair of fairly generous eyebrows. His thinning blonde hair had fallen onto his brows as he bent down from his Olympian heights to extend his right hand out to her. Who was this man who knew her by her name? He looked vaguely familiar but she just could not place who he was and where they could have possibly met. Her fingers smelled of butter and cheese, she knew, and were soiled with breadcrumbs, what on earth was she to do with that hand that was being held out to her?

A person's upbringing stays on forever! And Nandita's upbringing had a very loud and controlling voice. Inhibitions of many a kind had been so deeply instilled into her mind that an act as simple as the shaking of a hand with a man whose existence lay beyond the immediate family was unthinkable for her. Yet the extended hand could not be wished away. She carried around the *Roy* of Prodipto's name but had never been able to adopt the uninhibited ways of Prodipto the person she had loved and married. To please the orthodox Gangulys, even he had had to pretend that never ever had they met prior to their marriage. In truth, his declaration that his grandmother's wish was his command and his grandmother's choice was as good as his own had provided him with a totally untarnishable halo that had crossed the boundaries of life and death and had never lost its sheen.

With the commands of so many generations programming her every action, she could not but feel uncomfortable finding herself trapped within such an impossible situation. Counting her sparse crop of blessings, she had thanked God that she had not bitten off a piece from the sandwich and started chewing upon it. The situation was as yet within salvageable limits. What would it have been like had she been compelled to face this blue-eyed giant with a mouth full of bread, cheese, and butter?

The retrieved sandwich once safely tucked away, she was able to think somewhat more coherently. This man knew her by name so they must have met somewhere; there was something vaguely familiar about him, but so nebulous was this feeling of familiarity that she just could not put her finger to it. More in control with the offending sandwich out of the way, she had been able to muster up an apologetic smile to take care of her memory lapse. But there was the problem of the outstretched hand that still needed to be resolved. She asked herself, 'Into how many heads have you yourself dinned in the commandment that you must do in Rome as the Romans do?' So presumably when in America you did as the Americans did! But even if she were to overcome her inhibitions, what was she to do with the state of her fingers buttered up and covered with crumbs all ready to be baked? The paper napkins she had brought along and had carried around all day and the most versatile of all garments, the sari, which could have stood in for a towel, were all forgotten by her.

And she had stretched out her cold and none-too-clean fingers towards the extended hand and he had enveloped the proffered hand, butter and all, into a warming and comfort-filled grasp. And a voice warmer than a hot cup of tea offered while you sat curled up under a *razai* on a cold winter's day had enquired, 'How've you been doin'? The grandkids must be quite big now?'

So he knew she had grandchildren. Did it mean that he had met her somewhere where the children were with her? Should she be alarmed? So many questions, with not a single answer in sight! But little wisps of remembrances had come floating into her mind, reassuring her that she in truth had met him somewhere, but before she could put these wisps together to create a decipherable pattern, they would scatter away and go out of her grasp. With a part of her brain scurrying around in search of links, she had hesitated a moment before finding her tongue. 'I'm fine, thank you. And the children have grown,' then with considerable pride, 'my grandson though not yet eleven is already almost as tall as I am.'

'You don't say. Kids grow up fast, don't they?' he had exclaimed and, indicating the empty space beside her, said, 'May I?'

Rendered shy and diffident by her own want of social niceties, she had murmured 'Oh, I'm sorry,' as contrite, she had begun dusting the vacant part of the bench with the trailing end of the *pallu* of her sari.

'Thank you. But should you be doing that with that lovely dress of yours?' He seated himself with a wide smile. 'These blue jeans of mine don't deserve all that cleaning up,' he said. 'And shouldn't I be the one doing the apologising here?'

'Why?'

'For keeping you away from your sandwiches.'

'Oh, that?'

'But more'n that, I must have managed to give you a crick in the neck by looming over you with all my two metres or so of height.'

'Two metres high? Really?' Her curiosity aroused, she had exclaimed.

'I was just kidding. I'm no Sears Tower.' Touched by the innocence of her reaction to his little joke, he had smiled a quiet little smile. 'Come on, pull out your sandwiches and I'll fish out what I have here with me.' Then in all seriousness, 'You don't mind, do you?' Nandita, while indicating that she had no objection, had yet thrown a glance his way, and looking down upon the changing expressions upon her face, he had caught on soon enough that she had been unable to place him exactly. This discovery had come as a total surprise to him for he had recognised her even on that other day when she was dressed to fight off the cold in the strangest amalgam of garments.

'I can see you haven't placed me, ma'am. I should have introduced myself, but you never let on, so I presumed . . .'

'I know . . . that I know you . . . but . . .'

'Hope you've been able to get a fix on me now?'

She knew they had met but where?

'I can see you haven't. I shouldn't have barged in without introducing myself. I am William Brady and we met at a do in New Jersey.'

'New Jersey!'

'Yes, at the Duttas' for the ceremony of their little son's first grown-up meal. Not so surprising, I guess, that you couldn't place me. It's been a while.'

A giveaway flicker of dawning recognition must have flit across Nandita's face and reassured he had helped her along on her path of re-discovery of an event that had thrown them together. 'Good, I can see that you have started recollecting that day when we met.'

'Yes, of course, we were there I remember we had motored down for their little boy's *annoprashon* . . .'

'That colourful ceremony where you guys officially give a kid his first taste of cereals.'

'Yes, we like to make a ceremony of almost everything we do.' She had accepted with a little laugh. 'That must have been . . . let me see . . . at least seven to eight years back.'

'But even so, you haven't changed much . . .' A look of appraisal was in his eyes.

'How can that be?' she had averred, totally unable to go along with his flattering observation. 'I've a lot of grey hair now,' she had extended, trying to neutralise his disturbing observation.

He had shown no desire to extend the argument, but the expression upon his face and the smile that had accompanied it had conveyed the message that he had not been telling a lie.

And somehow that look on his face had stirred up her memory. And in a magical moment of total recall, she had remembered where and when she had seen this man, his open laughter, and his heart-warming smile. She knew no William Brady, but she remembered a man called Bill whom his wife called Meg apparently loved very much. And from there, an entire panorama of images had come rushing to her mind. The most prominent among these images that had come back to her was that of a lovely little woman who had been seated that day by this man's side. Nandita realised that somehow the frame within which her memory had placed this man was not complete without that woman by his side. No wonder it had taken her so long to place him within a context. And there was some other nebulous difference that had come about in his face that had made him look the same yet not quite the same as before. It was later, much later, once back at home that she had recognised what the difference was. The smile, though it was still as large and generous as she had observed it was then, did not now quite match up with it. It hovered around his lips and remained there, never once riding up and into his eyes. Why was that so?

And then with recognition slowly dawning upon her countenance, she had questioned, 'I remember now, you are Dr William Brady, aren't you? The famous professor the Duttas were dying to show off.'

'Not as famous as all that, believe me, but thanks for the nice words, it makes me feel real good. Now that you have recognised me, allow me to tell you how pleased I am to have met up with you today.'

'I'm also very pleased to meet you, Dr Brady.'

'Shall we get on with our meal then?' And he had promptly dived into his copious coat pocket and brought out two bars of chocolate. Both pieces of confectionery, bedraggled and worn out and somewhat the worse for wear, had looked far from inviting.

Long years of homemaking and caring to the fore, on firmer grounds now, all self-consciousness set aside, she had asked, alarmed, '*Is that your lunch?*'

'Sure. High in calorie, low in volume, fits into my pocket, and goes wherever I go. Shall we eat?'

She looked on in surprise as he had really and truly settled down to eat a couple of bars of chocolate, and unable to hold herself back, she exclaimed, 'I'm really surprised to meet a doctor who eats a balanced diet of chocolates for lunch!'

'Not a doctor-doctor but a doctor of philosophy. Philosophers, as you know, are allowed to do all kinds of strange things,' he had responded immediately to her little bit of raillery.

She had smiled at his explanation and without another word had brought out her hidden meal and handed him one of her two sandwiches, placed neatly upon a paper napkin. Then cutting the shiny red apple in two, she had given him one half and then gently urged, 'Come, eat.'

Taken aback by the sudden transformation that had come about from timidity to total assertiveness in the woman seated beside him, he had fallen silent for a moment. That such a major metamorphosis in behaviour should come about all because of *what he was planning to have for his midday meal* had, strange to say, not left him completely surprised and had left him wondering why if at all it felt so familiar. The realisation as it had dawned, had hit him like a sledgehammer blow aimed directly to his heart. He knew he had to get an immediate hold upon his sentimentality for what he hid within his heart was not for the world to look upon. Holding on to the sandwich in one hand and the portion of the apple in the other, he had begun to laugh. As a cover-up, what could be better? It was but an outburst of a moment; sobering up, in a voice tinged with nostalgia, he had observed, 'You women do have such a god-given gift of bullying.' She had looked startled and he had acquiesced, 'Sure, I'll share your meal, only provided you allow me to offer you one of these badly mutilated bits of compacted calories . . .' She had stretched out an accepting hand. 'I'm sorry they don't look any too appetising.' And wearing an apologetic smile upon his face, he had passed over one of the bars to Nandita.

As they had sat eating their simple shared meal, Nandita had remembered his wife with a clarity that was surprising. She remembered that she was petite and well padded while he, her husband, a study in contrast: though generously built had not an extra ounce of flesh upon his frame. Yet a better-matched couple could rarely be seen. One could sense that apart from being husband and wife, they were also the best of friends. Seated side by side, totally absorbed in the ceremony, they had laughed together in joy at the sight of the infant dressed like a Bangali bridegroom being given his first official taste of cereals. His tiny little *chelir jore* and his white-as-popcorn *topor*, the headdress made of pith, had left them awestruck. Nandita had been seated in a chair just a few seats away, and leaning across his wife, he had asked, 'No kidding, is that how a bridegroom dresses in India?'

'Not all over India, but in Bengal and in some other parts of the east as well.'

'A bridegroom in red, that's quite something.'

'The genuine bridegrooms only wear white.' And with a little laugh, she had added, 'These babies can't protest so we make them dress up in bridal red.' Turning to the petite woman, she had asked, 'But doesn't he look really sweet?'

'Real cool, I must say.'

And then someone had called Nandita away to officiate as consultant to the proceedings. There always was a shortage of expert advisors on the nitty-gritty of those never-ending ceremonies that ruled a Hindu householder's life. And Nandita with her superior status as mother to Sudipto was much in demand. And as such, apart from those few words they had spoken regarding the attire of the star of that day, they had had no further social exchanges. But she had watched them from afar as they had sat companionably together, laughing and joking and pulling each other's leg as if they had been married just the other day.

As she had watched them interacting happily with each other, she had known with deep regret that had her Dipto not killed himself, they could have also grown into middle age companionably together and, from there, on to old age as well.

Then she had laughed at her own fanciful visualising, for there could be nothing more sacrilegious than to think of her Prodipto as anything but vibrant, ebullient, and forever young!

But however far-fetched the scenario might have appeared to be, how alluring was its possibility.

Was it possible that with him by her side, she too could have drunk of the elixir of eternal youth? On occasion she did encounter that little girl and that other girl who, having come to bloom, had emerged as a desirable young woman with newly discovered bodily needs of her own. The carapace of self-denial that she had donned at twenty had never been able to evacuate these personas of her own self from the recesses of her heart!

Oh, the physical anguish of those first few years after her Prodipto's death, when her body would cry out for him; with time, the intensity of the pain had diminished but the emptiness it had left behind had left her hollowed out.

Oh, how it hurt then, as it did even now, not to have her Dipto! Why had he so assiduously taught her every lesson of love and left her to lead a lonely passionless life?

Society could efface all the emblems of your sexuality from your person. You could change your attire and dress yourself up in cold white in a show of denial to all sensual needs, but you knew that it was just a façade put up to fool the world. For no change of attire, no removal of embellishments upon one's person, no change of lifestyle could cool down the heat of the red-hot blood that flowed within your veins once you had tasted from the cup of love. Oh, the pain of not having anyone to turn to, whose eyes would light up with love at the sight of you. Oh, the agony of not having a chest upon which you could lay your head and put all your anxieties and care to rest. Oh, the anguish of not having a body against which your body could place itself to meld, melt, and merge into and become one. Oh, the trauma of not having a friend, a companion, a lover who was your very own. The togetherness of that couple had filled her heart with a deep regret for all that she had once had and so speedily lost.

And the next day after the *annoprashon*, on reaching home and having retired for the night to the sanctuary of her room, she had lain thinking in bed, her eyes fixed upon the darkness gathered up near the ceiling. And strangely enough, in that gloom she had felt the presence of her mother, of whom she had thought so seldom. And if at all, when she did think of her, it was always with little or no sympathy. But that night for the first time in her life, transcending her own personal preoccupations, she had thought of her mother as a flesh-and-blood person with all the needs that flesh and blood demanded. How had she handled her husband-less life? Had she yearned for the embrace of a husband? If so, how had she managed to traverse those arid years filled with yearning for a husband who had left her for another passion and gone away forever out of her life? He had disappeared but left behind all the symbols upon his wife that proclaimed to the world that she was a woman who had a man and therefore had social sanction to participate in bodily pleasures. The blazing red *shindoor* in her parting, the bangles of *loha*, *shankha*, and *paula* (iron, conch, and coral), each with their inner hidden meaning, the embellished multicoloured borders of her saris—in these, a woman's sexual rights had been distilled into platonic visual symbols for the world to see. Strangely enough, though she had lost the core of what those symbols stood for, she had nurtured them with the greatest of care. They were the status symbols of a value and worth that only a Hindu woman could quantify and appreciate. For without them, she was reduced to a veritable social outcast.

Nandita had always resented her mother's total preoccupation with pleasing her mother-in-law. Propitiating her elder relation by marriage had become such an obsession with her that Nandita, her only child, had been completely sidelined in the affection stakes. But the reason for this inequitable distribution of her mother's time had dawned upon her much later, only when her mother was no more. A letter, *that letter* which she had handed to her grandfather one day, had come back into her hands, still faintly imbued with the perfume of piety. While she sorted through her mother's worldly belongings, it had emerged from within the folds of her mother's clothing housed safely within a steel trunk. From it, she had been able to unravel many a mystery that had all along shrouded her life.

Her father, having disappeared without a word of warning from his wife's life, had in a moment of extreme generosity remembered her existence. And had granted a reprieve to her from widowhood, but even so, being a still better son, he had given the power of attorney to seal Nandita's mother's fate into his own mother's hands. It was all a question of priority that had made Nandita's mother into what she was. A daughter could have given her affection and love but the mother-in-law, if neglected, could have robbed her of the only status that really counted for a married woman, that of being a *shodhoba*. And she had made her choice. She had decided to leave this earth when the time came without the attendant stigma of having outlived her spouse.

Nandita hardly knew her father, for she was but three years old when he had left home. But as she kept growing, his ever-present absence had begun to haunt her. She had very desperately wanted to have a father of her own but where was she to go in search of him? The match between what he wanted and what she desired was never to be. For, thirsting after immortality, he had gone in search of his father in heaven, denying her, his mortal daughter, her need for a simple embrace from him, her father on this earth. She had asked in vain to know where her father was and had never been able to get a reply.

The injustice heaped upon her beloved Boroma by her great-grandfather's suicide and the eternal absence of her father from her own life had angered Nandita all through those growing years of her life. And that was the reason why she had told Prodipto that he would have to change the rules of the world before he could begin to play about with his own life.

He had put the ball right back into her court by asking her to fight for her rights. 'For rights and privileges, my dear Nondu, have to be fought for and wrenched out of the hands of an unwilling adversary.' Becoming serious for the first time since she had known him, he had asserted, Holding her close to him, he had continued, 'My dear Nondu, however careful or careless I am with this life of mine, I believe that I will only live for as long as I have been assigned upon this earth, so that is why I live as I do.'

'Excepting when you are up in the skies.'

'There I am linked to my country's fate, not mine.'

'How well you can argue yourself out of a corner.'

'I am dead serious about everything I have just said. There are no guarantee certificates given out with life, so if one day the occasion does arise for you to stand up to the unjust laws of society, *please do put up a fight*.' He had looked down upon her with persuading, piercing, bright eyes. Then in gentler tones, he had concluded, 'For those in positions of power and privilege rarely, if ever, hand over a portion of those advantages that they have all along been enjoying without a fight.' Nandita, though drawn to his argument, had yet felt that he was diverting her attention from the point that she had wanted to make. However, point given or point taken, the opportunity to test her strength against society, alas, had been given to her by fate without much ado soon after that.

So angry was she with all the generations of men whom she had seen letting women down that, driven by a deep sense of hurt, she had caught on to the wrong end of the stick while designing her own revolution. And she had herself thereby inadvertently managed to let her own team down. Her symbolic black-badge, sporting not a word-voiced kind of satyagraha, had taken her nowhere. Her total acceptance of all the orthodox laws governing a Brahmin widow's life had not managed to repeal any laws but had instead caused embarrassment enough to make people avert their eyes from this uncomfortable face of reality. And soon even that had ceased to be! And so, where she had thought she was taking a step forward, she had in truth made a retrograde move and taken a step backward for her own self, and in consequence for womankind.

So many memories and so many thought-provoking ruminations linked to those memories had been generated in her mind that day at New Jersey as she had watched this man and his wife seated in happiness together. And because he was but a half of what she had felt was a perfect whole, she had been confused. And now here they were sharing a meal that hardly deserved to be called a meal at all.

That single sandwich was done with soon enough. With the help of the apple, Nandita had felt her hunger pangs fade away, but as she looked at the well-exercised form of her bench-mate, she wondered how his six feet plus of height could possibly be nourished with what he had eaten. She felt guilty holding on to the offering he had made. How could she possibly bring herself to eat it all alone? It just did not happen that way in the world from where she came. Big or small as the size may be, you just broke the bar in pieces and shared those segments with the people around.

'I couldn't possibly.' She attempted to return the bar of chocolate she had been handed at the beginning of the repast.

'Come on, a deal is a deal, and I've kept to my end of it . . .'

She broke off a piece and held out the rest of the bar to her companion. 'Please . . .' was all she said.

'And leave *you* feeling hungry?'

'Look at *your size and mine*,' she argued, with a look of something bordering playfulness in her eyes.

'You sure are a persuasive talker,' he observed, smiling widely.

Lunchtime over the benches had slowly started emptying out; he had looked down at his watch, shrugged, and sat on. Abruptly changing track, he asked in a nostalgic mood, 'Do you remember what a beautifully colourful and bright fall day that was?'

She had nodded agreement, remembering more than just that particular day. Tukun at the wheel and the car awash with Robindro Shongeet, and the children seated in their car seats as usual, anointing her with their grubby paws, they had set off. A relaxed Tukun had opted for the scenic route because he said the woods were indeed beautiful in and around the New York region during the fall season.

Unlike the highways with their rigid sense of purpose, these roads meandered playfully on in search of the wonders of the wooded world gifted by some propitious god to America. The woods around were unbelievably, incredibly beautiful, and getting to one's eventual destination was but an excuse for taking that passageway. Without any rush or bluster, these roads did eventually get you to your destination but attaining the chosen destination was but an additional bonus point notched on to the journey. You traversed those roads not to get anywhere but to take in the breathtaking, awe-inspiring magnificence of nature. That ride through the wooded roads of America, trees resplendent in their multihued fall attire, had been one of the most sublime experiences that Nandita had ever had.

'Yes, the fall season in the United States is beautiful beyond belief,' she softly reaffirmed.

'What's the fall like in India?'

'Timid in contrast. I lived for a while in North India; there the trees do shed their leaves in preparation for the rigours of a blazing hot summer, but that can come nowhere close to the show of colour you have on parade here.'

'Do you write?' he asked, enquiring seriously.

With a smile tinged with just a suspicion of regret, she denied ever having done so. 'The only writing that I've ever done, apart from writing letters, was for the taking of exams. I remember once having got carried away, I had almost rewritten Keats,' she informed him, with a twinkle in her eyes. The reminiscences of an earlier epoch, an epoch from which she had separated herself long ago, had suffused her face with a strange glow. It was strange indeed that she was sitting sharing near-forgotten vignettes from her past with this near stranger. How long was it since she had spoken of anything but mundane everyday matters to anyone? It was as if a dam had burst and words were coming spewing out of the breach!

He smiled. 'You sure had a huge crush for Keats, I can see, but wasn't Shelley the one young females used to drool over at one time?'

'You are right; Shelley had quite a following, but I had a preference for the poetry of Keats. When I arrived here ten years back, I'd thought I would be able to at last take a look upon his "season of mists and mellow fruitfulness", but nowhere could I find the languor of Keats' opium-drugged autumn here. The Bohemian splurge of colour of the American fall, I think, needs as much an artist with a palette overflowing with colour as it does a host of poets whose hearts are overflowing with variegated shades of ochre, red, and gold.'

'Are you an artist?' he asked with genuine interest.

'No, I was a schoolteacher.'

And with that, she came down to earth. What was she, a widow, a staid retired schoolteacher, the mother of a grown-up son, a grandmother to two growing grandchildren, doing sitting here, chatting away with a big, huge man whom she had but met once many years ago? She must leave, she told herself, but the civilised creature within her had wanted to know should she do so without enquiring about his wife? But then another voice asked her to tread with care. In this civilisation, one never knew what one could ask of a person and what one could not. Which question and at what turn a simple enquiry could be construed to be an invasion of a person's privacy, she was not fully aware of. But that there was but a very slender thread that lay between the two, she had come to learn of, if not from any personal interaction with live people, then from the soaps that she saw quite often on TV. Her own upbringing urged her on to make a polite enquiry. 'How is your wife?'

His blue eyes clouded over with the reflection of a patch of grey clouds that were just then drifting past up there in the skies. Clearing his throat after some deliberation, he spoke. 'I . . . I don't know exactly? She must be fine, I suppose.'

What did he mean by those uncertain, unsure words? Had she left him? Or had he left her? All that love on show for the entire world to see had evidently gone up in smoke. She knew all along about the fragility of the bonds of marriage and how easily they snapped in the countries of the West. But this one, no, not this one. Having built so many dreams out of their togetherness, she was unable to handle the grotesquery of this separation. She looked down at her watch and, making pretence of being startled, mumbled a few words indicating that she must leave immediately and rose to leave. If he was surprised by the sudden change in her demeanour, he did not show it and rose courteously and allowed her to go on.

As she plodded homewards, countless conjectures kept ploughing their way through her mind. Bill and Meg divorced! She just could not reconcile herself to such a sordid ending to what had appeared to be such a wonderful relationship. She just could not visualise a woman like Meg being unfaithful to him. On the other hand, Bill seemed to be such a nice man as well. But men, she gleaned from her personal experience, managed somehow to always let a woman down. Had he perhaps strayed, she asked herself as she let herself into the house. She had decided then and there that she would never again venture downtown, for what if she were to meet him again?

Having been out for the whole long day, she suddenly felt overwhelmingly tired as she took off her shoes. Moreover, Bill's strange reply had added its own burden of despondency upon her fatigue. Her throat was aching from the burden of her unshed tears; she made herself a cup of tea and went and sat on the bench in the yard. The house felt terribly closed in after her daylong sojourn in the outdoors.

5 ALL ALONE IN A HOME BRIMMING WITH LIFE

Weekends tended to be rather more tiring than the days of the week in the life that the Roys now led in the United States of America. A frenzied exchange of cordiality between friends and acquaintances kept everyone in a constant whirl of arranging social events. You went for one and gave two, or you gave one and went for two; whatever the mathematics of it, you never quite got round to getting off the carousel that had been set in motion.

Yet another weekend was looming large and the time had come for the Roys to do their bit towards the cause of perpetual socialising that now took up such a large chunk of their life. Patkar was throwing more than mere hints that it was time some fish curry be cooked, and the sumptuous meals partaken of at several other homes over the past weekends were also tipping the scales the wrong way for them! And so a guest list had to be decided upon, but a guest list that would be able to keep Patkar's special demands in mind.

Since the divergences of eating habits among the peoples of India were legion, bringing together guests who thought alike and ate alike was not that easy. Having juggled around the names of all those who were avid fish eaters, Meeta had eventually settled with four other couples and their children, apart from the Patkars of course! Even so, despite all the fine-tuning, you could still end up having a problem, for some only ate freshwater fish, while others would have nothing but the harvest from the sea!

'What should I cook? Tell me, Tukun, tell me, please,' Meeta wailed.

'Dal . . . rice . . . and now let me see . . .'

Sarcasm dripping from each gesture and word, she countered, 'How very helpful!'

'I gather you don't want to make dal and rice. Then I suppose we could get some takeout Chinese,' he summed up with a chuckle.

'Go away before I kill you.'

'Anything, Meetu, anything, but no shivery jellies and blancmanges, please.'

'So it will have to be the inevitable ice cream, I suppose.' Not that Meeta had any particular love for both these quivering desserts, even so, a total embargo upon them annoyed her no end. 'Jellies and blancmanges are so easy to concoct, Tukun.'

'But ice creams, you don't even have to concoct. And they don't move!'

'What's this fixation?'

'Ma hates the stuff and so do I.'

'What a strange man you are, just because your mother hates the stuff, you hate it as well.'

'And your son will not eat any mangoes because . . .'

'Mangoes have such a funny smell,' she said with an absolute straight face and then laughed.

And Tukun, while laughing along with her, said no more.

He strolled back whistling into the kitchen, where Meeta was pottering around with some recipe books and asked, 'What do the kids get to eat?'

'The kids are easy to please. They'll have their usual stuff. It's the big bad dads and mums who create the problems.'

It was true that the children posed less of a problem than did the adults, for their initiation into savouring Indian food had not developed beyond imbibing the daily homespun meals of *dal/chawal/sabzi* that their mothers made them eat. Fun eating for them had an altogether different connotation from that of their parents. Pleasing them as such was not a difficult matter, for the Italian pizza in its American incarnation was just a phone call away. And if they wanted a change, the ubiquitous burger and potato chips, ice cream, and Coke were also well within easy reach of the hostess.

Nandita going past the kitchen had heard the exchange. It surprised her that not one single parent among the lot she knew was making any effort at all to initiate their children into learning to enjoy the vast and varied and flavoursome food that India had to offer. En masse, the children would turn up their noses at Indian food and the parents, taking an easy way out, would succumb to their demands. Nandita had tried to inveigle them away from their pizza and burger routine by creating several culinary wonders which had involved putting in a great deal of work. Oh, what a ruckus the young ones would create:

'Oh, Ma, Mom, pleeeeze, we don't want this stuff.' And then a chorus of little voices would join in with 'Please, please, puleeze . . . let us have some pizza, please.'

The peer pressure in the United States was so strong that getting out of its stranglehold was near impossible, Nandita had eventually recognised. She knew from experience that for the human species, the need to know and to acknowledge one's roots was an inescapable psychological drive embedded deep down in its subconscious. This need, becoming an acute hankering, caught up with one sometime or the other within one's own lifetime. It surprised and alarmed her to see how hard these children (perhaps aided and abetted by their parents) were trying to integrate and become one with the fabric of the nation where they lived. Their public rejection of all overt symbols that separated them from the mainstream showed the children's desire to be accepted in totality as a genuine part of the whole. Would this denial of their own roots really and truly make them acceptable as an integral part of this predominantly black-and-white world? She sincerely hoped and prayed that one day these little brown creatures would not have to face disillusionment and hurt at the hands of time. What if America was not to accept them as wholeheartedly as they had the United States of America?

Of late pondering upon her own predicament, she had begun to wonder whether the strategy adopted by the children and their parents was in truth the correct one. Would her own life have been as dull and moribund had she been closer to the heartbeat of the life that the people led here? But how was she to get closer to that heartbeat? Her aching blistered feet were a mute but painful testimony to that first attempt she had made at familiarising herself with this land where she now lived. She had come back into her lair bruised but mollified by the mere sight of that which lay outside the four walls of the safe and secure home where she now lived. And the second attempt she had made just the other day and her encounter with Dr Bill Brady, so buoying at first, at the end had left her ever so sad and confused that she had begun to wonder if at all she should attempt to venture out again. So it was not her feet alone but her heart as well that was holding her back.

Sunday morning dawned crisp and clear; the sting had gone out of the tail of spring. The trees, now clad in a whispery shade of green, had made the yard look festive and inviting, and after a very long time, the windows had been thrown wide open. The tide could still turn at any time; why not enjoy the warmth while it lasted.

The familiar mechanics of a weekend brimming over with visitors that normally irritated her with its extreme boisterousness had served as a reprieve this time round. She had helped with the cooking as she always did, but with an added bit of enthusiasm this morning.

And then the guests had begun to drive up to their door. In the vanguard like a tornado, the Tandons had arrived with their two sons and their minuscule dachshund pup. A strange choice of pet, for a larger-than-life family! It was a marvel that the little pup had not yet been mowed down under the trampling feet of the two mega-sized little boys. But completely unaware of any threat to its life, fearless in its ignorance, it clip-clopped around on its noisy little feet wherever the two boys went and little puddles marked the progression of the strange procession. 'Hey, Tom, hey, Tammy, get out of the way, here we come,' the giant-sized mites had called out as they had hurtled past Nandita, dog in tow. And without so much as a greeting to the grandmother of their friends, they had gone out of sight. And Nandita, looking towards their disappearing backs, had marvelled at the norms by which children and their pets were being brought up these days.

Their father, Dinesh Tandon, renamed Danny in this land which he had adopted as his own, while cruising through his teen years, had almost forgotten to stop growing. His skyward surge, to the relief of his parents, had come to a stop at last when he was just short of the six-and-a-half-feet mark. He now wore a fulsome moustache and a flourishing beard, perhaps to cover up the floridity that suffused his face, thanks to an excessive fondness for alcoholic beverages. But this was one man who never forgot his niceties towards those he would term as the 'elderlies'. Having arrived at his adult stage, he had observed that the world abounded with older people and that these people were a temperamental lot who needed to be treated more like children than adults. Paying large dollops of condescending attention, in his opinion, was the thing to do. And having done so, your conscience allayed, you could then safely set them aside to get on with a life replete with more adult and interesting activities, such as the quaffing of large quantities of chilled beer.

Nandita knew what was coming as he loomed large over her as she stood chopping some cabbage in the kitchen. Barely allowing her to rid herself of the knife, he wrapped her in a huge bear hug. Rubbing his beard upon her cheek, he boomed, as was his custom, 'So, *how are you, auntie?*' A rhetorical query, for he went on to add, '*As beautiful as ever,* as I can see.' Nandita was none too sure of the sincerity of his comment yet had smiled. So unused was she to being embraced that his hirsute hug had managed as always to bring a flush of colour to her cheeks and a slight speeding up of her heartbeat as well. Shamed by her own bodily responses, she struggled to free herself from his grasp. Dressed as usual in a pair of shorts, his long-legged wife Neelima, now called Nelly, intervened, and the twosome, having done their duty towards her, disappeared towards the living area of the home to join their real host and hostess.

The next to arrive were the Kidwais with their daughter Saba. Nusrat and Nafisa, with Saba hanging on to Nafisa's dress, had paid their respects with all the courtesies due to the mother of a friend, and Saba too had been coerced into doing the needful. For a moment or two, she had stood peering from behind her mother with beautiful large eyes but had very soon found her voice and produced an indistinct *adaab*. Sighting her friends, she had found her feet as well and had rushed off where fun beckoned.

Just as Nandita got to the point of putting the finishing touches to the prawn curry simmering on the stove, a smiling Milind Patkar, sniffing dramatically, put his head into the kitchen. While in Calcutta, Tukun and Milind Patkar had studied together in the same college for just a short while; at that point however, they were mere nodding acquaintances. Tukun and Milind had met up quite by chance one day in a supermarket and one of them had called the other over. From there, the exchanges between the two families had developed and grown into a regular affair and had come to a point where they had become more family than friends, one to the other. Wearing an ecstatic look upon his face, Milind chortled, 'Thank you, Kakima, thank you,' as if the curry was being cooked just for his personal benefit. 'I can smell my favourite *chingri macher malai kari* on the boil.' His near-Bangali status had made him a purist when it came to Bangali cuisine. And so, 'If you need an official taster, please do send for me,' he suggested.

Patkar's wife Suhasini could be heard saying, 'Milind, don't be so greedy,' in a hushed but admonishing tone as she entered the kitchen. 'How are you, Moushi?' she asked of Nandita, and then, 'Can I do something?'

'Later, with the *luchis* perhaps. Let me see: my, what a pretty sari you're wearing, Shuhashini,' she said, fingering the delicate fabric. 'What fine and intricate checks your weavers create in Maharashtra.'

'When next I go to India, I'll . . . oh, sorry, but, you don't wear anything but white. Don't you get bored?'

'Perhaps I do, but then . . .'

Then someone had called out to the Patkars and both of them had left.

The other two couples had not bothered to take a detour through the kitchen, and Nandita had been able to get back to where she was. The cabbage *chenchki* out of the way, she wondered what next to do. Should she go and join Tukun and Meeta's guests or should she go and take a peep at what the children were doing? Nine children up there together and not a sound! That, in her opinion, certainly needed some investigating!

Nandita was aghast at the sight that met her eyes as she stood at the door and looked upon the scene laid out before her. All nine children lay sprawled out on the carpet in different angles and in different poses; Coke cans and potato wafers were just about everywhere. Most of them were devouring comic books as if this was the only opportunity they would get in their life to read them. Three of the boys were intensely preoccupied in trying to kill their imagined enemies in their handheld Nintendo sets and the puppy was busy chewing a slipper. The children and the pup were all doing exactly what they would have done had they been marooned companionless at home.

'Tanmayee, Tomal,' Nandita called out softly at first, then a little louder!

Both the children looked up with a frown from whatever they were doing.

'Why don't you go out with your friends? It's such a bright and beautiful day.' Her suggestion was met with little or no response. 'It's so lovely out there, I'm sure you'll enjoy—'

'Aw, Thamma, please, we *are* enjoying ourselves.' The little girl, setting aside her comic book, rose from where she had been lying, and turning her grandmother around and placing her hands gently upon her back, slowly but steadily started pushing her out of the room. Once outside, she asked belligerently, 'Why do you call me Tanmayee when my friends are around? They always laugh and make fun of me when you . . .' And she trailed off with a pout.

Confronted with a rebuff, Nandita withdrew and went into her room and sat listless upon her favourite chair near the window. What a beautiful day this was, all gold and green and alive with birds and bees and butterflies. But what could she do if the children would not listen? She remembered her own childhood when the very suggestion of an elder was as good as a command.

Today a little girl of nine could dictate by what name you should address her. And as for the little boy, her grandson, he had merely looked up from his Nintendo and gone back to it without even making an attempt to give a reply. And his eleventh birthday was still a clear six months away!

Slowly, Nandita rose and took the stairs to go down. In a home brimming over with life, she just could not bring herself to remain alone any longer. Days on end, she remained in solitary confinement within the confines of these four walls, but not so today! Standing at the foot of the stairs, she heard the babble of voices and the sound of laughter carrying happiness with it to her ears. She wanted to be there where laughter and happiness was! Yet an invisible barricade put up by whom she did not know made it impossible for her to make an entry there. Why was it so, she wondered, as she stood unsure, undecided, and unable to move towards her desired goal, the company of some fellow human beings? Still hesitant, she asked, was it she herself who had set herself apart? Was it perhaps that she, Nandita, had never made effort enough to find companionship among the people who came and went in this home? She would find out today what it was that had isolated her and left her hankering for company. How had she, Mrs Nandita Roy, who had been a part of the heartbeat of all those people who had lived around her little flat back there in that block of LIG flats in Calcutta, come to this pass?

She went back into the kitchen and stood a moment pondering the problem. If her dignity were to be kept intact, then some ploy would have to be created. She needed a valid reason to make an entry; walking in without a passport, so to speak, just would not do. She took down a container marked *besan* and placed it upon the counter, and then bending to reach down under the counter, she brought out a few large onions. Preparations over, she dipped and fried, dipped and fried till she had a mound of golden-hued, hot and crisp *pakoras* piled up invitingly in a shallow dish.

Tidying herself, she picked up the plate full of savouries and came and stood at the door of the room from where a babble of speech and an occasional burst of laughter was flowing out. Through the slightly parted folds of the curtain screening the door, she could see that a muted videotape of *Sholay* was soundlessly unwinding its tale upon the small screen, while the raised voices of the occupants of the room made up for the lack of the soundtrack. No one was paying any attention to this history-making movie. It had perhaps been put on just to lend an aura of Indian-ness to the gathering! And skirting its colourful presence, an animated conversation was going on.

In response to something Meeta said, Milind warned, 'Watch out Meeta, this much-touted Mahadevan of our Tukun could very well turn out to be some lissom Mahadevi.'

'Playing mixed doubles *yaar*,' drawled Danny.

Meeta's muted response was drowned out by a burst of laughter and Tukun had attempted a fitting response.

'I wish I . . .'

At that point, parting the curtains, Nandita entered, alibi in hand. And the laughter filling up the room died an untimely death! And all the smokers facing the entrance to the room immediately shifted their smouldering cigarettes out of sight. The rest, alerted by the changing stance of the herd, also swiftly followed suit and placed their lit cigarettes away from Nandita's view. Four out of the six women in the room were not smoking. Of the two who were, one had got rid of the evidence as promptly as possible, leaving only one among the lot that had held on to the lit cigarette, wearing a look of amusement upon her face. Refusing to fall in with the instinctive reactions of the pack, she continued to puff on, looking the new entrant straight in the eyes. Nandita had never met this young woman before but could sense that she was a breed apart. It was more likely than not that she had been born and bred outside India, Nandita felt. It was clear from her reaction to this little bit of drama that to her, this strange so-called courtesy towards an elder was totally incomprehensible and therefore a needless act. Nandita remained unperturbed, but all the men in the room, with their upbringing lying in distant India with its unique social mores, looked none too comfortable with this unconventional behaviour on the part of one among their women.

As if struck by a severe drought, the conversation that had been comfortably flowing around the room had precipitately gone dry. The silence reigned but for a moment, for immediately afterwards as if by the command of a conductor's baton, it came back with a rush creating a veritable flood of words.

Meeta rose from where she was seated and came forward to take the plate from her with a 'Ma, you should have called.' Was there perhaps a slight frown chasing those words?

Flipping his cigarette out of the window as unobtrusively as possible, Tukun came and stood beside Nandita and, addressing the couple she had not met earlier, said, 'Vivek, Sue, meet my mother.' Then, 'Ma, this is Vivek and this is his wife Sujata: they have moved here quite recently. The rest of the lot I think you already know.' She nodded in agreement.

Vivek had put his palms together in a *namaste* while Sue, shifting her cigarette from her right hand to the left, came forward and shook hands with Nandita and cordially said, 'Glad to meet you, Mrs Roy.' To Nandita's surprise, the words had rung true to her ears. Another couple whose names she just could not place but who looked familiar beamed a smile apiece her way, and then Danny boomed, 'What happened to the *pakoras*, Meeta? Are you polishing them off quietly or what?'

A ripple of laughter followed, and an indignant Meeta, pretending to be outraged, promptly began circulating the plate around. On the small screen, the story had silently moved on and reached the historic moment where Hema Malini had begun to dance on broken glass to save the life of her beloved. At one end of the screen, Dharmendra the hero of the tale, not so heroically tied to a stake, squirmed red-faced but remained tethered exactly as he was. And as Hema danced, making cinematic history, a gloating Amjad Khan, playing the arch-villain Gabbar Singh, looked villainously on. But no one paid any attention to this trio of cinematic big guns emoting together on celluloid for posterity.

A place had been made for Nandita and a great deal of disproportionate praise was heaped upon the *pakoras* that she had cooked up.

'Just what we needed,' boomed Danny.

'Your *pakoras* never turn out this crisp,' a none-too-diplomatic husband going overboard complained to his wife.

And the creator of a million *pakoras*, Nafisa, even suggested that she take some lessons in *pakora* making from Nandita.

Discomfited by this condescending posture of the younger people, Nandita wondered why these people could never be natural with her. Why could they not accept her as a *person*, as a human being? They either heaped excessive amounts of attention and praise upon her or completely forgot her existence. She wanted to scream *I'm an intelligent educated woman, talk to me on equal terms*. But all that she had been able to get from them were banal inanities.

'So, auntie, what have you been doing with yourself?' asked one among them, not particularly interested in eliciting an answer. But then as far as conversations went, it was not such a bad gambit to fall back upon. Another discussed the welcome changes that had come about in the weather and what she was planning to do with it. Only Sue, wanting to know why she still draped herself in six yards of material that came right up to the ground, posed her a question that deserved a considered response. And while these questions were being asked of her, their long-extinguished cigarettes had gone cold and their chilled beers at the point of turning warm had gone haltingly back into circulation once again. Meeta, however, had chosen not to take up her glass! The whole set-up was too uncomfortable by far to make Nandita want to stay on with it for any prolonged length of time.

Conceding defeat, she smiled benignly upon the congregation of young people and moved out and away from the stifling air of formality that she encountered there. While among Tukun's friends and compatriots, she was not an individual called Nandita. She was just a species called *Mother*: nameless, personality- and individuality-less, with no introduction of her own. She was just nineteen years Tukun's senior and many among his friends were closer to her in age than they were to his. Yet the generation gap assigned to her by virtue of her status as mother to Tukun had remained as an unbridgeable void between them.

It was a fact that could not be disputed that the greatest distance that lay between two generations was the gap that lay stretched out between children and their parents and in turn that which lay between parents and their children. Friendship was a person-to-person affair that saw no boundaries of age, colour, or sex, nor of language, religion, or nationality, for all it sought was a kinship of feelings and emotions between two persons. Nandita the individual had numberless friends back there in the life that she had left behind in far-off Calcutta, but the mother of Tukun did not have a single friend here in this life that she now led, not one friend whom she could claim as her own. Her hankering after meaningful human company quashed, come Monday she would settle back more comfortably into the accustomed smoothed-out groove that the movement of time had cut out for her.

Seated in an empty home, Nandita sat thinking. Mondays always left her bemused, for the weekends full of activity that should have left her energised seemed instead to leave a flat aftertaste in her mouth which she could never really logically explain. Why was it, she wondered, that the lonely days of solitude were never as lonely for her as were the days when the house brimmed over with company?

Having tasted many failed encounters setting herself apart, she could perceive clearly through a prism of heightened awareness this morning that she was a total misfit whichever way she moved. Like Daminidi, she had also come to a point where though she was *a part of the whole, she really was not quite a part of anything!* She closed her eyes and let the sun's warming rays play upon her face and suddenly felt that she was no longer alone. Ahead of her, she found Damini seated dejectedly upon the single step that took one into the coal-room. A hint of tears hung upon the faithful servitor's eyelashes. Nandita stretched out a hand to brush away the glistening beads hanging upon her eyelashes.

'Why are you crying, Daminidi?' Her question had been met by a sniffle. 'But Thakuma is not here, so who could be scolding you to make you cry?'

Wiping her eyes with the end of her sari, she had surprisingly come out in fierce defence of Thakuma. 'Silly girl, your Thakuma is not a tyrant, she scolds me because I deserve to be scolded. When she is here, I never feel so lonely and unwanted. I can work all day long without any rest but I cannot live with the silence I have endured since the last six days.

Coming out of her reverie, Nandita murmured, 'You were right, Daminidi. The silences that engulf us are indeed painful to endure! I do not like it, I do not want it, but what am I to do?' She wanted desperately to break out of this stultifying existence, but she did not see how. She had watched in wonderment as the long since dead and buried bulbs of the daffodils and the crocuses had broken through the frozen crust of the earth and come back to vibrant life with the advent of spring, but she had learnt no lessons from them. Steeped in self-pity, Nandita could see no path before her that she could take to bring herself out of this impasse where she had wandered willingly into one day. She had conceded defeat and thrown up her hands long ago, for having sold her flat and given up her job, she had literally burnt all her boats.

Winding down a social weekend was heavy work. Weighed down by the cumulative fatigue of all the hectic housekeeping, Nandita sat down, a cup of tea in hand, wondering what exactly she should do with herself and the bright and beautiful day that lay ahead of her. Her limbs were stiff and heavy, and her resolve of sorts to stay away from all disturbing encounters that lay beyond her home was making her wonder what she should do.

But the beauty of the glorious springtime day had broken through the armour of her tepid resolve. Remaining within the safe confines of a prison is extremely habit-forming but freedom once tasted is far more difficult to eschew. And so she had been unable to hold herself back from going in search of human contact. Carrying a little bite with her, she pulled the door shut and moved towards the rose garden.

Grace had assured her that if the sun were to be out, then so would she, and there she was, court shoes, camel-hair coat, plumed hat, full complement of make-up, and all. Nandita, in her eagerness to meet her newly made friend, almost ran the distance that remained between the entrance to the garden and the bench where she was seated. As she arrived panting, she saw that she was not alone today. Grace, who was in fact rather spare of frame, looked quite fat in contrast to the reed-like thinness of the woman who was seated beside her. Her elderly crumpled-up face was made-up as painstakingly as her friend's was. And akin to Grace, she too was turned out in formal wear. A pair of well-polished pumps, a well-styled but well-worn coat out of another era in a subdued checked material, and a hat with a narrow ledge running around it where a variety of fruits sat huddled together, made up her attire.

'Hi, honey, I was kinda hopin' you'd be comin'. This here is my friend Kate,' she said, pointing to the woman beside her. 'Kate, meet Nan.' Nandita and Kate shook hands. Nandita would have much preferred sitting facing the two aged women, but a garden with a semicircular array of benches left one with no such option. The bench was large enough to accommodate three and so Nandita had been compelled to fit herself in, like the filling in a sandwich, between the two of them. Nandita, clutching her satchel with its component of sandwiches and a fruit (an orange today), felt like a little girl out on a picnic with her guardians.

'Sure does feel good to have a young person around,' observed Grace with some satisfaction.

And Kate, more parsimonious with words, echoed her feelings with a very economical 'Sure does.'

There was need for some correction here, Nandita felt. Grace seemed to have somehow got the wrong impression that she, Nandita, was a young person. It made her feel like a fraud, having her repeatedly refer to her as if she was someone just past her girlhood. A grandmother of two and young!

Trying to catch their attention, she said, 'You know,' avoiding the use of either of their two names. For never in her life had she had the temerity to address anyone who was senior to her, by name; *it was just not done that way* where she came from! You assigned a relationship to each person who was elder to you, and then addressed that person by the nomenclature of that given status. It could be as elder sister, elder sister-in-law, mother or aunt, grandmother, elder brother or elder brother-in-law, father or uncle or grandfather, but never ever did you commit the social faux pas of addressing a senior by his or her given name. And here were these two women older by far than her mother would have been had she been alive, whose attention she was trying to attract. She cleared her throat. 'You know,' she said again, 'I really am not all that young, in truth I'm quite old.'

Grace broke into a peal of laughter and Kate did her bit by donning a smile. And then Grace, taking Nandita's hand into her own, convincingly stated, 'You ain't old, honey. You ain't old by a stretch, believe me. There's no rush, if you go on living, you'll get there sure enough,' she assured Nandita.

'But . . .'

'Trust us, honey, you haven't got there yet.'

Nandita smiled at the words and then mumbled, 'I really don't know.'

'We do. You know, Kate, when Nan and I met yesterday, we hardly got to talk. You know how it is at lunchtime. Margaret's cooking had begun to call.' She smiled broadly, revealing the splendour of her pearly dentures. Turning to Nandita, she informed her, 'Margaret cooks for us, believe me, hon, she is a real whiz with whatever she whips up.'

'Nan's from?' asked Kate.

'Nan here is from Pakistan, am I right, honey?'

'No. I'm from India . . .'

'Just imagine, Kate, she is from India and I thought she was from Pakistan.'

'Are they two different places?'

And Nandita had gone into a short speech on the partition of India and the ever-increasing divide that had come about thereafter. When she surfaced from her little talk, she found that she had lost the twosome somewhere along the way. They really did not want to know about India and Pakistan. They would not mind knowing more about Nandita, however.

Grace had had quite enough of the combined history and geography lesson that she had been droning out to them. There were more interesting things that she would like to know about India and she stopped Nandita in midsentence and asked, 'I've heard y' have a lotta snakes and tigers there, how do you guys ever get about in that there country of yours, honey?'

It was no easy matter for Nandita to get out of the tangle of snakes and tigers; it was like being back in school teaching class again, but rather more difficult, all in all! Dislodging preconceived notions from the minds of children was difficult enough, so it can be well imagined what she had got into.

Once the snakes and tigers had been removed from the streets of India, they had failed to remain a matter of curiosity for the old ladies. The talks reverted to the daily concerns of Nandita's companions. Kate left soon after; a great-grandson's birthday was coming up and she had to mail him a cheque.

'Things are getting mighty expensive these days, Nan, Kate'll be at least five dollars out of pocket, believe me.'

Nandita nodded agreement. She knew very little about the value of five dollars under these circumstances, but she very well knew that five rupees had long since gone past being a sum of money you could gift a grandson on his birthday in India.

They spoke for a while on this, that, and the other but finally Grace asked, 'Do you live alone, honey?'

'No, I live with my son and daughter-in-law and their two children.'

'What, with your daughter-in-law? She must be quite some kid, for the world of me, I'd never have agreed to live with a mum-in-law.' She paused, then, 'Not too easy for you either, Nan, I suppose,' she had observed with a deep perspicacity.

Nandita, steeped in self-pity regarding her position in the home of her son, was surprised to find her daughter-in-law being projected by Grace as a martyr to circumstances. She herself had eschewed living with her parents-in-law and yet had never looked upon Meeta's position with any sympathy, where a mother-in-law was a fixed point in her family that she could never remove. *They* had asked her to come because *they* needed her, so wasn't the case different? Disturbed beyond measure, she fell silent. Was she really such a selfish person, she asked of herself, self-doubt welling up within her heart!

Grace was not one to remain silent for long and broke into her reverie with a demand for photographs of the entire family as she rose to return for her afternoon meal and rest. 'Make sure you come with those snaps tomorrow, honey. I'm dyin' to meet that family of yours.' And she hobbled off. And Nandita sat on, wondering what she was to do with the sandwiches she had brought along with her. The meal she had shared with Bill just a few days back had made her greedy for company. Unable to eat alone, she retraced her steps and went back home where of course she had eaten alone as always.

Would she ever again meet Bill, she wondered as she went through the mechanics of eating a meal. She neither knew from where he had come, nor knew where he was going. She had not asked for a point of reference, nor had he given any. Maybe it was better this way. It would have been better had they not met at all, for she would have been far better off without the knowledge of *that* couple drifting apart. A human being needed a few illusions to anchor on to so as to make life's journey a bearable one.

Just a bit of neglect and the house had begun to look a little listless and lacklustre. Guiltily, she whisked through the house, putting things in order as she went along. Having completed her normal contributory quota of cooking for the night-time meal, she had just sat down with a book when the children came in, and soon after, their mother arrived as well. It was nice to have them back, she thought as she closed the book and went and joined them in the kitchen where they sat snacking.

'A cup of tea, Ma?' asked Meeta, putting the kettle to boil.

'Shall I make it? You must be tired.'

Meeta looked up with a faint look of surprise. 'No, Ma, I can see you've already cooked dinner, so *you* must be the one who's tired.' It was Nandita's turn to look surprised. Tea in hand, they had sat chatting together for a while.

As she walked into her room later that evening, Grace's observations came to her mind and she had to concede that it was perhaps not all that easy for Meeta to have her around forever as well.

Late that night, she pulled out her stash of photographs in search of the best among the snapshots that could most flatteringly project her family to Grace. And her Dipto emerged from his hiding, from within the folds of her clothing in her chest of drawers. He was smiling as mischievously as he always did. He was young and fit and handsome; yes, he was so achingly handsome and young. He had been made to go into hiding after three to four enquiries regarding this handsome man in uniform had been made of her by the friends of her son and their spouses. On straying into her room and sighting the photograph on the dresser, they would invariably ask where this handsome younger brother of Sudipto was. And soon after, Flying Officer Prodipto Kumar Roy had been banished from the counter atop her dresser and made to live in the topmost shelf of her chest of drawers.

Should she take him along tomorrow or should she not? She really did want to show him off, but what if their reaction were to be the same as those other people's had been? Looking at herself in the mirror, she wondered how an ageing Nandita could present such a vibrant, exuberantly youthful person as her husband. The man in uniform with a generous smile lighting up his face was far younger in that photograph than his son was today, for his life had been scorched with but twenty-five summers, no more. After many long years of loneliness and longing, that night Nandita shed some unchecked tears upon the altar of her beloved's memory. For whatever the mirror might say, whenever she looked upon her Dipto's smiling face, the young unsatiated woman just into her twenties who lived trapped within her ageing frame, cried out from within her. That was one of the reasons why she rarely undertook the task of looking at old photographs, and why still more seldom she showed them to anyone. For old wounds, once disturbed, caused much pain. Undecided, she set it apart.

Photographs of the family taken against the backdrops of Disneyland and the Niagara Falls were more joy-filled subjects, and she carefully picked a selection and, putting them into an envelope had set them aside for her visit to the park the next day.

As usual she was the first to awaken and come down to the kitchen to brew herself a cup before the rest of the horde descended to taint the environment with alien aromas. Little Tanmayee, now renamed Tammy, whom she preferred to call Tanu, was the first to make her appearance in the kitchen. Having woken earlier than she normally did, she came where she knew she could get a little petting. Eyes half closed, hair tousled, cheeks warmed by the residue of sleep, she tumbled straight into the open arms of Nandita, who held her curled-up form close to her heart.

Away from the eyes of the rest of the world, she was still her very own little baby, the baby whom she had held close to her and brought up with care from the very first day of her birth. Today the child's mother frowned upon all such overt signs of 'babying', as she liked to call it. And as a consequence, Nandita had distanced herself to the extent possible from her grandchildren. They appeared to be none the worse for it, but she herself had felt totally marginalised by this moving away. Having brought up an only child who was left fatherless at the tenderest of possible age, whom she had not allowed to get away with any misdemeanours, she felt spoiling anyone was the last thing she was ever likely to do.

Energised by that buoying hug from her granddaughter, Nandita had tripped more lightly when she left home later that day. She carried no sandwiches with her, having concluded that eating alone on the benches of an emptied-out rose garden was not such a good idea at all. But she carried a couple of oranges as emergency thirst-quenchers, and a small pouch filled with grains in case she was to chance upon a congregation of pigeons! Was she then planning to go to the centre of town where the people and the pigeons of downtown Saisborough congregated?

Grace, who had been awaiting her coming with acute eagerness, welcomed her arrival with the promised bunch of photographs with uninhibited glee. Kate too had delayed her departure from the garden to take a glimpse at the snapshots; that was a very major concession on the part of Kate as she had a very important appointment with a morning soap which just could not be missed! Having made appropriate noises of approval, she had flipped speedily through the photographs and left on spindly legs for her rendezvous with the superstars of the little screen.

These photographs, however, for Grace were the centre point of her concern for that morning. She crooned over the beauty of Nandita's grandchildren and declared that they were the loveliest babies she had ever seen. Nandita knew that Grace was exaggerating beyond limits but let it pass because her response to those photographs had made her feel so very good. But when it came to their names, Nandita discovered with a certain peevish amazement that the names Tomal and Tanmayee were not going down any too well with her dear octogenarian friend, for never had she heard such strange-sounding names in her entire life. Facing defeat, Nandita eventually handed over Tom and Tammy, two names that she abhorred without any reservations. 'Oh, Nan honey, you should stick to these cute little names and forget those formal and difficult ones.' Grace's reaction to these two new names came as an eye-opener to Nandita, who had always resented the takeover by them of their beautiful, meaningful given names. Quick to observe Nandita's look of disappointment, she quickly went on to add, 'Not that they ain't pretty names, but kinda difficult for an oldie like me to . . .' Since then, Nandita, when among her newly found friends always referred to her grandchildren by their new Americanised names! But it had not been easy for her for she sensed a feeling of betrayal towards her own self while doing so.

Turning to the snaps of Tukun and Meeta, Grace had complimented her on the intelligent looks of her son and the grace of her daughter-in-law. Nandita had taken just a single photograph of her husband with her, but among all the photographs, the one of her Dipto in his winter blue barathea uniform adorned with his hard-won wing had completely stolen Grace's heart. 'Bring some more snaps of this handsome young man,' she had commanded. Her Dipto was wonderful, she knew, but Grace seemed to have a weakness for a man in uniform as well, Nandita had surmised from her reaction to his attire. And what was wonderful, Grace seemed to have had no problem at all in pairing her with this dashing young flyer. And in return for that little bit of consideration, Nandita had promptly given that generous old woman her heart.

Grace was one of the most interesting events that had come to pass in a long stretch of years in Nandita's famished-for-friendship life. She had filled up the haunted spaces within her with light and sent the ghosts scurrying that had settled down there.

And the very next day, Grace replied with a return volley of snapshots that faithfully snared and tamed myriad moments of happiness that had been left behind forever in time. And at every turn, Nandita would encounter two persons, Dave and Chuck, whom she could sense were at the centre of Grace's universe. She wanted to be introduced to them but so engrossed was the old lady in showing off her treasured photographs that Nandita hadn't been able to interrupt and to ask of her who they were. And at a given moment marked out by the needles upon her watch, a happy Grace, having shared her precious spoils with her Nan, wobbled off to keep her appointment with Margaret's culinary offerings. And Nandita, her mind a-jumble with a host of new characters that had just been introduced to her with little or no reprieve, stumbled preoccupied in thought down the garden steps and walked straight into Dr William Brady, who was just then walking past.

6 BILL BRADY HAS SOME UNFINISHED BUSINESS

'Hello there, we meet again,' he said with a smile, while steadying her with a firm grasp.

Nandita was embarrassed beyond measure at finding herself in such a disadvantageous position. She wondered what he would think of her cannoning into him as she had just done. 'I'm sorry . . . I . . . I . . . didn't see you.' She saw him wince. 'Did I hurt you?'

He smiled off her improbable assumptions. And she realised how ridiculous her words must have sounded.

'Off somewhere? If you're not too busy, I'd be grateful if you could spare me a little while.'

Nandita, having vowed to eschew his company, gave no reply.

'I'm real glad that I've found you, for I do believe we have some unfinished business to transact.'

'Unfinished business?'

'I think you misinterpreted something I said that day.'

She frowned, trying to understand the underlying meaning of his words.

'My fault entirely, but would you please allow me to explain?' Nandita continued to stand silent where she was, and taking that as an acceptance of his request, taking her gently by the elbow, he propelled her up the steps and back to one of the benches in the rose garden that she had just left.

'Would you prefer to be in the shade, or is this place OK?' he asked as if the location of the seat was of paramount importance.

'I'm fine, thank you,' she replied somewhat abruptly. 'And why should you explain anything to me?'

'Please,' he pleaded as he urged her to take her seat. 'Thank you,' he said as she sat down. Seating himself beside her, he said softly, 'I guess I know why you left so abruptly that day.'

'I'd been out for too long; I had to go home. There was no reason other than that,' she offered, face expressionless while nervously twisting one end of the *pallu* of her sari around the index finger of her left hand.

'I had seen a look on your face so I know it was more than just that. Drat! Why am I beating about the bush? You had asked me how Meg was and I . . .'

'It was none of my business; I shouldn't have asked . . .'

'There you go again, turning into an iceberg on me. Why can't you understand,' he pleaded, 'that what I am trying to tell you is very painful for me to speak of.'

'Then why must you speak on such a subject at all?'

Brushing aside all further prevarication, he abruptly came to the point. 'I *hate* telling anyone that Meg is dead.' Face averted from her, he threw to the winds in a harsh pain-filled whisper, 'Yes. Meg is dead! It gives me a strange sense of comfort to pretend that she has just gone away somewhere out of sight.' The pitch of his voice changing, he had gone on. 'There you have it all, the reason why I gave you that spiel about how well she must be somewhere else. From the look you wore on your face just before you left me that day, I realised immediately afterwards that you had come to some strange conclusion, that I had in some way let my Meg down.' He plucked a blade of grass and subjected it to a close scrutiny before going on. 'I have been looking for you downtown where we met the other day; having failed, I was planning to go through the phone book today. I just couldn't let you go on thinking that I could have done anything like that.' And he still continued to look away from her.

Too stunned for words, she sat on beside him in silence. Pain is very clannish by temperament, so his pain, having traversed the boundaries of the two selves, became one with her own stockpile. The myriad agonies that life had inflicted upon her and the sad blow that life had dealt him had flown into one another and become a solid mass of anguish within her heart. She wanted to express her sympathy and concern to him in so many well-chosen words, but words had abandoned her like false friends do at times of adversity. She wanted to look upon his face, but her eyes too refused to obey her command.

Head bowed, she instead stretched out her hands towards him and covered the hands he held in his lap with her own. And only then did he look her way. To his utter surprise, he saw that a surge of silent tears, which had welled up in her eyes, was coursing unchecked down her cheeks. She was crying as if she had just learnt of the passing away of a very dear friend of hers. And her hands remained covering his hands with their comforting cloak of caring. And for a while longer, they sat on together in silence.

And then he stirred, and as if slowly coming awake out of a trance, he uttered a very simple 'Thank you.'

'Oh, Bill, forgive me, please, for my thoughtless thoughts.' It had not even crossed her mind to address him as Dr Brady at that point. The name Bill that she had heard his wife call him had come spontaneously upon her tongue. She forgot all the tenets of formality; this sorrowing man seated beside her had become 'Bill' to her.

Gently removing his right hand from within her folded hands, he delved into his pocket and offered her a handkerchief. She accepted it but did not make use of it. So he gently took the handkerchief back from her and wiped the tears away from her eyes.

'Giving vent to one's feelings has gone out of fashion these days, thank you very much for the tears you just shed for my Meg. My mother was from Italy, so that little bit of Italian who lives within this American accepts your tears as a tribute to the girl he loved so dearly.'

'I cried because I just could not hold back my tears, I had seen you together and had sensed how much each of you meant for the other.'

'We had been together, squabbling, and fighting and loving each other since we were both eighteen,' he told her, his eyes brilliant with unshed tears and his voice gone heavy with emotion.

'Why did you allow her then to go out of your hands?' she demanded, forgetting that she had no right to do so.

'I should have been more careful, knowing how fragile Meg was. She was always hypertensive. I had no idea that she had been playing hooky with her medicines, she had a stroke one day, went into a coma, and three days later, poof, she was gone. I blamed myself for not having checked her weekly pill dispenser more often, but what use was my remorse then?'

And then she told him about the helmetless driver upon a motorcycle who had ridden out of her life one day.

'He made me fall desperately in love with him and left me to fend for myself without his loving presence when I was not yet twenty. I don't know, Bill, whether to love or to hate him for having played around with his life as he did. And that really hurts. A fighter pilot should have gone down in glory, performing daring exploits up in the sky, not upon a motorcycle that had gone headlong into the rear of a parked vehicle. He was a fantastic flyer, and if he had to make a dramatic exit, then he should have done so riding upon the wings of some outstanding exploit, an exploit such as the world would have cared to remember, and I myself could have cherished and cosseted and hung on to for the remainder of my life.'

'Yes, there is a great deal of anger and petulance mixed with regret and despair when one loses a person who was really close to oneself. I too have hated Meg at times for that bunch of leftover pills that was found in her medicine cabinet once she was gone.'

And then a little bird hopped into their sight; his spirits lightening, he asked, 'No sandwiches with you today?' She indicated that she was carrying none with a shake of her head.

'Where are your chocolates?'

'I have a sweet tooth, but not that sweet; I didn't bring any. Have you eaten?'

'I'll go home and eat.'

'Why don't you let me buy you a salad or something?'

She hesitated, not knowing how to handle the situation. Never before had she been confronted with such a situation in her life. It was bad enough that she was sitting talking to a near stranger, discussing the most intimate details of her life. How could she possibly become so bold as to go for a meal with him in a public place, she asked herself. She was tempted to accept but her upbringing interceded and made her refuse.

'I really must go back home.'

'If you must, then I won't keep you. But tomorrow around one, I'll be there on one of those benches downtown, most probably eating a bar or two of chocolates all by myself. It would be nice if we were to bump into each other, wouldn't it?'

She was shocked by his assumption that she would accept his invitation to join him the next day. With a little grunt denoting nothing in particular, she collected together her wits and her little bag full of photographs and beat a hasty retreat from the rose garden as yet bereft of roses.

She took the steps down more carefully because she knew there was no one ahead of her who would be there to steady her if she were to stumble or to fall.

When very young, Nandita had been bred, like most children, upon fairy tales; in these tales, sorcerers and witches abounded who went about casting spells upon certain hapless souls. These unfortunate persons coming under the sway of these spells would have all kinds of strange things happen to them, and trapped in time, ensnared within bodies other than their own, they would linger on. But then one day a benevolent spirit would come along and wave a wand or, with the utterances of some magical words, release them from the incantation within which they had been caught and then all of a sudden as if coming awake, all would be buoyant, bright, and beautiful in their little world once again.

The unexpected arrival of Bill in her firmament and the friendship that had been offered unconditionally by Grace and her compatriots worked like the proverbial magic wand of fairy tales. And out of the blue, Nandita discovered a new person who had been living unnoticed in hibernation within her. And to her utter surprise, this newly discovered persona of her old self was not an old and stodgy female who could be ignored and set aside; she was a woman imbued with confidence enough to reach out to people and forge links with them at first hand. Of late, she had observed and then accepted that it was always via media that people would place her when they positioned her within their sights. She was always *someone to someone, and only then was she something to someone else.* She never stood alone as an individual without these peripheral props.

As her legs began getting her closer to her destination, a longing to get back to the familiar surroundings of her home had begun to stir within her. And by a strange act of transmogrification, the prison walls of home had even begun to acquire the aspect of a sanctuary by the time she got there. She was not aware of the whys and wherefores of this changed perspective. In truth, she was not even aware that a change of perspective was coming about in her mindset at all. Just a few short jaunts away from home had imbued the place in which she had been living listlessly for years with an entirely different allure to Nandita. At the turn of a key, a haven of assuring sameness of scents and sights welcomed her back. She shut the door behind her and stood a moment savouring the joy of being back home.

It was well past her normal mealtime and the exercise added on to it had made her ravenously hungry. Removing her shoes, she uncurled her toes and went into the half-bath downstairs. Dripping water she had emerged refreshed, and gone directly to the kitchen. A combination of *dal, bhaat,* and *torkari* was her preferred choice when it came to an afternoon repast. She measured out portions of all three onto a plate and microwaved the mix into a piping hot state of enticing edibility. She added a sliver of fresh lemon and a dash of mango chutney to give an extra edge to the meal she had served herself. And having poured a glass of cold water, she picked up a spoon and went out to the yard. The trestle table and bench were none too clean but she had eyes for none of that. As she raised the first spoonful up to her mouth, she felt as if someone was eyeing her.

It was an eerie feeling. Relieved, she saw that it was the fat cat gone fatter still, who was observing her closely as she ate. Apparently, he felt that she was invading *his* private domain. He looked her straight in the eye as only cats can do, his eyes belligerent, wanting to know why she had diverted his attention from his chosen pursuit. He seemed to lose interest in her soon enough and was back to his wildlife-watching vigil. He was seated under the tree where she had seen him so often eyeing the savoury mouthfuls of squirrel gambolling up above. Looking at the widening girth of the vigilant tabby, Nandita wondered how many of those squirrels he had managed to kill and to feed upon. She didn't like the idea very much, because she felt the squirrels living under the protection of the Roys should not become snacks for the neighbourhood cat! A few birds alighted and soon flew off, and the cat went off chasing their shadows. The squirrels were safe, at least for the moment.

She went in and, with feet up, sat down to rest for just a very little while. Half an hour later, she woke with a start thanks to the clock striking the hour in the living room. Should she stay at home for a day or two and make amends, she asked of herself.

The children returned soon after, ate carelessly of whatever she gave, and dashed out again, variegated gear in hand. Tomal was to be picked up by 'mother number 1' for gymnastics, while 'mother number 2' was to come by for Tanu to take her for a ballet lesson. Meeta's turn to cart around myriad children from one destination to another would come around soon enough, she knew. Mothers these days, Nandita had seen, were perpetually on the run behind their children. Pampered as they were, the children of the generation of her grandchildren seemed to have lost the art of entertaining themselves. If they were not off to do something 'meaningful' where they were slated to acquire some additional skill, then they would have to be transported to wherever 'company' was to be found. What a restless lot they were!

Meeta returned, and the children stormed in soon after; spreading their shoes, socks, satchels, and sundry gear, they rushed off upstairs. Their mother had not said a word to them. Tukun as a schoolboy, she remembered, had had an entirely different set of rules to abide by. His chores were clearly earmarked and he had always carried them out in their exact given order. Barring a stray occasion or two, she had never had to remind him to fulfil his given tasks. Those habits of order and obedience had stood him in good stead; why then had he not imposed those disciplining rules while bringing up his own children?

The children had been in her keep during those first few years. And then affluence had come, and with it, the norms of normal living had also changed. The children had slowly slipped out of her grasp, and Meeta and Tukun, far more embroiled in their work and with it their newly acquired social responsibilities, had also little by little begun to drift away. She had tried on occasion to point out where she felt they were going wrong in the upbringing of their children, but the lines of communication were already filled with static, and except for generating resentment, it had done nothing else.

She had voiced her opinion regarding the upbringing of the children to her son one day: 'Don't you think, Tukun . . . a little more discipline', he had looked towards her, 'should be instilled into the children . . .'

'Are they undisciplined?' It was more a challenge than a question.

'I didn't say that! But now that they are growing up . . .'

'Yes, they are growing up and . . .'

'Remember how you used to look after all your own things when you were young?'

'So I did. But things change, you know. All the same, if you feel that way, why don't you tell Meeta where we're going wrong?'

'I'm sure both of you know.'

'Do we?' And 'Meeta,' he'd called out going up the stairs, and his wife had met him halfway down.

'Why're you shouting?' she'd asked, standing at the halfway mark. And Nandita caught just below had heard the entire exchange.

'I'm not shouting. I was just calling you.'

'Why?'

'Ma was saying the kids are getting really spoilt.'

'Spoilt?'

'They don't put away their shoes and things.'

'Oh, that? The kids are quite fed up listening to the tales of what a perfect kid their dad was. "He used to polish his shoes every evening," she tells them, forgetting that they wear sneakers.'

'Shhh!' he cautioned, knowing full well that his mother was within earshot of this exchange. 'But they could surely put away their clothes.'

'Whatever for? Why waste time when they are destined for the next day's wash in any case.' The voice had been lowered by a jot but was audible enough to anyone who was interested to hear what was being said.

'Tell them to put their clothes into the laundry basket then.' Choosing a solution that sat right on the fence, he had made an attempt at buying peace on both fronts.

'Why don't you tell them yourself?'

Tukun's brows had creased together. He *knew* that what his mother had taught him one day had made him the man he was, even so. And perhaps Meeta's argument was just as tenable in its own place, and trapped between these two opposing viewpoints on child-rearing, he had just ceded ground and kept quiet, and had shelved the matter for then, and perhaps forever. And Nandita too had chosen not to repeat herself.

The evening had worn on and rolled onto night-time, she remembered, and the shoes and the socks and the satchels had lain sprawled around right inside the entrance to their home, and no one save her had found anything amiss in this state of disarray!

Tukun was loading the dishwasher and Meeta was occupied in wiping the kitchen counters clean when Nandita went into the kitchen to have her night-time meal. Both of them looked up in surprise, and Tukun looked down at his wristwatch and, seeing Nandita put some food onto a plate, asked, 'Eating early?' And then coming up to her and touching her forehead, he murmured, 'Not unwell, I hope?'

'I was feeling a bit tired, so I thought I'd eat early and go to bed.'

'You should drink more milk, Ma,' Meeta had advised, looking closely at her mother-in-law. 'Post-menopausal women have too many problems with weakened bones.' She did look tired today, she felt, and turning to her husband, she asked, 'Doesn't she look tired, Tukun?' And Tukun had nodded his agreement. Though touched by their concern, Nandita had flinched. But why must Meeta discuss such personal matters pertaining to her bodily functions in the presence of her son! Throwing a glance Tukun's way, she busied herself, and Meeta had gone on, oblivious to her discomfiture. 'What you eat is not nutritive enough on its own.'

'I am used to the food I eat, so why' (a look of surprise flitted across Tukun's face, for he had seen his mother eat differently from the rest of the world all his life and never thought of it as being anything but adequate and right for her) 'should it make a difference now?'

Tukun had programmed the dishwasher and switched it on. Standing beside the humming machine, he looked at his mother then at his wife and then back at his mother again. And he, a full-grown man of thirty-five, wondered for the first time in his life why his mother ate differently from the rest of the people around her.

'You know why, Ma. The bone depletion after menopause . . .'

To change the topic, she found so embarrassing, she conceded, 'I'll have an extra glass of milk from tomorrow.'

'Why not from today?' Tukun asked, going to the refrigerator and pouring a glass. And then they remembered the news that had to be watched, and Meeta, nodding in agreement, followed him out of the kitchen.

Nandita finished her two-chapatti meal soon enough and, looking around to see that no one was watching, poured the milk back into the container from where it had been taken. She had no desire to have a bout of gas poking her in the ribs and bringing her awake in the middle of the night!

As she was falling asleep, she acknowledged that at some level the young people did care. They said she was looking tired and had offered remedial measures; perhaps she should not push herself too much or too far all at once. She would give a break to her wanderings, she told herself sagaciously, and fell into deep slumber there and then.

Heralding the arrival of a new day, a ray of sunshine escaping from the sun bounced off her face and went straight across the room and fell directly upon the photograph of Flight Lieutenant Prodipto Kumar Roy resplendent in his winter blues. She was surprised to find his mischievous face smiling down upon her from there, and then realised that she had forgotten to place him back in the drawer where he had been residing for ever so long! Light of heart, she smiled back apologetically towards the dresser and rose, and her Dipto, released from his incarceration, smiled on.

Morning tea, bath and *puja* over, she went directly into the tidying up of her room. She could faintly hear voices strident and soft, a chuckle here, a chastisement there, followed soon after by the clink of cutlery and crockery: the delicate, delightful morning sounds that brought the day alive. Humming softly to herself, plumping her pillows, she had drawn the bedspread tightly across the bed, feeling inexplicably contented.

Once all four of them had left, she came out of her room to confront the emptiness of the house. Nandita wandered aimlessly from room to room, desultorily picking up the detritus left behind by the departing army. But after a while of whiling away time, she began to get restless and began to ask herself why she had decided to sit it out at home today. What was she to do with the long day that lay yawning with boredom ahead of her? Snapping out of her lethargy, she assessed the work that had to be done and, speeding up her actions, got down to completing them as fast as she could. She had no desire to face a house in turmoil on her return.

She draped her sari with far greater care today than she took these days. She was a good seamstress and the blouse she had stitched for herself was a complete fit, she observed as she shrugged herself into it. Having pleated the length of the sari that formed the skirt, she tucked the pleats into the waist of her petticoat, seeing that it fell to her feet in a uniform line. Then taking the trailing end left over for the *pallu*, she carefully draped it across her breast in neat folds and then pinned it to her left shoulder. She let the remaining swath of unadorned fabric fall in a straight line up to her knees at the back. She appraised her figure critically as she smoothed down the pleats lying flat over her tummy. How long was it since she had taken a good look at herself? The strict regimen of work she had apportioned herself, and the prescribed widow's diet that she ate, had allowed her to hold on to a near-perfect figure. And so a sari worn with care, she realised, looked elegant upon her even today.

She tripped lightly down to the kitchen and pulled out the satchel that she had tucked away into a drawer. She found the grains that she had carried for the pigeons the day before were still sitting there; she let them remain.

She was none too fond of cheese and so she had built up a couple of sandwiches with a filling of a dry cauliflower *chenchki* left over from the previous night. On the verge of leaving the kitchen, she pulled out more bread and, scraping the remaining curried cauliflower onto it, made an additional sandwich. The other compulsory add-ons like a couple of fruits and a couple of cans of thirst quenchers were finally added to the lot making the bag heavier than she would have liked it to be. But she was not planning to go very far; she would meet her friends, relax and then eat at the rose garden, and come back home.

The days were fast warming up, but the leaves having grown more luscious had woven a cooling canopy up above. Her legs were getting more used to walking, but even so, she wished sometimes that it was as easy to get about in America as it had been in Calcutta. No wonder one got totally isolated without a vehicle and a driver's licence here. The ubiquitous hand-drawn rickshaw and its more elevated cousin the bicycle rickshaw that had been so abundantly available in Calcutta had begun to take on an acute aspect of desirability to her plodding feet.

As she entered the garden, she could see that Grace was holding court. She had brought along two of her companions, Emily and Helen, to show off her newly acquired friend. Nandita, in her elegant white sari and her delicately brushed-by-Bangla English, was quite a matter of curiosity to them. Moreover, her 'youthful aspect' made them warm to her, forgetting all differences. Her reluctance to call them by their names dawned upon Helen soon enough.

'You don't like our names, honey?' she asked in mock seriousness.

'No . . . It's not that . . .'

'Then?'

'You have beautiful names . . . but . . . how can I address you by your names?'

'Did I hear you right, honey? By our names of course.'

'I know, but in India . . . in India it would be considered very rude if I did not . . .'

'Did not?'

'Add at least an "Aunt" to your names, but I know I can't do that here . . . so tell me . . . what am I to do?'

'So that's what's troublin' you,' Grace twinkled. 'When we go visitin' India with you—' And a spluttering laugh followed by a wheezy cough ended the sentence at the halfway mark.

'But right here you just do as everyone else does,' Helen advised.

'Just go ahead, honey, and call us by our names.' Getting her breath back, Grace had ruled.

And Nandita, breaking the stranglehold of tradition had haltingly at first, then more comfortably taken to calling them all by their individual names within the hour.

In the presence of her two compatriots, both Chuck and Dave, who had made a brief but meaningful appearance upon Grace's lips the previous day, remained out of sight. Her curiosity aroused, Nandita had been dying to learn more about these two men. She had been amazed to see how the very mention of these two names had lit up the elderly woman's face! Nandita had enjoyed meeting both Emily and Helen, but somehow, having the company of Grace all to herself was far more enticing to her.

Lunchtime was approaching, and in a while, all three melted away, leaving Nandita holding on to her satchel, wondering what she should next do. And then, eureka, she remembered the grains of cereals that she had been carrying around for the pigeons for the last two days. Since her childhood, she had been taught that on every morsel of food, however humble or grand it be, the maker had imprinted a name. Those birds must be awaiting what was their due, she recognised, as she began marching forward towards the centre of the town. And a bubbly effervescent feeling buoyed her on.

The pigeons were there, and though she was not seeking him out, so was Bill.

She had come to feed the birds, not meet him, but as he was there, she had to be polite, didn't she? A man as sad as he was needed to be cared for, besides. He was deeply immersed in a book, so she was wondering whether or not she should disturb him at all, and then he had looked up. The smile of welcome wreathing his face was invitation enough, and she sat down beside him without being invited.

'I came to feed the pigeons,' she said by way of explanation while pulling out the little pouch of grains. 'Would you like to feed them some?'

'Sure,' he said, getting smoothly into the game of pretence. It was but a matter of minutes, for the birds were a greedy lot and polished off all the seeds they had scattered before them.

'What are you doing for lunch?'

'I'll go home and eat,' she lied. 'Have you brought your standard lunch of chocolates?' she asked with a smile.

'Buying chocolates is no problem, I thought I'd wait for you and then decide.'

'You were expecting me?' she asked in some surprise.

'Let's put it this way, I was hoping you'd come. Can I buy you something to eat? I forgot to eat breakfast so my stomach is growling.'

'You can forget lunch, but never your breakfast,' she admonished as she went into her satchel in search of the sandwiches, forgetting for the moment that she had told him that she was going back home to eat. 'There's enough here for both of us,' she reassured him.

Hiding a smile, 'So I see!' he said.

'You don't mind sharing these sandwiches with me, do you?'

'I'd be crazy to deny myself the privilege.'

'They may taste strange to you; I made them with a cauliflower curry I had cooked.'

'To get to eat home-cooked food, a man has to be lucky indeed.'

'I . . . don't know. If you don't like them, please tell me.'

'I am a boor when it comes to taste; I'll go buy myself a burger if I don't like the stuff.'

At the point of taking the offered sandwich from her, he suddenly retracted his hand. 'Hold on,' he warned, 'I need to know your name before I go laying hands on your lunch yet again.'

'My name? Haven't I told you?'

'When?'

'I'm sorry, I thought I'd told you. My name is Nandita Roy, and I live with my son and his family on South Woodford.'

'Nun . . . deet . . . aaaa.'

'Is it too long and unwieldy for you?'

'We-ll . . .'

'You can call me Nan if you like, some of my other friends do.' With a sudden burst of speed, she had added 'some of my other friends'; just a very few uncommonly common words yet how nice it sounded as it fell from her lips, echoed, and returned to her own ears, and from there into her heart!

'That would be easier; I think I'll settle for Nan. And may I have that sandwich you were just offering, please?'

'Oh, the sandwich, I'm sorry. I didn't realise . . .'

After a short while, he spoke up, 'Believe me, Nan, this tastes real good, I am going for no burgers today.'

'Have another, please, I brought two for you.'

'Didn't you come just to feed the pigeons?' he queried with a playful smile as he took the second sandwich from her. And Nandita's face suffused by heightened colour looked far younger than it had in years.

After the meal, they sat chatting together for a while. And then he told her, 'I'll be gone for a few days. But I would like to meet you again, so could I please have a number where I could call?'

Reluctant to give her home number for a variety of reasons, she suggested, 'Tell me when you're returning, and if it's possible I'll come.'

'I'll be away till next Tuesday. Shall we meet here on Wednesday then? And, no excuses, please, you'll have to allow me to buy you some lunch then.'

'We'll see about that.'

'No, we will not. So twelve in the afternoon on Wednesday right here where we are now seated, and Brady buys the meal.'

And it was then that she shyly asked, 'Please don't mind my asking, but don't you work?'

'Work?' And he took a longish pause. 'No. No, I'm not working very much at present.'

'You don't have to tell me.' She stammered, 'I shouldn't have asked. Please don't . . .'

It was as if she had not interrupted him at all for he went on in exactly the same tone as he had begun giving her an answer. 'Work was all I did after Meg left me and went away. That was my only escape, so I just worked, worked, and worked and nearly killed myself in the bargain.' He sighed deeply and went on, 'I was so exhausted working without any break that in a while I couldn't sleep at all. I started taking sleeping pills, but apart from making me feel kinda woolly in the head, it did nothing else for me, believe you me.'

Desperately wanting to retract her question, desperately wanting to make amends, and stricken with remorse, she apologised, 'I'm sorry. I shouldn't have asked. I shouldn't have pried and caused you so much pain.'

'I'm glad you did. I need to talk, and am I glad you are here to listen to me.' A bunch of pigeons had just then hopped up close to where they sat, and turning his attention to the birds, he carefully collected together the few breadcrumbs that were scattered around and fed them out of his own hand. They fluttered off in search of better offerings, and turning to Nandita, he picked up his narration from where he had left off.

'After a whole string of sleepless nights, one morning when I tried to get up, I found that I was just not able to function. I was barely able to dress and drag myself to the doctor; and there, I believe, I just flaked out. When I came to, I was surprised to find myself in a hospital bed, attached to a very serious-looking drip.' Lower lip caught between her teeth, twisting the end of her sari *pallu*, her throat gone heavy, eyes smarting from unshed tears, Nandita sat listening quietly as he spoke on. 'The doctor, an old friend of mine, when he came to see me later that day was as officious as any doctor possibly could be. Not an extra word did he waste on me on that first encounter! But once I started improving, what a lambasting he gave me.'

'Oh no!'

'Oh yes! He called me a coward and several other unmentionable names and reminded me that I was not the only one in the world to have lost a dear one and told me in no uncertain terms that what I was doing with myself was tantamount to attempting to commit suicide.'

'Need . . .'

'He also told me most helpfully that there were far better and speedier ways of achieving the objective if that was what I thought was the best way out of my predicament.'

'Need he have been so harsh?'

'Well, he was! He picked me up by the scruff of my neck and roughed me around so bad that I saw nothing but red murder in front of my eyes.'

Concerned, she exclaimed, 'Did he really have to do that?'

'There were moments when I wanted to kill him for having dared call me a coward and all those other names besides. I still feel angry about his behaviour at times. But he healed me, so I . . .' And on the tail of the unfinished sentence, he heard a drawling voice within him say, *How foolish can you be? Can't you see that with his harsh and cutting words he turned that inward-looking rage that was corroding your soul onto himself and forced you to look outwards again? He saved your life, Brady, he literally saved your life!* And turning to Nandita, he said in hushed tones, 'He saved my life.'

'I'm glad he did.'

'He is a good man, and a good doctor besides, and knew exactly what he was doing. In truth I realise, Nan, that it was not the treatment but his tongue-lashing that saved my life.'

'You really think so?'

'Yes, now I do. And once he had pulled me out of the woods bit by bit, one little thing at a time, I began to take my life back into my hands once again.'

'Even so, need he have been so cruel?' she murmured, saddened by the tale of his traumatic journey away from his death-wish-filled days. She knew exactly what it was like to have to go on living when all you wanted was to die. But she had had a child in her arms and he had given her no reprieve. Even if she had favoured death to a life without her Dipto, she had been forced to remain connected to the land of the living because of that child's needs.

'I think . . . sometimes . . . cruelty is the only weapon of kindness a man may have.'

'I wonder whether my husband Prodipto had a premonition of his own early death.'

'It's possible he sensed something. Human beings are far more sensitive than we . . .'

'Was that why he goaded me on so cruelly to be a fighter?'

'It's possible.'

'But how can it be . . .'

'With the advent of civilisation, we have lost a great deal of what could be called our sixth sense, but at times it does show up.'

'And, Bill, I thought all along that he was being frivolous in his responses to my concerns. Poor Dipto.'

'Life's too complex by far, and you were far too young then to unravel those complexities. Don't blame yourself. That's one thing I've learnt: not to blame myself for every goddam thing that goes wrong in life.'

'You're right but . . . but you haven't told me what you're doing here. Or shouldn't I ask?'

'Ask by all means. I was born and brought up in and around Chicago; I needed a change of scene so I took some leave, picked up a couple of bags, and like a homing pigeon, drove myself down to these familiar pastures that I'd left behind a long time ago. I had a couple of weeks of doing nothing, and then some of the guys in the universities around here got wind of the fact that I was knocking around in these parts. I was reluctant at first to get into work so soon again. But then . . . they were a persuasive lot . . . so . . .'

'They were able to change your mind.'

'Fortunately so, because work in small doses was just what I needed. I'm teaching a few courses here and there. I'm pretty busy at times and at others I have very little to do.' He shrugged. 'At the end of these six months I'll go back to Columbia again.'

A scab had long since grown over her wounds but she could perceive that his lacerations were still open and weeping. Compassion welled up within Nandita's heart for this man who had suffered and was still suffering. And Nandita, scaling the barriers of her restraining upbringing, feeling a mounting affinity for this man, suppressing a flutter of apprehension, promised to be there when he returned, come Wednesday. A woman born and bred to orthodoxy had committed herself to a luncheon date with a man she had just begun to come to know! How strange are the circumstances that govern a human being's actions!

Back within the four walls of her home, pacing up and down in her room, she rued the moment when she had succumbed to her emotions and agreed to join this big white American called Dr William Brady for a meal. Never before in her entire life had she done anything as outrageous as this! Had she but known where to contact him, she would have backed out of the appointment, having handed him some age-old excuse over the ether! And had not Grace's overwhelming affection drawn her out of her home, there was a possibility that Nandita might have taken fright at her changing ways and retracted into her shell once again.

And one such day, while retracing her way home from the rose garden, Nandita meandered her way into a garage sale. What an eye-opener it was. Was it possible that Tukun and Meeta had been unaware of this most interesting and entertaining aspect of American life when she had joined them in the

United States? For had they been aware, she would surely have known about it; she was an integral part of the family back then in those happy days.

In those early years of her being with them, the sojourns the family took outside their home had but a very few assigned destinations. Drive to the shopping mall, go straight into the selected supermarket, buy the most economical grocery items, eat baked potato, and wend your way home. Or drive to a Bengali friend's home, eat a far more elaborate version of what you ate every day, and back home to the usual grind. Her son and his wife did not seem to have had either the time or the inclination to go in search of new openings to the world that lay around them. And as she went where they went, she too had remained uninitiated to the little snippets that made up the everyday life here! Blinkered by the constraints of their straitened circumstances, they possibly had seen little beyond what lay right ahead of them!

Getting to know Grace, acquainting herself with the people and the fabric of America apart, there still were too many hours left with her to mull over the problem of the luncheon that was looming ahead of her. The Damini that had been revealed to her by Damini herself would not approve, she felt, but the Damini she had chanced to look upon when her guards were down, what would she have to say? She would never know now for Damini had also slipped away out of reach of the living, leaving Kakima behind in that rambling, crumbling mansion of her ancestors. And then transiting from the living to the dead, her head in a whirl, she tried to contemplate, what would all those ghosts of her foremothers and forefathers think of her behaviour if they were to take a look down earthwards from their establishments in heaven? She shuddered at the very thought of it. When she thought of her Dipto in the same milieu as that of her long-departed ancestors, she just could not make a mental match out of it. And so she guessed that he must have somehow contrived to be reborn to escape from their staid company and come back to earth again. He must be a strapping young man, no less, by now. Whose terrace was he landing his kite upon, she had wondered.

Would he be upset as her Thakuma and her ilk surely would be? Would he have either the time or the inclination to be upset with the innocent jaunt downtown of an elderly woman? With pain, she accepted that whether she liked it or not, for the newly recycled Dipto, she and her little outing with Bill would be of little or no interest. Of what account would she be for him now? None, perhaps! Then why was it that a religion that believed in rebirth chose so explicitly to tie down its widows to the ghosts of men who had once been their husbands? Her Dipto was long since gone and yet society demanded that she and others like her live on forever mourning their deaths.

A quiet voice wanted to know of her why *she* herself had chosen to follow all those unjust tenets. And pondering upon the unjust tenets of the society into which she had been born, she remembered one poignant sorrow-filled page out of the not-so-crowded diary of her life!

It was just a few months since Prodipto and she had been married and her tousle-headed husband was doing what he least liked to do. Pinned down to a spot, he was studying for an examination. Poor Prodipto Roy, aficionado of the outdoors, flyer of kites and still bigger kites, was trapped indoors, trying to retain an imprint of Air Force Law within his brain.

Her voice heavy and blurred, she had called out softly, 'Dipto,' as she came and stood alongside him.

Looking up from his books, he had put his arms around her waist and cajoled, 'Let me study, please, Nondu, we'll talk later.'

Strangely docile, she had taken her seat upon the bed a short distance away but, disregarding his request, had asked of him, 'Don't you think the rules of society are totally unfair, Dipto?'

Prodipto was busy studying for one of those promotion examinations that the Air Force kept throwing its officers' way. 'Really and truly unfair, there you are sitting pretty, asking me all kinds of philosophical questions while I'm being forced to mug up for a stupid promotion exam. Nobody asks you the rules that govern a court martial, now do they?'

'I was not talking about such simple matters.'

'You think a court martial is a simple matter? Ask the johnny who gets court-martialled and you'll change your mind.'

She had brought out 'Perhaps!' accompanied by a big sniff.

He had looked towards her, and seeing tears in her eyes, he'd asked in alarm, 'Why're you crying, my poor little thing? Why?'

Nandita had broken down; in her hands was a tear-stained letter. He had opened the letter and given it back to her. It was in Bangla and he had never learnt to read the language.

'It's from Dadu. He has written to say that Boroma has passed away. Oh, Dipto, you don't know how much I loved Boroma,' she had sobbed, holding on to him. 'Do you know she was no blood relation of mine?'

'No blood relation of yours!'

'My great-grandfather lost his first wife and was forced to remarry. He did so against his will, and hours after his wedding, he committed suicide.'

'How could he?'

'And left Boroma my step-great-grandmother a widow when she was just ten or eleven years old.'

'A mere child, how terrible.'

'And for having outlived her husband she had been awarded a life sentence of eternal tasteless, colourless, escapeless existence of a Brahmin widow by the Bangali Brahmin society.'

'Why did she not rebel, Nondu?'

'How could she? The rules have been laid down by men, and all in the favour of men, and so Boroma had to follow them or become a social outcast . . . or so my Kakima told me.'

Becoming uncharacteristically serious, he had pleaded, 'Maybe *she* could not rebel but *you*, Nondu, can. If one day the need for it arises, do please put up a fight. If you want something, even if it is change, you'll have to go after it yourself. No one will give you any space, no, not a single inch, without your fighting for it all the way.' Never had Nandita seen him as serious as he was that day and she had looked up at him, bemused, as he spoke on. 'And as for the unfortunate life of your beloved Boroma, I suppose you are right when you say that she had no options whatsoever.'

'It's so unfair!'

'Who said life was fair, Nondu? But fortunately for your Boroma, your Dadu was there; he is a good man, he took on his father's responsibility and cared for his young widowed wife all through her life.'

'Isn't it terribly unfair that she . . .' she'd asked in frustration and anger.

'Yes. But it could have been much worse. An entire family assigned her the status she had acquired by marriage and went on with life, having positioned her there. I wonder whether such a thing could have happened anywhere else in the world.'

'But I still think if men make the rules that rule society, then they must be responsible for the outcome of their actions. My great-grandfather should never have married again. And you too . . .'

Switching back to his normal jocular tone, he had assured her, 'I promise not to remarry if you die, but please, Nondu, please don't die.'

'And don't you dare leave me in the lurch my ancestor did his wife,' she had thrown at him, eyes ablaze.

'I'll change the rules of society as soon as I find some time and only then will I die. Satisfied?'

But he had not been able to keep his promise!

In a flash, her mind was swamped by memories of that terrifying, tormenting, terrible, tear-stained day out of the diary written for her by life when she had lost her Prodipto. For days on end, she had wished for death with every breath of her life! But unlike Prodipto, she was not to be granted the boon of eternal youth; she had a son, and for him, even her grief knew she must live on. In search of channels through which it could flow out, her grief had transformed and turned itself into anger. How dared he make her fall in love with her as he had done, how dared he love her as much as he had and then recklessly ride away out of her life?

When she had surfaced from the first stinging whiplash of her anguish, she had been surprised to find that the world had remained much the same as it was before the passing away of Prodipto. Boroma, Kakima, and Daminidi were positioned as they always were. Thakuma was still filling her parting with blazing vermilion and wearing saris with brilliant red borders; after all, though Dadu was very old, he was still alive. Ma had earned her reprieve from widowhood by a divine sanction that had come by post one day, so she too continued to wear her *colours* with aplomb, while she, Nandita, had stood before them deprived of all right to the use of colour. And for her, they had bought an entire wardrobe of new saris with inch-wide borders, black, brown, and grey, but never red. She, who had told her Kakima one day that she would never allow society to treat her as shabbily as they had treated her, had chosen a strange path to concretise that revolutionary resolve! She had turned upon the powers that be and asked that they take away the clothes that they had provided for her. If this was the way they wanted her to dress, then she would do one better.

Damini was driven to distraction at the sight of Nandita dressed in the starkest of possible widow's weeds. 'We were powerless, but you are not, why, why, Didi, are you doing this to yourself?'

Kakima had cajoled, scolded, and admonished her, but she had not moved by an iota from the stand that she had taken. 'Kakima, you must have read about how the Japanese workforce protests.' The older woman had nodded in agreement. 'They don't down their tools, they voice their displeasure by silently putting in some extra amount of work. And so I am wearing some extra amount of white!'

'Will that help?'

'I don't know! But I am angry and disappointed and so very unhappy. I have been let down by both the families. Dadu looks the other way and my father-in-law the major general is no longer the man he was. My mother-in-law has exited from her very modern, very Westernised ways and re-entered the Middle Ages. Having made me, the daughter-in-law, in some strange way responsible for her son's sudden passing away, she has stepped aside, while he stands helplessly by, with a wounded look in his eyes, but neither says nor does, anything! I always thought he was a strong and upright individual and would object to the ways I have adopted.'

'And so?'

'I want to hurt all those who have hurt me: I want them to wince each time they look upon me. I will stringently abide by the rules that govern a Brahmin widow's life, and make that my silent protest!'

'Stupid girl, this is not Japan, this is India, and silent protests get swallowed, chewed up, digested here. No one will listen to you unless and until you stand on a rooftop and scream.'

'Why aren't you screaming?'

'How can I?'

'When fighting with one's own people, the only voice one is left with is the silent one. And that's why, Kakima, both of us are fighting our own silent battles.'

'I am fighting no battle, my child, but beware you don't hurt yourself more than the people you have set out to hurt.'

Strangely enough, Kakima had been right. She had given up everything, and people had noticed that for just a little while and then shelved it aside and gone on with whatever preoccupied them most. And once again a quiet voice within her had wanted to know of her why *she* herself chose to follow all those unjust tenets. She thought she was emulating the Japanese brand of black-band-wearing silent protest by eschewing every bit of embellishment, every touch of colour, but had instead ended up cementing further the unjust mores of society!

Who was that young woman that Prodipto had asked to stand up and look society in its eyes and give it a fight: Nandita? A woman who could not even decide whether or not she should, or could, go out for an innocent meal with a friend?

Disappointed and angered by her prevaricating self, she had decided that come what may, she would go for this lunch! All the same, she had told herself that this was to be her last meeting with Bill. She would contrive somehow never to again meet him: a Bangali Brahmon widow who was a grandmother had to behave more decorously than she had been doing of late.

And accompanied all the way by a host of butterflies playing softball in her stomach, she had arrived at her destination to keep her appointment! Seven days, she had not realised, was such a long span of time. It had almost made her forget how handsome and young Bill really was. Seeing him from a distance as she approached him, she felt he was far younger than what she had thought he was when she had first met him. Somehow that feeling that he was younger than her had made her feel far more comfortable. She approached him with a smile and he had stretched out a hand and taken her hand into it.

The little restaurant was cool and comfortable with not too many tables to it. As she entered, she had remembered the little place where her Dipto had taken her, fully pregnant then, on his motorcycle to celebrate her nineteenth birthday. Tukun was to arrive a month later.

'What a nice place this is!' she said as he pulled out a chair for her.

'Have you been here before?'

And she had truthfully stated she had not. How many restaurants had she ever been to in her entire life, in truth? They could be counted on her fingertips, with quite a few fingertips left over for future computing, she thought, smiling within herself as she made herself comfortable.

The food was being ordered; when she stated that she was a vegetarian, the waitress had hummed and hawed and suggested she have a salad. It was somewhere along halfway through her meal that she discovered the little pink shrimp that was sitting under some lettuce leaves. After more than three decades, she had gone and broken her vow to remain a vegetarian for the rest of her life, all because of what a young waitress thought were the right components of a vegetarian meal! She blanched momentarily, gulped hard to get down the morsel sitting in her mouth, and steadied herself.

'Anything the matter?' Bill asked, having observed her halting movements.

'No, nothing, I'm fine.'

'Is the salad OK?'

'Yes . . . yes . . . it's delicious,' she lied. She did not wish to clutter up everything just because of a stupid little crustacean or two having found their way into her stomach.

'You know, Bill,' she said, 'the last time I went out alone with a man to a restaurant was on my nineteenth birthday.' And then she told him about how her Dipto had taken her, heavy with pregnancy, pillion riding on his motorcycle to eat a Chinese meal and the reaction thereafter of the elders in the family. They laughed together imagining the situation that must have prevailed.

'I can barely remember when I was nineteen, after all it was, let me see, a good thirty-two years back that I became nineteen.'

'You really are very young, Bill.'

'Not so young really.'

'No, you are young, Bill, you have an entire life lying ahead of you.'

'And you?'

'I don't know, but the people around me think I'm old.'

'What do *you* think?'

'I don't know, I really don't know.'

And then she told him a little tale. She told him about her kite-wielding pole-vaulting Prodipto and the stratagem he had had to adopt to bring about their marriage. 'I still don't know how he had persuaded his Didima, his maternal grandmother, to break away from tradition and go visiting my Thakuma.'

'Must've been a persuasive guy.'

'That he was.'

'It's a fascinating tale. What happened after that?'

'Slowly word seeped out that, that courtesy call had been accompanied by a marriage proposal. And Mukherjee Didima's eldest daughter's anglicised grandson was the prospective groom. Saving face was a very important factor for that lot . . .'

'So, how did she manage?'

'She had let it fall that her daughter was on the lookout for a bride for her son and so had condescended to look our way. After all, neighbours had to do neighbourly things!'

'Wonderful machinery, this human brain!' And he laughed.

'I wonder what Dipto's grandmother, having broken protocol, must have felt, Bill, because my imperious grandmother had refused even then to descend from her Olympian heights. It was reported that straightening her imperious back, she had said in honeyed tones to the exalted emissary from next door, "Sister, my poor little Nandita is a pure and simple child, *it just would not do* if your *shaheb* grandson were to ask to speak to her. Normally we don't show our daughters to the prospective groom; but in the case of your grandson . . . provided of course her grandfather agrees to a *military match* . . . I may . . ."'

'Your grandma, I can see, was a Queen Victoria of sorts,' Bill observed.

'Oh, Bill, it really was very funny, for my Dipto's grandma was quite a strategist on her own rights, she stole the thunder from Thakuma by projecting her grandson as a young man steeped in tradition. I got excerpts of the historical conversation from Daminidi, our maid of endless years of service in the family. The conversation went something like this: "Sister," she is said to have stated in honeyed tones, "my little angel of a grandson has left the entire matter to me; he says if the girl is to my liking, he will marry her to please his mother and me."'

'All this is so far removed from our lives that it sounds like a fairy tale . . .' And he shrugged.

'But you haven't heard the best yet! Thakuma, harking back to tradition, I believe, had queried, "Don't you think your grandson is too young for my little Nandita? She has already completed her eighteenth year, and your grandson you said was . . ."'

'Prodipto's grandmother had supplied no numbers; even so, falling in line she had stated, "Twenty-three."'

'"Just five years difference, normally everyone prefers . . ."'

'This is really hilarious, Nan, what a pair of grandmothers that twosome was.'

'Now can you see why I think you are ever so young? At eighteen I was supposed to be too old for a very young Prodipto, who was already twenty-three.'

'Meg's and my romance was in no way as colourful but . . .'

'Just as romantic.' And they laughed together as they turned back to their meal.

'But tell me, Bill, how you ensnared your Meg.'

'I had to work pretty hard at it. You see, for me it was love at first sight. As soon as I saw her, I knew she was the girl I was going to marry. You know how it is with big men; they fall for these cuddly little petite girls.'

'I wouldn't know. I am not a big man!'

'Thank God, Nan, that just wouldn't do!'

'So you fell in love and then?'

'Falling in love was all very well, but it wasn't as easy to win Meg as falling in love had been. She was a year my junior at school, and the more I chased her around, the more she ignored me. Pregnancies out of wedlock were still not quite the done thing in those days. So in desperation I even thought of getting her into a compromising situation. But when you haven't got round to holding a girl's hand . . .' And he chuckled recollecting those fretful, foolish days of his youth. Nandita was embarrassed but managed not to show it. 'Then I started dating a curvaceous six-footer and that seemed to do the trick. My plump and petite girl was just stringing me along; she had fallen for me just as hard but you know how it is with women . . .'

'Eat,' she said with a smile, 'your food is going cold.'

They wandered off from there onto many other different topics of discussion and she learnt of his two children: a daughter and a son. They had come to be with him when their mother had died and again when he had fallen ill. But as they were both working and the daughter married besides with a child, it was not possible for them to hang around their dad, was it?

And then he suddenly said, 'I think, Nan, I would have liked to have met your Deep-toe. He seemed to have been quite a guy. So he lands a kite on you and disappears from the terrace and then accuses you of . . .'

'Pretending to study. I had to object that I was doing nothing of the sort, but he insisted that I was doing just that.'

'Weren't you? Admit you were, Nan,' said her listener with an amused look hovering upon his face.

'Not you too, Bill.'

Bill laughed loud and long and Nandita was happy to see that the dark clouds that always shrouded his blue eyes had drifted away.

She was really glad that she had come. She was really glad that she had been able to make him laugh. She was glad that she was alive! She was glad in a way that she had been forced by circumstances to take the first step forward towards making some changes in her life. She was not unhappy that she had unwittingly broken her vow of vegetarianism. She accepted that what she ate or what she wore made little or no difference to the rest of the world! For the first time in years, she felt unshackled! And the voice of the Bangali Brahmon widow quietened and quelled, Nandita the individual had found herself at long last.

And from there, she had begun to resurrect herself little by little in the company of all her newly acquired friends. And the days piled up one upon the other and a very different Nandita from the one who had stepped out of her home alone for the first time in years that early spring day took over from there. Little by little, Grace became a need and an addiction for her. The days when the weather played foul, Grace would not venture out to come to the garden; that and the two days of Saturday and Sunday when she herself did not venture out would chafe like a leash around Nandita's soul. Sometimes, Nandita would ask herself what she would do if one day she were not to find Grace in the garden. Though she went to meet the professor almost as often as she did Grace, she liked to believe that it was compassion, and compassion alone, that drew her to him on those days. She had not asked herself what it would be like if one day he were to disappear from her life altogether!

And her son Tukun and his wife Meeta and the two children, immersed each one of them in their own occupations and preoccupations, failed to notice the change that was coming about in the woman called Nandita Roy. That she walked taller and spoke with greater assurance had at times flitted across her son Tukun's mind, but he had assigned the change to the near advent of summer and dislodged it from his thoughts.

And so a pattern was set; whenever the weather was fine, Grace would hobble to the park, and Nandita, having made it a habit, would sit a while with her in the rose garden. Oh, the wondrous variety of things they would sit together and discuss. The old lady tired rather soon and Nandita, having kissed her a fond goodbye, would move on to her own favoured bench downtown. Whenever Bill was free, he would be there, and on those days, they would discuss the world and its vagaries and eat their simple afternoon meals together.

And thus her life fell into a comfortable pattern where, leavened by the yeast of friendship, her dull and stodgy days had become events to be looked forward to. The ghosts who had peopled the lonely daytime hours of her life had long since fled in search of more hospitable lodgings. For they had recognised that there was no place left for them in a life so full of happenings and happiness as hers was.

7 SWAPPING MEMORIES AND MEMORABILIA

The outdoors with its many-splendoured allure beckoned, but the pampered Roy household wearing a fretful appearance was giving Nandita a hard time. She would perhaps have to stay at home and make amends; but a mischief-filled thought had interceded and made her shelve her transient resolve. Throwing on a light wrap and slipping her feet into a pair of shoes, she pulled the door shut and, a smile wreathing her face, took off down the road.

Spring was on show everywhere! From somewhere, a soft and seductive tune with a string of picture-perfect evocative words adorning its cadence emerged as if by magic from the rusting archives of her brain and came upon her lips. Tagore had feted the seasons: his festooned-in-flowers springtime was a season in robust bloom, holding no resemblance to the just-emerging show of life that signified the season that lay burgeoning around Nandita. And yet! Softly humming that so-familiar yet near-forgotten tune, she bent and plucked a pale green blade of grass and, cradling it within her palm, gazed in wonder upon it. It was as poignantly beautiful as a newly born child was.

With each progressive day, the roads were filling up; gone were the days of empty sidewalks. It was good to be out among so many other human beings! With a wry smile, she thought, 'If the people of Saisborough don't watch out, this place will soon start looking like Calcutta with its milling populace.' Visions of the throngs upon the ever-crowded Howrah Bridge swam before her eyes; the comparison was so ridiculous that it brought a chuckle out of her that mingled with the effervescent joy of the changing season!

And joy of joys, Grace was there at the garden with Kate beside her. Was she perhaps looking out for her? The smile that broke out upon Grace's face at first setting eyes upon her reassured her and she moved forward with a sense of joy towards the two elderly women seated in tandem right in front of her.

'Your hands are cold, why don't you wear gloves?' Grace scolded as she felt the icy coldness of Nandita's hands.

'But, but you . . .'

'I'm not from India.' And all three laughed and a little baby going past in a pram broke into a chuckle that mingled and became one with their laughter.

'Come sit,' Kate invited, making place for her between the two of them.

'See what you left behind.' Grace was brandishing a photograph of Prodipto in his winter blues.

'I left it behind?'

Wearing a teasing smile, 'Not quite. I took it away along with my stash.' Contemplating the snapshot for a while, she said, 'Some gorgeous hunk that there husband of yours was, no wonder he stole your heart, Nan.' Nandita's vision blurred, and Grace looked at her and looked away and prattled on, 'A lady-killer, I can tell from that mischievous twinkle in his eyes. What do you say, Kate, isn't he?' And she placed the photograph of Prodipto into Kate's hands with a wobbly little laugh. Though the words were light and frolicsome, the clouding over she had spied in Nandita's eyes found a resonant chord and moistened the edges of Grace's mascara-laden lashes. The damp had spread and had placed a couple of blemishes upon her carefully coloured cheeks. It looked so much like the *kajal* marks a mother puts upon her baby's just-washed face to keep all evil eyes away! It was a touching sight that had made Nandita feel a surge of protectiveness towards this frail old woman who belonged to another race, another land. Nandita wanted to stretch out and wipe the marks off with the loose end of her *sari*, thought better of it, and held back! It was possible that those tears were not to be put on record at all, for had not laughter capped every word she had so far spoken?

'How old was he when you lost him?' Kate asked in matter-of-fact tones.

'He was not yet twenty-five,' Nandita said in a small voice.

Grace stretched out and took Nandita's hand into her own and softly said, 'It's a pity he had to die so soon. But what is one to do? There really is no logic to life and death.'

'But why?'

'We don't know why but I wonder at times, Nan, why God chooses to be so thoughtless!'

And Kate, emerging from a reverie, asked, 'Have you made a beautiful headstone for your sweetheart, dear Nan? You must have.'

And Grace added, 'A fine gravestone helps; it's better than having nothing to hold on to, nothing to look upon.'

Nandita, at a loss for words, choked back the rush of tears that had come straining somewhere behind her eyes. She did not want it to spill over and give her away. Oh, the world and its different ways, what was she to tell these old women: that there was no burial site, that there were no headstones for the kind of people they were! Would they be able to handle the bald fact that when you were a Hindu, no plot of land marked your exit from this earth? You died and were consigned to flames, and even the ashes were scattered to the four winds or immersed in the rushing, gushing waters of the revered rivers of India. All you were left with were nebulous memories. Grace was seeking no answers, so Nandita was saved the need to give any. But in those few moments of silence that hung between them, she tried to visualise her Dipto in a grave and shuddered, for she had known with a surety that a grave with a headstone would not have suited her Dipto's personality at all. His memory was better left unconfined, untrammelled, unfettered by boundaries!

'The generation that went to war at Vietnam, and the ones who sent their dear ones to fight that war, know the real worth of a memorial.' Pulled out of her reverie by the words, Nandita looked up with a start and detected a strange glitter in Grace's eyes that she had not been able to decipher. 'So many were lost without a trace in those inhospitable marshlands. So many homeless souls knocking at our hearts asking for a place of rest.'

'Then?'

'Then though belatedly a memorial was raised to their memory.'

'Have you visited the Memorial, seen the Wall?' asked Kate.

'Yes. We went one summer soon after I came to the United States. There are so many, many names etched in stone.'

'You look up and up, and the names just keep going on up and up into the sky,' Kate added, sighing softly.

'Yeah, Kate, there are too many names up there.' Then turning towards Nandita, 'Did you touch any of those names that have been engraved there?' Grace asked.

'No. Something held me back,' Nandita replied, remembering that bright and beautiful day when she had seen that imposing monument.

'Did you feel you'd be intruding, and held back? That was really thoughtful of you, honey. Each one of those names carved there on stone is a living person . . .' And her voice had gone heavy.

Nandita, feeling a complete fraud, murmured some reply to cover up her confusion. She was ashamed that those names had evoked no such feelings or sentiments in her. Was she so insensitive as to have felt nothing, standing there under those rows and rows of names of men who had lost their lives in one among so many useless wars? She had read a few names but, as there was no connectivity, had moved on; the garden had held her interest far longer, as had the picture-perfect blue of the sky! How terribly selfish was the human race that a fallen hero for one nation was but an unknown name for another.

'You see that woman sitting there?' Nandita saw Grace pointing towards a bench at the far side of the park. And on that bench could be seen a huddled-up plump figure bundled up against the cold in a flowing cape-like garment.

'Yes, who is she?'

'Her name is Rose. Rose Dillon,' supplied Kate.

'Is she someone special?'

'No, just one of us.' And then there was a pregnant pause. 'She lost both her sons at Nam, and not one of them came back home.'

'How terrible.'

'She had gone kinda crazy,' Kate informed them.

'It's terrible to feel that your dear ones are wanderin' around homeless,' Grace had qualified. 'Now that those boys of hers have a place of their own, she is happier.'

'Yeah, that she sure is,' agreed Kate.

Then a man in naval uniform came up the steps, went up to a woman seated on the far end with a baby in a pram, spoke a few words, and went away. That pristine white uniform had thankfully brought the earlier discussion to a close, for it joggled Grace's memory and brought forward a hero of yesteryears into her mind.

Eyes lighting up, Grace wanted to know how that handsome guy who was taking care of India was doing. 'Is he still around?' she ended a trifle breathlessly.

'He was a handsome guy who was taking care of India?' Who could she be asking about? 'Jawaharlal Nehru?' Nandita had quizzed.

'No, no, he is a very handsome British prince.'

Handsome . . . British . . . prince?

'I think his name was Prince Monty, or Mounty or something. Come on, Kate, give me some help.'

Prince . . . Prince . . . which prince? She had never heard of any Prince Monty; was it perhaps . . . and then, her face lighting up: 'Lord Louis Mountbatten! It must be Lord Louis Mountbatten,' Nandita, pleased with herself, exclaimed.

'Yeah! That's the name, I think.'

'He was the first governor general of independent India. He left India a long time ago, Grace, and I am sorry to say the ire of the IRA reached out and got to him some years later.'

'Got to him?' asked Kate.

'They blew him up along with his boat.'

'Oh, no! How terrible!' exclaimed Kate.

'Tread on someone's toes or what?' Grace asked.

'You know the Irish tangle that has been going on forever.'

'I don't know if I've heard of it, but once one of these "I hate you, you hate me" stuff gets started it just goes on and on and on. What a shame though that fairytale prince had ta get killed, he was such a heart-stopper in his gorgeous white uniform.' And Kate, recollecting at last, nodded in agreement. Sandwiched between the duo of oldies from the Home Nandita had sat on like an exotic Oriental filling between two meagre slices of white bread.

Veering sharply away from Lord Louis Mountbatten, Grace observed, 'Talking of white, you were in white yesterday, Nan, and here you are in white again today.'

'Must be Nan's favourite colour,' Grace threw across Nandita to Kate, pulling her taciturn friend into the conversation.

Kate, a matter-of-fact person, liked to have her equations well measured out. A trifle short on imagination, she had little or no patience with all this guessing business that Grace had chosen to get into. Favourite colour, indeed! As far as she was concerned, the colour white stood for christenings and marriages, and she reaffirmed the point by coming out with a very matter-of-fact 'I wore white when I became John's bride.' And within her heart, Nandita had echoed, *And I, when I became Dipto's widow!*

Prodipto and she had been married on a lovely November evening and everyone had remarked upon her good luck! He had come into her life wafted in by a cool breeze that was soft scented with the perfume of the fallen *shiuli*. And then one hot tar-melting day, robbing her of all laughter and joy, he had disappeared and gone away without warning, out of her sight. And even though she had once promised herself, never would she tread the path that society had laid out for its women, she had done exactly that. The declaration had been wrenched out of her when she had seen Kakima adhering to all manner of demeaning customs after Nandita's Kaka, her husband, had passed away.

But then, 'never', 'ever', 'forever', though words replete with immutable promises were yet contrary, fickle, and changeable at their very core. How often had she said 'never' and gone back on it? With the first bit of resistance that had come the way of her resolve, she had fallen in line like a dog upon a choke chain and had halted just where she was! Her anger and frustration had caught hold of her hand and taken her away from her resolve. She had been ousted from the select club of the *shodhobas* even before she had fully savoured the privileges of that sorority and had entered into the realm of drab white. But not a voice had been raised!

The ways of Grace and her friends were full of surprises to Nandita, but then, had she, the mother of her husband, come as less of a surprise to her than had the painted-on faces of her newly made friends? When first she had set eyes upon Prodipto's mother at Delhi, she had been dressed in her traditional best. But once the houseguests had left, she had emerged as a butterfly does from a chrysalis and donned a different image altogether. There was this distinct dichotomy in Sujata Roy's persona that was out there in the open yet not quite there. that had fallen, yet not fallen to Nandita's ever-so-young eyes. Trying to placate her past and her desire to live in her modern and liberated present had endowed Sujata Roy with a chameleon-like changeability of personality.

There was blazing red lipstick upon Sujata's lips and a hint of rouge upon her cheeks and the sleeves of her till-then-staid blouses were now missing, leaving on show a bare expanse of unseemly flesh. Heroines of Bangla cinema had introduced these *bogol kata* blouses on the silver screen way before Nandita's times. It was indeed incredible that coming from those roots that lay at Bhabanipore, she could have transformed herself into this utterly modern film-star-like personality. No wonder then, that Grace and her compatriots' painted-on faces had come less as a surprise to her in comparison.

Someone had coughed at a near distance, and rescuing herself from the currents and eddies that lay within the undercurrents of her thoughts, coming back to the present, softly she said, 'You must have looked lovely in white, Kate.'

And Kate, looking as pleased as pleased can be, repeated, 'Yeah, I wore white when I married John.'

Grace, not to be outdone, gave a reply that had quite taken Nandita's breath away. 'So what's new, we all wore white, didn't we? *We had to wear white* to show to the world that we were untouched, unbesmirched virgins.' And she followed up her repartee with a long cackle of mirth that created havoc upon the painted-on mask that she was wearing as always upon her face. But the old lady, Nandita could see, was having too much fun to really care. And latching on to Grace's infectious outburst of mirth, Kate went into a lively spate of laughter that also had an equally detrimental effect upon her carefully made-up face. And Nandita, totally out of her depth, had wondered whether it was all a very big joke.

Unable to contain her curiosity, Nandita asked hesitantly, 'And were you?'

'What? Oh, that? Crazy or what, what were all those barn dances designed for?'

Confused by the teasing look in her elderly friend's eyes, Nandita whispered softly to herself, 'No, they are joking.' And after that single slip-up where her curiosity had got the better of her, she straightened her face and listened on with a cover-up smile wavering at the corners of her lips that had a nice sitting-on-the-fence quality to it!

'What say you, Kate?' Grace egged on, and a stream of tears induced by her laughter had welled out of her eyes and coursed down her cheeks. This was not the day for Grace's make-up. The black blemishes, and then the *batik* cracks and now the rivulets running down her cheeks!

And Kate echoed, 'Yeah, whatever for?'

Were they pulling her leg, she wondered; perhaps, even so, she was at a loss to understand how the minds of these two old women worked! Nandita, brought up within the stays of absolute prudery, where even the mere mention of a natural bodily function like menstruation was to be spoken of in hushed tones, was amazed and shocked by the ease with which these two women could hold forth on a conversation that was strung out around premarital sex, no less. It was incredible that women older than her mother could talk so freely on subjects that paradoxically one pretended did not exist at all in that highly overpopulated land from where she herself hailed.

With each new encounter, new vistas opened up to her that revealed a way of life that was distinct and set apart from her own. Yet despite the vast differences that lay between the world these people inhabited and her own, a point of convergence at an emotional level always did manage to come about. Human beings and their joys and their sorrows were one and the same the world over; the rest was so much window dressing, a touch of cosmetology! That household of the Roys in New Delhi had opened her eyes to this fact. They were Bangali Brahmins as were the Gangulys of Bhabanipore and yet their ways of life had nothing in common one to the other. But in truth, deep down were they really so different? Nandita, to her detriment, had realised that their modernism, their Westernised ways had been no more real than a painted-on drop-scene upon a stage. It had but needed a cruel gust of wind to bring that cover-up crashing down to reveal the real persons it was harbouring behind its colourful facing!

'Sowed no wild oats of your own, honey?' chuckled Grace as she rose painfully. Nandita, coming out of her reverie, just laughed along with her. 'Kate has a soap to ketch up on; I'm goin' along with her to see who is romancing which guy now.'

'It wasn't like that in our times,' Kate, at her pompous best, stated as she rose from the bench, 'once you married a guy, you stopped playin' around.'

'Yeah, people have changed, they don't think the way we did; but what's one to do, Kate?'

'I don't like it,' Kate, at her sanctimonious best, pontificated.

'All the same, we rush to the TV to take a look at what they're doin', don't we?' Grace concluded mischievously. 'Come on, let's get going, we don't want to miss the beginning, do we?' And tip-tapping along on their walking sticks, the two old women walked off towards the steps leading out of the garden.

And Nandita, collecting together her wits and her little bag, beat a hasty retreat from the rose garden as yet bereft of roses; coming to a stop at the foot of the steps, undecided, she looked this way and then that. Depending on which way she faced, both her home and the benches downtown lay straight ahead of her! And she would have to choose one out of the two straight paths that lay before her.

She woke early with a multi-pieced orchestra of birdsong filtering in upon her ears. Treading softly, she tripped down and, brewing herself a cup of tea, had come up again.

What a wondrously bright and beautiful day this was, Nandita thought, as she looked through her window down upon the yard and then up, up into the trees and from there onto the blue of the skies! Putting down the cup of tea she had in hand, she threw open her window and took a long deep breath of the cold, crisp, aromatised air. What a splendid sparkling clean day this was! Why had she looked upon the weather of Chicago and Saisborough with such deep disfavour for so many long years? There must have been other such magnificent days to wonder upon in the course of the ten long years that she had been in the United States? Beautiful days, wondrous days that she had never once perceived, never once seen? She had abhorred the long and dreary winters and hated the acute heat and humidity of the long sticky summers and had chosen to not notice the more clement moments wedged in between times. And somehow once that obstinate viewpoint had been formed and got cemented into her consciousness, she had never once allowed herself to deviate away from that standpoint.

Why had the resplendent white of freshly fallen snow, the gradual clothing of the naked arms of the ivy embracing the buildings turning later to flamboyant red and gold, the green of the freshly sprouting leaves of grass, the beauty of the changing seasons eluded her vision? Was it perhaps that in some long-forgotten dreary moment of deep disaffection, she had decided that the Chicago weather was irredeemably, irrefutably, incurably foul?

Nandita was in a thoughtful frame of mind. Moving from the window and taking up the fast cooling cup of tea, she sat down, cup in hand, in her favourite location, the chair beside the window overlooking the yard. The sun was out and some of the landmarks that made the yard the special place that it was were up and about! The fat cat was on the prowl but unconcerned the bushy-tailed squirrels scurried around upon the branches of the apple tree that was well out of the reach of the ever-watchful feline. The interaction between the visiting cat and his ever-elusive prey was more like a familiar musical piece created by design as a background score for the lively screenplay that her thought processes were busy creating that moment. She was thinking back upon her visit to the rose garden on the previous day. That conversation held between Grace and her companion Kate with herself as an intermediary had come to mind over and over again and had left her totally confused! A part of that conversation had indeed dealt her a severe culture shock! What would her forefathers and her foremothers have thought of the mindset of these people, she had wondered!

Nandita's upbringing had a very compelling conservative presence to it. So like a spawning salmon, she had had to fight against the flow of the currents to cross the barriers of her prejudice whenever she was confronted with norms and mores that were not the ones she had been taught to look upon as acceptable. Though it had faced many an assault, it had refused to lay down its arms and accept defeat. An occasional retreat perhaps, but never defeat! And so, at each turn, she had faced some kind of a culture shock. Culture shocks! Yes, Nandita's life had had its share of culture shocks. Even so!

As long as she had remained within the four walls of her son's home away from the rest of Saisborough and the real world that lay beyond its boundaries, she had not been so much as touched by its very own particular-to-itself vagaries and values. But her interaction with the visitors from the Home at the rose garden, and her recent encounter with Dr William Brady, had opened her eyes to a world apart from the one where she had been born and bred. Nandita had realised but recently that the ten years she had so far spent in America had been wasted upon her, for in her self-chosen incarceration, she had not allowed herself to even stretch out her fingers to feel the fringes of its ever so exhilarating, powerful, and lusty personality!

The very first knock upon the well-guarded citadel of her way of life had been dealt by Prodipto when, riding upon a mischievous streak, he had come flying down to invade the very tightly barricaded bastions of her ancestral home. Sharing her life with Prodipto had suddenly opened up a world to her that was so different from anything that she had known that it had shaken up the very foundation of her existence. She had but recently read a book that claimed that men and women hailed from different planets. If one was from Mars, the other half, the author claimed, was from Venus! Extending the analogy, she could bring herself to believe that if the Roys were from Mars, then the Gangulys were from Venus!

Her father-in-law, the major general, was in no way anything like a prescription father-in-law ought to have been; after all, he was a Martian! She had realised sooner rather than later that the father was privy to all the strategic moves that his son had made in order to win the hand of the fair maiden called Nandita. A Nandita on whom a dragon-like grandmother had placed all manner of restraints to keep her from getting into the company of dangerous creatures called *young men*, with whom she could slip up and possibly fall in love. 'Love marriages', as they were called, were all right within the pages of a novel, or up there on a screen in a cinema theatre. But when it came to marriage, the arranging of it in no way was to be the concern of the ones who were to be married.

They really were so intriguing. And different, or so she had thought!

Delhi was the destination, and after a short honeymoon on wheels, they had arrived there. When the train had steamed into the railway station, a wide-eyed Nandita had stood at the door of the compartment and had looked in wonderment upon the capital of India for the first time in her life. Stepping out of the station, she had breathed in large lungfuls of the air with its different scent and allure. The Delhi air was pregnant with an air of expectation for the arrival of its favourite season: winter. The dry air was heavy with suspended dust, the aroma of hookahs and smoked *biris*, and the smoke of myriad *chulas*; and all of these had intermingled with the smell of horse dung that had come upon the air from the direction of the tonga stand. Yet quite surprisingly, there was still a certain sweetness of scent lacing the acridity of the air. The horses black, white, brown, and mottled, bells jingling with each movement of their heads, decked out in plumed headdresses, harnessed each to their tonga, had such a romantic allure to them that it had filled Nandita's heart with the desire to ride on one of those. 'They are being pushed to extinction . . .' the Major General pointed to a rash of monstrous heavy-duty motorcycle rickshaws, 'by those,' he had stated.

And reading the wistful expression upon Nandita's face, Prodipto had soothed, 'I'll take you for a ride in one of these tongas before they vanish altogether.'

And driving along in her father-in-law's black-as-charcoal Vauxhall, she had begun taking in this new environment into which she had been catapulted. If the land and the landscape, the buildings and the boulevards, the shores of the larger-than-life lake upon which Chicago stood had come as a revelation to her, so had her arrival at Delhi filled her heart with a similar feeling of otherworldliness.

As they were going past the India Gate, her father-in-law had turned to Nandita and said, 'Very few people know this, Nandita, but during the war years, they used to grow vegetables where.'

'Really, Dad?'

'Did you know, Prodipto, that we even had some tents here for the officers of the Indian Army for a while?'

'Unbelievable!'

'The vegetable patches have disappeared and so have the tents. Things have changed,' and then with a short laugh that had a tinge of wistfulness to it, 'but then, change is inevitable!'

New Delhi with its wide and majestic roads canopied by magnificent trees and with its battery of gardens at every roundabout was beautiful but not like a city at all. Cities had to have confusion and people aplenty to give it an impact-making personality. And to Nandita's eyes, New Delhi had none of these! No wonder Chicago with its set-to-a-pattern ways had smacked of pallidity to her. And when she had seen the life the Roys led, that sense of otherness she had felt at the New Delhi railway station had been further ingrained into her mind.

And here she was wondering what her ancestors would have thought of Grace and Kate, and the things of which they spoke. For that matter, what would her ancestors have thought or said had they been to visit Mummy and Daddy when she had first gone to them at their home? Were they Christians, they might well have asked, for Bangla was spoken but occasionally, while the English language reigned supreme! Had they known that the man who cooked for them was called *khansamaji*, there was a possibility that Nandita's marriage with Prodipto might well never have come to pass! And they would have surely wanted to know why she had abandoned the accepted appellation of 'Ma' and 'Baba' and taken to calling her parents-in-law Mummy and Daddy.

Married into an apparently modern and Westernised home, she had had to unlearn a number of things. Whenever she slipped into calling his parents 'Baba' and 'Ma', her young husband would say, 'Come on, Nondu, my dad the major general and his wife the lieutenant general have never been Baba and Ma to me.' Turning to his mother, he'd ask, 'Isn't that right, Mummy?'

'Stop troubling her, Prodipto, let her call me Ma if she likes. And why have you turned me into a lieutenant general, may I ask?'

'You know that's the rule in the services, Mummy, the wife always carries an extra rank. Look at Nondu's shoulders closely and you'll find that she is already sprouting the rank badges of a flying officer there.' Nandita had inadvertently turned to peer at her own shoulder and Prodipto had taken her into a quick embrace and laughed down upon her upturned face. And from that day on, the parents of her husband had become Mummy and Daddy to her as well.

Just ten days before her wedding, she had become a graduate. But degree or no degree, when the family Roy spoke in English, she was left completely tongue-tied. Never having learnt to make use of the language as a viable means of verbal communication, she had been left both metaphorically and literally speechless! Transplanted from her totally Bangali milieu where Bangla was the only legal tender one used within the four walls of one's home, she had felt like a bankrupt facing the reality of his dried-up bank balance. The Roys, the Indian Air Force, and her sense of inadequacy had soon taught her to speak English, but try as she might, she had never been able to shed the subtle nuances of the Bangla tongue that overlaid her speech.

Come late evening, the Roys dressed for dinner and ate at table with knife and fork. Khansamaji, their super-speciality cook, had a large repertoire of Western dishes to his credit, and one was duty bound to eat those when one ate after sundown. And so, one sipped soups and dined only on *side dishes, cutlis*, and *chaaps* along with elaborately engineered main dishes! How otherworldly could it have been for Nandita!

Was it a small wonder then that just yesterday she had been able to cover up her confusion when confronted with Grace and Kate's small talk around sex out of marriage? But even so, it had not been an easy task for her, for her training had just begun when it had come to an abrupt end! Moreover, that which she had thought to be liberalism in the Roys was but a thin layer of pasted-on veneer, and it had peeled and fallen off with the first lashing of rain that had beaten down upon it. And so disillusioned, she had moved abruptly back and, losing her foothold, had fallen into an abyss of orthodoxy! Dipto had left her far too soon for change to have really taken root, and wallowing in her grief, she had regressed to her learnt-at-the-feet-of-her-grandmother ways.

Cup in hand, she made her way downstairs to an empty home. A vacant home was a good place to be in when your brain was spilling over with your distant yesterdays that had been brought forward to you by your most recent yesterday!

All that ruminating before open windows had done no good to the brew she had so carefully made and taken up. Her hankering for a proper cup took her to the kitchen; the brew readied, a dash of milk remained to be added. She looked upon the so-very-familiar can of milk with a questioning look as she poured herself a small amount. Was it not strange that she had no inkling as to what the milkman behind this milk looked like? The legend on the can made no secret of the fact that this was cow's milk.

Prior to her marriage, she had no idea that human beings ever drank anything besides the milk of the cow. But the cow's milk that she had drunk since birth had a cow and its attendant milkman always attached to it. Panchu *goyla* came at the crack of dawn and along with him came his cow! Nandita had no idea whether or not the milking was done in the near dark of the night somewhere at the rear of their own home, or whether the cow, the milk in the shiny brass pail and Panchu all came along as an entourage. But the cow came and the shiny brass bucket full of foaming milk came to the door. Was it possible that Panchu *goyla* used to bring his cow along as proof of authenticity of his product? And now, here in America, they were all drinking milk out of plastic cans with no proof at all excepting that which was provided by the written words upon the label on the can!

On her arrival as a bride at Delhi, she had discovered for the first time that there were animals besides the cow that produced milk that was to the liking of humans! She smiled at the remembrance of her first reaction to buffalo milk. 'How can anyone drink the milk of such a black and beastly-looking animal?' she had asked of her husband.

'Just try it once and you won't go back to cow's milk ever again,' was his smiling reply!

'Never.'

But then, 'never' is a word that is ever so mutable. Once she had crossed over the hump of her inbuilt prejudices and tasted the thick-as-liquefied-cream milk of Kisan Lal's black-as-midnight buffaloes, her abhorrence had turned to adoration for its nectar-like sweetness.

That Kisan Lal, unlike the denizens of the imaginary well that turned into toads, was a real entity had dawned upon her one day when she had seen what had looked like a headless man riding on a bicycle come in through the gate and go on down the driveway. The man wearing a very economical-sized *dhoti* with a *charpoy* with two fully loaded gunny sacks balanced somewhere above his shoulders was pedalling on at a steady pace towards the rear of the bungalow.

'Dipto, look,' she had croaked, 'a headless man has just gone away to the rear of the bungalow.'

'It must be Kisan Lal,' was all he said while turning the page of the book he was reading.

'Kisan Lal the buffalo man?'

'Yes!'

'But it looked as if he is headless.'

'Nondu, Nondu, Nondu,' he exclaimed, 'what am I to do with you? Come, haul me up, let's see how strong you are; come on, give me a hefty yank.' Pretending to take her help, he had come up on his feet and, putting an arm around her shoulders, said, 'Let's go.'

'Where?'

'To check out why Kisan Lal is going around impersonating a headless ghost.'

'I'm not coming.'

'Yes, you are, come give me your hand.'

Imprisoned within the crook of his arm, Nandita had been propelled along down the driveway, past the kitchen garden with its rows and rows of the tiniest of white-as-pith cauliflower nestling within their housing of the darkest of green leaves. Past the bed of the just emerging purple as *jamuns* brinjal, smaller as yet than the beautiful mauve of the flowers from which it had taken life. Past the tomato bushes with their star-like sunny-gold flowers with just an occasional ruby-red tomato peeping out from within the clusters of its serrated leaves. And past a bamboo and jute-string fencing upon which the tenderest of tendrils of a timid green creeper was climbing up.

Never having seen a vegetable patch, she had stopped abruptly and touched the harp-like strings of the fencing and asked, 'What is this?'

'Mummy's green peas will grow on these. And we'll harvest a few seers of peas just when peas are at there cheapest in the market. Daddy and I have a good laugh at Mummy's horticulture outputs but, Nondu . . .' And he'd rolled his head heavenwards.

'How lucky you are, Dipto,' she had said with a catch in her voice!

'But you are a part of all this now . . . Come, let's go and take a look at why Kisan Lal has chosen to lose his head.'

'I didn't say . . .'

A somewhat straggly *mehendi* hedge, no match to the hedge that grew alongside the compound wall, demarcated the staff quarters from the main bungalow. That hidden from view there was a bustling township lying beyond the kitchen garden was beyond imagining for Nandita. Half a dozen habitations lay in a cluster before her eyes. Prodipto explained that the *dhobi*, the *mali*, and the *jharuwali* lived at one end of the enclosure, while the *khansamaji*, the *masalchi*, and the *dudhwala* Kisan Lal lived on the other. At the sight of the master's son and his bride entering the enclave, a flutter had passed along the spine of the community. The tremor had reached out and touched Kisan Lal as well who was taking some well-earned rest at that moment upon the charpoy, which had, till but so recently, served as a luggage carrier!

The *dhoban*, abandoning her ironing, had stood with folded palms, the *mali*, the *malin*, and the *jharuwali* and *jharuwala* were not there, but their children had looked on shyly at the visitors. Khansamaji's wife had ventured to invite them in; the *masalchi*'s young wife had gone to visit her parents and was thus unable to participate in this 'royal' *darshan*. And the *dudhwala* Kisan Lal, rising abruptly from his place of rest alongside his sleek buffaloes, who stood placidly chewing cud, had called out urgently to his wife. As the wife was busy giving a lusty draw to the nicely going *biri* she had just lit, had paid no attention at all to the urgent summons of her lord! And in the meanwhile, Nandita while following *her own lord* having hit her foot on one of the gunny sacks that had just been pedalled in, had realised how heavy those sacks lying on the floor really were. No wonder the charpoy had curved over on either end of Kisan Lal's head and covered all but his bull-like neck from sight. Forgetting that she had come to check out the state of Kisan Lal's headlessness, she had looked on in wonder upon this man with the strength of an ox. Her Dipto, a tall and well-built man, had looked puny in comparison to the owner of the wonder buffaloes with the creamiest of milk in New Delhi!

'Ram, Ram, Kisan Lal*ji*, I have brought your *bahurani* along to visit all of you.' Turning to Nandita, he said in a whisper, 'Look for yourself, he has a head.' And a blushing Nandita had looked down. But all thoughts upon Kisan Lal's strong head had flown out of the window at the sight of the woman who, head decorously covered, was seated upon the floor a short distance away. Completely detached from the world around, eyes shut, she was contentedly puffing away at a *biri*. Nandita's eyes had almost fallen out of their sockets, for never before in her life had she seen a woman smoking! The woman preoccupied with her tryst with the fast-diminishing *biri* had failed to notice who the visitors were. So many people came to her husband for milk; was she to get diverted on each occasion?

'Ram, Ram, *Chote Sahib*, Ram, Ram *Bahuraniji*,' Kisan Lal had replied, all the while dusting vigorously upon the strings of his just-vacated bed with his *pugree* to make it a suitable seat for the honoured visitors. 'I am honoured, really, really honoured, that you are visiting this poor man's home. I have nothing better to offer, but please sit down and make yourself as comfortable as you can,' And then, looking towards the seated woman, Kisan Lal had called out, 'Imarti,' this time in a more commanding tone of voice. The increased decibel at which he had pitched his voice, the changed tone in which he had called out to her had alerted Imarti that this was a command that was not to be ignored, for an angered Kisan Lal was as dangerous as a lion on the prowl. Even so, being no less than a lioness herself, she had turned to him only after she had wrung the last comforting puff from the *biri* that she had been smoking.

'See who has come to visit us,' the husband had pointed out to the wife, 'Make some *malai wali lassi*, woman,' he had growled. A confident Imarti, not to be hurried along by any random orders, had looked towards Prodipto and his wife, risen, given a shake to her *lehenga*, and then voicing a 'Ram, Ram,' saluted them with folded palms. Only then had she gone in to fulfil the command of her husband! When Imarti had handed them a half-seer glass each of creamy *lassi* aromatised by the lingering odour of the *biri* left over on her hands, Nandita had wanted to flee from there. How could she possibly down so much *lassi*? But how could she possibly refuse to drink that which had been offered most obligingly to her by a woman who had wrists that must have been easily double that of her Prodipto's?

Kisan Lal and his Imarti had surely been eye-openers to Nandita, and so once again, it had come home to her that one did not have to travel over the seven seas to face up to the reality of otherness. No wonder that she had not turned her back upon Grace and Kate and run back to the safe harbour of her home. She was a seasoned legionnaire with a great deal of experience under her so-called belt! After all, even in the long-distant past she had not turned her back upon Imarti, her magnum of *lassi*, and her *biri*-smoking ways, had she?

8

GRACE GIVES A
TERRIBLE SCARE

With her caring, an ancient woman with a painted-on face had shaken up Nandita's well-cemented viewpoint upon the state of her own life. And slowly, hesitantly, she had begun to take a closer look at her own self. True, Grace had two persons, Dave and Chuck, who really cared for her; even so, here she was almost nudging ninety with countless infirmities, spunkily facing the world while she, steeped in self-pity, had accepted a lacklustre, moribund existence. Where had Dipto's darling, Tukun's mentor, Boroma's *chander kona*, Dadu's pet, Kakima's chosen one, Daminidi's very special protégée, the well-respected teacher, the much-sought-after neighbour gone? Was it possible that in her thoughtlessness she had neglected those bonds of companionship that had sustained her through the years? She was none too sure, for so many of those who had once cared for her were no longer alive, and those who were very much still there had moved on with their own particular occupations and preoccupations.

Very few among her close friends had telephones to their name, and even if they did, long-distance calls were expensive. Letter writing took time on both ends and the communicating links, fallen into disuse, weighed down by the grime of time, had sagged and then lain crumbling along the way. Malnourished, the roots of those relationships had withered to a point where they did not have strength enough to rejuvenate themselves today.

Those first five years when the family was still overwhelmingly close to her, she had lulled herself into believing that she needed no other ties besides the ones that emanated from her son and his family. So embroiled was she in giving support to the young couple by caring for their two children and their newly set-up home away from home that she had forgotten to allocate any time or space to her own need for self-actualisation. And sadly enough, the young couple had also not looked beyond the immediate present.

The future that lay beyond that phase where she was needed at every turn had arrived sooner than anyone could have visualised, and had turned itself into an arid present. And once again with the percolating away of time, she had found herself perched precariously upon the periphery of other people's concerns. Five years of staying aloof had rendered her incapable of unfolding her wings and even hopping along, wings half open, across her very own front garden to take a peek at life as it was lived by the people here. And for that matter, nor had the life lived beyond their own circumscribed territory ever made an attempt at taking a peek at this little enclosed world of hers. Alas, life in this country left one alone as the life in Calcutta never did. If you chose to get isolated, no one came and bullied you out of your corner. And then she had remembered those days out of her past when she had faced absolute aloneness for the first time in her life.

The fledgling had grown up; he was to leave for college in far-off Bangalore. A long journey lay ahead of him; she had given him a hot cup of Horlicks and told him, 'Go to sleep, Tukun, you have a long journey ahead of you.' And retiring to her singleton bed, she had lain awake, unable to cope with the emptiness that henceforth lay ahead of her. Eyes squeezed tight, she was trying to squeeze in some sleep when the thudding arrival of a missile halfway upon her startled her out of her forced stupor! Her son had landed beside her. He was clutching a pillow close to him. 'Move over, Ma,' he said gruffly, 'that fan in my room . . .'

'What's happened to the fan?'

'It's making too much noise.' And moving to one end of the bed, she had accommodated him beside herself and both of them had soon fallen asleep.

And then the bird had flown away! It was four months since Tukun had left home! And for the first time, Nandita had been alone in her flat during the festive season of Durga Puja. She had curled up tight within herself and decided to stay home and wait out the end of festivities. If she stayed out of sight, no one would disturb her, she thought; but she had been proven wrong!

Four-year-old Ronen, unable to reach up to her doorbell, had come scrabbling at her door with a message from his parents. Ronen and his parents the Sens lived just two flats away from Nandita's; he must have just about woken because he still looked cherubic with the leftover vestiges of the night's sleep.

'Ma said, tell Dida to get ready.'

'Why?'

'I don't know,' he said, peering into the interior of her home. 'Where's Tukun Kaka?' he asked, and before Ronen could be handed an answer, the door to the flat across the landing had flown open and the young family of three were commanding her, toothbrush in hand, across the tiny landing to get dressed for a day's outing.

Not a soul had forgotten that she was alone during Durga Puja that year, and invading her privacy, the city of Calcutta had also come in search of her. Dressed to kill, she waited outside while her emissaries, the very air perfumed by incense and flowers, had crept in and forced her to look outwards. She had covered her ears but the loudspeakers cacophonously spewing music, the beat of the *dhakis* drums accompanied by the long drawn-out song of the conches, the clashing of cymbals had not agreed to be kept out! And pulling her along by her hand, the city and its people had taken her along!

People the world over were different, and that difference in the manner in which America conducted itself had made her stand hesitantly aside. Transplanted from an entirely different milieu with no reference points of her own to fall back upon, she had not known that she would have to go at least halfway out in search of companionship. Long months of inclement weather had further cemented her stay-at-home approach to life, and when the weather did improve, where was she to go when she had neither friends nor money nor means of locomotion other than her own legs to take her anywhere? She had somehow not got round to interacting with Chicago as she had with Kolkata, and the city had got along fine without her interaction. And she in turn had gone further and further into her own shell.

You retract your hand and place it within a pocket and go around complaining that no one shakes hands with you!

Goaded on by Tukun, she had fortuitously stepped out of the confines of her home that early spring day and had very soon found hearts aplenty that were willing to give a little place to her. The fact that they sought her out because she was she, a woman named *Nan*dita, who had one day by sheer chance walked into their lives, had indeed come as a very pleasant surprise to her! Lonely persons one and all, they each served a purpose in the others' life! But there was something special about Grace that drew Nandita to her, and soon Nandita had become the ear that Grace had long been in search of.

And with Bill, was it his pain that drew her to him? With him, she managed to have a more equitable exchange. She had very soon learnt a great deal about him; the layers of experience that made up Bill's life were in no way as complex as Nandita's had been. A happy childhood followed by an early romance in tandem with a brilliant academic career culminating in a satisfying vocation in teaching and a happy marriage had made up the foundation of his life. The two children had also arrived without much ado and flown away from the nest even before he was forty-five. So unused was he to face up to sorrow and disappointment that the death of Meg had almost jolted him out of his moorings. His anguish and his loneliness were a pair of companions that he had picked up but lately. Nandita, on the other hand, had long since made her acquaintance with both these entities. They had quite often taken over her life and at other moments, pushed aside by joyous events, had stood apart but never quite gone away. And so she had experienced his pain, as if it was her very own, and had veered towards him with a want of reserve that would have been quite frightening had she but given it a closer look.

Grace loved to speak, and in Nandita, she had found the one receptive ear that would hear her out patiently and without interruption. When you lived year in and year out with the same set of people, there remained very few tales to tell that had not already been heard. With similar stockpiles of memories circulating within the Home, it was hard to find a listener for those near-matching memoirs that perhaps still remained to be told. So many little incidents and events, the milestones of her life, were seething around within Grace in search of an outlet when Nandita had arrived out of nowhere, a willing receptacle into which these could be poured!

The terrain through which Grace's life had sojourned was so far removed from Nandita's own that quite often she felt that what she was listening to were but fairy tales. So fine-tuned was Grace's art of telling her tales that in the recounting, even the saddest moments of her life had been imbued with a patina of joy in the telling! Having sensed that a strain of sorrow lay hidden away within Nandita's heart, she had deliberately painted over the pain-filled moments of her life and turned them into colourful snippets before passing them on to Nandita. And the subterfuge had worked, and Nandita had believed that no sorrow had ever even brushed past Grace in her journeying through life.

Chuck and Dave, Dave and Chuck, and Chuck again had dominated every little anecdote that she liked to spin. To better highlight the importance of her main protagonists, Grace did allow a few other subsidiary players to take a minor role or two, but the top billings had to be always theirs. Chuck was the butt of so many jokes. Grace laughed so much while speaking of Chuck the baby, Chuck the schoolboy, and Chuck the young university lad that it made her eyes well up with tears of joy. Nandita often wondered that if Chuck was such a wonderful son, why then did he not look after his mother better? But Nandita had asked no awkward questions.

It was not as if it was one-way traffic all the way with Grace, for there were moments when she would invite Nandita to bring out a word or two about her life as well. Faced with Grace's burnished-gold recapitulations she had been compelled by pride to bring out an untarnished tale or two herself. In a spirit of competitiveness, Nandita had slipped in a tale or two of the son who in his school years had been no one else's but hers. A smile would flit across her countenance as she spoke of the schoolboy Tukun. Though Grace much preferred to talk of Chuck, she had magnanimously allowed Nandita to get an anecdote in edgewise. And then it would be back to Chuck again.

Nandita's account of some mischief that had been played by Tukun had brought out a laugh-filled response from Grace. 'Nan, these only kids are a real pain. I suppose we end up spoiling them right and proper and then blame them. I can see your Too-koon too gave you quite a few turns.'

And Nandita had smiled, remembering the little boy who had at one time been her shadow. 'Isn't it a pity, Grace, that children have to grow up?'

'And we have to grow old,' she said with a big wide smile as if it was the funniest joke of all that she could find to tell. And from philosophising, she had shifted gear and gone swiftly back to the telling of the saga of Chuck again. 'Chuck had a way of not doing his assignments on time and then, feigning a bellyache, taking to bed.'

Nandita chuckled, remembering an incident or two where she herself had tried it out on her grandfather. The difference was that a girl's education was never important enough in that milieu to have made anyone take a closer look and she herself had got away. But Tukun under her hawk eyes had fared far worse when he had tried out the same trick on her.

With a twinkle in her eyes, Grace carried on with her account. 'I got conned once or twice, and in retaliation one day I ended up sending him to school when he was really and truly unwell. I felt guilty as hell but I was not one to own up to it.'

'Was he really very unwell?'

'Unwell enough, but then kids have to have some discipline dinned into them, don't they?'

'That they certainly do.'

'When the doctor, my Dave, and even Chuck tried to emotionally blackmail me into feeling guilty, I stuck to my guns like Annie Oakley.'

'Annie Oakley?'

'Never heard of her? You don't know much about this country of ours, do you? I'll tell you about her another day, she was quite a gal, believe me. So as I was telling you, there were these three males trying to browbeat me; I squared my shoulders and told them right on the face that, big or small, any guy who tried crying wolf on me would end up gettin hurt.'

'You must have been quite something at one time, Grace?'

'I haven't too many persons left to terrorise now, otherwise I could have still given a person or two a run for their money.'

'I can well imagine that,' Nandita acknowledged with a smile. 'What was I to do, Nan? Dave was too soft-hearted by far. Left to his own devices, he would have spoilt Chuck rotten, so I had to become the gun-totin' mama at times. Did your Deep-toe do the same with your Took-oon?'

'Tukun was just a few months old when he lost his father,' Nandita choked out and Grace gathered her to her bosom and said, 'Oh, my poor child,' over and over again and held on to her till she had regained her composure again. 'How stupid of me to have forgotten . . .' And with that embrace, Grace had entered Nandita's heart to stay on there forever. And the little bit of reserve that Nandita had erected between herself and Grace in order to keep hold of her inner privacy had begun to melt away.

Diverting her attention away from her gloomy thoughts, Grace asked, 'Know any American cooking, honey?' Nandita gave a shake to her head in the negative, and aghast, Grace proclaimed that something would have to be done about it and, taking her in hand, started her culinary education in right earnest. The promotions were fast, and the very next day, she found herself being initiated into the nitty-gritty of putting together a Thanksgiving dinner. 'Once you are in America, you just have to learn to fix a proper turkey dinner, Nan. You know, honey, don't you, that the cranberry sauce has to be just right?'

Nandita had not let on that she had never tasted cranberry sauce in her life. And Grace had gone on, 'I can give you a tip or two, so bring along a notebook when you come tomorrow. My Dave used to say that the stuffing I made was better than his mama's ever was.'

'You must be a very good cook, Grace.'

'Good enough! But I didn'a have to be a super cook to earn myself that there compliment,' and then she confided mischievously, 'my mum-in-law didn't know no cooking, Nan.' And then spotting Kate at a distance, Grace called out, 'Hey, Kate, I'm tryin' to teach this gal here some good old American cooking.' Kate came up and joined them, and a lively discussion on the making of a worthy pumpkin pie ensued and then Kate remembered the soap she had to see, and they were back to the cooking of a stuffed turkey once again.

'See that you get the right ingredients, Nan,' Grace warned. 'What's the matter? You haven't been looking too bright since you came, not unwell or something, I hope.'

'I'm all right, but . . .' She fell short, and *I never do any shopping so how can I . . .* remained unsaid.

'Something the matter?' Looking at her closely, Grace asked.

'Oh nothing, nothing, I'm fine.' And she beat a hasty retreat, fearing that she had already given away too much, and Grace on her way back to the Home wondered what exactly was the matter with young Nan!

Weekends for Nandita normally were stay-at-home days. But once in a while when the younger people would go off to be with their friends, she would go wandering off to take a look at as many garage sales as she could spot. She had even picked up a gift or two for Grace, Helen, and Kate from one of them. Garage sales always left her in a thoughtful frame of mind. She just could not adjust herself to the ease with which the people of this country could rid themselves of things no sooner than they had gone past being of use. Her ancestral home in Bhabanipore not only housed four generations of Gangulys; it also housed the junk that those four generations had accumulated in the course of just leading their lives.

Generations of used-up exercise books, of tattered and torn textbooks that were no longer prescribed, pens with bent nibs, still more pens with bent nibs, inkpots stained red, black, blue, and blue-black all long since gone dry had taken up precious shelf space. Since she had become conscious of her surroundings, she had seen two broken bicycles positioned against a wall in the cavernous courtyard of her childhood home. When she last had visited the mansion of her ancestors, she had still seen some bits and pieces of those bicycles holding on to the land that had been bequeathed to them. There even was a spot where earthen water pots gone into disuse were stored. Why they were stored, no one knew, but that they had to be stored everyone knew with a certainty. There even was a certain amount of affinity for the cobwebs that had festooned themselves onto corners in that sprawling home in which she had been brought up. Generations of spiders must have lived, spawned, and died there, and they had still hung on undisturbed. It was as if a misplaced sense of sentiment and loyalty had fettered all hands. Once an item entered a home, it always remained there.

Her own little flat had no cobwebs in sight, nor were any water pots given a place to rest their bones there, but when it came to old textbooks and used exercise books, Nandita herself had followed the same route. If one were to so desire, the academic journey of young Sudipto Roy could easily be traced from the mounds of material available upon a narrow concrete shelf in the little living room of Nandita Roy's minuscule flat. Prodipto's uniforms, his other clothing, and Tukun's childhood clothes had taken up an entire cupboard while her own clothes had to find room on a clothes horse, a tin trunk, and the lid of the same tin trunk!

Nandita had very soon come to recognise that the items on display in a garage sale were very good indicators of the stage of development at which a family at that point of time stood. She had soon become an expert in gauging the mechanics of the whole thing. When she saw a crib, a car seat, and a baby bathtub up for sale, she knew at once that the babies in that home could no longer be called babies. And it was quite possible that another such sale being held perhaps just a few homes away would have something on display to fulfil some of their needs now. You did not have to go to hundreds of these sales to realise the speed with which America recycled itself. What had become one family's junk had by a simple sleight of hand become another family's coveted possession.

The frame was tarnished, and one end of it had come loose, but the print that it had kept together for who knows how long was as beautiful and bold as only a Van Gogh could be. She was none too familiar with the Impressionists yet had fallen in love with the baroque boldness of the artist's brushstrokes and had wanted to give the painting pride of place in their home. She had hesitated awhile, never having bought anything for this home of her son ever before. But the whirling fragments of colour like the sparks of a Catherine wheel that the artist had filled the background with had tempted her along, and succumbing to temptation, she had bought the print, damaged frame and all. It was cumbersome and heavy and had a coating of dust upon it that had come off onto her white sari. She dragged it into the house and placed it leaning against a wall in the dining area. It still looked as good as she had thought it was in the garage from where she had hauled it here. She had sat a while gazing upon its beauty, feeling good at having bought something as beautiful as this painting was. The frame would have to be repaired, she knew, but what of that?

She could hardly wait for the return of the young people; anticipating their joy and surprise, she went around happily looking for a place where it could eventually be placed. On Sunday, they came in somewhat late and each rushed off to their own room to freshen up. The painting had quite naturally gone unnoticed that evening. The next day and the next day and the next day and the next day and the next day after that were busy days for one and all, and the print leaning against the wall had stayed on there without being noticed at all. On Saturday morning a week from the day it had been bought, it entangled itself into the running feet of Tomal and came to the notice of the family at long last.

Tomal had gone rushing out to the yard, and 'Where has this come from?' asked Meeta of no one in particular.

Tukun was drinking coffee and reading the day's paper at one end and had raised his head and taken a look at what his wife was pointing at. 'Looks like a piece of junk brought in from a garage sale. But how on earth did it come here?'

'I've no idea, maybe someone has thrown it out and the kids have dragged it in here.' And she had called out to the children in the hope of eliciting a clue from them to the mystery. And it was then that Nandita just next door in the kitchen had come to the dining area and confessed to the crime.

Incredulous Meeta had laughingly asked, 'You bought that, Ma, whatever for? Where do you think we can hang that?' She was neither being sarcastic, nor wanting to hurt; she really was surprised at this sudden purchase her mother-in-law had made. But her want of sensitivity hurt. And Tukun sat on, silent, not interrupting nor interfering even once.

'I bought it because I thought it would look nice on one of these empty walls.'

'Oh, Ma, how could you possibly think we can put up a print bought at a garage sale now? Your son has a status to maintain, what would people say if we were to hang up prints that have been discarded by others? Say something, anything, Tukun, why do you always leave me to do all the talking?'

Nandita had picked up the print and was dragging it towards the huge garbage bin kept at the rear of the house when Sudipto rose and took it from her. There was a look of shame in his eyes that she was not able, alas, to interpret. But the very next day, she found that the frame within which it sat had been repaired and the painting had been placed upon a wall in her room. She had taken it down and pushed it into her closet.

The next day when she met Grace at the rose garden, where the roses were now reigning, she waited for a slot in Grace's flow of words to pose a question or two to her.

'Tell me, Grace, have you ever been to a garage sale?'

'Who hasn't?'

'Are all the things worthless that you get there?'

'What a crazy idea, Nan, if they were totally useless, whoever would buy them, tell me?'

'Do you think I'd be acceptable as an item at one of these sales?'

'You kiddin' or what?'

'I'm still not that old, am I? Surely I'd make a very good stay-at-home grandmother for some family that takes me in?'

Grace looked closely at Nandita's face in search of some clues to what had brought about these strange pronouncements and then, taking hold of Nandita's hands in her own, asked, 'Hey, what's the matter now, the kids not treating you right or somethin'?'

'No . . .' she brought out with a certain degree of uncertainty. 'It's not that they are unkind or do not take care of all my needs . . . I think, in truth, I've simply gone past being truly useful to them. I still do a lot of work, but I certainly am no longer indispensable as I was at one time.'

Cocking her head to one side, Grace sat looking at Nandita, anxiety and concern showing in her eyes, on her face, and in every contour of her body.

Nandita did not wish to alarm the old lady and, contrite, tried to make amends for her thoughtlessness. 'Dear, dear Grace, can't you see I'm absolutely all right?' Hugging her close to herself, she reassured her, 'I have just become sentimental watching all those unknown people getting rid of items that had at one time been so closely tied up with their lives. It just woke up the philosopher that has been sitting quietly within me, that's all. I promise it was nothing more serious that prompted me to speak.'

But Grace had been around in this world for a while and summed up what ailed Nandita with a single telling sentence. 'I know it can be a pain living with the kids once they have made a life of their own. But unfortunately, dear Nan, it is no less painful living without them.' And though Grace was smiling all along as she spoke, Nandita felt for a fleeting moment that her eyes had filmed over with unshed tears.

And then a child had come into sight; his mother was chasing after him and he was chasing after a ball. A bird frightened by the commotion flew off its perch with a raucous squawk and Helen arrived navigating her aching joints. Arthritis took over from garage sales and sentimentality, and the grass continued to grow under their feet.

Grace spotted a skinny man in a suit and called out from across the garden to him while waving her arms, 'Hey, Ted, how're you doin'?'

'I'm doin' fine, just fine,' he threw across, 'is that Helen I see there with you?'

And Grace looked at Helen and then laughed, 'Your boyfriend's a-callin', Helen, you better be gettin' along.'

Nandita blushed an unbecoming beetroot, as if an indecent proposal had just been made to her.

'Boyfriend indeed,' Helen said gruffly and Nandita was surprised to see a tinge of colour come creeping up onto her face. The grass was green and the roses were red and romance was right there in the air. And Helen, walking somewhat more upright than when she'd arrived, went off across the garden, to join the man whom Grace had called out to as Ted.

'I've been encouraging Helen to get hitched up with Ted, so what if she's no spring chicken, it's nice to be held close by a man, whatever your age, I tell her.' Nandita thought she must be joking, yes, she must be joking, how could it be otherwise? She had seen Ted from a distance and had no idea how old he was, but Helen, she had heard in passing, had been hanging on for a while now to her seventy-ninth year with a great deal of tenacity. According to the grapevine, she had taken a vow never to cross into her eighties. 'Good

for her,' Grace had twinkled while on the subject, 'crossing eighty is so ageing.'
Nandita, aghast, had burst out laughing.

Her curiosity was aroused, stilling her laughter. 'And what does she say?'
Nandita wanted to know.

'She goes around blushing to the roots of her dyed blonde hair like a
teenage gal. I tell her, you're gettin' a chance, go grab it.'

What a strange world this was, Nandita had caught herself thinking. She
had no idea whatsoever what the man called Ted thought of all this, but Grace's
endeavour towards advancing a romance and Helen's blushing response to it,
as she could see, was real enough. Having escorted Grace back to the Home,
she went thoughtfully down the road to meet Bill downtown.

Bill had been away for almost a week, and to her surprise, she had really
missed him. She had wanted to see his blunt but comfortable features, his
blonde thinning hair, and his ever-welcoming friendly smile, to reassure herself
that he was not a figment of her imagination. And then with a burst of
happiness surging through her heart, she had seen his tall and robust frame
looming large at a distance. He was real and so was the smile that lit up his
face on sighting her.

He had cajoled her before leaving town to join him when he returned for a
pizza lunch in a small place he liked. A vegetarian pizza implied a cheese-laden
meal, and though cheese was not among the things she really liked, Nandita
had agreed to the suggestion. Bill was sporting enough to forego his pepperoni-
festooned favourite and shared the cheese pizza with her.

'Would you like to have some beer, Nan? It's vegetarian, you know,' he
qualified, gently pulling her leg.

'Vegetarian or not, I've never had any alcohol in my life, Bill. So . . .'

'This beer has no more than a drop of alcohol in it, so what do you say,
should I pour you just a dash?'

'I'm not feeling bold enough today, I'll have plain water, please.' Cutting
off a piece from the triangular segment on her plate, Nandita forked it and,
holding it aloft, contemplated the Parmesan covering its top end. 'I wonder
sometimes, Bill, how those pundits who laid down the rules that rule our lives
forgot to include milk and all the innumerable milk products in the list of
things that would not do for a vegetarian to eat.'

'Shall I take it up, and see if it can be expunged from the list? But come to think of it, wouldn't be in my interest at all. I am a widower, so those pundits would force me to give up all the stuff I like to eat.'

'No, they won't, there are no rules that curtail a widower's life,' she corrected him in dead seriousness.

'That means I can go ahead with the movement without damaging my interests,' he said with a mischievous smile to cover up his faux pas. And coming under the spell of his charming smile, she was forced to pull herself out of her dudgeon.

Little by little, he was coming to understand this woman who had helped him with her companionship to tide over the most difficult period of his life. Under the carapace of conventionality that she wore with such dignity, he had deduced lived a young and inexperienced woman, angry at the generations of men that had peopled her life. In the course of their conversations, Bill had learnt the reason why Nandita was an isolated island hugging on to vegetarianism in the sea of non-vegetarianism that her home was.

'Why did you accept the verdict passed by society that you lead the life of an ascetic?' he had asked of her one day. 'Ascetics should be ascetics by choice, not by compulsion.'

'I made a deliberate choice.'

'Why?'

'Because I wanted someone, anyone among the men in authority in either of the two families to object to what I was doing. May I have some water, please?'

'Here you are.' Pouring some into the glass and putting down the jug, he asked, 'And?'

'And I found out that they were weak men with strong facades, with no courage in them to bring about major changes.'

'And you're still hurting.'

'I don't know! Perhaps I am. I did feel very let down, Bill.'

'I can understand.'

'But they were not always like that. You cannot imagine how kind Prodipto's parents were to me when I first went to stay with them after my marriage. And when my baby was to be born, they took care of me as no one else could have. My father-in-law fussed over me, pampered and cosseted me and treated me as he would a favourite daughter of his own. And my mother-in-law was no different. And seeing the kind of life they led, detached as it was from the reality that I had known till then, I went and mistakenly thought that liberalism was the cornerstone of their existence.'

'But it wasn't?'

'It was, up to a point,' she said, pondering the question, 'and then their only son got killed and everything changed.'

'Grief does strange things to people, Nan. Come eat; the pizza is going cold.'

They sat eating for a while, and then as if swept along by the flow of her resurgent thoughts, she had gone back to the telling of a tale to Bill. 'Dadu, I mean my grandfather, had taken ill, and so I was at my ancestral home when the terrible disaster came to pass. And the Gangulys had gone tradition's way and transformed me, as was their wont, into a traditional widow of Bengal. I waited for a word of protest against this life of asceticism that had been imposed upon me from someone, anyone, but none had been raised. But Dadu's silence had hurt me the most. The averted eyes of all those who crossed my path were all that I got from them. And in anger, I accepted all the humiliating norms that ruled the lives of women who had dared outlive their husbands in this life! But from the Roys and the Major General in particular, I had had an expectation of an entirely different set of reactions than the ones I had faced in the home of my ancestors. But he too had failed me!'

And toying with a morsel of pizza, she remembered how when she had next met the Roys, stripped of colour, devoid of joy, the entire fabric of her life tattered and torn, she had discovered that they were no longer the people she had earlier known. True, Prodipto's parents had not once asked her to give up the trappings of normality, but then for that matter, neither one of them told her specifically to hold on to them. Why had her father-in-law not insisted that Nandita should lead a normal life? With the loss of their son, their love for Nandita seemed to have suddenly petered out and run dry. It had flown through a channel, and once that conduit had been removed, the flow had fallen into a chasm and lost its way. The major general, her father-in-law, stunned by his loss, had said nothing and that was a betrayal for which he had never been forgiven!

And aloud she said, 'It was as if there was a crater where their heart had earlier been and whatever had been housed there had fallen through, Bill.' Her eyes were glittering with unshed tears he could see, and he stretched out a hand and took her hand into his own.

'I'm dying to have an ice, care to join me? The answer, I think, is yes. Chocolate or vanilla?' Bill asked. She smiled but said nothing. 'Chocolate, I think, will do fine for both of us. Come on, cheer up, Nan, we can talk of all this on another day.'

And wistfully she said, 'My dad-in-law used to love chocolate ice cream.'

'I can see you really loved him a great deal; no wonder you have been punishing yourself for his weakness. What a stubborn girl you are, Nan.'

'Yes, stubborn enough to have stuck it out.'

Bill wanted to ask what end had her stubbornness served. A Gandhi might have brought about a change through satyagraha; for Nandita, it had certainly not worked. He felt she should have taken the bull by the horns and given it a twist or two and gone on normally with her life. She had wanted desperately, he could see, to cock a snook at society but had ended up further cementing its norms. But he said nothing to her.

She had fallen silent for a while and then suddenly asked, 'You know, don't you, that my father left home when I was three?'

'Yes, you've told me.'

'Bill, you are a very learned man, could you please help me sort out some of the questions that have plagued me all my life?'

'If I can, I will.'

'Why did he go away, Bill? Did he have no love for me at all?'

He had sensed immediately that there was deep-seated hurt somewhere within her that had prompted this question from her. He wanted to soothe away the pain that had settled into her psyche. 'In truth I think he loved both you and your mother rather well, but his quest for that unknown something that was eluding his grasp was greater still.'

'His action did not make either of us feel loved.'

'Your father had to function within a milieu, and being a perceptive man, your father—'

'Perceptive? Or as thoughtless as his own grandfather, my Boroma's husband?'

'I think, Nan, in some way you have been unfair to your father. You have equated his going away with the suicide that ended the life of his own grandfather. Your step-great-grandma, what do you call her?'

'Boroma.'

'Yes, your Boroma, did she not have a horrible life?'

'I don't know. It was not horrible perhaps, but it certainly was most unfair.'

'Your father had finesse, Nan; he had to do what he had to do, but he chose to give your mother a carte blanche to lead a life of normality right to the end of her life.'

'But what of me?'

'Forgive him if you can, Nan, sometimes even when it hurts, one has to sever oneself, away from people and from places one loves, to move on.'

'It had hurt many when I moved myself away from the protection of the Roys and the Gangulys, perhaps it was something like that for him as well.'

'He was a man with a purpose, I think, and taking from him, so were you.'

The use of the past tense in relationship to her own self had evidently hurt, for forgetting her father's desertion, she had gone directly to her own self. 'I think, Bill, you're right that whatever I was, purposeful or otherwise, is now in the past.'

Stretching out his hand to cover Nandita's with his own, he looked her in the eye. 'I didn't mean to hurt, Nan . . .' And unfinished sentence hanging in the air, a shadow fell across them and their clasped hands.

A Yankee drawl followed the shadow that had fallen across them. 'How're you doing, Mrs Roy? What a surprise meeting you here.' The voice was American of Caucasian descent, but the expanse of bare brown flesh left on show beyond her pale skimpy shorts and her just-as-skimpy top told another tale. She was of Indian origin, and she knew she had met her somewhere before.

A flustered Nandita snatched her hand away from Bill's as if she had suddenly found a coiled-up serpent in there. Guilt pulsating through her every vein, she was left completely wordless. And that giant of a girl, what was her name, was looming large over her. Images of Hema Malini dancing painfully upon bloodied feet on glass, a Dharmender tied to a stake and of a leering Amjad Khan had all landed up within her head. And with that, she was able to place when and where she had met this young woman, but her name continued to elude her grasp. And then slowly it came to her; it was something like Susan, or was it Sue? Yes, it was Sue; she knew she should introduce Bill to her, but how could she? What would she think of her? Bill had risen in the meanwhile; Nandita, he could sense, was lost for words and had introduced himself.

'I'm famished, I'll grab myself a bite, see you, Mrs Roy, bye, Mr Brady.' If she was surprised at Nandita's silence, she did not show it and was gone.

Shaken up by this sudden encounter, Nandita had risen, made an excuse, and left abruptly. Bill, a man from another civilisation unable to understand the vagaries of the tradition-bound Indian mind, felt somewhat confused by her sudden change of mood and did not stop her from leaving. And once out of sight of Bill, Nandita almost ran all the way back to her home.

Throwing herself into a chair, she sat with head in hand for a long time. What had prompted her to behave so contrarily, she asked herself over and over again. What if this girl, or her husband, were to tell Tukun or Meeta about this meeting? What would her son and his wife think of her? What would they say to her if they were to learn of her frequent meetings with Bill? With a heavy heart, she resolved never to venture out to meet Bill again; henceforth she would only go to the rose garden and return home from there. Hoping and praying that that girl Sue would not think this encounter important enough to repeat it to anyone, she sighed deeply and rose from the chair and went to the kitchen.

Meeta was back from work; hands busy, phone tucked in between her collarbone and cheek, she was busy dispensing and catching up with the gossip making the rounds. Nandita had come into the kitchen, seen her daughter-in-law on the phone. A tremor of disquiet passed through her heart. Were they discussing her? She took some raw vegetables out of the refrigerator, sat down, and started chopping some zucchini. Ears cocked, she sat working.

'Oh, tennis!' said her daughter-in-law to the caller. 'Tukun's still onto that trip.' There was silence for a while and then she heard Meeta say, 'No. Thankfully there's no Mahadevi,' and laugh. And Nandita let out a sigh of relief. 'This guy Mahadevan,' Meeta went on, 'is trying to get rid of his paunch; and it's doing no harm to Tukun's figure as well . . . what? There's nothing wrong with his figure? I'll let him know. He'll be flattered.' The conversation shifted to the other end and then Meeta spoke up again. 'No, I don't mind. I get to hear some howler or the other every day. Tukun was saying the parents of this guy seem to be fighting like teenagers. You won't believe this but the television programmes . . .' And then Meeta went away, out of earshot, and

Nandita was left wondering about these unknown people and their childish quarrels.

For the next few days, she feared every glance that was thrown her way. The feeling was a familiar one, reminiscent of those days when she would come down tiptoeing from the roof, fearing that some aura left over from her deliciously forbidden meeting with a young and brash youth would give away her assignation to one and all. She feared to show her face to anyone; what if they were to find a reflection of Prodipto there? Trembling with apprehension, she passed her days expecting at each turn to be caught like a criminal and brought to book. The thought of having to face the steely gaze of Thakuma and the rest of the coterie in positions of power in the hierarchy had sent cold shivers up her spine. But even so, the very next day, she had gone back to the roof again. But her Dipto had shuffled the cards like a magician and brought out a winning card and no one had ever known of her outrageously forward behaviour. Not a single person in that ancient home of theirs, no, not even Daminidi had even suspected that Prodipto and she had ever met. It was a perfectly admissible arranged marriage into which she had walked in head bowed, with the blessings of one and all.

The people in authority were not the same today; but she was not in the position of authority then, nor was she now. She feared her friendship with Bill might well be looked askance by the people who now ruled her life. Their collective unconscious was replete with orthodoxy, what if it were to suddenly come alive in them? She had no desire to get into any ugly controversy over a friendship that she had dared to enter into with a man. It was better to step aside and go back to her boring existence once again. The decision had hurt but she had felt unequal to the task of handling a question-and-answer session with her son and his wife if one day they were to question her. But her fairytale friendship with Grace—that she would keep up at all cost.

Grace would be waiting for her, she knew; otherwise, she would not have been able to coax herself to go out from home the next day. Would Bill be waiting for her, would he be disappointed because she had failed to show up? Perhaps he would but what was she to do? She was not courageous enough to fritter away the little bit of peace that she had accumulated in her account. Taking two steps forward and then two steps back and then forward and back again, she had almost settled with the idea of staying back at home. But so unused had she become to spending an entire day alone that she had been compelled by habit to move on to her destination at the park.

The garden was bereft of Grace that day and the next and for three other succeeding days after that.

Kate and Helen had also not come. Heart filled with apprehension, she gazed each day in fear at the seat in the park that continued to remain bereft of Grace's presence. But so afraid was she of the terrible possibility of hearing that she had lost her friend forever, that she asked no one. Right from the beginning, Grace had taken her right into her heart and kept her without any reservation there. With Grace, Nandita had never ever had to remain perched on the periphery of her concerns.

And so she would come each day in the hope of seeing the face that she had come to love so dearly. But the seat had continued to remain forlorn and empty. Where was Grace? Had she gone away somewhere, but where? Gritting her teeth, she had curbed her yearning to move on from there to her usual destination downtown. One unfulfilled meeting notched up to her account, she deliberately turned her back upon another. Winning an argument against her own inner voice was a very disappointing experience, and downcast, she would turn around and move the opposite way and go back to her empty home. How long she would have held out against the magnetic pull that downtown Saisborough held for her was never put to the test because on the fifth consecutive day of her absence from there, she received a call.

Was it Tukun, she wondered as she went towards the trilling telephone. Who else could it be? Everyone else who called knew that there was no one at home except for her in the daytime. Rekha had called up once; it could perhaps be her. She picked up the phone, and though she had been told time and again to identify herself by her telephone number, she mouthed an innocuous hello into the mouthpiece.

And without preamble, she heard a familiar ripened-in-the-sun voice ask, 'Why have you abandoned me, Nan? Not been well or something?' Where had he got her telephone number, flustered, she asked herself. A saner part of her told her: from the telephone directory, where else? It was so wonderful to hear his voice. It was so, so wonderful to hear his voice. In that instant, she acknowledged the extent to which she had missed hearing that solid dependable voice.

Voice almost down to a whisper, she offered only 'I could not come'!

'You've had me that worried. Why didn't you call?'

'I didn't have your number.' A wondrously light and effervescent feeling coursed through her. He had missed her; he was worried about her. What a beautiful day this was!

'You had my name, you could have found out. Never mind, tell me how you're doin'?' he asked with genuine concern.

'I . . . I'm . . . fine.'

'Then you had no business to worry me, did you?' He was scolding her, how strange!

'Sorry, I didn't realise . . .'

'I'm as much to blame. I should've given you all my contact numbers. Do I see you today? I've a couple of hours in the afternoon that I could easily spare.' A prolonged silence hung in the ether between them. And only when he had cleared his throat a couple of times did he get a reply.

'Not today, I won't be able to come . . .'

'Why? What's keeping you?'

'There's too much to do here.'

'I see. If not today, then when do I get to see you?'

'I'll come on Monday, no, Tuesday would be better.'

'What's with you, Nan? Tuesday's almost a good week away.'

A trifle querulously, 'I told you I've a lot to do.' She was buying time, time in which she could take a closer look at her own wayward desires. She had to know who Bill was and why she hankered after his company as she did. *And should she go at all?* was a question that her head had thrown her dithering heart's way! *Have you forgotten that encounter with that woman Sue?* It next wanted to know *Hey, Ma Kali*, how difficult life was. But Bill was her sounding board and she needed badly to be with him to open her eyes to the world. Why did that girl Sue or Sujata, or whatever her name was, have to land up at exactly the same restaurant where Bill and she were sitting together sharing a simple friendly lunch? What if the news was to travel through her to Meeta and Tukun? Did she have strength enough in her to protect her own self? She wanted to meet him, but to go or not to go to meet him had now become the question.

Cutting into her chain of thoughts, 'Not Tuesday, Nan, make it Wednesday week. Tomorrow I'm off to New York to attend a seminar. I'll only be back next Tuesday week.'

Sue forgotten, cautioning head set aside, she exclaimed, 'You'll be away almost ten days.'

'Make sure you're there when I get back, life tends to get boring when I don't see you.' He sounded like a child who had misplaced a favourite toy!

'I promise I'll be there.' Leopards, they say, never change their spots; an eighteen-year-old Nandita, though fearful of the consequences of her daring, had yet gone up to roof to meet Prodipto day after day after day. She was glad to have the assurance of a continuing friendship with Bill and happy that she would have time enough in between to resolve the mystery of Grace's absence from the garden. Light of heart, she made her way to the rose garden, confident that fate having been kind to her this day, she would also find Grace reinstated upon her seat. But it was not so.

When two more days of brilliant weather had filed past and the chosen seat where Grace sat to hold court had remained vacant, alarm bells began to ring in Nandita's head. Grace, she realised with a sudden clearing of her vision, had become for her the mother she had at one time had, but never really had! She did not want to lose her; rendered fatalistic by the lessons that life had chosen to teach her, she feared the worst. Bill could have helped; she wished he had not gone away to New York. Why had he gone away when she needed him so terribly?

Finding herself facing a blind alley, she was forced to overcome her fears; she just had to find out where Grace was. And then as if in answer to her prayers, she spotted Helen at the other end of the garden. But approaching her was not that easy for she was sitting cosy as cosy can be with that man Ted, whom Grace had designated as her boyfriend. Perhaps he was, Nandita thought, for they did look rather comfortable together! Butting into a budding romance was not quite the thing to do, but her anxiety forced her to overcome her scruples and to barge in upon the romantic duo. And setting her inhibitions aside, taking courage in her hands, she went up to Helen.

Hesitantly approaching the couple, she timorously greeted the elderly woman, 'Hello, Helen.' Startled at the unexpected intrusion, both of them looked up and into her face.

'Oh hi! How've you been? Ted, this is Gracie's friend . . .' An awkward pause ensued; poor Helen had misplaced her name.

The brand-new incarnation of Nandita did not hesitate a moment; stretching her hand out towards the elderly gentleman who had risen from his seat by then, she offered, 'I am Nandita, most people though prefer to call me Nan.'

Introductions over, Nandita asked, 'Helen, where's Grace? I haven't seen her in days.'

'Don't you know she's sick? Real bad bout of flu has flattened her out.' Nandita's heart lurched painfully on hearing that Grace was ill.

'Oh no!'

'I'm afraid, yes. She's been givin' us some bad moments, the doc was lookin less grim yesterday, so we are kinda hopin she's outta the woods now.'

This was good news and bad news for Nandita. But certainly better news than what she had feared it would be.

With a proprietary air, Helen gave a playful nudge to Ted and made him move to make room for Nandita. 'She's as weak as a kitten,' she informed Nandita, while patting a place next to her.

'Thank you, but I hope I won't be making you uncomfortable?' Nandita, glancing Ted's way, posed the question.

'Come on, sit down. Ted don't take up too much place, and you ain't no Amazon either.' From the coquettish look Helen had thrown Ted's way, Nandita could see that Helen was in her element. There was an air of self-assurance about her today that had been missing earlier on. Grace was absolutely right; there was romance in the air. Smiling apologetically at Ted, Nandita took the proffered place and Helen was back to giving an account of Grace's state of health. 'I'd told her, "Watch out, Gracie, mind you don't catch a chill." She said she was feelin' that hot and had thrown off the light wrap that she had thrown across her shoulders. And then a cool breeze had sprung up, and there we were, the rest of us, all nicely parcelled up and she without her wrap.'

'Is she very sick even now?' Nandita asked fearfully.

'Not so good. That chest of hers is still wheezing so loud that you'd think you're at a train station.'

Nandita blanched visibly and her hands flew to cover her mouth to block out the cry of alarm that had risen within her heart. There was fear in her eyes, and Helen had seen it. 'Don't worry, honey, our Gracie's a fighter she'll pull through fine,' she reassured her. 'Tell me, Ted, won't she?' Ted, a man of few words, though not quite sure, nodded in agreement.

'Has Chuck been informed, has he come to see her?' Nandita, concerned, wanted to know.

Ted broke his vow of silence and quietly rumbled, 'Not possible for him to visit her from where he is.'

Nandita, aghast at the callousness of Grace's son, asked no more, and Helen, intent on changing the subject, suggested, 'Why don't ya come and see her for y'rself? She'd be that pleased to see ya. I'll tell the guys who keep watch over that there place of ours that you're expected. You can come today, tomorrow, anytime. Just ask for me or for Gracie and they'll let you in.'

Helen had graciously cleared the path for her to go and take a look at her ailing friend, yet Nandita hesitated. For though she was on the best of terms with the visitors who came to the rose garden, she had never ventured into the premises. What was the need when she met them so often, she had told herself! But in truth, she knew deep down that the reasons that kept her away lay elsewhere, in a location filled with fear deep down within her.

Though Grace and Kate had on occasion invited her to come and join them at tea, she had made some excuse and sidestepped the issue. It was a transparent place, for the whole world to see. And what she had seen had filled her heart with trepidation. Massive glass walls let the light of day and the gaze of curious eyes into the premises. She had seen them at table, their movements painfully slow and laboured, the reaching of each morsel of food to their mouths a triumph in itself equivalent to the conquering of Everest! Locomotion on their own was a thing in the past for far too many of the people who could be seen moving around; they were tied now by ageing to their wheelchairs.

Whenever she went that way, this naked show of ageing frightened her beyond reason and compelled her to turn her face away and move on as fast as she could past that edifice enclosed in glass. She had realised that the persons she constantly met at the garden that lay spread out just adjacent to the old age home were the more mobile and therefore the more fortunate among the inmates of the place. But a package deal was far more daunting; once inside the premises, she would have to face up to the abject and absolute reality of ageing. She did not have the courage within her to see the naked bared face of old age. She was already into her fifty-fifth year; what if she were to continue to live on? She could very well get there in a not-too-distant future! It was a reality that lay ahead for all those who managed to win the survival game; she sincerely hoped she would not come out a winner in the longevity stakes.

She had lived among the old and the ageing; Boroma, Dadu, Thakuma had all been images of extreme old age when viewed through her very young and fresh eyes. And with the passage of the years they had, each one of them really and truly grown old and died. But placed as they were within the context of a multilayered family comprising of the young, the very young, the middle-aged, the old, and the very old, they had been an important fragment of the mosaic that made up life. They were a part of a whole, not a grotesque reality to be set aside and put away out of sight. In isolation, and set apart from the rest of humanity, old age took on a very fearful face.

The images Nandita had seen within that glasshouse had haunted her at every turn, and she told herself that she did not wish to live too long. The very next instant, she would question her assumption that she was unique in some way. Philosophising on the mystique of life and death, she recognised that it was perhaps not she herself alone who wanted to opt out of life while the going was good! But questioning herself once again she asked, was that in reality the truth? Perhaps her assumption was all wrong! Had she ever in her encounters with the elderly really felt they were hankering after death? She was not sure, but what she knew for a surety was that people, once born, had only the experience of living, however bitter or sweet, that life or living may have been. So how could they want to rush on to face the unknown, unmapped region that was death without some apprehensions? The further you thought you were from death, the less fear of death you had; the closer you got to it, its unknown-faced veracity terrified you. So she had come to the conclusion that human beings tended to cling on and on and on to the wisps of tattered life that lingered within them. For though tortured by life and the fact of living on, they dared not voluntarily enter into that dark and fearful region that was so completely unknown to them.

Nandita would never have entered the old folks' home had it not been for the fact that she loved Grace so dearly. She did not have courage enough to face up to the ultimate reality of ageing that she would have to face once there. But the bonds of love that she had wrought with Grace forced her hesitant steps to turn that way. Seeing so many really old and ailing people with their manifold problems of ill-health and frailty, so many men and women confined to wheelchairs, so many people waiting for nothing more exciting than the ultimate release of this their burdensome life shook her up completely. But this heart-wrenching, soul-searing traumatic experience turned out to be one of the most positive experiences of her life when she stood beside Grace's sickbed and looked down upon her.

A frail hand came up and grasped her proffered hand; holding on, Grace said, 'Nan, my dear Nan, how happy I am to see you.' Sickness had shrivelled up her already wasted frame, but the smile was that of a lovely girl, for starting from her eyes, it spread across her entire face and made her look ever so beautiful and young again. 'I knew you'd come, I knew you'd come to see your Grace.' And a teardrop trickled out of each eye and made its way slowly down the dried-up terrain of her cheeks.

'I thought I was a goner when breathin' in and out had become the most difficult job I'd ever done. And believe me, Nan, I was that there scared of dyin'. I had no contact numbers, no addresses, no directions which way I was t' go to find a familiar face when I got t' this new place.' And she clung on to the solid reality of Nandita's outstretched hand.

And as she bent to pass her hand upon Grace's forehead, Nandita's eyes fell upon a pair of photographs that were sitting upon the top of her bedside dresser. Nandita knew both the men in those framed snapshots from the pictures Grace had shown her of her family one day. Dave, Grace's husband, she knew, had died some eight years ago when he was well advanced in years. Evidently, Grace liked to link her memory to the young and handsome husband she once had, for Dave was no more than fifty in the photograph she had placed beside her bed. And next to him in a silver frame stood a smiling Chuck, their son, resplendent in a Marine's ceremonial uniform, and a bunch of bright and burnished medals lay alongside that frame. Where was Chuck, why had he not come, was it really so difficult for him to leave whatever he was doing to come and see his mother? And then the meaning of those medals sitting like an offering at an altar came and hit her with its terrible pain-filled meaning. Those medals, won with blood and sweat, had been placed by Grace at the feet of a slain hero, and with a terrible jolting blow upon her heart, Nandita realised that Chuck really and truly could not come to see his ailing mother from where he had gone away.

Nandita bent down and embraced Grace, and the tears that had sprung to her own eyes blended together with the tears coursing down the older woman's cheeks as she spoke on. 'What if I were not to find Dave and Chuck when I got there? I was really, really scared, Nan,' she finished with a watery smile. Placing a gentle kiss upon her forehead and brushing aside her tears, Nandita tried to lighten the burden of the fear of the unknown that was shrouding her dear friend's heart.

'Be brave, Grace; you've always been brave, haven't you?'

'Promise you'll keep coming,' pleaded Grace, taking hold of Nandita's hand.

'Of course I will. I won't come on the weekends but I'll come to see you on all other days.'

'Thank you!'

'And once you're up and about, we'll meet at the park once again,' she encouraged. 'Won't that be lovely?'

'I guess I'm kinda weak now. But I'll come for sure to meet you at the park again.' Though she had wheezed with the effort, a twinkle had appeared in Grace's bleary eyes as she had mouthed these hope-filled words.

'That's my girl, come let me comb your hair. And how about a touch of lipstick, shall I get it? I hope I'm not hurting you?' she asked while gently combing out the wispy strands of Grace's hair. Having completed the task, handing her a mirror, she asked, 'There, doesn't that make you feel good again?' The old lady replied with a heart-warming smile, and for Nandita, yet another tier of mothering began from thereon. Through the years she had transited from child to mother, then from mother to child and now back to being a mother once again. It was a liberating, buoying experience! And with that, she grew back into adulthood, a status she had ceded somewhere along the way.

From that day onwards, Nandita made it a point to visit the home for the elderly for two hours each day. And she found her languid, aimless days turning into very busy and crowded ones indeed.

And having come close up to them, she slowly began to discover through random words, through gestures, and through the photographs that stood beside so many beds, the trials, the tribulations, and the tears of their lives. Had she but known what the smiles upon those heavily made-up faces hid, she would never have let out a whimper or made a complaint in their presence. But it was already so much water under the bridge, for she had used Grace's warm and welcoming bosom to unburden herself of her frustrations and sorrow time and again.

# 9   NANDITA FORGETS SUE

Nandita, entering the Home on confident steps, going past the foyer and then a series of rooms, came and stood at the door to her ailing friend's domain; she waited a moment there, looking appraisingly towards the recumbent form of Grace and remembered Helen's reassuring words, 'Don't worry, honey, our Gracie is a fighter, she'll pull through fine.' Yes, Helen was right; she was a fighter all right. She could see that her dear friend was picking up and, that too, rapidly.

And Grace, sensing her presence, had sat up and thrown a look her way. 'Is that you, Nan? Come on in. I wasn't sleeping. Do come in.'

Later, much later, fears set aside, Nandita plucking up courage asked a question that had been tormenting her since she had discovered that photograph upon Grace's bedside table. 'Why, Grace, why did you make me believe that your Chuck was alive and safe?'

'Did I do that? No, I don't think I . . .' And she trailed off.

'Every tale you told me of your Chuck was in the present tense,' Nandita protested.

'No, Nan,' Grace said, shaking her head, 'I told you the tales of his schooldays and of his early youth. And you made what you wanted to make of . . .'

'And I went and jumped to the conclusion that one of these days, he would pop in to meet you and I would see him here.'

'It's possible I led you on.' She took Nandita's hands into her own. 'I like to think he is around somewhere, so when a friend thinks the same way, I let it ride.'

'You are so brave, Grace. You never dropped a hint that you had . . .'

'I'm not alone, Nan.' And she sighed, 'There are a whole bunch of us here, who've lost someone or the other in Nam. And of course when you live too long . . .'

'And I have been pestering you with my own miseries as if I was the only one singled out by fate to face a loss.'

'Now, now, Nan, whether you lose a beloved person on a battlefield or upon the daily battlefield of life, it's just as painful: for each loss is a loss. Losing a husband you love at that tender age can't be brushed aside as an ordinary incident, can it?'

'Thank you for being so understanding of my weepy ways.'

And then through the door of Grace's room, they saw a man trundling past in a wheelchair. He was seated ramrod straight upon his perambulating chair. His bristling moustache brushed with a flourish into an upward wave was reminiscent of the moustache that Nandita's late father-in-law the major general had worn upon his upper lip.

Grace called out, 'Hey, Colonel, come in and meet this young friend of mine.'

The elderly man seated in a wheelchair brought it to a standstill, turned it around, and was right there beside Grace's bed. 'Yes'm,' he said, giving her a salute.

'This is Nan, a very good friend of mine. She is from India, not Pakistan, I understand they are two different places,' she twinkled.

'Getting your geography straight, Grace,' he teased with a mischievous smile.

Ignoring his rejoinder, 'And he's the Colonel.'

'I did have a name,' he said with a twinkle in his eyes, 'but today I am just the Colonel because these guys here just refuse to call me anything else.' And he extended a hand towards Nandita.

Shaking hands, she said, 'Pleased to meet you, Colonel,' and then with some hesitation, 'I too come from a military background.'

'Really? In that case we are kinfolk in a way.'

'My father-in-law was a major general in the Indian Army . . .'

'You don't say!'

'And my husband was a fighter pilot in the Indian Air Force,' Nandita offered with pride.

'Was!' he exclaimed, looking closely at her. 'What a pity it's all in the past tense.'

'Yes, it's a pity. I learnt with sorrow from Grace that she has lost her only son in Vietnam.'

'Ah! So she's been telling you about Nam.'

'Not really. Perhaps one day I should find out more about it.'

'Perhaps!' And so saying, he raised a hand and brought it to his lips and, looking mischievous as a schoolboy, blew a kiss their way and moved on. Nandita laughed and Grace smiled looking on at the tableau. Then becoming suddenly thoughtful, she said, 'You know, Nan, that jolly Colonel of ours . . .'

'Yes?'

'Lost two sons and his mobility, right there back in Vietnam. And his wife couldn't handle the blow, or so we've heard, and died soon after.'

'Oh, no! But, but he's so jolly?'

'Yes, he hides his pain very well.'

And then a contrite Nandita rose, seeing the ashen look upon Grace's face. 'Dear, dear Grace, how thoughtless of me to ply you with so many questions.'

'I'm all right.'

'Even if you are, I must not tire you any further. I'll come tomorrow, and will write those letters that you were telling me about.'

'I'll be waiting for you, and thank you for offering to do somethin' with those letters that have been sittin' there naggin' at me.'

The very next day as Nandita had entered the Home, she bumped into the Colonel, but that day she looked upon his smiling face with different eyes.

'So?' he challenged. 'You are planning to get interested in that war we fought out there in the marshlands of Nam?'

'Grace and I were talking together and it just came up.'

'No need to apologise, if you really want to know something about the mess that fellow Lyndon Johnson got us into by messing around with other people's problems, then tell me and I'll give you a book or two to read. But I hope you have a strong stomach to stomach the stuff, because believe you me, those books won't tell you sweet scented tales of romance and roses.' His customary smile wiped off his lips, he goaded her.

She looked him in the eyes and said, 'Give me the books and I promise I'll read them.'

'That'll be a good thing! Not too many people care to know about that horrible misadventure today. Come pull up a chair and sit down, you are giving me a crick in my neck,' he said testily. He waited till Nandita was seated and then went on, 'I still keep dashing off letters to the papers, voicing my anger against this amnesiac nation, but who bothers. Who is interested in what happened thirty or forty years back, tell me?'

'Yes, it's only those who suffer directly who remember those terrible political blunders that have affected their lives. In 1947, India was partitioned, and a part of it became Pakistan. I was born around those years so I was too young to have even been aware of this terrible upheaval that was taking place in the life of our country. But I've heard of the bloodbath that followed and the displacement of the millions of people that took place then, because of that decision a handful had made, to divide a nation in two.'

'I'm sure only those who were mixed up in it can ever know what the price of that partition really was.'

'My husband died in a road accident, so in truth he died for no particular cause.'

'The cause that's life is cause enough.'

'It's really strange, Colonel, but for a very long while, I resented his dying in such an inglorious manner.'

'It happens . . .'

'I felt a warrior's death should have been on the battlefield rather than upon a metalled stretch of road.'

'A death is a death, Nan. And the death of a near and dear one is always painful.'

'I'm mature enough to understand that today, but at that moment of time,' and she sighed, 'when I was not yet quite twenty, I wanted a little bit of honour and glory to cling on to, to make the terrible loss of my young husband more meaningful.'

'Of what avail is a glorious death when people forget so easily?'

'I've realised that since then. When a number of my husband's friends died during the war that was fought to liberate Bangladesh, I came to know that this so-called glory that attached with those deaths was ever so fickle and transient.'

'Do they deserve to be forgotten? Is that correct? Is that right?'

'No, they don't,' she sighed and went on, 'so many of my husband Prodipto's course mates never returned from those encounters; but a nation *was born* with the help of the blood *they had shed*. But I think neither the Indians nor the Bangladeshis remember them with any clarity today.'

'You are an intelligent girl, Nan. I have enjoyed speaking with you. I have a large collection of books. Feel free to make use of them.'

'Thank you; I will.'

'Though sometimes I do say that this country of ours is lousy, I know deep down that it is one of the most astounding feats of collective nation-building that has ever taken place in the history of mankind.'

'Deep down you are very proud of your country, aren't you?'

'Yes, it surprises me sometimes, but I think I am.' He sounded angry but soon, becoming thoughtful, concluded, 'I think perhaps our generation was just born at the wrong time, otherwise tell me, Nan, what were we doing out there in that godforsaken place so that we could get caught in that godawful crossfire?'

No answers were being solicited and Nandita offered none.

And with that, he trundled off without another word and then changing his mind at the entrance to his room, turning round, threw the cryptic command 'Wait.' He returned soon after and handed Nandita two books. One was on the war that had been fought at Vietnam and the other was a concise history of the United States. Nandita was back to studies all over again and her guru was to be a very stern colonel!

The next morning, she rose as usual and, with a song on her lips, performed all her early morning activities in their precise given order. A surge of happiness kept time with her singing, for Bill would be back, and he had made her promise that she would be there to meet him. A promise had been made and a promise, she believed, had to be kept. But her hesitant self was back with its timorous voice, with its litany of *you can't do this, can't do that; don't do this, don't do that.* However, confronting her cowardly self, she had asked a simple question or two of it. Was she a grown woman or was she not? Did she have the right to decide who should be her friend and who should not? Did she need the permission or the approval of her son and his wife to choose the path on which she should tread? The answer, though none too boldly voiced, was yet a *no.*

So lost in her thoughts had she been that it was only somewhat later that she realised that it was a while since the entire family had left for school and for work, and that the cacophonous presence of the companions of all their waking hours was still stridently speaking on. The radio was soon silenced and the voices within the multiple TV sets were also stilled. Calmed by the all-pervading silence that she had wrought, she wandered from room to room, savouring the soothing salve of solitude that had spread out, little by little, bit by bit with the percolating away of the grains of time. A sense of calming aloneness seeped through her entire being as she anticipated her suzerainty over the entire domain that now lay around her. People changed and so had she. Today, she went out of her home in search of caring, among people who were strangers to her till but yesterday! Happily there were few strangers in her life today. The warm glow left over in her heart from the friendly overtures she had encountered from all the friends she had so recently acquired had kept her company as she dressed for the day. The Colonel's gruff handing over of a precious book into her care had touched her deeply. She stood awhile and recaptured the expression upon the Colonel's face as he had commanded her to wait. And she was imbued with a deep feeling of tenderness for this man who had suffered so much and even so had not lost his zest for life and living. A quick visit to the Home would have to be worked in if peace was to continue to prevail in her life.

Trying to please one and all yet not quite managing to please anyone, a trifle perturbed Nandita, breathless from rushing around, had gone directly from the Home to meet Bill downtown, hot and flustered from the exertion. *So many days, so many, many days have gone by since that day when that encounter with Sue sent me fleeing from Bill,* she reminded herself while wiping her face with the loose end of her sari. *And I have made a promise besides that I would never meet Bill ever again.* Just a single telephone call had been enough to undo her resolve and here she was. And there he was at a distance, but he had not seen her as yet; she stood a moment observing him. How very young and handsome he was; why did he seek out a decrepit woman like her, she agonised. Should she turn back and return to her earlier resolve? And then he looked her way, and all resolves forgotten, she moved forward and he, spotting her, covered the space between them at a near trot.

It was but natural that he open his arms to her, and she walk into its protective embrace. A gruff 'Am I pleased to see you, Nan,' fell to her ears and brought her alive to the ridiculous situation she had positioned herself. Separating herself from him, she looked up into his face. And what she saw there made her wonder what he had been doing with himself. He was smiling as usual, but once again today, it was not rising up to his eyes. Saddened by this throwback to those days when they had first met, she took his hand into her own, and took him towards an empty bench.

'Not well, Bill?'

'I'm fine, just fine.'

'Then why so sad?'

'Am I sad? No way. I'm doing good.'

'Then?'

'Want to know? You girls keep giving a guy a hard time then ask. You abandoned me and then Meg decided to pay me a visit. I'm a tad confused, that's all.'

'What happened, Bill?'

'I went home, Nan, and you won't believe this, but Meg was there. I could feel her presence but she wasn't speaking to me. It felt kinda weird because with Meg you had to find yourself slots to put a word in.' He laughed as if it was the funniest thing that he could think to tell Nandita.

And she was glad that she had broken her promise to her own self and had come to meet him. During his visit to New York, he had spent several nights in his home rendered lifeless by the absence of Meg. He needed someone to talk to. And she was there.

'I know, Bill, these silenced voices can be quite troublesome.'

'Troublesome? Who said anything about its being troublesome? It was hilarious, Meg and wordless!' And he guffawed. 'Some days from now I'll be fifty-two. Had she been around, she would bake a cake and stick fifty-two candles onto it to remind me how old I'm getting to be.' And as if suddenly out of words, he fell silent.

'We will have a birthday party. I'll bake you a cake,' and with a wide smile, 'to remind you how old, or perhaps how young, you really are.' Bill looked up at Nandita with some surprise; he had sensed some change in her. She seemed somehow more in command.

'Why don't *I* take you out for dinner?'

'The promised lunch is still pending, Bill, shall we get on with that first?' Nandita was feeling grown-up but not that grown up. Venturing out with Bill for dinner did not fit in with her agenda as yet. 'I think it would be nicer to have a picnic on the lawns of the Lake Shore; for your birthday, I want to cook you a proper Indian meal.'

'That sounds great, thank you. Sure you want to slog?' Tentatively, 'The dinner offer's still open,' conspiratorially, 'want to change your mind?'

'No way!'

'Say that again. How *wonderful*, since we last met, you've turned American with a luscious Midwestern Bangla accent, Nan.' She laughed at his reaction to the small deviation in her vocabulary, and a chuckle emerged from within him and exploded into a laugh, and seated side by side, they laughed together long and loud and the pigeons on the make for crumbs got startled and flew away. And the sweet old pair of ladies seated on a bench alongside had chuckled in unison for no reason at all.

And then she told him about how ill Grace had been and how she visited the Home for two hours at least each day. 'So many people besides my beloved Grace, I now find, need a younger person's presence. They need a little touch of love, a gentle smile, or even a word or two with someone who will listen.'

'Yes, human beings, young or old, do hanker after a little emotional exchange.' And within himself, he marked the change that was coming about in Nandita. The word 'young' had slipped unselfconsciously out of her while referring to her own self.

'Grace's illness served a purpose. I had to overcome many of my preconceived notions, face up to my fears to step in there. What had been a fearful place filled with a million fearsome images has now been revealed to me as a place of compassion that is overflowing with love.'

'How tremendously exciting, Nan, I've just been away for a handful of days and you've found yourself a vocation. I'm really very, very happy for you.'

'Thank you, Bill, I think more than a vocation, I have begun to find myself once again.'

'We must continue with this chat, but you must be getting hungry, I sure am . . . shall we go find ourselves something to eat?'

'Let's.'

Strolling along companionably, they entered a small eatery. Once seated, the ordering of a simple meal out of the way, he urged her to tell him more of her recent journey of discovery.

'Some other time, Bill.'

'Why not now? I really want to know why we find it so difficult to face up to the reality of old age. Are we that scared?'

'Perhaps, it was difficult to begin with, Bill, but now as you know, I find it to be a warm and friendly place. Unbelievable though it may seem, it is a happy place full of camaraderie and fellow feeling. They really are a brave lot for standing beside them in their home, where their guards are less well placed.

I have discovered a sad page out of American history that has touched their lives as well. So many of those people who live there have so many sad tales to tell that are linked with that war the US fought in Vietnam, which, in their magnanimity, having sensed my insecurity, they had never told me anything about.

'Yes, Nan, that generation of Americans has indeed suffered a great deal.'

'And besides, when you live to be really old, there's more than war that robs you of your loved ones. But they are not . . .'

'Making a song and dance of it,' he completed for her. 'In truth I missed being drafted by a mere whisker. Had I been a bit older and the war not come to an end when it did, I too may well have stopped a bullet.'

'Stopped a bullet?'

'With my heart perhaps.'

'Oh no, please, Bill . . .' she cried out, alarmed at the very prospect. 'It makes me very desolate and unhappy to even think . . .'

'Sorry!' Stretching out a comforting hand towards her, he said, 'Our toasted sandwiches are turning cold and our cold Cokes are turning warm, come let's eat. When do I get to eat some more of those lovely pea-filled savouries you brought along one day?' He had skilfully manoeuvred her away from the uncomfortable topic into which they had inadvertently strayed. In a moment, she brightened at the unexpected compliment. She loved to cook, and like every good cook, she needed someone to appreciate and laud her skill. He had been indeed very complimentary of all that she offered him out of her tiffin box, but how was she to know that it was not a mere act of courtesy and politeness on his part?

And going back to her pet obsession, she told him how, without fail, day after day she now went to the Home, setting all else aside. 'And though I give so little to those who live there, I feel I get so very much more from them in return.'

'You do have a wonderful and busy life, I can see, Nan.' Was there perhaps a tinge of forlornness in the words?

Nandita, engrossed in telling a wondrous tale, had noticed nothing amiss and had gone on. 'When I go there, so many faces turn towards me sunny faced like sunflowers and my shortened Americanised name, Nan, can be heard on so many lips. Never before have I felt so central to anyone's well-being as I do now, Bill.'

So tied up had Nandita become with her new-found relationships at the Home that there were occasions aplenty when she would land up later than expected to meet Bill downtown.

'What's with you, my girl, a schoolmarm and never on time?' he teasingly chided her one day.

'Oh, Bill, you should have seen the number of letters that had to be written, and—'

'I was just kidding; you're doing a great job.' And he smiled. 'Even so, being human I do get a tad jealous at times, Nan.'

'Oh, Bill, you are so kind to understand.'

'Me and kind? No way! Come, take a breather, you look exhausted.' And taking her by the arm, he took her to a seat. 'And you look hungry besides. Care for some potato salad?' And he offered her some.

The next day was more relaxed, and after their shared meal, they were seated companionably together with a Coke apiece in hand when, as if pondering the imponderable, he said almost to his own self, 'I wonder whether I could have overcome my fears as easily as you have done.'

'It was not easy to begin with, but once I'd gone in and been among all of them for a while, the frightening shadows of gloom and despair that the wheelchairs, the walkers, the guard-railed beds, the bedpans, and all those other orthopaedic props that propped up these lives soon fell into their correct perspective, Bill. It was the semi-darkness of my ignorance that had thrown up those shadows that frightened me.'

'Yes, ignorance and misconceptions do play havoc with our ability to reason out things.'

'The realisation that living out a meaningful life for those people not fully able to take care of themselves had been made possible, because of these . . .' Waving her arms around and clearing her throat, she went on, 'After a few false starts, I've now been able to place the props behind the people. The light that I'd been throwing had been upon all the wrong things! You know, Bill, all the props still remain but I hardly see them now.' Her tone awestruck, she continued, 'I had to but reposition my chair and light up the play that I was watching, to make me understand what was what. The ropes and the pulleys and the cardboard and the hardboard cut-outs, the brooms and the brushes, paint pots and the flowerpots, all the artefacts and artifices that went into putting up a stage presentation had to be kept in the background. They were important, but not as important as the finished product, the final presentation upon the stage.'

'So true, what an eye-opener, dear girl,' and then with a wicked smile, 'Tell me, how do you manage to make poetry out of all of this?'

'Being a Bangali helps,' she replied with a twinkle in her eyes. 'Thanks to Tagore, we Bangalis have a franchise on poetry.' And they laughed.

Today the woman who had thrown a challenge to society and walked out with her son to bring him up alone, the woman who had carved out a career for herself sat before him. The savant in him lauded her ability to concretise the abstract and to make it into a palpable entity and softly he added, 'Yes, the play that is life has to go on, Nan.'

'Yes, it does, doesn't it?'

'You are a very perceptive human being, Mrs Nandita Roy. I'm real pleased to have you as a friend. But how come this friend of mine who speaks so much of the Home and its inhabitants never really lets me into her own life, her own home? I know I'm intruding, even so . . .'

A confused Nandita fell silent for a bit. What was she to tell him, that her son's family and his home of which she spoke so little today had at one time been the very centre of her universe, that she had invested her entire self in its well-being? But it had not been as if it was one-way traffic in those early days, for in return she had been enveloped in caring and love by the young couple and their little ones. But slowly, unbeknown to her, things had changed and suddenly one day she had found herself holding on to the shell of past warm and bonding familial ties. And having bitten into the bitter kernel that lay within the heart of those failed and faltering once-sweet relationships, she had perforce stepped back. Today she went out of her home in search of caring among people who were, till yesterday, no more than strangers to her. For in her own home, none was to be found.

The silence between them stretched out; repenting his lapse from acceptable social conduct, he apologised, 'I'm sorry, Nan, I had no business to ask. Please forgive me for becoming so personal.'

'Please, Bill, there's no need to, I was wondering what I was to tell you. What is there to talk of when a relationship has drifted away from its moorings? Today the earlier glowing cheering place of warmth and caring that our home had been has turned into a chilling bone-numbing cold zone of indifference. Who knows who is to blame?' She paused a moment. 'My fate perhaps.'

Bill felt otherwise but said nothing. Even on earlier occasions, he had sensed a certain degree of hesitancy, a certain degree of coolness on her part while she spoke of her son and his wife. She was far more ebullient when she touched upon the subject of her two grandchildren, and softly he asked, 'Are there any problems that you'd like to share with me, Nan?

'If you don't wish to talk about it, that's perfectly all right with me, but as you can see, I have wide shoulders, feel free to make use of them,' he ended with a gentle smile.

'Problems—do I have any problems? Not really, no one ill-treats me . . .'

'Then?'

'But my son and his wife have changed a great deal. They no longer make me feel a part of their lives. I feel so trapped and isolated in their home.' She fell silent for a moment and then hesitantly added, 'I feel like a guest who has overstayed his welcome.'

'Have you?'

Startled, brows furrowing, she looked up at him eyes misted. 'I didn't ask to come.' Her voice had gone husky with unshed tears. 'They made me uproot myself and brought me here.'

'And you came.'

'Did I have any option faced with my only child's appeal? And besides,' he looked appraisingly at her as she hesitated for a moment, 'it had been so long since I'd been on my own. I allowed myself to be persuaded.'

'Yes, loneliness does wear one out, come take a sip,' he said, holding out her glass towards her.

'It was really nice in the beginning. I had lived alone for so long that it was wonderful for me to be wanted so much. The children, with the parents away at work, developed a special bond with me.'

'I can imagine.'

'And I allowed myself to believe that they loved me more than they did their parents.'

'A normal grandparently delusion. Come take a bite, you've hardly eaten.'

'I'm full. And, Bill, with the kids hanging on to me, Tukun, Meeta, and I did everything together then. We talked a lot, and we laughed a great deal. With very little money in our purse, that was the only way in which we could entertain ourselves. But slowly, imperceptibly, everything began to change. I'm still there, a fixed entity in their lives but they make no effort to make me feel a part of their lives.'

'Do you make an effort, Nan, to make them feel you appreciate all that they do for you?'

And seeing the expression of astonishment upon her face, he bit his tongue as she responded with 'What do they do for me? Nothing, so what is there that I should appreciate?' And with a very curt and formal 'Thank you for the sandwiches, it's getting late. I must go home,' she, hurt, had risen to leave.

Want her to walk right out of your life forever, you idiot, he asked his none-too-bright self. And moving swiftly away from the tricky subject of familial relationships, he asked, 'Hope you'll not forget that in ten days from today, it's my birthday.' She kept standing where she was but said nothing. 'Come on, you've promised to cook me a birthday feast, remember.'

'I know I have, but . . .'

'Please, Nan, no buts, please, I'm looking forward to my birthday party, don't disappoint me, please.'

She was angry and disappointed that he too had not understood her anguish, but seeing how he was missing his Meg, she had decided to forgive him, though not completely. 'No, I won't forget your birthday, or the promise I've made,' came her brusque response.

He let out a sigh of relief; that was a close call. 'Good. I'll be off to Singapore: day after, there's a conference there that I'm to attend. And as I'll have to put together some papers, I'll be tied up tomorrow, so I'll only be seeing you on my birthday.'

'That means I won't be seeing you for ten whole days, Bill.' Peeve forgotten, she sounded so forlorn that he looked towards her in surprise. *So I'm forgiven,* he thought.

'I'll miss you, Nan.'

'So will I, please do take care.'

'I'll take good care, I promise. Shall I pick you up from your home on D-Day? You'll be carrying party fare with you, remember.'

'Let me see, I'll let you know if I need your help,' the thoughts of what the prying eyes of the neighbourhood would think of his visit made her say.

'Suit yourself, and suffer a backache if you must. And what'll you tell those guys at the Home? They seem to expect a visit from you on all weekdays.'

'I'll tell them a very special friend's birthday is going to keep me away.' It felt good to be called a very special friend, and he smiled as he heard her. It was good to see he was smiling again, and Nandita smiled back into his eyes in return.

Late that evening as she sat reading, Tukun peeped into her room. 'I called this afternoon, Ma, and got no reply. Where were you?' he asked.

'I'd gone for a walk.' It was the truth, but only a half-truth! The light was positioned upon her book, so her face was in the shadow; otherwise, the telltale guilty flush riding up onto her face might have given her away.

'In this heat?'

The coolness of spring had been left behind and summer could be spied standing right around the corner. 'It's not all that hot, Tukun, if you step outside your air-conditioned car, you'll find it's still very pleasant outdoors.'

'Perhaps!'

'You told me to go out of the house, so . . .'

The look on Tukun's face was something akin to 'Did I?' He had forgotten the conversation that had taken place between his mother and himself sometime in the early days of spring. But he had been able to at last pin down the reason why his mother had started looking so much more fit and young and alive these days. The long walks she had started taking and being out in the fresh air were doing her a lot of good he could see. In truth, even Meeta had remarked upon the changes that had come about in her.

'The exercise is good for you, I can see, but why don't you go out earlier in the day?'

'I like to go out after having got done with my work, Tukun.'

'A lot of people get heatstroke in summer.'

'I've been going out regularly since early spring.' He looked surprised. 'And the heat has come on gradually so I'm quite comfortable with it.'

'Suit yourself, but I still think the afternoons are too hot to go out on foot.'

'Don't worry. I'll take care. But why did you call?'

'Nothing important really, Meeta asked that I pick up a few things on my way back; and I'd left the list on my bedside table.'

'I'm sorry I was not here. How did you manage?'

'Simple, I called up Meeta.' And he smiled.

And with that, he left the room, and a pensive Nandita sat on, book in hand, ruminating that one of these days, she would have to reveal the parallel life that she was leading. Even so, she did not feel like sharing that secret part of her, peopled by so many interesting persons, with anyone, fearing that the revelation would deplete those warm bonds in some way.

No, the time was not yet ripe for her to tell them about her life beyond the four walls of this home. In another month or two, Bill's leave away from his university would be over and he would be going away. The very thought of his going out of her life for ever had been depressing, but that was the reality and she would have to face it. So what need was there of her telling them about Bill? What if they were not to understand? What if they were to question her? Would she be able to take their questioning? Having reverted to adulthood once again, she knew that she would not be able to face up to any questions being posed to her by the younger generation with equanimity. She rose and, placing a bookmark at the open page, had shut the book and put it down upon her bedside table and gone downstairs.

As she sat eating in the kitchen, she wondered whether she should reverse her decision to eat alone at night. Now that she had such a hectic daytime schedule, she tended to get tired earlier these days. Yes, it would be nice not to eat alone, she thought as she finished her meal. Placing her soiled plate and glass in the dishwasher, she had gone upstairs. She could hear the children as she went past her grandson's room and peeped in to see what was going on. A yawning Tammy, no, Tanmayee, she corrected herself, saw her, smiled, said 'Goodnight,' and went across the landing to her room to go to bed.

Tom, no, Tomal, she said, bringing herself into line, also looked sleepy but very distressed. Nandita took him into her embrace and asked, 'What's the matter, Tomal, why're you looking so upset?'

'Oh, Thamma, our class is doing a project on American literature and I've been asked to submit a report on Mark Twain. And there is no one in this house that can help. Dad has no time and Mom doesn't know a thing about American lit, and the information on the Internet is too confusing. What am I to do?'

'When do you have to submit this report?'

'In three days.'

'There's plenty of time then. But, young Tomal, are you sure that you've not been putting off this work for too long? You're a very lucky boy to have got such an interesting author to write about.'

He smiled sheepishly, and then excited, he asked, *'You know who Mark Twain is?'*

The awestruck look on her grandson's face brought a smile to Nandita's face. 'And so do many, many other people of this world.'

'How awesome! Did you know about him even when you were in India, Thamma?' the young boy asked in a voice replete with rising interest.

'Yes, so I did. But just recognising the penname of Samuel Clemens will not do for that report you have to write. Will it, Tomal?'

'No, it won't, Thamma.' And he smiled a smile that evoked memories of his grandfather in her.

She ruffled his hair. 'What do you say we put our heads together tomorrow and see what can be done. You gather as much information on Mark Twain as you can, and I'll get something as well.'

'From where?'

'Does that matter? I'll give you help, but the report you'll have to write on your own.'

'Wow, Thamma, you are great, I promise I'll do all the hard work. But please do give me your help,' he coerced as he gave her a tight hug.

'I promised, didn't I? Go to sleep.'

'Thank you, Thamma, you are the best grandmother in the whole world.' And with that, he jumped into bed. And Nandita, overwhelmed by his generous words of appreciation, bent over and placed a kiss upon his forehead, and left the room thoughtfully. Her little grandson had asked her for help; she would have to get the right kind of information that would help a boy of ten to write a meaningful report. Yes, she must!

An unaccountable sense of excitement bubbling in her veins, Nandita stepped out of her home at the usual time. On the way, she passed so many known faces whose names and identities were unknown to her, yet they had become a part of her entity now. Why they should care that she 'take care' of herself, or that she 'have a good day', she did not know. But ritualistically they would shower their benisons upon her as she walked past them. Hesitantly, timorously she had joined in the litany of distributing goodwill and good wishes all around her as well, and slowly, unbeknown to herself, she had begun to become a part of the whole.

As she approached the edifice that housed the Home, though she was still a fair distance away, she could spot the Colonel hovering around the entrance. The Colonel was wheeling himself in as she came up and, on spotting her, had smiled at her and said, 'Hey, Nan, glad ta see ya.'

'Where've you been?'

'Not as far as you've come from, honey, just up to the gate and back. I was feelin kinda darin' and adventurous, so I thought, why not check out the world outside the gate?' Though he was smiling, his voice had a giveaway wobble to it that hit hard as a hammer blow upon Nandita's heart. And then she had done something that she could have never brought herself to do in her life before the Rose Garden and the Sandwich on a Bench, at Downtown Saisborough. Bending from the waist downwards, she gave the Colonel a kiss upon his forehead and then, smiling right into his eyes, straightened up and, laying a hand across his back, began walking alongside his wheelchair and into the Home. And as he trundled along, she told him about her predicament.

Interest awakening, moment's despondency forgotten, he deflected his preoccupation of the moment to the immediate need of his friend Nan. Nan's grandson Tom needed some help, so some help would have to be given, was his clarion call! And like the good military man that he was, he immediately launched a military operation to obtain his objective.

And the combing operation had proven successful and had yielded an expert who was living right there in their midst. And as a result, Nandita found herself facing David Whitfield, a schoolteacher from the state of Missouri. Twain had done their state proud, and so for him, he was an icon and an exalted being. He knew everything that was worth knowing about the writer and spared no pains to acquaint Nandita of these details.

Tomal, she was pleased to see, had worked hard and gathered together a great deal of information about the famous writer. Nandita held herself back and handed over only that information without which he would have been at a disadvantage. And encouraged by his grandmother, the little boy, feeling very important, produced a real good bit of work. And Nandita reaped rewards galore, for apart from the joy of seeing her grandson perform so well, she had, after a long leave of absence, found herself being reinstated in the position of heroine in her little grandson's life.

And at the Home, she now had two teachers who wanted to make sure that she knew more and more about their motherland. It was all very well to be handed books to read, but quite another when you were to be interrogated upon the contents soon after. Thanks to the Colonel and the good teacher David Whitfield, Nandita was back to school again.

What Bill would say when he would hear of her enforced return to studentship, of that she had no idea! But that he would be amused, she knew with a certainty.

There was so much to tell, and Bill was away at faraway Singapore. Oh, how she missed Bill whenever he dropped out of sight. Thank God she would have to wait just a few more days to have him back. And then she remembered the rash promise she had made to him.

'We'll have a birthday party. I'll bake you a cake.' Now why on earth had she said *that*? Nandita scolded herself. It was all very well to have a birthday party, and it was just as fine to promise that she would cook a very special meal, but should an amateur in baking have promised that she would bake a cake? And that too for an American who must have been gorging on perfect cakes and pastries baked for him by his mother, and then his wife. Definitely not, for the only cake that she knew how to bake was a sponge that tended to be somewhat harder than any self-respecting sponge would ever want to be. And when was it last that she had baked one of those as well? Must have been years now. The oven and its mystique and whatever little she knew of it had long since given her the go-by.

And in her enthusiasm to pour oil over the troubled waters of Bill's heart, she had gone and promised that *she herself* would bake him a cake *with her very own hands*. Cakes galore could be bought, she knew, but in her lexicon, a promise was a promise; if you said you'd bake a cake, you did not go out into the market and buy one! She could produce culinary wonders provided she was not asked to stray away from the *karai*, the *tava*, and the pressure cooker ensemble that went directly onto flame of a stove. Even so, it was not as if she had had to come to the United States to make her acquaintance with an oven!

She had left behind the coal, the charcoal and the wood fires, in the home of her upbringing at Bhabanipore. When Prodipto and she had set up home, they had taken a technological leap ahead and acquired a kerosene stove to cook upon for themselves. Having seen the fuss and the clutter of cooking on coal, she had marvelled at the inventiveness of the modern brain that had thought up such a convenient device. The only thing she had not liked about this fantastic gadget was the after-smell of acrid fumes that it left behind when the wicks were put out. Though kerosene had given way to gas soon after, Prodipto, alas, was no longer by her side. And the widowed Nandita had had to wait a while to acquire a gas connection for herself, for it had cost far more than she could really afford with the meagre schoolteacher's salary that she had at her disposal at that time.

And then slowly, electric ovens had also begun to appear in the kitchens around her. But those early entrants in those Calcutta flats had come in more as a status-enhancing device than as a useful item for cooking one's meals. Only very few among those who owned one of these magical gadgets ever really put them to any use. A person who baked cakes and other such alien eatables that emerged from the oven aromatising the atmosphere were as such held in a certain degree of awe, she remembered. And one day she too had succumbed to the lure of modernism and had bought herself one of those contraptions that had just then sprouted in the market that were called 'Round Ovens'. Tukun was still a boy in school and her lean purse had groaned with the strain of the amount that she had had to part with to acquire one. But once installed in her home, it had lent the place that certain aura of modernism that nothing else could have!

It was round in shape as its name 'Round Oven' implied. It had a cover as tall as a top hat with a circular glass window atop it, through which you could watch the rise and fall of the cake you were attempting to bake. It had three stumpy little black legs upon which it stood lording over the world. The outcome, in her own case, in terms of baking a cake had never been particularly satisfactory, but it had served a certain purpose that she had not thought would come her way when she was acquiring the contraption! All of a sudden, she had risen in esteem in the eyes of her own son Tukun. For with the emergence of each cake from the hot entrails of that little oven, she had become very special person in the eyes of his visiting classmates. With the help of those flattened-out sponges he had become *that boy who had a mother who not only taught in their school but also baked cakes!* No wonder she had specially crocheted a cover for its beautification and had given it pride of place in her home. But that had certainly not made her into a master baker, so what was she to do?

Baking cakes had never been within the purview of Nandita's responsibilities since her arrival in the United States. She knew her limitations and had ceded ground with no regrets whatsoever, for she felt the cooking of exotica was best left in the hands of the younger generation, who tended to be more adventurous and Westernised. So her non-rising sponges had surely gone flatter still with the passage of time! But considering the circumstances, she could not even ask Meeta to give her a hand of help to bake a birthday cake for Bill. Just eight days to go, what was she to do?

And then she remembered an untapped help-line, her cookery teachers at the Home. She had called up and asked for any one of the half a dozen persons whom she felt could help. Helen was the first to be spotted by the emissary of her message, and had arrived panting and quite short of breath, at the telephone. She was convinced that Nandita was in some kind of deep trouble to have called up as she had done. It took Nandita a while to convince her elderly friend *that she was in trouble* but not of the variety she was thinking of.

'I need your help, Helen. I've promised to bake a cake for a friend's birthday and don't know how. The last I baked was at least fifteen years back.'

'You kiddin' or what? Not baked for fifteen years, how's that possible?' she demanded.

'I really haven't, Helen, believe me.'

'Of all the funny things,' the older woman chuckled into the phone. 'If that's all that's troublin' ya, honey, go and get y'rself a packet of cake mix, follow the instructions right, set the oven at the right temperature, pop it in, and watch the cake come up. Some of them even have the icin' in a little packet. Slap it on and take all the credit ya want.'

'Won't that be cheating?'

'Cheatin'?' And she laughed. 'No one bakes cakes and pastries the way we used ta do any more. For us it was measure this, measure that, weigh this, weigh that, be sure of the size of the eggs, separate the yolk and then keep beating the egg whites till your hand falls off! Go find y'rself a packet of cake mix and bake y'rself a perfect cake, hon.'

'Thank you, Helen, thank you so very much.'

'What did ya say? Thank you? Thank that gal on the cover with the wooden spoon in her hand. I am only lettin ya into a little secret, that's all.'

'God bless you, Helen, I'll let you know how the experiment went once I bake the cake and see the results.'

'Believe me, honey, you can't go wrong with one of them packets. Hope your boyfriend likes it,' she ended mischievously before going off the line.

'There's no boyfriend,' Nandita remonstrated but who was listening! Helen was feeling romantic these days and could see nothing but romance whichever way she looked.

Her memory jogged by Helen, she remembered all those packets that she had seen Meeta ferreting away on the days she baked one of her fancy cakes. She had never given the matter much thought. She went straight to the huge cupboard tucked away at one end of the kitchen that served as a storeroom and found not one, but a stack of different cake mixes at the rear of the cupboard. So this was the *mantra* to Meeta's infallibility at the oven! The photographs of the readied cakes on the cover were most alluring and she chose the one that looked the most tempting to her and took it up to her room and put it away in her cupboard, fearing it might disappear if she let it out of sight.

The deed done, as soon as she returned downstairs, the doorbell rang and she opened the door to let the two children in. They had entered in a rush, strewing school bags and shoes along the path of their entry. Smiling indulgently at the disarray, she asked, 'Hungry?'

And together they replied with a big 'Yes!'

'Go and wash your hands and feet. I have made something special for you.'

Tammy ran out of the room but Tom came and put his arms around the middle of his grandmother and nuzzled her, and then, moving away, with a big grin on his face, said, 'Thamma, something awesome happened today. My paper on Mark Twain was read out to the whole class.'

'Really? Are you sure?'

'Yes, Thamma.'

'Come here, let me give you a big hug!'

'Mrs Mitchell, our class teacher, said that it was very, very, good.'

'I'm so very proud of you, Tomal. See how rewarding it is to do a good job of work.'

'Yes, Thamma, it felt real great to be told how good my work was in front of all those guys in my class.'

Tammy returned to the room just then and objected, 'Stop showing off, Tom, it was all Thamma's work and . . .'

'No, Tanu, I only helped a bit.'

'Will you help me, Thamma, please, we are doing a study on our National Parks, and I've to find out about the geysers at the Yellowstone National Park.' Tammy was demanding her pound of flesh. The word 'our' had touched somewhere painfully within Nandita's heart but she said nothing and reassured her granddaughter that she would help her research the subject.

They were hungry and Nandita gave them something to their liking to eat along with a glass of milk and sat down beside them as they ate.

'Where did you get all this stuff on Mark Twain, Thamma?' Tom asked.

'Books. Make time and read more books and you'll find all the information you want from them.'

'Thamma, what did you do today? Don't you get bored when we all go away?' Kind-hearted Tanu wanted to know.

'No, I don't get bored. I have so many things to do at home and then I go for a walk.'

'Where do you go, Thamma?' Tom, becoming inquisitive, wanted to know.

'Nowhere in particular,' she lied, lowering her eyes and, wanting to change the subject, took the conversation back to Tom's project and the kudos he had received that day.

'I'm going on the comp.' And the little boy melted away.

Meeta returned soon after and, after a few desultory exchanges, was on the telephone, catching up with the world at large. And Nandita drifted away up to her room.

But goaded on by the memory of the question that she had once been posed by Bill, 'Do you make an effort, Nan, to make them feel you appreciate all that they do for you?' She took a step forward later that very same evening and came up if not a winner then a runner-up at least!

Finishing with her meal, she went and joined Meeta and Tukun in the family room where they were watching TV. They looked at one another with looks of conjecture but said nothing. Tukun had pulled a chair closer to the circle so that she could join in the viewing, and without exchanging a single word, she had sat down. It was a long time since she had done anything like this, and she had been surprised to find how enjoyable it was for her to just be there with them.

But the feeling had been short-lived for the movie they were viewing had moved on soon after from blazing guns to the beginnings of a blazing-hot love scene. The hero and heroine had gone into a record-breaking spell of kissing. Then the heroine had begun to scrabble at the hero's clothing, breaking off the buttons of his shirt as she went along. And the hero, not to be outdone, began a clumsy foray into the removing of the clothes of his partner. An embarrassed Nandita had caught on immediately that there was no room for delay here; it would be wiser to retreat, she recognised, while the protagonists were still at least partially clothed. She rose as unobtrusively as possible from her chair to flee the scene, as the hero lifted the heroine into his arms and began marching off towards a bed that lay just beyond a half-shut door. She sensed, if not heard, the sigh of relief that the young couple exhaled as she left the room. So much for the joys of companionability!

The weekend had not been so bad really, thought Nandita, but these two days were really not her own, to do what she chose to do with. The abhorred lonely weekdays of one time were now the favoured days upon the calendar for her. It was towards the weekdays that she now looked forward with an intense longing. It was a damp and drizzly Monday, the kind of day when one needed plenty of motivation to venture out! After aeons, she had acquired a number of friends; a little bit of uncomfortable weather could not possibly keep her from meeting them! Saturday and Sunday had been full of myriad activities. Guests had come to spend the weekend so the rounds of cooking had been endless. With cooking came clutter, and to be rid of the clutter came the clearing away and the cleaning up. To Nandita's utter surprise, she had caught herself humming as she had gone around taking care of the endless chores. Meeta, entering the kitchen on an errand, had caught her in mid-tune. Surprised and pleased, she had come up to her mother-in-law with a smile, and gently said, 'Please leave some of the work for me, Ma, or you'll get trimmer, and I'll get still more fat.' Nandita, unaccustomed to such exchanges for such a long time now, had smiled back at her with a hesitant uncertain look upon her face.

Oh, what a furore there was when she got to the Home that Monday.

'Did the cake work out all right?' Grace wanted to know. Ah! So, Helen had wasted no time in letting the entire Home know that she was baking a cake.

'The birthday's a long way off as yet. You'll know when it comes up because I won't be coming that day.'

'What? Whose birthday is it, Nan, that you have ta stay away for a whole day?' demanded Grace in a complaining tone of voice.

'Must be a boyfriend she's hidin' from us,' conjectured Kate.

'He is not a boyfriend, just a friend,' she muttered in her own defence.

'You are making me jealous. Who's the guy? And why do you have to make special things for him?' asked the Colonel mock-seriously.

'Just a good friend, that's all. And I will have to bake a cake for him for there's no one else here who will bake one for him,' explained Nandita.

'So why don't you bring him over?' demanded Grace. 'Scared we'll steal him from you?'

'He's not mine, so why should I worry about anyone stealing him from me?'

'Is he young? Is he handsome?' Helen wanted to know.

'Yes, he's young, much younger than I am, but I don't know whether he is handsome or not.'

'Don't ya go coy on us, honey, we can see from your looks that he is quite a handsome hunk. And quite a heart throb besides.' Helen drew a conclusion and placed it before the congregation.

'Leave the kid alone,' the Colonel, going all protective, commanded.

'I'll bring him over one day and then you can see for yourself that I am telling no lies. He's just a friend, and nothing more than that.'

'Come, Nan, let me rescue you from these biddies before they drive you crazy. I have some wonderful shots of fall at Vermont that I'd taken when I was courting. I've been wanting to show them to you since I dug them out of my cabin trunk.'

'Thought you was a landlubber, what'r you doin' with a cabin trunk?' Ted, emerging from his usual state of silent communion with the world, asked with a laugh that soon turned into a spasm of coughing. A concerned Helen flew to his side. And what with one thing and the other, the photographs taken of the fall season at Vermont had not been seen by Nandita that day.

But the chapter had certainly not been closed. The man for whom their Nan was going to bake a cake had continued to ride high in their minds and the question-and-answer session had been taken up with enthusiasm over and over again. She might have been piqued at times by their persistent, insistent sleuthing, but bored she certainly was not! Boredom for her was a thing of the past! But she did remember a time when each succeeding day used to be the veritable tasteless clone of the other.

With so many interesting things happening in her life, she could hardly believe that till not so long ago her life had been completely enclosed by the four walls of her son's home. And there was a time even further back when, warmed by the importance of being needed, that hemmed-in life had sufficed. Today, having taken a few steps away from the centre of her existence, she had been able to acquire a changed perspective and could now see the mechanics of this turnabout. There were no villains in this little drama, except for time. Little by little, as the years had piled up one upon the other, the need for her ministering to the family had gone on reducing till such time as it had dwindled into insignificance. And that home which had at one time been a haven of joy for her, her last port of call, had changed its personality and turned itself into a heartless prison. Unable to see any path of escape from within this maze in which she had got trapped, she had fallen into despair and had allowed apathy and boredom to completely take over her life.

But once she had looked out beyond the parameters of her circumscribed existence, she had found options galore to carve out a niche of her very own. And Nandita Roy the rebel who had at one time carved out a life for herself with a little boy by her side had once again emerged as an individual. Giving enough time to all her interests and all those who cared for her was fast becoming her biggest problem.

Life was getting to be rather more busy and fulfilling than she could have possibly imagined. Apportioning time between home, the inmates of the Home, and the man with an empty home was fast turning her into a master juggler of the commodity in question.

And it was at this point of her life crowded beyond measure that fate was about to heap a little bit more of spice into her life.

How it came to pass was that the game of tennis over, Tukun said to Mahadevan, 'Why don't you come home and meet my wife? Meeta has heard me speak of you so often that she's been asking me why I don't bring you over. And a quick cup of tea won't take that long.' Like a reprieve to a well-known song, Mahadevan had been cropping up far too often in far too many conversations of late! He had not forgotten how loudly Meeta had laughed while receiving the Mahadevi joke. With wives, one could never be too careful! She had better take a look at Mahadevan in the flesh and clear her mind of all doubts.

Mahadevan looked down at his watch and said, 'I have a long drive ahead, but I would love to meet your wife; and a cup of tea would be most welcome.'

And that is how Mahadevan son of Neelakanthan and Parvathi, imported from Madras, citizen of the United States of America was introduced into Tukun's home, and our heroine Nandita's life.

10 TUKUN'S PAL IN NANDITA'S DOMAIN

Life, as we have seen, was getting to be rather more fulfilling and busy than Nandita could have possibly imagined it could ever again be. And as we have observed, apportioning time between her own home, the inmates of the Home, and the man with an empty home was fast turning her into a master juggler of sorts. And it was at this point of her life, crowded beyond measure that Mahadevan, having floundered into her home and set eyes upon her, decided that she was the medicinal herb that he had been in search of.

What was ailing him? In truth, nothing in particular!

But of late, like the sluggish flow of the unctuous contents of a bowl of split *payasam*, a thin layer of slow-spreading disquiet had begun to stretch itself out like a sticky puddle from Mr Neelakanthan, his father's otherwise comfortable armchair-borne persona. And some of that stickiness had managed to reach out and touch the comfortable existence of Mahadevan as well.

The genesis of the disquiet lay in the fact that the old man hated being disturbed even if they were by thought waves. And Mrs Neelakanthan, named Savithri in the family of her birth and renamed Parvathi in the family she had acquired by marriage, had of late been beaming too many of these the old man's way! Why couldn't this woman of his understand that he was a busy man with a great deal to occupy him? She had nothing much to do but potter around the house! Well, she did cook the meals, and she appeared to be doing some other meaningless chores besides, but with all those machines at her command . . .

Newspaper in hand, a frown creasing his brows, he sat thinking. How many years was it since had they been married? His brain came up with an unbelievably huge number. Could it really be that many? Eyes screwed up, he began computing the years in right earnest and had wafted himself back into the far distant past. He fondly recollected the young man of twenty-five that he then was. One day, falling into a reminiscent mood, he had told Mahadevan, 'Looking at me now, you may not believe it, but a lot of people used to call me MGR when I was young, my son.'

'Your moustache did resemble the great cine actor's in your earlier photographs, Appa.' Mr Neelakanthan, falling into a sulk, had discontinued the conversation there and then. Huh! MGR's moustache indeed! He knew without being particularly conceited that he was a pretty dashing young fellow when he had tied the *thali* around Parvathi's neck. And Parvathi, he recollected with a sudden misting in his eyes, was such a sweet and compliant nineteen-year-old then. She still was sweet at times but certainly not compliant, he thought ruefully, throwing glance kitchenwards, where he could hear her moving around.

That dashing youth with his carefully cultivated moustache had long since left his matinee-idol image behind, and become a parched-out old man. Without any fuss or fanfare, just the other day he had crossed his eightieth birthday as well. Parvathi had been none too pleased with the want of ceremony on such an exceptionally auspicious milestone in their lives. 'An eightieth birthday needs to be properly celebrated, not a prayer has been offered by anyone, is this civilised behaviour?' She had queried in high dudgeon.

Shushing her into silence, he had offered, 'This is America,' in hushed tones. It was as if he was accepting that being in America was reason enough to give up on all one's traditions.

And to that she had said, 'Then let's go back to Madras, where people are civilised and know what is to be done on what occasion.'

Alarmed at the prospect of having to set up home once again at this age, with undue vehemence, he had spat out, 'Are you mad or what, woman?' But he had known that though the matter of going back to Madras had remained unmentioned from then on, somewhere deep down within Parvathi, a desire to go back to her roots had simmered on. Crossing boundaries, this state of perpetual discontent had begun to make its presence felt in Mahadevan's life as well! From whence it came, Mahadevan had some idea; something was ailing his Amma, but what? These days, the *sambhar* she cooked was not quite *comme il faut*, so something would have to be done and, that too, really fast!

Mahadevan had sensed that he and his wife had somewhere fallen short and had asked of his wife, 'Sumu, do you think we should have done something more for Appa's eightieth?'

'Both of us work, going into a whole lot of ceremonies, how was that possible! I baked a cake, made some *paal payasam*, bought him a tweed coat. What else does he expect?'

What Mr Neelakanthan expected on the occasion had remained unsaid but his wife Parvathi's critical comments had rekindled memories of another milestone that had marked the passage of the years in his life. He could not help but remember the pomp and grandeur with which his sixtieth birthday had been celebrated. According to the laid-down dictates of tradition, he had married his Parvathi all over again on that day. That was no mock wedding; the priest was as serious as the groom and his bride were, and the wedding feast had gone on and on. At the end of the ceremony, a number of pockets were seriously lightened, but it had refreshed their jaded marriage and given it an aura of newness. And the euphoria built up by the thanksgiving ceremony carefully garbed in ritual, pomp, and ceremony had carried them forward with renewed vigour towards the years that were yet to come. Those elders of theirs did know a thing or two about life, he had had to concede on sensing the outcome of the entire exercise!

He came out of his reverie with the harsh crashing of pots and pans reaching his ears. He had been married to Parvathi for fifty-five years, so he understood each gesture, each word, and each and every non-word that she sent his way. Or so he thought! He believed in all innocence that with the help of all the modern amenities she had at hand, she really had very little real work to do. He also believed that he was not a fussy man. After all, all he expected her to cook for him and the family was no more than a *rasam* and a *sambhar* full of titbits of tasty vegetables. A dry vegetable to go along with it was a *must* of course! It was true that he liked the coconut garnishing she used on the *porial* to be freshly grated, nothing out of a packet for him, please. And quite naturally, the curd that wound up the meal had to be set to perfection as well!

There went the orchestra again. He knew she was putting on this grand performance with the pots and pans in the hope that he too would start believing in the myth that life was hard for her in this so very soft and comfortable environment. He, for one, loved being in America. She and her *kirtana* of 'Madras, Madras, Madras,' irritated him no end. He, for one, *did not mind, not being in Madras at all.*

In search of a way out of the impasse, he had demanded of her one day, 'Why don't you learn English from the grandchildren?'

'At my age?' was all she had said!

He had thrown 'Where on earth am I going to get Tamil newspapers and magazines for you?' to her receding back. One had to make some effort to adjust. '*And that* you will not do,' muttering to himself, he had settled down, remote in hand, in front of the TV set. But later the same evening, he had told Mahadevan to search out an agent who sold Tamil newspapers.

'I've no idea where they are available. I'll see what I can do.' But why was his father looking out for a Tamil newspaper, he had wondered: were his parents missing Madras or something? Not likely, see how comfortable they were here. But one day after a game of tennis, Mahadevan had asked Tukun, 'Roy, do you know where I can get a Tamil-language paper?'

'I haven't got round to finding a Bengali one . . .'

'I was joking, forget it.' And he had laughed. 'Shall we play another set?'

But Parvathi Neelakanthan hadn't been joking. She really and truly hankered after the life she had left behind in Madras. While the very thought of this possible move homewards had sent icy shivers down Mr Neelakanthan's spine! He had absolutely no desire to go back to what he had so thankfully left behind. Oh, the innumerable unpalatable chores he had had to perform while there!

With unerring precision, a host of bills would arrive each month, causing the elderly gentleman a great deal of distress. And his litany of complaints would begin: 'The phones are dead almost all the time, the electricity is cut off just when I want to take a little rest, and the taps let go of water so stingily that you'd think that the water board was supplying liquid gold.'

He had earned but modest amounts, and after retirement, making both ends meet had become more and more difficult as the days went by. And as for the weakened state of the currency, the less said of it, the better it would be. Depleted it may have been, yet to his surprise and horror, it had always added up to become a sum that made it necessary for him to part with an income tax. He hated those income tax forms with their infinite capacity for curiosity. It wanted to know your darkest little monetary secrets with not a touch of a blush crimsoning its cheeks. Mr Neelakanthan and his income tax were forever on a collision course. He resented all those people who could and did evade income tax. It angered him to think of all those people who were getting away scot-free, even though they had incomes large enough to make Mr Neelakanthan's income look in comparison like a black flea upon the back of a big black dog.

So an invitation from his son Mahadevan asking the parents to come over and stay with them in the United States of America had appeared to be no less than a boon to him. He needed little or no persuasion to put all of these irritants behind him to move in with his dear son. Neelakanthan's son had also weighed all the pros and cons of his present-day New World existence and come to the conclusion that small inconveniences apart, the addition of Mother Dear to their household would indeed be a very beneficial one for one and all.

Like his father, Mahadevan too loved his daily Tamil fare, but sadly for his craving interior, his wife Sumathi was not quite willing to go beyond the very basics that went into the making of a genuine Iyer meal. For Mahadevan, the entity his mother Parvathi was had long since blurred into an indistinct person with an indistinct personality. But the *sambhar* his mother had always cooked had remained clearly etched in his memory. The succulent vegetables submerged in the unctuous many-flavoured, blended body of the creation made up of lentils piquantly seasoned with just the right amount of tamarind, with just a whiff of asafoetida aromatising it had to be savoured to be believed. Having Mother over just for her *sambhar* would have been reason enough to ask the parents to join them in the US.

And so he had penned a sugary letter in his rusty Tamil and invited the parents to come over and stay with them. Mr Neelakanthan was overjoyed, but his wife Parvathi, as obstinate and unimaginative as she always had been, was none too pleased at the prospect of bidding farewell to her beloved Madras. 'The house is small, but it is our own,' she had thrown at her overjoyed husband. The words had doused his buoyant spirits like a bucket of cold water. 'You can go if you like, I'm staying on here.'

'Stupid woman, can't you see your son needs you there with him?'

'Where has this son of ours been all these years, may I ask?'

'Have you forgotten the dollar cheque that comes in *your* name every month?'

'I can do without his money.'

'No, you can't.'

'So let him keep sending that money, it may make him feel a little bit less guilty about never coming home to see us.'

'I always knew you were stupid, but I had no idea that you could be this stupid. What is all this senseless grouse you are carrying around against him? And that too when he is asking to take care of us in our old age.'

'Taking care of us, are you sure?'

'No, to take care of our neighbours.' The sarcasm dripping from the words had a sharp and cutting edge to it.

'I don't want to go into that *mlechh* land where everyone eats beef. And what about the temple I visit every day?' Parvathi had ended in a wail.

'They have temples in America. Come on, stop making such a fuss over a mere nothing. If only you would read the paper sometimes, you would have come to know this simple fact.'

'I will not go.'

But the dissenting voice of Parvathi had been stilled. Once the formalities had been got over and the visas had arrived, they had sold their home and all that went into it to make it their home. With their life's belongings crammed into two suitcases, they had caught a flight from Bombay.

And now she wanted her uncomfortable life back in Madras! What was he to do?

How many times had he told Parvathi to learn English from the grandchildren? Just too many to be kept count of. He harked back to those arid, television-less days back in Madras. The Doordarshan channels had been started, but where did they have the money to buy a TV set? If you could immerse yourself in the colourful lives those characters in the serials led, you had no need whatsoever to go in search of companionship or to look so bored and left out. She may or may not have watched television but she certainly kept a watch upon what he was watching!

Parvathi seemed to have extrasensory perception, which drew her to the room where the TV was positioned just when he was immersed in watching something interesting. A female character had to just get to the point of shedding some clothes, and there she would be. It irritated him beyond measure to have her creep up behind him so that she could quietly watch him watch all those scenes of intimacy that were shown in such explicit details upon the little screen. She managed to leave him feeling guilty, where in his opinion there was no guilt to be felt at all. He was merely trying to integrate with the culture of the nation in which he now lived, so what was wrong with that? Not that she said anything to him directly but she had developed this habit of late of making disapproving sounds and repeating '*Deva, Deva, Deva,*' as she would leave the room abruptly. Mr Neelakanthan felt awfully peeved at this intrusion into his pleasurable communion with his newly found companions and friends.

Ah! Friends! That was what she really needed. If only she had some friends to distract her, then she would not plague his life as she was doing these days. Something was certainly ailing Parvathi, and a cure would have to be found sooner or later. In fact the sooner it could be, the better it would be.

That evening, Mr Neelakanthan ventured out of his meshed-in sanctuary. Braving the attack of the countless bugs that had taken to the air as soon as the sun had set, he hovered around the garage, in wait for his son. Mahadevan had arrived soon after and looked with some surprise at this unusual behaviour on the part of his father.

'Appa?' he called out questioningly. 'There are too many bugs around, why are you wandering around in the dark? Please go in.'

'I have to speak to you.'

'We can do that inside. Once I've had a wash and a change, we can talk.'

'No, wait,' said Mr Neelakanthan, restraining him.

'What is it, Appa, are you unwell?'

'No, no, I'm quite all right. It's your mother who's causing me some anxiety.'

'Is she sick?'

'No. She is bored.'

'Bored?' *Ah-ha!* He thought, *This is where the discontent is seeping out of: no wonder the sambhar. . .*

'She can't read English, and she understands very little of the spoken language as well. All she ever does, she says, is cook, cook, and cook.'

'So what do you want me to do? It's Amma and you who need Tamil *sapar* every day. The rest of us can get by with soups and things.' Mahadevan, who had 'imported' his mother from India, with an eye upon her culinary skills, had suddenly, standing in the dusky stillness of his yard, emerged as an aficionado of soups out of cans and packets.

'No, no, that's not what I was saying,' an alarmed Neelakanthan exclaimed. He did not quite like the way in which the interview with the breadwinner of the family was going. Mahadevan had not understood what he was saying; he would have to be made to understand that *he certainly had no desire to rock the boat!* Mr Neelakanthan could not imagine one single meal, not to speak of a whole series of them, which did not have all the right components to make up an edible Tamil Brahmin meal! What an idea! Soup instead of *sambhar* and *rasam!* He wanted his son's help, not his belligerence; one surly member of the family was more than enough for him. He set about the task of mollifying his son and found, on patting him, that Parvathi's delicious cooking and the purity of the clarified butter that one got here had made him put on weight! He was glad to see that it was so! A man of substance must have some substance, he felt with certitude! And without any element of doubt, his Mahadevan *was a man of substance*. Reining in his tangential thoughts, he decided then and there that this was the moment when he must speak; *he had to apprise him somehow* of the perpetual state of discontent in which his mother now lived.

'Your Amma . . .'

'What's wrong with Amma?'

'There's nothing really wrong with her but . . .'

'Then?' Mahadevan asked with some impatience as he made to move on. A bottle of bourbon was calling out to him urgently!

Mr Neelakanthan acknowledged that come what may, he must put in a word with his reluctant son. He would have liked to build up a case, but Mahadevan was fast slipping out of his hands, so he blurted out, 'Don't any of your friends have their mothers here with them?'

'Why?'

'She needs some companionship.'

'Don't you talk to her?' the son asked the father accusingly.

'I do, but I think what she needs is some feminine company.'

'I'll see what I can do.' And then he added an afterthought: 'Why don't you encourage Amma to watch some television?' And he was gone.

Neelakanthan had done just that and burnt his fingers in the bargain.

His son had said, 'Why don't you encourage Amma to watch some television?' and so he had done just that. He had coerced his wife into taking some interest in the daytime soaps that he so avidly watched. Parvathi had made many excuses about the work she still had pending but had at times come and sat obediently by his side. Had he but known the outcome of this invitation on his part, he would never have extended it in the first place. The avid pupil wanted to know who each character was, and what each one of them was saying. With so much disturbance, he barely got round to watching anything while she was seated beside him. Relationships between the characters in the story being told on the little screen had soon become of paramount interest to her. And poor Mr Neelakanthan had rued the day he had decided to act upon his son's ill-considered brainwave. Watching television with Parvathi was as relaxing as having to walk on a bed of burning coals.

And Mahadevan's wife Sumathi, passing by the family room on one such day, had been surprised to find her in-laws seated alongside, facing a colourfully lit-up TV screen. There were two sets of dialogues taking place at one and the same time, one between the protagonists upon the little screen and the other between the antagonists who were seated facing the little screen! Overhearing some part of the exchange, she later told her husband, 'Your parents have started behaving like teenagers; you should hear how they squabble over the television programmes they watch.'

And Mahadevan, more surprised than amused, asked, 'What's the matter with them?'

'How should I know? But Appa was being bombarded with questions, that I could see.'

Poor Mr Neelakanthan—oh, the questions his wife could think up! 'Who is that young woman with the straw-coloured hair?'

'She is the daughter-in-law of the family, and her hair is not straw coloured. She is a blonde.'

'Well, to my eyes it looks like straw. And that must be her husband. Her husband he may be, but must they show them together in bed?'

Mr Neelakanthan was struggling with an answer to an awkward query when fortuitously for him, she moved on without waiting for a reply to that particular enquiry that she had made.

'They must be really very rich,' she observed under her breath, making note of the obvious opulence of the sets. 'Look at the grand house in which they live.' This observation was not made under her breath as it was aimed at her husband, just as was the question that came as a corollary to it. 'Did they show a grand wedding? You should have called me to see the ceremony, you know I've never seen an American wedding.' A break came at that point, and a series of advertisements came in to take the place of the narrative. Mr Neelakanthan, free for the moment, turned his eyes upon his wife and said with the authority of a man fully in the know, 'There has been no wedding as yet.'

'How can that possibly be? She is living in his father's home and sleeping in his bed and doing *everything* to become the mother of his child! And you say they are not married,' she spelled out in a horrified tone.

'They will get married very soon,' he assured her soothingly, as if he was in constant touch with the writer of the serial.

'I hope so! I really hope so!' she said, shaking her head dolefully. In search of further facts, she enquired, 'Do the father-in-law and mother-in-law know what's going on?'

'Of course they do,' he had said with the assurance of a person well in the know of the nitty-gritty of the plot. At that point, the break was over, and a duo of characters out of the soap opera once again came onto the screen. The woman with 'straw-coloured' hair and a man considerably older than the 'husband' of the woman with 'straw-coloured' hair could be seen standing cosily together. 'There, there, see for your own self, that is the father of the hero, see for yourself how much he loves the girl,' said Mr Neelakanthan, pointing with both hands towards the television screen. He liked to put the record straight; he wanted Parvathi to realise that this was a different world, a different culture, where the right and wrong of people's actions were measured upon a different scale of values.

In response, 'Does he have to go on kissing her? It is not becoming,' was all she had to say.

'Well, this is America, and this is a story about American people.'

She fell quiet for a moment. After a short while, emerging from the depth of her brooding, with a tinge of sorrow lacing her voice, softly she said, 'I think Devan should have stayed on in India. This is no place to bring up one's children.'

Just then, the telephone began ringing stridently, incessantly in the room next to the one in which they were seated. Mr Neelakanthan hurriedly rose to attend to it. This timely intervention was like a reprieve for the elderly gentleman. For it spared him from the need to carry on immediately with the thought-provoking, piquant conversation that his wife had thrown his way. When he returned after taking the call, to his relief, Parvathi with her uncomfortable observations was no longer in the seat where he had left her. The residual part of the serial soon drew to its end, but though he sat through to the very last, it failed to entertain him as it normally was wont to do. He felt disturbed, unsettled all of a sudden today.

It was not as if he was not aware of all the lurking dangers that lay below this life of comfort. He just ignored all that was going on around him and lived his days out without asking too many uncomfortable questions. He very often felt discomfited by the behaviour, the attire, and the conversation of the grandchildren. The challenging tone in which his grandson spoke to his own mother, he was surprised to note, was allowed to let pass without so much as a gentle reprimand. Why did they not teach him a more polite manner of speaking? Just because it was acceptable in an American child, should it have been acceptable in this Tamil Brahmin lad? He would have liked to bring about some changes in the upbringing of the children, but he was sagacious enough to know that there was not much he could really do.

Mahadevan and his wife Sumathi had chosen the American way of life in its totality; for them, the sun rose and the sun set over the United States, and in the United States alone. So what could he possibly do against such convictions as they had? Could he, would he ask Mahadevan to leave all of this to go back to an uncertain future, a far smaller rupee-salary job in Madras? And would Mahadevan move back? He knew with an absolute certainty that he would never go back from this life that he had carved out for himself here. He also knew that this was where they would all have to stay to the very end of their lives. Unlike Parvathi, he was a realist and had therefore decided to make the most of this uncluttered life, where he was not dogged with myriad problems. He knew of an endless number of elderly couples who had been abandoned back home in India by their children. Parvathi should be grateful that they were being sheltered in their old age by Mahadevan, their one and only son.

He sat thinking, rationalising the position in which they were now, fixed for the rest of their remaining lives in the home of their son. He was neither insensitive, nor was he an ignorant fool that he did not understand the anxieties that assailed Parvathi's mind from time to time. He did quite often ask himself, What is this milieu going to do to the grandchildren? And today more than any other day, the question had come back to plague his peace of mind. The TV had been meandering on in low key as he sat thinking; switching off the set, he pulled down upon the crotch of his trousers to dislodge and rearrange his wandering balls.

He knew there really was no escape from this life that their son Mahadevan had chosen to lead. Whatever was to happen to Mahadevan's children in this life had already been pre-assigned to them by their own past *karma*, he rationalised. True, it was not one's past *karma* alone that shaped one's life; the life one lived and led here and now would also come to bear upon it. He sighed, got up, and went in search of the horoscopes that he had so carefully had drawn out by a great *pundit* in Madras when the three grandchildren had in turn been born. Reassured to an extent by what they predicted, he wandered out onto the yard. The patch of green was soothing to his ruffled senses.

When Mahadevan came home after a long day's work, he was surprised to find his father out in the yard where he rarely ventured after sundown. He was normally to be found glued to the TV. What was it, he wondered, that had drawn his father away from his magnet? *Was Amma still on the warpath? Had the TV failed to work its wonders upon her?* He had thrown a tentative glance his father's way and while loosening his tie but, as he had said nothing, had walked into the house through the mesh door at the back. Mr Neelakanthan had wanted to voice his concerns to his son; but what was he to say? He had gone in a little while later. The gnats were out, and a sudden chill had crept into the air!

Life continued to go on in much the same way. The son and the daughter-in-law at work, the grandchildren at school, he immersed in his newspaper and his lifeline, the ever-entertaining television, and his wife in her kitchen. But once too often, Parvathi had continued to ruffle his equanimity. She managed to make him feel guilty where there was no guilt at all.

Here he was, married for centuries (or so it appeared) and not once, yes, not once had he strayed from the straight and narrow, except perhaps in a chance thought or two! 'But then, a man is not like a woman that at forty-five or fifty, he should cease to have any interest in, uh, hum, interest in,' under his breath, he muttered to himself. His puritanical upbringing had not allowed him to mouth, even to himself, what exactly it was that a man wanted to continue to be interested in! Life without a little bit of excitement was like eating a meal made up of cardboard. Surely a man should be allowed to sprinkle a little spice onto that cardboard to make it edible? Television as it prevailed in America had certainly spiced up his life to an extent.

But the last straw, which had broken the camel's back, had been the last cross-questioning session he had had to undergo when Parvathi had decided to join him as she did on occasion to watch some television. The selfsame serialised soap opera in which the young woman with straw-coloured hair was the heroine had evinced her interest. Though she understood very little of the English dialogue, the familiar faces upon the screen had drawn her to his side. She sat cutting beans, and Mr Neelakanthan sat hoping that she would not notice any discrepancies in the storyline. Since she had last sat with him, the characters had been busy changing their allegiances. All was well for a while, but only for a while; her hawk eyes had fallen upon a scene that had shocked her beyond measure! The knife had slipped out of her hands, and the chopping up of the beans forgotten, she had let out an anguished expletive of disgust in the purest of Tamil.

Turning accusingly towards her husband, Parvathi had demanded, 'What is that young woman doing in *that* fellow's bed?'

'She is his wife.'

'What, do you think I'm a fool or something? I remember very clearly that you told me she is his daughter-in-law, and now you tell me she is his wife.' The tone was accusative, and a riled Mr Neelakanthan had not liked it at all.

'*I did not tell you that she is his daughter-in-law. I merely told you that she was living as a wife with his son.*' He had no idea why he was trying to put the record straight, but there he was, trying to do so as if he himself had done something wrong.

'What has he done to his wife and his son?'

'Nothing, they have accepted the situation. The wife has divorced him and the son has got himself a new girlfriend.'

'*Deva, Deva, Deva,* what a horrible unholy society this is. I've been telling you all along that this was not a fit place for civilised people to live in. But no, you had to come here to besmirch the last years of our lives. You can stay here if you like. Ask Mahadevan to get me a ticket. I'll go to Madras and live out the rest of my years with my brother there.'

'You think your brother is waiting for you there with a band of wedding musicians?' Sarcasm dripping from every word, he challenged her.

She rose and went away inside without uttering another word. And the long drawn-out silences that had followed thereafter had spoken far louder than any speech could ever have. And some part of that silence, oozing discontent, had poured out into her *rasam*, and her *sambhar* had continued to touch both Mahadevan's taste buds and his life!

And then Sudipto Roy had invited him home and Mahadevan had accepted, saying, 'The offer is tempting. I'll call my wife and tell her.'

'Meeta,' Sudipto called out on letting himself and his companion in. Lowering his tennis gear onto the floor, he made Mahadevan comfortable and then went in search of his wife. 'Meeta,' he called out a little louder again, 'could we have a cup of tea please?'

It was his mother who had responded to his call, in Bangla, and out of Mahadevan's earshot. 'Meeta has taken Tanu to her ballet class. I'll make you a cup . . .'

'Could you make that two, please?' Lowering his voice, he added, 'I have brought along the Tamil gentleman with whom I play tennis these days.'

'Shall I fry a few *pakoras*?'

'If it's not too much trouble. Will you please!' And he went back to his guest.

When Nandita came into the living room, tea tray in hand, her first thought was *Tukun should have put on some lights, I hope I don't trip over something.*

In the descending gloom, all that Mahadevan's eyes had caught was the slender and tall frame of the woman who had just entered. 'How many years did his in-laws manage to hide while marrying her off to this fellow,' he conjectured as he rose and did a *namaste*. 'Sorry to have caused you so much trouble, Mrs Roy.'

'Making a cup of tea can hardly be called trouble,' she said, while putting down the tray with a smile. Suddenly becoming aware of the shortage of light, Sudipto rose and went towards the light switches.

'I'd better put on some lights. It has suddenly gone rather dark.' Turning to his guest and pointing to Nandita, he said, 'And, Mahadevan, let me introduce you to her, she's my mother.'

Mahadevan swallowed hard, composed himself, and made a shallow drive for Nandita's feet and lay arms outstretched, completely prostrated at her feet. He had to make up and, that too, swiftly, for his recalcitrant thoughts.

Nandita, taken by surprise, had rocked back on her heels. Regaining her balance, she took a step or two backward.

Of late, all was not well with Mahadevan's neatly docketed and structured world. His father had been sending out signals to him, as had the downswing in his mother's culinary outputs. And his father had suggested that he 'find her a friend'. Living as he did in a housing estate (more an empire) where both the colours black and brown were but scarcely to be seen, he did not see where he would find this friend his father had ordered him to acquire! Having seen Nandita, an NRI mother in the flesh, he felt hope burgeon in his heart. Rising from his prone position, with folded palms, the penitent stated, 'Ammaji, I am your son's friend. So please do treat me as your son. I shall be honoured if you would condescend to do so.'

Nandita was disconcerted by this sudden show of respect and devotion on the part of a total stranger. She was hard-pressed to decide how she was to handle the situation, as she was not feeling in any way maternal towards this portly middle-aged man. Yet, as he was a friend of Tukun's, she did not wish to make her feelings too obvious to him. So she had showered as benign a smile as she could muster upon this man with a bulging belly, standing before her.

What Mahadevan saw standing before him, on the other hand, was the panacea to all his ills; she was the herb from the Gandhamadhan Mountain that his father had asked him to find for his ailing mother. Unlike Sri Ram, he did not have a faithful Hanuman who would rush off and fly back carrying a whole mountain, from which just the right medicinal herb could be plucked off and administered to the ailing patient, in that instance his brother Laxman. The words of his father spoken to him in the gnat-infested gloom of their backyard came back to him in a total recall. Neelakanthan his father had asked him to produce a magical entity called a mother, specifically an Indian mother, the progenitor of an Indian living in the United States. And here she was, right there in front of his eyes.

There must have been an endless number of mothers of immigrants from India tucked away in boundless homes, but where was he to go in search of them? Thankfully the search was over. Though he had rashly told Appa that Amma cooked Tamil Iyer *sapar* only to please his and her own palates, an inner voice had told him that it was not the truth. An Amma on the warpath was equal to a rainless monsoon season afflicting their lives. He could visualise the drought-ridden barren state of the dining table if that were to come to pass. His stomach had churned at the very prospect and he decided then and there that this lady standing before him would somehow have to be recruited towards bettering his cause!

'It was nice meeting you,' said the panacea to all his ills, 'but I have a little work to do, so if you don't mind . . .' And with a smile and a *namaste*, she was gone.

As Mahadevan drank the tea and ate the just-fried *pakoras* and conversed in monosyllables with his host, a part of his brain had kept weighing up the elements of the medication which he had just discovered. Had this fellow Roy's mother been a little bit older, a little bit less modern, then he would have felt a trifle more comfortable. He would have been better pleased had the lady in question not had such an apparent air of self- assurance about her. It managed somehow to take the authenticity away from her *Desi mother stuck at home* image. And finally, he thought it would be totally improbable that she would be speaking any Tamil at all. He sighed heavily, lamenting the fact that all Indians were not fully civilised; otherwise, they all surely would have spoken some Tamil! All the same, he took a long shot, not just a long shot, but a very long shot.

'Does your mother speak Tamil?' he asked without going into any preamble.

'I'm afraid not, our family has never lived in South India. Did I by any chance give you the impression that we had lived down south?'

'Not at all, Roy, I was just wondering, or rather hoping, that is all. My parents live here with me and my mother could do with some companionship, so I thought perhaps . . .'

'I think my mother is also very bored. None of us are here at home, you know how it is? And even when the kids get back, they have their own things to do. Does your mother speak Hindi?'

'Yes, a little,' lied Mahadevan, sensing some interest on the part of Sudipto as well.

'That's interesting.'

'They should meet, I think,' Mahadevan added, pinning down the advantage he supposed he had gained.

'We'll have to fix up something,' Sudipto muttered in a vague non-committal tone.

Mahadevan, pressing his point, said, 'It would be nice if your mother could come and spend a day with Amma. I am sure they would both enjoy one another's company. You see, as Appa is at home, it would be more practical if . . .'

'I can understand. It would be easier, I think, for my mother to go over.'

'They should be able to find many a point of common interest between them,' said Mahadevan.

Looking towards Mahadevan, Tukun offered, 'I suppose I could drop her off on my way to work and—'

'Don't worry,' cut in Mahadevan ingratiatingly, 'my wife Sumathi comes home quite early from work, she can drop your mother back in the evening.'

'That sounds good. I'll speak to my mother about it. I'm sure she'll be happy to get this opportunity to meet some other people apart from us.'

When Mahadevan had gone home and gleefully informed his parents of the impending visit of Nandita, an Indian mother living in 'exile' in the United States of America, the reactions of the two parts of the whole that made up his parentage were diametrically opposite to the other. Mr Neelakanthan barely held himself back from chortling with joy, and Mrs Neelakanthan left the room in deep dudgeon.

'*Deva, Deva, Deva,*' she could be heard muttering, 'this Devan has gone completely out of his head. What does he think I should do with this totally strange Bengali woman the whole day? And who is going to cook for this guest, may I ask?' Emerging from her room, she had thrown, 'Tell that son of yours to tell her not to come, she speaks no Tamil and I don't know a single word of the strange tongue in which she speaks.'

'Don't be stupid, after having invited a person, how can you tell that person not to come?'

'I didn't ask her to come, so why should I carry her around on my shoulders for a whole day? And if Devan insists on her coming here then *his* wife can cook for this favourite guest of his before going to work. *I refuse to do any more work than I am already doing.*'

'Who is asking you to work?'

'*Hah! No one.*' Those three little words were replete with sarcasm. She glared down upon him.

The disconcerted husband, attempting an unaccustomed hand at mollification, said, 'I will ask Sumathi to cook for her. Satisfied?' She still kept looking down angrily at him, so raising his voice he threw, 'Devan goes out of the way to find a friend for you and see how you react.'

'You want me to dance the *Bharatanatyam* or what?' she hurled back.

'You are impossible, all Devan was trying to do was to help you.' He paused for a moment to get his breath back and then, trying to reason it out with her, went on in a cajoling tone, 'Once she comes here, you'll realise how nice it is for you to have a friend.'

'Huh!' was all the response he got from her as she left the room in high dudgeon.

Obviously, this friendship business that they had engineered was not going off as well as Mr Neelakanthan and his son had anticipated. They had thought it would bring the stars to the eyes of the most senior lady of the house; instead, it had gone and placed a frown upon the face of the next in command as well. Womenfolk were so contrary, mused Mr Neelakanthan as he settled down, remote in hand, before the television set the next day. Do them a good turn and find out for yourself how it boomeranged on you! Mahadevan also was none too happy with the way the womenfolk of the household were reacting. His mother, he could see, was even more on the warpath now than she had been before. Sumathi had got into a bad mood on hearing that she was expected to cook for this guest who was being brought into their home from god knows where. Cooking a meal or two once in a while was all very well, but just supposing this were to set a precedent and she would be expected thereafter to cook every single day for the whole family before going out to work? It did not affect Mahadevan's life, so why should he consider the far-reaching consequences of his rash action?

Sumathi's ruffled feathers had continued to remain ruffled, and Mahadevan wondered why on earth he had listened to his father and got himself into this uncomfortable mess. At fifty plus, a man needed some harmony and peace in his life. In trying to defuse some imagined tension thought up by Appa, he had gone and generated some real tangible tension in his own life. Life was not as easy as it appeared to be on the surface. No one in this family of his understood how difficult it was to work in an environment where a wonderful job could be here today and gone tomorrow. Keeping his grip from slipping in the slippery job market always kept him on tenterhooks. On top of that, a middle-aged spread had also emerged and become rather worrisome of late. He knew a bulging belly could well give a butt in his bulging belly in this highly competitive dog-eat-dog work environment! He hated exercising, he hated games and sports, and he hated knocking tennis balls around with men far fitter and far younger than he was, in order to combat the growth of his runaway girth. And now Sumathi's frowning face had been added on to the list of his bugbears.

And Sudipto, having somehow been swept along by Mahadevan's enthusiasm to bring the two mothers together, agreed to take Nandita over to their home very soon one day. With utter short-sightedness on his part, it had not once crossed his mind to cross-check with her to find out what she felt about the whole scheme. As far as he knew, his mother was a lonely person in need of some company, and here was company being offered to her upon a platter! Mahadevan had left soon after and Sudipto allowed the proposal that had just been made by Mahadevan to lie simmering awhile within his brain.

He knew all was not as it once was today; a yawning chasm of silence lay between him and his mother. He did not know how this state of non-communication between them had come about. It had happened so slowly, so insidiously that he had sensed it only when it had come upon him in its full-blown form. The chill winds that blew between them with each attempt at communication that they made with one another and the silences that reigned between them at all other times had surprised and hurt him. As far as he knew, he was a good-enough son; he had not left her behind to fade away alone in her lonely far-off Calcutta flat, as so many had done. He took care of her every need, didn't he? Then what was it that had made her so remote and uncaring?

He had thought long and hard upon the matter and come to the conclusion that *there were no genuine reasons* for this change in behaviour on her part. Yet his mother, his one-time most reasonable mother, was growing more and more unreasonable as the days were going by. Perhaps it was the effects of ageing, he rationalised; but in truth, he really did not know. But she was somehow no longer the person she earlier was.

When she had arrived from Calcutta to live with them, things were quite naturally somewhat different; Meeta used to be far more at home, and the children were always there. But then, life was not a static, unmoving, unchanging veracity. Things had changed for one and all and so also for Meeta. Today she had moved out of her earlier circuit of half a day at work, once-a-week visit to the supermarket and back into her home for the rest of the time left with her, schedule. A more time-consuming job, new friends, newly found interests, new associations had all come in to fill up her days. And living with a mother-in-law forever and ever was not an easy job, Meeta had impressed upon her husband. And Tukun had had to admit that Meeta had no way out with her to opt out of the situation! Meeta was for sure stuck with his mother, with no escape at all available to her. Seeing how his mother had changed and become these days, he could not help but feel sympathetic towards his wife. She was a very good wife indeed! His American colleagues marvelled at how his mother and his wife were coexisting at all.

And as for the children, well, children did grow out of their babyhood to grow up into independent little things. Yes, independent little things, with schools and school friends, with games and sports and studies! Yes, independent little things, with television programmes of their choice attracting them like magnets. With game gear and video games turning them into fiercely competitive, bloodthirsty killers with lethal weapons spewing death in their hands, they had little or no time left to spare. They had neither the time nor the inclination to interact with anything or anybody that lay outside the boundaries of this exciting world. Gone were the days when they would cling to their grandmother and trail around behind her wherever she went, whichever way she moved.

Sudipto himself had been climbing the ladder of success at more than just a steady pace, and with success, his responsibilities in the workplace had gone up by leaps and bounds. The manifold pressures of this career of his on the upsurge had left a mark on his personality and had perhaps robbed him of some of his sensitivity! With the passage of time, he had also acquired a bigger and better home, a pair of shinier cars, more fashionable friends, and a few new pastimes besides. Time was always in very short supply with him now, but it was not just that. For even had he not been as short of time and even if he had made time to sit down to speak with his mother, what would they have spoken about beyond two sentences to each other?

At one time, his mother had been such an interesting person to be with; today, the same woman had somehow dwindled into being a very boring and repetitive person. What was it that had made her change so much? He really and truly had to make an effort to get into any genuine conversation with her. He could not quite condone this attitude of his, and so at times, he felt guilty that he spent so little time with her. But that sense of guilt did more harm than it did good, for it drove him on to an undue shortness with Nandita his mother, whenever the two of them happened to exchange a few words. And nagging, his conscience once again would come up with the old question, why had she changed so much?

What he did not recognise or realise was that his mother cut off from all her earlier intellectual sources was, in a manner of speaking, subsisting on a starvation diet. For a long time now, she had not been in a position to accrue the wealth of new experiences, so where did she have the wherewithal to deposit any residue into her account? She had already withdrawn all the earlier deposits and today no credit remained with her to draw upon.

And he knew nothing of the remittances to her account that she had so recently made!

Mahadevan, a man with whom he thrashed around a ball on a tennis court, had thrown an idea his way, and willy-nilly, Sudipto had decided to go along with it. All that remained now was for him to inform his mother of this forthcoming visit. Should he ask her to go over to meet them tomorrow, or should he propose another day to her? Before making any decision, he would have to take a look at his own early morning fixtures, he reminded himself as he drove into his garage. When he let himself in, Nandita was the only one at home. Meeta had gone on a ferrying duty; the children seemed to have so many appointments that what they really needed was a full-time chauffeur. In the meantime, the mother was filling in for the post. Nandita was seated, book in hand, in the family room. She looked up from what she was reading and asked, 'Shall I make you a cup of tea, Khoka?'

'Let it be, Ma, it's already quite late, Meeta will want us to have dinner as soon as she gets back.'

Nandita chose to keep her council; dinner at seven in the evening for a grown-up man because his children would have to go to school at seven the next day was not her idea of a sensible practice. A man needed to take a breather when he got back from work. She had learnt a long time ago that subjects such as these were best left untouched. The violent reactions that she had encountered in trying to air her opinion had taught her that silence was the language of the sagacious. As Tukun did not want anything, she went back to her book. Her interest in Vietnam and the war that had been fought there had been kindled through her constant interaction with her friends, so many of them the victims of this major misadventure. This was the book that had been lent, in tandem with a book on the history of the United States of America, by her friend the Colonel. It was heavy work getting into reading a book such as this; but once it had got hold of you, it allowed no path of escape.

She remembered his words of caution as she had ploughed through its harrowing yet engrossing pages. 'Read the book if you must, Nan, but I sure do hope you have a strong stomach.' Sorrow had seeped through her entire being but she had read on. So engrossed was Nandita in that chronicle of war that she did not observe her son observing her as she sat reading. He had not paid much attention to her in a long while. His mother was there, and that was all there was to it! He was surprised to note a look of tranquillity upon her face that had been missing for a very long time. Come to think of it, he had sensed in some way that a change was slowly coming about in his mother. What that change really was or what it augured, he really did not know. He studied the passage of expressions flitting across her face as she sat reading. And suddenly transported back in time, he remembered his young mother the teacher, as she had sat reading preparing for her Master of Education exams. He must have been eleven or twelve, no more, at that time.

He would sit beside her and work at his maths while he could keep awake. One bulb was all that would be put on at a time, she had told him, and it was just the light of that one bulb that they had shared between them. It was from her that he had learnt the art of giving total undivided attention to the job that one had at that moment in hand. He remembered those days when waking in thirst sometime late, late into the night, he had found that single bulb still glowing on. Her daytime hours were already leased out but the nights were even then hers to use as she wished. When the results were declared, everyone asked where had Nandita found the time to do what she had done. She had topped in her subject in the entire Calcutta University! And for this brilliant performance, her school had rewarded her with a fifty-rupee increment in her salary, he remembered. Just a book in his mother's hand and he had been transported back to those days full of happiness and the remembrance of *that* unique and wonderful mother that was, had filled his restless heart with nostalgia.

The wash was done; the shrill whistle of the washing machine had fallen jarringly upon his ears and jolted him out of his reverie. One look at his watch and he knew he had only a little time in which he would be able to speak to his mother without interruption.

'Ma,' he spoke up, attracting her attention.

She looked up and, placing a bookmark at the right page, shut the book and put it down upon the nearest table.

'Yes, Tukun?'

'I know you're lonely so when a friend of mine suggested you visit his mother . . .'

'Yes?'

'I said you'd love to meet her.'

'Without asking me?' frowning, she asked.

'I didn't know you'd feel this way.'

'No, no, it's nothing like that. I really don't have time to spare, that's all.'

'You don't have time in the daytime, Ma? Are we loading you with so much work?'

'Will she be coming here . . . or will I have to go?'

'She won't be able to come; her husband is there at home. I understand he's quite old. They are the parents of Mahadevan, who came home with me that day.'

She remembered Mahadevan and his *shashtanga pranam* very clearly. 'I see,' was all she said!

'I'll drop you off in the morning and Mahadevan's wife will reach you back in the evening.'

'As you've already told them, then . . . I suppose . . . I'll have to . . .'

'I can tell them you won't be able to come.'

'No. Now that you have promised . . . don't do that.'

'Thanks!'

'Let me see, Monday and Tuesday are absolutely out for me, if it's suitable for them, I'll spend Wednesday with Mahadevan's mother. But in the future, please do not commit on my behalf without asking me.'

Sudipto was taken aback by her tone of quiet dignity and assurance. The gentle reprimand underlying her words were not lost upon him, and he wondered, what had brought about the resurgence of his mother as she was in those years of her struggle back in Calcutta? A nonplussed Sudipto felt like a child rebuked for a misdemeanour as he saw her gather up her book and leave the room. It was long years since he had felt this way!

His wife and children returned soon after and he set aside the conundrum and got down to the business of getting over and done with the meal at hand. Nandita had never accepted the dinner-at-seven regimen imposed by Meeta upon the family. She would come down much later when the rest of the family would have moved on to doing their own things, and eat her simple vegetarian meal in isolation. Though she had toyed on occasion with the idea of making a change, she had not got round to doing it yet. One day perhaps she would; but at present, she would let things be as they had been for the past so-many years!

But as of now, what was she to do with the immediate problem of handling her very demanding, very childlike elderly friends? Having just handed them the news of her impending absence from them on Bill's birthday, she was in a quandary as to what she was going to tell them. She dreaded the prospect of adding yet another day of absence to the one she had just had sanctioned from them. Juggling all the demands upon her time was getting to be a real problem.

What had prompted Tukun to design a social life for her, she wondered, as, book in hand, she sat on, bemused by circumstances.

11 RUFFLED FEATHERS

'A birthday party for some unknown guy and now this,' grumbled Grace. 'I'm kinda gettin' jealous of all these new friends of yours, honey.'

'Friend! I don't even know her.'

'Then why're you going?'

'I have to,' she pleaded, 'my son has gone and promised that I would.'

'Why?'

'Because I think both his tennis partner and he think that their mothers are pining away for India.'

'Are you pining for India?' the Colonel, seated alongside, asked with a tinge of belligerence in his tone.

'Why should I, when I have all of you?' And then a thought flitted through her mind: *perhaps Mahadevan's mother has no friends at all.*

'Does she live alone?' someone asked.

'With her family. She even has a husband, I know.'

'Then?' demanded the Colonel.

'I have no idea, Colonel.' And within her heart, she said, *We all know that one doesn't have to be alone to feel alone, don't we?*

Slowly, the news of her impending visit to Mahadevan's home seeped out and reached a number of ears. 'A birthday party and now this, is Nan planning to abandon us?' was the war cry.

'Make sure you're here on Thursday,' Grace admonished.

'You've got us used to havin' you around, so report back in time, otherwise I'll have you marked AWOL,' the Colonel warned.

Kate smiled a limpid smile and urged her in her vapid way to come back as soon as possible.

And Helen, holding hands with Ted, mischievously enquired, 'Are you sure, honey, you're goin' to meet a countrywoman of yours? And not goin' a-jaunterin' with that there boyfriend of yours?' And Nandita marvelled at how perky and vibrant this Helen in love had become in comparison to the Helen she had first met. And then holding on to Ted's hand, Helen enquired, 'A little get-together before the birthday bash perhaps?'

Nandita felt heat rushing to her face and, like a schoolgirl caught cheating in an examination, denied the charges most vehemently.

'I really am going to visit a countrywoman of mine.'

But as she remonstrated with the laughter-filled questioning voice and all those questioning eyes brimful of amusement, the face of Bill, his eyes alight with life, had come floating in and made her heart skip a beat. She was confused at this intrusion and her reaction to it. Why should the memory of his blue eyes crinkling at the corners make her react as she had done? He was younger, yes, a good bit younger than her! And incongruously, out of context, she remembered Thakuma objecting to a *very grown-up* eighteen-year-old Nandita making a match with a *very young* Prodipto who was then already past twenty-three.

Bill her boyfriend indeed!

He loved his Meg and missed her. He had needed a friend and a companion to help him tide over his sense of utter desolation. And she had been discovered at that precise moment of his acute need, sandwich in hand, seated on a bench in downtown Saisborough! And she, feeling lost and vulnerable, having just posted that letter to Rekha screaming warnings to her to stay away from this misadventure that was called *joining one's children to give them a helping hand*, had welcomed, without realising, this intrusion by an outstretched hand into her life.

And from there had begun her journey away from the stranglehold of traditionalism into which she had enmeshed herself. The person she was today and the person she had left behind on stepping out of the confines of her home were apparently the same individual, but in truth, they were no longer one and the same person today. So far had their personas drifted apart that had they met by accident on a lonely road, that other part of Nandita's self might have had some difficulty in recognising this new manifestation of her own self!

Bill and she had come together because his loneliness had met up with hers. It was no more than that; and from there, their friendship had bloomed and become . . . become . . . what? Her mind in turmoil, facing an uncomfortable question to which she preferred not to give an answer, she once again denied the charge made in jest by Helen, but this time with far greater emphasis than such a simple little question really demanded.

'No, Helen, I have no boyfriend, how could you possibly think I could have one?'

The vehemence with which she reiterated her earlier denial was so marked that it made Grace look at her young friend's face and wonder.

'Because you're young and beautiful, and . . . life's so short. Get yourself one, honey, if you haven't got one yet,' Helen urged, 'just as I've got myself this wonderful man.' And Helen gave a resounding kiss on the wonderful man's nearest available cheek and proved her point.

'Young and beautiful?'

And Grace looked on and thought, *Yeah, why not? This girl Nan should as sure as there are seven days to a week get herself a man! She's a lovely girl, yeah, she really is a lovely girl.* She would have to urge her to move on with her life.

'Hey, Nan . . . Helen there has a real good idea, believe you me,' chipped in Grace. 'It's a pity though that the youngest guys around here have all said their goodbyes to their seventieth, years ago.' And she chuckled like a little baby enticed by a rattle in its hand. Everyone laughed at Grace's huge joke, but all of them agreed that doing some matchmaking for 'young' Nan would be a real fun thing, except for Nandita herself, who did not think that it was such a funny matter at all.

'I am a grandmother twice over and certainly too old for all that stuff now, so . . .'

'With so many great-grandmamas around, you're impressing no one,' spoke up a voice from somewhere behind.

'No more talk about boyfriends, please.' Nandita, brooking no interruption, concluded.

'Just as I was thinking of proposing to her, she says, "No boyfriends, please." I'm barely past eighty and can do with a gal. Can't you change your mind for me, please?' the Colonel coaxed, and followed it up with a chuckle as he pirouetted playfully in his wheelchair.

Nandita, though embarrassed, laughed along with the rest. Then to the utter relief of Nandita, the subject veered around to the weather and how hot it was getting to be day by day.

'We go to the rose garden but only in the evening. Thank God, Nan, that you came to see me when I fell ill, otherwise we may never have met again. You usually run home as soon as we go to rest, so . . .'

'The kids get home before their mother gets back,' she justified. The word 'kids' had slipped out smoothly: the United States of America, now that she had opened her arms wide to it, was absorbing her little by little by little into its embrace! 'Take care,' she said, kissing Grace on both her cheeks on her way out.

'Don't play hooky on the way, see you get home safe and sound,' Grace ribbed Nandita. 'We'll wait for you on Thursday.'

And having somehow appeased her friends, Nandita made her way home.

But there was no appeasing Mahadevan's wife! If her mother-in-law was so desperate for company, then it should be *she* who should *do the needful*, Sumathi indicated to her husband. Mahadevan had invited Sudipto Roy's mother without realising that that there was more to a simple invitation than that which met the eye. Arguments had flown back and forth between the husband and wife, but even so, come late evening, Sumathi had found that she was still holding on to the portfolio of provender of a luncheon for the historic visit between mothers that was to be held at their home. As of now, Mahadevan, though mauled, had won the round, but he knew he would have to pay for his folly sooner rather than later.

The day was more or less done, and having retired to the confines of their own room, Sumathi asked Mahadevan, 'What do these Bengalis eat?' Her brows crowding together, she had a pot of wrinkle-eradicating cream in hand. Mahadevan was reading one of those Deepak Chopra books to see what really made them sell. Could he not write something similar to this, he was questioning himself when his wife's voice asking this weird question caught hold of his wandering mind and brought it back down to earth.

Placing a bookmark at the right place, he took off his glasses; putting them aside carefully, head aslant, he pondered the sight of his wife rubbing some wrinkle-eradicating cream into her face, wondering where all that stuff went, considering he had seen the contents of a series of such jars disappearing without making any obvious difference to that selfsame face for so many years. And then he replied, 'I've no idea,' with a shake of his head.

'Thank you for the help, Mr Mahadevan.'

Touched to the quick, his brain had gone into a whirl. He could almost see and smell the hostel dining room teeming with students, at the IIT, where he had eaten for four long years. The food was far from satisfactory but the Bengali component among the students had more complaints to make about the food than anyone else ever voiced. There was one segment of their complaint, however, that had stuck too far out to go unnoticed. And pleased with himself, he decided to exonerate himself by displaying that bit of retrieved information to his wife. 'There were a few Bongs with us at Powai and I remember clearly that they were forever cribbing about the absence of fish in the meals the canteen manager served us.'

He was rudely cut short. 'So? What do you want me to do, cook fish for this old woman or what?' Sarcasm dripping in every word, Sumathi asked her already harassed husband as she screwed the cap of the jar of cream onto it and thumped it back onto the dressing table where it normally resided. The missile had gone haywire; forgetting that it was not a boomerang, it came and landed back from where it had been fired.

'Why are you being so difficult, Sumu? *Fish and our home*, what a crazy idea,' he remonstrated while a part of his mind wondered whether labelling Sudipto's mother as an old woman would be the right thing to do.

'That's just it; the whole idea of yours was a crazy one. Why don't you cook for her yourself?'

'I don't know how to cook, and Amma is on the warpath; otherwise . . .'

'*You're the one who has invited her*,' she reminded him promptly as she got into bed beside him and, covering herself, lay down. 'Hope this is not going to be the beginning of a permanent tools-down by your Amma,' she grumbled, pushing her pillows into a more comfortable position. 'You can take it from me *I'm not going to cook all that stuff that you and your father can't do without every day.*'

'*Don't I know that?* For heaven's sake, cook a potato curry or something, and get done with it, please. I don't know why I allowed Appa to talk me into this messy situation. All I was trying to do was to bring about some peace in this home, instead I find a battle of Kurukshetra raging around me.' Muttering in disgust, he turned on his side and shut his eyes, thereby putting to an end the troublesome conversation. Sumathi had known all along that she was fighting a losing battle. With her mother-in-law launching a non-co-operation movement, she had known she would have to produce a meal whatever argument she might put forward against the motion. But she was glad that she had given Mahadevan a thing or two to think about. *Why should I let him off the hook without giving him a few uncomfortable turns?* she asked of herself as she drifted off into sleep. She rose earlier than she normally did and went into the kitchen and managed, by cutting corners, to produce a meal of sorts by expending a very economical outlay of time. *But that she, Sumathi, wife of Mahadevan, was cooking was audible to one and all.* And eventually more than just a potato curry was produced, for whoever had ever heard of a single-instrument orchestra? Trust Mahadevan to make a suggestion as senseless as that!

Parvathi had quite enjoyed the commotion that had been orchestrated by her but had not shown her face outside her room that morning. Mahadevan crept around looking sheepish while his father looked extremely cross as he sat around with the newspaper, waiting for the storm to abate.

On the other hand, no cymbals had crashed in the Roy household, nor had any protest flags been hoisted, for though Nandita was none too enthusiastic about this outing, she had no desire to let her son down. She had risen earlier than usual, bathed, performed puja, and worn one out of her many white-blouse-and-white-sari outfits. Her wavy hair was still damp when she had parted her hair down the centre, combed it down flat on either side of the parting, and tied it into a loose bun at the nape of her neck. Devoid of any jewellery, her slender neck stood out in a clear classical line upon her shoulders. She picked up a small purse, stuffed in a few dollars, a pen, and a handkerchief and went down to wait for Tukun, who was to transport her to the home of Mahadevan.

The kitchen was empty, and the house emptied of the three voices on collision course lay silent. She had toasted a slice of bread, smeared a dash of butter on it, and eaten it accompanied by a small glass of orange juice. She looked down at her watch and, satisfied, had sat back.

Mr Sudipto Roy, dressed appropriately to give battle to the day, had come down from his room soon after and was pleased to find his mother already there. Pausing at the entrance to the kitchen, unobserved by her, he stood a moment looking at her. She reminded him today of someone he had known far back in time. A familiar friend of his from long ago! And as he stood there, he had a sudden throwback into his past and felt for a fleeting moment that she was waiting patiently to go to school together with him, as she had done for years. There was a major departure from that routine though, for she had arranged no breakfast for him today, and that had hurt. That apart, the woman in white seated in his kitchen at Saisborough looked in the early-morning light very much like the mother who had waited for him each day in her kitchen in Calcutta. Was it so surprising really that she was ready and waiting for him today? Had she not always been very particular about punctuality? How hard he had tried as a schoolboy to beat her to the kitchen, but had never succeeded. Even today, he, a grown-up man, had not been able to change the odds.

Way back in those days, he remembered how confident she had been of the discipline she had instilled in him. She would never once call out to him during those intervening minutes between her arrival in the kitchen to set out his breakfast and his joining her to eat it soon after. She had never once doubted that he would join her in time to leave for school. No wonder the noise and commotion that always preceded Meeta, Tom, and Tammy's departure from home perturbed her. Maybe the times had changed, and one could not discipline children the way one did in those days? Even so, the marked difference in his own behaviour and that of his children had made him pause and think a moment.

Pretending to have just come down from his room, he entered the kitchen, gone up to his mother, and placing a hand upon her back, said, 'I won't take more than five minutes and then we'll be on our way.' Surprised by his show of affection, she smiled up at him and, touching his hand, said, 'I'm in no hurry to go anywhere, take your time and eat a proper breakfast.' The mother was the mother, and the son the son, once again today!

He shook some Raisin Bran out of a carton into a shallow bowl, put a dash of milk onto it, and then picked up a spoon. He took a seat at one end of the large deal table that sat in the middle of the kitchen. From there, he stretched out and picked up the newspaper. As he ate, his eyes strayed from the cereal in the bowl to the headlines, and then onto his mother, who sat impassive at the other end of the same table. He had for years seen her dressed and waiting for him as she was today. But there was an intangible something of late about her that he had observed yet not observed that he could clearly see today. She looked, to his eyes, to be almost as young and fit and energetic and self-assured as the mother he had left behind somewhere in the distant past.

And then a ray of sunshine fell directly onto her face and the illusion was broken. But even so she looked fresh and beautiful and poised but, alas, distant. Having remembered that mother from the past, a deep feeling of protectiveness surged through him for the mother who now inhabited his present.

The BMW was in the garage, and having shrugged himself into his suit jacket, he picked up his briefcase and the car keys. By the time Nandita had checked the rear door and let herself out, Tukun had brought the car and parked it in front of the house. Leaning across, he opened the right-hand front door for Nandita and, as she got in, inquired, 'I hope you have your key with you, Ma, it's possible no one will be at home when you get back.'

In reply, she showed him the key. Looking around appreciatively, she settled herself in. 'This car is very nice, Tukun. Really very nice.'

'You have been in it before, haven't you?' he asked, frowning in his effort to recollect the series of events in relationship with his new car.

'Yes, we all went for a test drive.'

'Never been in this car after that?' he asked, surprised by her response. 'How strange! Please do belt up, Ma, the cops keep their eyes wide open, and in particular for the passengers in the front.'

'True, I have little or no experience of sitting in the front seat of a car. It really is quite a different experience all together,' she commented as she belted herself in and examined the understated opulence of the dashboard. And Tukun, caught on the wrong foot, wondered whether she was being sarcastic or merely indulging in small talk. He fell silent and turned out onto the road fronting their home. The beautiful sleek car picked up speed, and a soft-as-a-whisper sitar piece by Ravi Shankar filled the leather-bound luxurious interior of this classic vehicle with its classical presence.

Nandita was pleased that she had come; she could hardly remember when last she had been with her son alone. Having him by her side with none to share him with was a near-forgotten experience. Luxuriating in its warmth, she had taken a look at the handsome man seated beside her. Yes, Tukun did look very much like his father, but people said that he had a great deal of her as well. She had never been able to spot *those similarities*, but that he looked like Prodipto had given her a great deal of solace while handling the trials and tribulations of single parenthood. She looked at him from the corner of her eye to see whether time had obliterated any of those familiar landmarks upon his countenance that so clearly marked him out as his father's son. There were no changes as such, yet the changes were there! Today, Tukun looked like the venerable elder brother of Flight Lieutenant Prodipto Kumar Roy. It was inevitable that Dipto would be left behind by his son one day, but Nandita was saddened by this inevitability.

Today seated beside him alone under different circumstances, in a different location, she was the same person yet not the same person at all, thought Sudipto. Casting a glance her way, he could see her hair was damp as usual; *Ma*, he thought with a smile, *will never change.* He remembered those days with nostalgia, when come summer, come winter, each morning she would bathe, against her better judgement, pouring water onto her head. Her hair used to be thick, curly, and very black with a streak of obstinacy to it and would never dry in time for her to get dressed for school. Oh, the endless times she had caught a cold because of this habit. *Did she catch cold even now or did she not?* He thought, *perhaps not, she goes nowhere these days.* He remembered how she would comb her damp hair flat upon her head as if wanting to wish the waves away. But her hair, being less obedient than her students, would invariably escape out of their straitjacket and spring into waves all over her head quite soon again. And a few among those wavy locks would even manage to escape from their bonds and fall across her forehead. He had not liked those tumbled locks at all, for it had made him self-conscious to have a mother who looked as young as she did.

Glancing her way, he was pleased to see she did exactly the same with her hair even today. How strange, her hair had not changed much, and for that matter, nor had she. She was as slim and upright as she had been then, and her hair, though it had a few greys to it now, was almost as thick and wavy and obstinate as it was in those days. And even today, it was not willing to obey her command. The waves were springing up and soon he knew some of the locks would begin to stray out of their restraining bonds.

None of this had caught his attention for ever so long. She was always there at home visible yet rendered invisible by the inevitability of her presence. A mere shove, a little push given to his memory by a minor relocation had brought forward so many images that were long forgotten. And it was then that he remembered his meeting with that boy out of his schooldays in Calcutta.

'I forgot to tell you, Ma, I met Monoj Sirkar the other day. I was there at a sports gear outlet and there was this guy buying a racquet. I didn't recognise him but he pounced on me from behind and was all over me.'

'Monoj Sirkar?'

'Our math's teacher's son. That fat boy who used to keep running behind his mother.' And with the recollection of the fat boy's feats, his school and his schooldays had come back with a nostalgic rush into his mind. 'I must go and visit my school one day,' he murmured to himself.

'Did you say something?'

'No, I was telling you about—'

'Some Monoj Sirkar? Yes, I remember now, that must be Nomita's son. He must have grown up by now.'

'Grown up?' And Tukun was laughing, as she had not heard him laugh at anything she had said, in a very long time. 'He must be thirty at least. He was in class five or six when I was in my tenth.'

'That's true, he must be a full-grown man by now. Is he as fat as he was then? Is his mother still teaching at our school?' Here was a world where no one had dwelled but Tukun and she, and she and Tukun. Where they were at home alone together after such a very long time today! And holding hands, they comfortably strolled down memory lane, remembering, recollecting little snippets out of their unshared-with-anyone-else past.

'Nothing much has changed, he is still fat and his mother still teaches math but his father has just retired from his job in the railways, he told me. You remember we went once or twice to that railway quarter where they lived?'

'Yes, I do, was it near Howrah or was it somewhere near Sealdah?'

'That I can't remember, but I do remember that it had smelt just like a railway station or the compartment of a train when we went there.' They laughed together and fell silent. After a short while, he turned to her and said, 'Monoj was reminiscing on how good you were as our deputy headmistress, I agreed with him totally.'

'I must thank him if I ever do meet him.'

'I told him you'd become headmistress just before you left. He said he was not surprised.'

'I would like to meet him.'

'He said he'd be coming over. He wants to meet you, Ma, for him you still are a very major entity. He wanted to know what you were doing these days.'

And, for you! she thought, as she asked him, 'What did you tell him?'

'Oh, I?'

Nandita was waiting for a reply, curious to learn what her son thought she did with her days. But the moment was lost, for an impending change of direction in their journey brought about a change of direction in their conversation as well.

'Ma, please see what's written on the board up there, is it exit number 1 or exit number 2?'

'One.'

'Then we must turn off from the next one and then take two lefts from there.'

'How do people live here? It looks so lonely.'

'Yes, these new developments are somewhat set apart. Vast tracts of land are required for these exclusive properties, so quite naturally . . . now which way do I go? That way I think: yes, what was I saying?'

'Aren't they kind of cut off?'

'I suppose in a way they would be. Ours is a reconditioned old house, so it is more or less in the centre of the town.'

'I'm glad you chose to live there.' As she had never once shown any likes or dislikes in the decisions he made, Sudipto was surprised and pleased that his mother approved of his choice of dwelling. Going back to the topic of shiny new homes, he asked, 'Have you ever seen any of these new places close up?'

'Wasn't the Duttas' place in New Jersey also brand new?' she asked, recollecting the house made of wood and glass that had smelt like the interior of a new car. *The house where she had met Bill for the first time!*

'Meeta and I had seen a couple of these before we settled for the place we now live in, so I know, these new houses are not what we had seen at New Jersey so many years ago. These are far, far more modern, much more flimsy to look at but functional by far than those were,' and with a short laugh, 'and way beyond my means as well.'

And then they came to a rise upon the road where Tukun halted the car for a moment to take in the panorama laid out before them. From where they stood, they could see acres and acres of land at a lower level rolling away from them to the edges of the horizon. Though just a stone's throw away from the highway, hidden from view, lay this vast green region dotted by tall trees and distant homes, where Mahadevan was said to be living. It was from this vantage point right up on a hillock that they were to descend for their destination. The carpet of green was so well kept and so well trained and so well held on a leash that it almost looked like a pet readied for a show. The sprinklers going round and round and round created myriad rainbows by throwing water mischievously onto the back of the sun's rays as they sprayed water upon this pampered piece of turf. And whichever way her eyes went, all Nandita could see was this veritable sea of absolutely perfect, manicured, pedicured, shampooed, trimmed, teased, and tempered and beaten-into-shape sheet of green. So perfect was its undulating expanse that it appeared as if it had been spray-painted onto the surface. As far as the eyes could see there was grass, grass, and still more grass. An occasional path would meander away through this perfect landscape and lead to a secluded home.

And sitting there atop a hillock, seated beside her son, she remembered that day when riding in a black Vauxhall, seated beside her newly made husband, she had seen another such lavish show of green. What she had first observed on entering the gate that led to the portals of her father-in-law's home at New Delhi was a magnificent spread of green. And that sea of emerald green, though beyond belief, was nothing but a luxurious carpet of grass. Had she not seen the lawns around the India Gate, she might not have recognised it for what it was! Nandita had seen grass, in ones and twos, and in small bunches upon platters readied for rituals; and in clumps and straggling patches in their very own courtyard in Bhabanipore, but never ever in such lavish and opulent and dramatic dimensions. A trimmed-to-perfection wall of green with the girth of a mammoth had been trained to run alongside the compound wall, marking the territory of the garden. Could this really be a garden attached to a home? Prodipto had told her that his mother had a lovely garden, but that garden had looked more like a park! A garden, what exactly was a garden? As far as she knew, gardens did not coexist with city-bound homes, and the 'garden' she had till then known did not go beyond the venerated *tulsi*, the single transplanted oleander tree, and a solitary banana palm that stood askew near the dripping tap in the enclosed courtyard at home.

And turning to her son, she said, 'Tukun, this brings back memories of your grandfather's garden at Delhi. Not a weed was allowed to stray into that beautiful lawn of his.'

'A lawn that big, Ma?' he teased, spreading out both his arms towards the horizon.

'No. Not this big but it was a beautiful lawn.'

'I can imagine how beautiful it must have been.'

And then he released the brake and let the car move forward. The downward gradient was so thoughtfully gradual that one barely felt that one had descended from any height at all. 'Is this where they live, Tukun? Are you sure?' she asked, as he took one of those paths that led to a hidden-away home.

She had wanted to ask a similar question when first she had seen the home in which Prodipto's parents lived. Because what had lain before Nandita that day was a habitation so far set apart from any place that she had ever seen that she could not believe that any ordinary mortal could possibly be living there! Did they not feel afraid to live here, she had wondered, for the house sat like an island in the middle of what appeared to her to be a vast ocean of empty space. The home in which she had lived since birth was by no means of ordinary pedestrian proportions, but it had held itself comfortably together for it had chosen not to contend with a fearful moat of emptiness all around. It went safely upwards from the very edge of the street upon which it had firmly planted its majestic feet, and rose three floors up, where it came to touch the very blue of the skies! And the rooms large and small, though they meandered hither and thither, came to rest in the embrace of the enclosed courtyard. It was frightening to see that nothing seemed to be enclosed in this home where Prodipto's parents lived. How could two persons, just two persons, live in a house as large as the one that was looming ahead of them, Nandita had wondered that day.

And once again today, she felt the same way. *How do they live here through the long, cold, and dark winter?* she asked of herself.

'I think I'm lost, Ma, Mahadevan did give me a few landmarks but everything looks the same here.'

And then with a little spurt of excitement, she said, 'Tukun, I think they do live here, I think I can see that friend of yours waving out to us.'

'Where?'

'There to the left.'

He took the path lying to his left and drove on towards the home that lay right before him. And Mahadevan dressed in a charcoal-grey three-piece suit, cornflower-blue shirt, and a marigold-yellow tie had loomed large, standing at the door of the house sitting like a little ship upon a vast pea-green sea. A driveway cutting a brick red swath through the expanse of green curved along the side of the home. A dark-blue Mercedes Benz stood pawing the ground like a thoroughbred raring to go.

And the house itself, though large, stood like a flimsy cardboard-and-silver-paper doll's house. How it kept out the cold of the intense winter and the heat of summer of Illinois was a wonder to Nandita, who had lived only in elderly homes with their thick and ageing walls.

Nandita stepped out to face an approaching Mahadevan. Her toes curled, remembering that act of homage he had performed at her feet when he had come to their home. But today, dressed in the full dress regalia of the corporate world, Mahadevan's mindset was on an entirely different wavelength. Tukun had entered along with her but had stood but a moment by her side and left, having made a mere salutary entry into their home. Nandita had looked at him with pleading eyes and he had turned his eyes away, feeling strangely guilty at abandoning her in the hands of these strangers. 'See you, Ma,' he had said quietly, slipping away. And Nandita had felt exactly as she had done on her first day at school as she saw her son drive away.

What am I to do among these strangers, was her anxious thought as Mahadevan ushered her in. The windows were all shut tight and a smell of stale cooked food bottled up within the four walls of the house had hit her nostrils. A carpet imitating the colours of a camel's coat had been poured onto the flooring and could be seen flowing away into the interior of the house.

'Sumathi was so anxious to meet you, aunty, but she leaves for work before I do,' Mahadevan said, fictionalising his wife's eagerness to meet this 'old woman', as she had liked to call her. Had this 'old woman' whom *he* had invited looked a little older, Mahadevan would have felt a bit more comfortable. However, as she belonged to the coterie of mothers, she could very well be clubbed along with his mother, he soothed himself.

'Had we met, it would—'

'But you *will meet her*, she comes home by four.'

A little smile hovering upon her lips, she said, 'That'll be nice.'

'She woke up very early this morning saying, "I must cook for aunty myself, she is coming to my home for the first time today." I told her, "Don't worry, Amma will cook something," but she just would not listen to me.'

And Nandita thought *that means his mother does the cooking on most days*. How old was Mahadevan's mother, she wondered, to take on such a huge load of work? But she said, 'I seem to have put your poor wife to a great deal of trouble.'

'No, no trouble at all.'

Mahadevan called out, 'Amma . . . Appa,' as they entered what appeared to be the family room. It was a room that was imbued with a personality similar to the area through which she had just come in. It was reminiscent of the mock-up homes, one created with hardboard and plywood upon a stage: the roof low, the walls thin, the windows aluminium and glass. The flowers in the vase plastic, the paintings on the wall expensive prints bought en masse and put up perhaps by the person in charge of the interiors of these luxurious but faceless homes. It was a room predominated by the selfsame camel-coloured carpet, with its own complement of aluminium and glass. The furniture too was so modern as to have almost overreached itself and, rocking on its toes, fallen into the future.

An old gentleman with his roots still attached to the Vedic era, carrying upon him the aura of a few thousand years left behind in time, sat incongruously amidst this statement of modernism made by some pricey architect. He sat impassive facing a blank television screen, reading a newspaper. He was lean, and his nose stood out like a beak from his face. Strangely enough, his hair was almost all black, but the little moustache that bristled atop his upper lip was well peppered by white. He looked Nandita's way, put his palms together in a *namaskara*, and nodded his head but chose not to smile.

And then Amma entered upon the scene. *She must have been a beautiful woman at one time,* Nandita thought. *Who had Mahadevan taken after?* She had remarkably clear-cut features and her light skin still had a lustre to it. *How old is she?* Nandita had wondered. *Seventy, seventy plus?* Unlike her husband, whose hair still retained most of its original colour, her head of hair had turned completely white. She had scraped it all together and put it into a tight knot at the back of her head. The earlobes, left uncovered, sagged under the weight of the diamonds she wore upon them. Both her nostrils were similarly adorned. Her nostrils slightly flared, the diamonds upon them flashed some message along with her eyes. Mahadevan broke into Tamil and Nandita could decipher 'Sudipto Roy' and the word *Amma* out of the flow of words he was directing to his mother. She nodded her head as she heard him out and her eyes continued with their appraisal of the visitor.

Mrs Parvathi Neelakanthan surprised both her husband and her son. For she who was said to have no English to her vocabulary suddenly spouted a word in that language. Pointing to a chair placed a safe distance away from Neelakanthan, she said, 'Sit,' to Nandita.

Mahadevan left immediately afterwards, almost as if happy to escape from the strange social hotchpotch he had himself cooked up. He had no idea that his mother could speak English; he sagged with relief on having seen the beginnings of a conversation between these two mothers in his home. He might have heard the adage that a single swallow doth not a summer make, but he was paying no attention to such inconsequential natter as he entered his car and drove off.

Having seated Nandita, the older woman disappeared somewhere into the interior of the home. Nandita looked down at her watch, wondering how long it would take for four in the evening to arrive. What were this fellow Mahadevan and her son Tukun thinking of when they had engineered this scheme of bringing together two Indian mothers floundering in a sea of loneliness in a land far away from their own?

Mrs Neelakanthan was none too happy with her decision to leave 'that woman' seated there with her husband. Old fools were such big fools; one never could tell what they would do faced with a little bit of temptation. 'Widows are far more dangerous than spinsters,' she opined as she measured out milk and water and put it on the gas range to boil. And all those curly strands of hair spilling onto that woman's forehead could not possibly be natural, she knew. 'A woman her age should know how to keep her hair from straying so coquettishly,' she grumbled under her breath, as she went about her task.

Why had Parvathi left her here and gone away? Had she not been brought in to keep her mind wandering off Madraswards? He cleared his throat and was deciding to call out to Parvathi to remove this obstacle in the path of his TV viewing when his eyes fell upon the hands of his watch. Visitor or no visitor, the programme that was just about to come on could not possibly be missed. The remote control was already in his hand, and without losing another moment, he zapped the set with it! The volume had been preset, and as soon as it had come alive, an ear-splitting medley of mixed sounds jumped out of the box and started bouncing around like a wayward squash ball within the confines of a tightly shut squash court. Nandita's hands flew to her ears to ward off the attack upon her eardrums.

But when the TV had come on, spewing sound like bullets from an automatic weapon, Mrs Parvathi Neelakanthan thought, dirty kitchen or otherwise, that woman would have to be removed from the proximity of her husband. Who knew what they were watching together? Men were so vulnerable to suggestions one could never tell when they would want to emulate what they saw. She had tried very hard to wean him off this bad habit that he had acquired after coming to America, but with nothing else to do, he would pick up the remote and go back to the TV again. Television sets, she had come to realise, were the veritable harbingers of evil; just imagine a father taking over his very own son's wife! Not that this woman was all that young, but young enough for a stupid man past eighty who was relentlessly fed on American TV shows and TV shows alone.

A Tamilian widow dressed decorously in red, she had heard this woman was a widow, and here she was dressed in white. *Strange were the ways of these North Indians, but was she a North Indian? No, she was not a North Indian, she was a Bengali, and that was in the east, wasn't it?* It was then that she had remembered those translated works of Sarat and Bankim Chandra that she had read when she was young; how surprised she had been to discover through the pages of those novels that their widows dressed in white. Why white? White was such a youthful colour. Bright colours on the elderly looked so correct! And this woman here brought in *to entertain her*, being a Bengali, was dressed most incongruously in white. To her eyes, it just did not look right. *Deva, Deva, Deva, what a strange country we come from,* she thought, *they dress their brides in red and we our widows in the same colour.*

The coffee done, she poured a part of the scalding brew into a mug for Nandita and the rest into two stainless steel tumblers and then, placing all of them on a tray, had gone back to the family room. Parvathi stood a moment and observed her guest closely. The pained expression she wore upon her face and the hands she had placed upon her ears to ward off the bludgeoning blows being dealt upon her eardrums brought a smile of sympathy upon the older woman's face. Spewing a string of words at her husband, she moved up to Nandita and, saying the single word *kapi*, handed the mug to her. Mr Neelakanthan, throwing a fiery look towards his wife, switched off the TV and turned his chair round to face their guest.

Parvathi his wife had made it clear to him that his services as interpreter would henceforth be required. They sat for a while drinking coffee, and then began the barrage of questions. How many children did she have?

'Just one, this son with whom I live.'

How long had she been in America?

'Ten years.'

'Ten years? As long as that?' Did she like it here?

Did she like it here? Nandita was none too sure what to make of that one. A few months earlier, she would not have hesitated while giving an answer to *that question.*

Did she ever want to go back to Calcutta?

'Yes, I do quite often, but what am I to do? To what or to whom would I return?' Mr Neelakanthan had approved of that answer. Sensible woman, he thought; she may even din some sense into Parvathi's head!

How many grandchildren did she have?

'Two, a granddaughter and a grandson.'

Did her daughter-in-law cook, or did she have to cook for everyone?

That was a tricky question that needed some diplomatic handling; whatever she said could be construed to mean something else. She didn't want her words travelling via media and landing up in an unrecognisable state in Meeta's lap. And she had bought off future possible hostilities with a non-committal smile.

How old was her son?

'Thirty-six, he married young just as his father did.'

Only thirty-six? Then how old was she?

'Fifty-five.'

'Running or completed?'

'Running.'

'*Poor child*,' thought Mahadevan's mother, for the first time looking upon Nandita with kindly eyes. Parvathi turned to her husband and said something, and as she spoke, there was a quiver to her voice. And he, in turn, turned to Nandita and told her that his wife wanted to tell her that she was not much older than their daughter would have been had she but lived. Nandita had felt a constriction in her throat in sympathy with their never-to-be-assuaged sorrow.

'She would've been fifty-four in a few months from now, had she lived,' said Mr Neelakanthan without any prompting. A year later, their Devan had been born, she was told, and they had had no other children after that. And Nandita's eyes had moistened in sympathy with their pain. The look of genuine sympathy upon Nandita's face touched a chord within Mrs Neelakanthan's heart. Sympathy culling sympathy, she had wanted to know a little bit more about this young person in widow's attire who was seated before them. Prompted by his wife, Neelakanthan asked if Nandita had been widowed recently.

'No, a very long time ago when I was not yet twenty. My son lost his father when he was not even one.'

Parvathi wished then that Nandita had been capable of understanding Tamil. Had it been so, she would have taken her to her bosom and told her how saddened she was by the tale of her life. These were not sentiments that one could convey with the help of an interpreter, she knew. Words such as the ones she would have liked to use were so delicate that they would not be able to take a change of vessels at midstream without getting shattered or misshapen in the handling. And finally having accepted her with affection, Mrs Parvathi Neelakanthan wanted to know what her name was.

Mr Neelakanthan, tiring of his role as interpreter, indicated that he had some pressing business to transact. 'Show her the house,' he said. Parvathi did not like his attitude and told him so. And he in turn said something else and so it went on. Defeated on the last round, the wife showed her disgruntlement and finally withdrew from the arena, with her guest in tow. Mr Neelakanthan sighed out a breath of relief and turned his attention back to where it belonged. The TV, when he had switched it on, came on as loud as a festival loudspeaker back home in India; Parvathi looked at Nandita to gauge her reaction, but Nandita gave nothing away!

Reluctantly accepting her husband's suggestion, Parvathi went upstairs and down, to the right and to the left, out onto the garden and back inside again, with her guest marching alongside her. To begin with, that chasm that lay for want of words between them had been bridged quite creatively by mime. And slowly, one at a time, a few simple words also began to erupt between them.

The time for the afternoon meal arrived far sooner than Nandita could have imagined. Parvathi went into the kitchen and Nandita followed, meaning to help as best as she could. Nandita's life was so devoid of multiregional experiences that she expected this meal cooked 'just for her' by Sumathi would be a new and exciting experience for her. The nearest she had come to South Indian food was the *idli/vada/sambhar* breakfast she had had along with Prodipto at a neighbour's place soon after they had got married. So deeply in love with Prodipto was she at that moment of time that the remembrance of that meal was not linked to the taste or the flavour of the food she had eaten that day, but to the look in Dipto's eyes as they had engaged her own eyes teasingly across the dining table. Seeing the sudden flush of colour upon

Nandita's face, the older woman mimed the question 'Are you feeling hot?' by dramatically fanning her own face.

No sooner than the food had been put upon the table, Mr Neelakanthan arrived as if by magic and took his seat at the table. It was evident from the expressions flitting across his face that Mr Neelakanthan was less than pleased with the culinary creations of the absent daughter-in-law. As she ate, Nandita looked from the husband to the wife and then from the wife to the husband. Mrs Parvathi Neelakanthan, Nandita could see, was considerably pleased with her husband's discomfiture.

The last round of rice was to be eaten with curd and Nandita looked around for sugar to go with it. 'Do you want something?' Mr Neelakanthan asked on being nudged by his wife.

'I was looking for sugar.'

'Sugar? Why do you want sugar?'

'For the curd rice!'

'With sugar? Is that how you eat curd rice in your parts?' Neelakanthan asked, cocking his head to one side. 'Doesn't it ruin the taste?' he questioned, and Parvathi, well aware of the word 'sugar', went and fetched some sugar for Nandita, thinking what weird tastes these Bengalis had.

'Spoil the taste?' How strange—without sugar, how could anyone eat sour curd, Nandita wondered as she ladled sugar onto her curd and rice.

Meal over, Parvathi took her guest to her room, opened a trunk, and took out an aged album. Indicating to Nandita that her husband would soon be coming to rest in that particular room, she drew her into a room across the landing. As soon as Nandita entered the domain, she knew that this was the room in which the two daughters of Mahadevan lived.

It was a teenager's room out of a Hollywood movie. A computer was endlessly scrolling a message that said 'Maddy is an idiot, Maddy is an idiot, Maddy is an idiot'. Whoever this Maddy was, no pains were being spared to inform her of her intellectual inadequacies. Her eyes moving from the computer monitor, Nandita flinched as her eyes fell upon a parade of glossy posters flaunting barely clothed muscular male torsos on show upon one of the walls. She moved her eyes away from those posters and took a peep at her companion; the older woman looked quite unperturbed by the presence of the male pin-ups.

The room was in a state of total disarray; a pair of tennis racquets, one sheathed, the other unsheathed, some tennis balls, and umpteen magazines on tennis were spread out upon one of the beds. Pennants blandishing favoured soccer teams, baseball caps indicating team preferences were stuck onto the headboard of the other bed. A music system pretentious enough to make do for a band and a plethora of compact discs upon a narrow shelf running along one of the walls, when put all together, gave something away of the world in which the granddaughters of Parvathi Neelakanthan lived. A pile of lacy brassieres and panties lying in a puddle at the foot of the beds and a packet of sanitary towels ripped open in a hurry that perched atop the heap caused a minor embarrassment to the old lady. A small nudge with her foot and the offending garments and the baggage atop them was deftly moved out of sight by the grandmother of the occupants of the room. And in that room, Mrs Parvathi Neelakanthan in her nine yards of brilliant silk and Nandita Roy in her six yards of white cotton moved in and took a place like a pair of false notes in an otherwise perfectly harmonised pop concert piece. Parvathi made room for both of them upon the less crowded of the two beds and, with a sigh of contentment, flipped open her treasure trove.

The young and personable Mr Neelakanthan and his lovely bride Parvathi debuted on the first page and kept growing into maturity with the turn of each page. With Mahadevan's entry into the US, the colours of the rainbow had visited the album for the first time. The black-and-white images that had started off this collection moved no further forward and it was colour all the way from that point onwards.

The photographs of Mahadevan's wedding had projected the extended family and the home: a simple abode, with very few frills to it. She showed off her retinue, the 'cook woman', and the 'servant maid' to Nandita, in the saris she had bestowed upon them, when her Devan got married. Her face glowed as she unfolded to Nandita the life of that dominant player back there in Madras.

And the exchanges between the two women, though held together by fragile and tenuous links, did not snap asunder even once. Parvathi had evidently not opened her heart to anyone in a long time and, overwhelmed by emotions, forgetting that the woman sitting facing her did not know her language, broke into Tamil on those occasions when she could no longer contain herself. But the language in which the older woman chose to speak did not matter to Nandita, for those hours she spent each day at the Home had trained her well to become a sounding board for the needs of all such people. Who said there was any need for her to understand exactly what was being told to her? All a lonely soul needed was a person who would show some interest in what was being said. And that was one service Nandita was well able to provide.

When Tukun had first told her about this visit, she, resenting his presumption, wanted to refuse outright; *how dare he*, she had thought, *make programmes without so much as asking me whether I want to be a part of it or not?* But having landed up, so to speak, in Parvathi's parched-for-companionship lap, she was glad that she had come today. However, she wished time and again that she was able to communicate with Parvathi with the ease with which she could with Grace and all those other inmates of the Home whom she regularly visited.

Slowly through the photographs, through words and gestures and the ever-changing expressions upon the beautiful ageing face, Nandita was able to decipher the old lady's hankering for her own home, her own environment, the temple where she had worshipped regularly, and the city she loved so well.

Nandita relived those years of loneliness that had begun to engulf her life, with the gradual growing up of the little ones and the growing away from her of the young people. She, more by accident than by choice, had managed to spread her wings and to escape from the monotony of that existence. But what were Parvathi and her ilk to do? They were educated and independent people who had been rendered totally unlettered and dependent and cloistered by these moves away from their roots. Nandita, empathising with Parvathi, knew that never ever in all these ten years that she had spent in this new country had she ever been as isolated as this elderly woman was. Her knowledge of English had always kept the door to the world outside her own home open to her. But for the likes of Mrs Parvathi Neelakanthan, there was no path of exit from within what could well be called a gilded cage!

Nandita could sense that an excess of emotion had tired Parvathi out, and she persuaded her to take some rest. She went silently into the kitchen and let herself out from the rear screen door onto the yard.

There were no clear demarcations of 'your yard begins there and mine ends here' in this home. The green of the surrounding rolled up to the doors of Mahadevan's home and rolled away to the far distance once again. The garden furniture beckoned to her but she chose to go past and wander down an uncertain path that went into an uncertain distance. Not a soul was to be sighted anywhere. That there were other living beings somewhere in the vicinity could only be assumed from the hum of a distant lawnmower going about its task somewhere at an uncertain distance. The scent of mowed grass hung enticingly in the air. It was beautiful and serene and set apart. So serene and set apart was it that a person could well feel lost in its abundant aloneness. And then she heard the booming bark of a large dog, and as she went along the curve of the road, she sighted a house as well. People other than the Mahadevans lived here but you had to journey out of your home to even get a glimpse of it.

What will happen when one of these two persons will die? How will the other live alone in this desert island when inevitably one of them would die ahead of the other? A shiver had passed through Nandita's frame at the very thought of such a situation coming to pass. With a sigh, she accepted that come what may, one day such a situation would surely come to pass. Incongruously, she voiced softly to herself, 'I hope Mr Neelakanthan will outlive his wife. He at least has his television set.' Turning around, she walked back to the house and let herself in by the door through which she had exited.

She had barely picked up a newspaper when the house came alive again. Parvathi came out of the room where she had been resting, wearing an enquiring look on her face. On seeing Nandita, the expression changed to a look of 'Oh, so this is where you are?' Tiffin-time was upon them and Mrs Parvathi Neelakanthan got down to preparing a meal of sorts in a matter-of-fact, what-one-did-every-day manner within minutes of entering the kitchen.

And then Nandita heard a car come to a stop somewhere close by. She heard a door open and shut and knew that she would be meeting Sumathi, wife of Mahadevan, who had taken the trouble to cook a meal for her that morning. She had seen a number of photographs of Sumathi, so she expected that she would have no trouble in placing her. The daughter-in-law of the household bounced into the kitchen with a flood of Tamil-flavoured English overlaid with a Yankee twang. There was such a lot of difference between the Sumathi in traditional wedding attire that she had met in the album this morning and the one she was meeting dressed in pseudo-American attire that had all the parameters not been pre-fixed, she would never have been able to place her.

The onslaught of her overwhelming presence and the deluge of English that she poured into the room instantaneously snapped the fragile and tenuous links that had created a pathway of communication between Parvathi and

Nandita. And Mrs Parvathi Neelakanthan, cowed down by the torrent of English, allowed herself to recede into the background and fade away.

It was time to go home; Nandita was happy to be going home. Yet Nandita was not happy to go home, for there was a strange sense of sadness in her heart at leaving Mrs Parvathi Neelakanthan. Mahadevan's wife looked on with surprise as her mother-in-law took this stranger into a warm embrace before finally letting go of her. Had she not been totally opposed to this woman's coming to their home? Strange were the ways of her mother-in-law, she thought as she waited for Nandita to get into the car.

Nandita, having thanked the elderly couple, got into the car and took her seat beside Sumathi. Sumathi had bounced into the kitchen on coming home, and her car, a shiny red Toyota Corolla, also took a bouncing leap forward before moving ahead on its course. And Parvathi continued to stand there at the entrance to their home. Nandita's eyes remained upon the frail figure of Parvathi till a turn in the road finally placed her out of her sight.

12 SEALED WITH A KISS

On return from Mahadevan's place, Nandita let herself in to find that Meeta and the children were already back. It was indeed a strange experience to come into a home that was awaiting her return. Had she returned before them, there was a distinct possibility that her daylong absence might well have gone unnoticed, but thanks to the timing of her re-entry, her day of adventure provoked some desultory questions, which in truth needed no particular response at all from her.

'How was the day?' Meeta asked, a cup of tea in hand.

With a non-committal 'OK . . .' she went upstairs to freshen up.

Once back in the kitchen, she found her grandson out in the yard, where he was busy shooting down myriad 'enemies' with a toy handgun that looked too real for comfort. Nandita, settling down to cut some vegetables, frowned as she pondered the sight of her gun-toting grandson. She had observed how empowered children felt as they spat out the words 'You are dead.' Why, she asked herself, do we so thoughtlessly desensitise our children to the lethality of firearms? With a little sigh, she went back to the task she had taken in hand.

A while later, having slain innumerable enemies, Tomal threw 'Was the stuff you got to eat OK?' her way as he breezed into the kitchen, where Nandita was seated, now chopping some zucchini.

'It was different, but nice.'

'Different?' He wanted to know, 'Different like what? Like pasta or pizza or burgers or what?'

Nandita was amused by his typically masculine gastronomy-centred curiosity regarding her venture into the unknown.

'Tell me, Thamma, tell me, how was it different?' he urged.

'Like our food but tasting different.'

'Oh!' he said, losing interest. Dal and rice and their accompanying curries did not tickle his fancy.

Tanu came in, a comic book in hand, looked at her grandmother, and asked, 'Did you have fun, Thamma? Isn't it nice you have a friend of your own?' Nandita was surprised to find how sensitive her little granddaughter was. How had she realised that she had no personal friends whom she could call her very own?

'Silly. She's not Thamma's friend, she's Dad's friend's mom,' Tomal told his sister. 'Is she your friend Thamma?' Nandita smiled at the differing responses of the two children.

And she replied with a hesitant, questioning 'I don't know, I don't know yet whether she is a friend or not.' It was possible neither of the children heard, and losing interest, they left soon after.

And from there onwards, the curiosity aroused by her unusual outing assuaged by that smattering of questions, each individual moved back into their assigned slots and life meandered on very much as it always did. Meeta was soon on the phone as she normally was each evening, communicating with the entire world, and the children were in the yard as she cooked a dal and a simple zucchini *chenchki*. Putting both the items into suitable bowls, she went upstairs again.

She sat on, a book in hand, wondering why Bill's observations upon her sense of alienation that, alas, had leaned towards the unsympathetic came back to mind at this moment. It was time perhaps for her to make some amends. But what shape those amendments should take, she had no idea.

Nandita knew that she herself and Meeta and Parvathi and her daughter-in-law Sumathi had all come to this land from the same mainstream that had flown out of India. Parvathi and Sumathi spoke in the same language just as Nandita and Meeta her daughter-in-law had been born to the same tongue! Yet, Parvathi and Sumathi in one case, and Nandita and Meeta in the other now stood at a point where they could not communicate with ease, one with the other! What was it that brought these strange changes to come about in relationships? What was it that created the divide between human beings? Whatever it was, it had opened her eyes to the fact that it was not a matter of vintage or culture or language that made or unmade relationships! But the key to what made them work was, alas, still out of her grasp!

As soon as Tukun got home from work, the foursome dined. She came down somewhat later and ate her solitary meal in the kitchen, with the open pages of a book keeping her company. But she felt far from alone! The sound of the TV next door and the voices of the children filtering down enveloped her in a cosy blanket of togetherness.

And lying in bed, she mulled over the day she had just spent with Mahadevan's mother. That mock-castle stranded like a desert island in the midst of a sea of relentless green had its very own captive princess with silver tresses, she had observed, but all the other parameters of this fairy tale were not quite as they normally were! The prince in this instance was located just there beside this distressed princess but recognised nothing of her desire to escape back to where her kingdom lay over the seven seas. The fairy godmother, having abdicated her post, had handed over a magic wand to the prince. But that wand had no powers beyond the ability to create an illusion of freedom, an illusion that appeared upon a little screen within a black box! But this magic wand could perform its magic only if one knew the magical language created by the Anglo-Saxons of yore! Poor Princess Parvathi, devoid of the knowledge of that magical tongue, with not an ally in sight, was doomed forever to live out her life of segregation in distant Illinois in the vast and varied land called the United States of America.

Nandita could understand the hankering in the heart of the older woman for a return path to all those well-beloved landmarks that she had had to leave behind. Forever distanced from the familiar, had she not herself experienced this total sense of loss, this total sense of entrapment as well? But one day, she had stepped out of her home more in anger than a spirit of adventure and had once again savoured the flavour of freedom. Since her arrival in the United States, she had never once gone beyond the pale of her immediate family in search of companionship. And it had indeed been an exhilarating experience when she had started exercising her volition once again.

The pangs she had felt in her heart on parting with the older woman stirred up a hornet's nest within her head and her heart. Feelings urged her to take a look afresh at the life of not only Parvathi and her own self but also that of a woman who had been left far behind in her life, her mother. That day for the first time in the years of her existence upon this earth, she wanted to know what her mother's life must have been like.

Had her mother ever had any freedom of choice in matters that were her very own? Never ever had Nandita seen her make a single move that had not been orchestrated by Thakuma, that did not have that matriarch's stamp of consent upon it! How dry and tasteless must it have been for her to live out a life that had been totally designed and directed by someone else. Who was that woman, did she have a name? She tried to remember what her mother's actual name was, and floundered. How strange it was that not one single person in that mansion of the Gangulys had ever called her by her given name. Shrouded in anonymity, she had lived on, clinging to the symbols of her marital status.

That woman, her mother, had been forced by circumstances to live out the life of a woman who had no husband. Yet empowered by a letter scented by the perfume of crushed marigolds and the scent of burnt-out joss sticks, she had been permitted to lead the life of a woman battened by the presence of a husband in her life. She had had to pay a heavy price for this little bit of make-believe. And she, the daughter, had understood nothing of the compulsions that made her mother what she was, and hurt and bewildered, she had withdrawn whatever little favours she could have showered upon her. How blind children are to the pain and anguish of their parents. Or else, was it just a matter of progression in time that had brought her to a point where she could perceive the pain that the generations inflicted upon one another?

With regret swamping her heart, she realised that not once, not once prior to this day, had she ever looked upon her mother with a feeling of sympathy or understanding. All her life, Nandita had resented the neglectful behaviour that had been handed out to her by the woman who had brought her onto this earth. With a sudden infringing rush of shame, she wondered at her own lack of concern for that woman who was her mother.

There was so much to tell, and Bill was away at faraway Singapore. What would he make of the strange day she had spent with Mrs Parvathi Neelakanthan and the surge of remembrance it had brought in its wake for a mother who had never been spared much thought by her? How she missed Bill whenever he dropped out of sight. What would she do when he would go away, never to return? She would have to grit her teeth and bear the pain. Pain—why did pain underlie so many human relationships?

A ray of sunshine cutting across her face had nudged her out of sleep this morning, but she lingered a while longer in bed, savouring the joy of just being alive! Her Dipto reinstated upon the dresser smiled down upon her from across the room. She no longer resented the face of eternal youth that he presented to the world.

A smile gently caressing her face, she lay back languorously watching the dance of the dust motes trapped in the rays of the early morning sun. There was a time in the not-so-distant past when she could not or perhaps would not have possibly allowed herself such a moment of luxury at the break of a new day! She revelled now in the tremendous sense of freedom that this unchaining from the early morning activities of the family had brought to her life.

It pleased the newly incarnated Nandita to distance herself from the rough and tumble of these mundane daily chores that she had been so involved with at one time. Why she had hankered after that rush and bustle of the early hours, she often wondered these days. She had moved to a position now where she could find humour where she had found none at one time. It amused her to see Meeta and her children working themselves into a state of frenzy each morning, wondering why the new world order worked itself into a coil over trifles. Had mothers lost their ability to give clear-cut directives to their children? Or had children changed so much that they had no need to listen to what was being said to them?

She wished sometimes that she and her dear Dipto could sit and exchange a few words, a few laughs together at this present moment of time: now! But if supposing they were to come face to face by some strange turnaround of the laws of nature, of what would they talk, she wondered. Had not the drift of time separated the points of reference to life and living for the two of them completely? Perhaps! Even so, these were his grandchildren as well, were they not? She wanted desperately to know what he would have thought of them, how he would have reacted to them, how he would have interacted with them as a grandfather. No. Trying to place Flight Lieutenant Prodipto Kumar Roy in the exalted position of grandfather to two growing children was for Nandita an impossible, imponderable task. What would a man who had worked out a perfect recipe for eternal youth have to do with such an ageing relationship as grandfatherhood?

But there were other people besides these two descendants of his whom today's Nandita would have liked to introduce to her beloved rogue of a husband. There were so many different things to tell about all her newly found friends that lay seething within her in search of a worthy ear. But Dipto stayed behind somewhere in time with his feet planted forever in her yesteryears, so what was she to do? The romance of young Helen who refused to cross her seventy-ninth year, and worthy Ted, who was well past his eightieth, she knew, would have surely tickled his fancy. And the tales of the barn dances of oh-so long ago, replete with indiscretions committed in the heat of youth would have brought a twinkle to his mischief-filled eyes. The altercations over the viewing of soaps on TV between old Mr Neelakanthan and his hawk-eyed wife, the tale of bravery of so many who had lost their dearest ones, the propositioning of the Colonel, and more besides. Yes, she would have liked to share all these myriad multihued experiences with that handsome young husband of hers.

And then with a start, she pulled herself short when a silent voice from within wanted to know what would Prodipto's stance be if she were to produce Bill, and present him as a friend to him? She held her breath and acquiesced that she really had no idea. What occasion had she ever had to test such a ground? For those short years that they had been together, he had been the centre point of her life. A friendship beyond what he had to offer and, that too, with another male—where did the question for that ever arise? So how could she possibly make a guess at what his reactions would have been? This was virgin land upon which she had not so much as placed a mark, so how was she to know? But somehow, she had sensed a certain sense of disquietude deep down while dwelling on Prodipto's possible reaction to the friendship that she had formed with this man called Bill! Had she not seen the sliding back into orthodoxy by his mother at the very first shake-up at the foundations of her existence? He was the selfsame woman's son, was he not?

But Bill was a reality of her existence now, so what was she to do of it? Pushing the uncomfortable thoughts out of her mind, she hurriedly picked up some clothes and went into the bathroom, closing the door with far greater force than it in any way demanded! Her mind skittering around in search of answers to a fistful of futile ifs and buts, like a wayward thought on the loose, frightened her with its restless ways. She stood much longer under the onslaught of the stinging spray of the power shower that morning, as if willing it to wash away all the troublesome thoughts that were creating a clutter within her consciousness.

It was no easy task to tether her mind to prayer as well this morning; but a habit of a lifelong of giving her all to her prayers soon dominated her obstinate thoughts and brought them under control. Eyes shut in total devotion, she gave herself over to the reciting of the Durga Stotra, hymn to the Divine Mother Durga.

sarva mangala mangalye sive sarvartha sadhike;
saranye tryambake gauri narayani namostu te.

srsti-stithi-vinasanam sakti-bhute sanatani;
gunasraye gunamaye narayani namostu te.
saranagata dinarta paritrana parayane;
sarvsyarti-hare devi narayani namostu te.

jaya narayani namostu te!

And soon, its lulling cadence having soothed and strengthened both her head and her heart, she was able to look forward to the rest of the day with far greater equanimity. And it was with snatches of a very well-known Shyama Sangeet in adoration of Ma Kali upon her lips that she came down to make herself her first cup of the day.

As soon as she crossed the threshold of the kitchen, she could clearly discern that the coffee drinkers had beaten her to the kitchen this morning. The coffee maker simmering happily upon the counter at one end of the kitchen and the newspaper in a state of disarray gave proof of the invasion that had already taken place. She breathed in a deep lungful of the all-pervading aroma of the perkily perking coffee that lay wreathed around the kitchen. And its energising ever-companionable perfume gave a joyous little lilt to her heart.

Forming a soothing backdrop to the waking hours, the sounds of a household on the go floated down to her in the kitchen, where she sat sipping her first cup. Rinsing the cup and setting it aside, she stepped out and took a few deep breaths of the fresh morning air. The fat cat was already there, grooming its whiskers; she hoped it had not eaten one of the tenants who lived up there in their trees! Somewhat relieved to see that there were no apparent signs of carnage, she heaved a sigh of relief and re-entered through the mesh door and went slowly upstairs, vacating the premises for the breakfast squad that would soon be coming down to eat.

The clatter of young feet upon the stairs, the shouts, the occasional screams, the reprimands and remonstrance filtered up to her as she went about tidying her own room, humming a few snatches of a song that she had learnt as a girl. With the departure of the threesome, a sudden silence fell upon the place and emerging from her lair, she went back to the kitchen once again. Normally, having straightened up the table, she would withdraw from the domain. But this morning she lingered on, in the hope perhaps of finding some remnants of the companionable moments she had spent after so many long years with her son on the drive she had taken with him the previous day.

A little later, Tukun dressed for the day entered the kitchen, picked up the newspaper, got himself some cereal, and got on with his breakfast. It was only when he was halfway through with his meal that he realised his mother was also there.

'Sorry, I didn't see you, Ma. Not too tired, I hope.'

'I'm all right.'

And then as if belatedly having come awake to the possibility that he had left his mother in a morass of non-communication the previous day, he put down his newspaper and asked, 'Was it too long a day for you? After I'd left, I was a bit worried.'

'Why?'

'I wondered whether Mahadevan's mother spoke English at all. Does she?'

'She only speaks Tamil.' The answer crisp and short held no reprieve within it.

'Somehow, Mahadevan gave me the impression . . .' And he shrugged. He mumbled, 'I'm sorry. I shouldn't have taken you there without finding out.'

'It's all right,' she said, as he picked up his briefcase and left for work.

None too pleased at her own shortness, she threw a reassuring 'We managed . . .' to his retreating back. But it was possible that he had not heard her at all. For he hadn't turned and smiled upon her as he had when they had journeyed together to Mahadevan's place.

Her outing of the previous day was already a thing in the past, and the minimal interaction that it had drawn in its wake was over and done with. It was a while since Tukun had left for work, but she sat recapitulating his enquiring statement, 'I wondered whether Mahadevan's mother spoke English at all. Does she?'

And pondering that question, Nandita recognised with some surprise that one needed very few words to express intense feelings. Why then had she not heard the silent cry of despair that must have emanated from her own mother? What was there in common between Parvathi and her own self? Apparently nothing, yet had she not felt a resonant chord of sympathy for

Mahadevan's mother? And in a moment of sudden perspicacity, she realised, to her surprise and wonderment, that though there was this vast difference of usage and language that stood between her and Mahadevan's mother, there was this delicate thread of cultural commonality that tied them together. It was a commonality that ran like an underground stream that lay out of sight and watered their sameness. Had she but a few more words with which she could have built a bridge, she would have told Parvathi that she, Nandita, too had made a similar transition and had tasted the same bitter fruit of non-communication in her life here. No wonder then that Parvathi and she had communicated despite the fact that they had but a handful of words between them!

And she once again remembered her short and crisp 'She only speaks Tamil.'

But his equally cut and dried response, 'I'm sorry. I shouldn't have taken you there without finding out,' had hurt her deep with its absolute formality.

This was not the Tukun Nandita had sat beside in his luxurious car just yesterday. He looked the same but was not the same person. He had reverted to being the cold and distanced son with whom she had been living for the last so-many years! Rendered myopic by her long drawn-out proximity to her one and only child, somewhere along the way, Nandita had ceased to perceive how those troublesome cryptic answers that she so often gave caused him concern.

And even today, those gaps left between the words she had just spoken had sent out some message to him that he was unable to decipher and make sense of. He wondered as he strode towards his car what it was that had brought about such a major change in his once warm and loving mother's temperament? She spoke very seldom to him, but when she did, the words she spoke emerged more often than not as conundrums to him. Conundrums to which he could rarely find an answer! And yet, she had almost been her old self yesterday as they had taken that long drive together to go to Mahadevan's home. How refreshing and relaxing had been those exchanges between them with no intervening intangible words marring the landscape of their true meaning! He wondered, as he drove on, what had made her revert once again to her usual near-monosyllabic responses so soon after?

Though he was not a stranger to this drought-like situation in communication between himself and his progenitor, somehow this drying up of communication between himself and his mother did at times hurt somewhere deep down within him. 'It's all right,' was all that she had chosen to say in response to his concerned query. They were but a trio of words but those words, few though they were, had so many undertones to them that he had been forced to mull over them in search of what they really wanted to tell. He had toyed with those non-words and then, untethering them from their moorings, had allowed them to float away like a released gas balloon up and away from his mind! For the sake of one's peace of mind, that which was unfathomable was best left to its own devices!

Reinstalled within their normal milieu, both the mother and the son had retreated to their chosen positions of minimal communication once again. Monoj Sirkar and the school in Calcutta had all receded into the background, and the only reality left with them was their life here in the United States. And with this realisation, the euphoria of that transient moment of bonding with her son as she had ridden with him to meet Mahadevan's mother soon faded away.

And with these questions and non-answers that came along in their wake, the chapter with the heading 'Grandma's Day Out' had been put away in a file and closed immediately after.

The day's outing put behind her, Nandita bursting with excitement stepped out to go and meet her friends at the Home. She knew deep down within her that she would have to make amends for her absence away from them, for as chance would have it, she would be absenting herself once again the very next day as well.

Bill would be back tonight and she had promised a birthday party with a cake to him!

The Colonel was the first to spot her as she entered, and his 'So you're back,' drew the attention of the rest of the congregation to her.

All eyes turned her way and smiles erupted on all the ageing lips, and a chorus of 'Hi, Nan' fell like a welcoming song upon her ears. So many persons waiting for her return from her voyage into the unknown overwhelmed her with its bounty. There were hugs and kisses galore and enquiries of how she was on so many lips; their abundant, unreserved affection for her brought tears to her eyes. And standing there among these people, she felt as if this was her family and she had come home. Even the nurse on duty stopped for a moment and asked, 'Where were you yesterday?'

There were no desultory questions awaiting her return from the unknown here. They wanted to know where she had gone, who had driven her there, how many people she had met. Were they nice people, had she liked being there, what she had eaten?

With a shade of jealousy peeping out from under her well-chosen words, Grace stated, 'It must have felt real good to meet a woman from your own parts, Nan. I can guess you'd be wanting to speak to someone in your tongue.'

And the grilling went on!

'Had a great time speaking Indian with your friend, Nan?' Helen wanted to know.

'And eatin' Indian food cooked by someone else. A change of hand makes such a difference to the same old stew,' Emily chipped in.

'Did you give her the recipe for stuffed turkey?' one of her cookery teachers asked. 'It will come in handy for sure. Thanksgiving's only a few months away.'

'Hey, Nan, why don't you teach us some Indian, please? I know some words of Vietnamese but . . .'

'The old codger wants to learn Indian now!' Grace groused.

'Yeah, it'll come in handy when she says yes to my proposal.'

'Getting ambitious, Colonel,' someone quipped.

Nandita, smiling at the Colonel's words and the rejoinder to it, had toyed with the idea of putting the record straight in the matter of the language called 'Indian' and the food that could be listed under the heading of 'Indian' per se. But better sense having prevailed, she let it pass.

'Yes, I had a nice time,' she said with a wry smile.

'There I told you,' said Grace, turning to Helen, 'that she must'a had a ball.' And then after a short pause, she threw 'Hope your jaw ain't painin', honey?' Nandita's way, at her caustic best.

'Grace, my dearest Grace, I can never make friends who can possibly be dearer to me than you and . . .' And she swept her hand across the entire room. 'I went to visit those people because *I had to* and I come here because *I love to be with all of you!*' There was moisture in the air; the possibility of a cloudburst could not be ruled out! Bringing about a downpour was the last thing she had in mind. 'Come on, shall we play some Scrabble? It really helps improve my English.'

'Liar,' the Colonel remonstrated, 'you speak the language kinda funny, but you know a dictionary full of big words. Otherwise, how do you win so often? All right, bring out the board, and let's see if we can get the better of her today.'

When Nandita lost outright at Scrabble, the Colonel was pleased but not so her mentor Grace. 'You sure you're not a-cheatin', you old fox?' she had demanded of the Colonel. A heated argument followed and then Helen remembered the birthday cake that was to be baked and the impending birthday party.

'Finished baking the cake, Nan? Isn't the birthday party tomorrow?' she enquired.

Nandita sagged with the relief at Helen's query; she had been dreading the task of having to remind this congregation that she would be absenting herself once again the very next day. And light of heart, with a shake of her head, she indicated in the negative.

'Not done yet, Nan?' Grace scolded.

'Go home and get down to it, girl,' advised Helen. 'That boyfriend of yours will be expecting a treat for sure.'

'Don't overdo it, Nan, no need to push yourself,' advised the Colonel. 'But bring him over one day. Must check him out and see if he's worth all the trouble.'

'Stop being so stuffy, Colonel. Our Nan has sense enough for sure to check out a guy,' Grace defended her. 'But do bring him over, Nan!'

'Yeah, bring him over,' Helen reiterated.

'I'd like to but—'

'But?'

'He's away on work quite often. When he has some time, I'll . . .'

'A busy body as we can all see,' added the Colonel in a crisp and dry tone of voice as Grace glowered at him.

Soon after that, the bell for the afternoon meal intervened on Nandita's behalf and took her inquisitors to table. She still had to visit those among the inmates who were tied to their beds because of their disabilities. One among them, Charlotte, who preferred to be called Charlie, had coined a phrase, 'bedpan beauty', for herself and the likes of her. 'We the bedpan beauties were a-wonderin' where you had gotten to yesterday,' she asked sternly as soon as she spotted Nandita. Explanations rendered, Nandita flitted from bed to bed, exchanging words, performing minor chores, arranging things as per demand, and left soon after.

That *virtual* cake housed within a packet would have to be transformed and brought into the world of edible *reality* if a promise made in haste were to be kept.

She selected the oven placed at the level of her eyes, positioned the thermostat at the correct temperature, switched it on, and got down to creating the batter. The instructions were simple enough, but Nandita followed them as if a slip-up on her part would transform it into an atom bomb or something worse than that. The batter looked good enough; the next step was to get it into the oven and then wait out for the final result. Perfuming the air, the cake eventually arrived. Smothering it with the icing, she set it aside. But it looked no way near as classy and ostentatious as its projected image upon the cover had promised it would be! She let out a sigh of relief, made herself a cup of instant coffee, and sat back, exhausted. This cake thing had really troubled her no end. Feeling very foolish, she carried the confection up and placed it within her wall closet, out of sight of inquisitive and questioning eyes!

Next morning, no sooner than the family had left for school and work, Nandita emerging from her room swiftly got down to the task of creating a meal that would be light on spices. She had decided upon some shrimp-centred *chops* as the central item of this simple yet tasty meal. In Bengali parlance, a *chop* was a cutlet, though a *cutlet* was not necessarily a *chop*! So what would she tell Bill they were: *chops* or *cutlets*? She smiled to herself as she set aside a batch of the shrimp-centred *chops* with their crisp coat of potato and breadcrumbs for the night-time meal of the family. *Puris* had to be hot to be enjoyed, so she made some soft and feather-light *parathas* instead to go with them. A near-dry chicken curry cooked in yoghurt, and boiled potatoes tossed in clarified butter and flavoured with freshly crushed pepper with a dash of salt were to play stellar roles in this meal she had cooked with care for Bill. With a sense of deep satisfaction, she thought that this evening when the family would sit itself down to table, it would also share in this birthday feast that she had put together for her friend. How could she possibly cook with care and leave the family out of it?

And as for the birthday gift, that had posed no problem, for that beautiful painting in swirling colours that she had fallen in love with and bought one day was sitting in her closet, waiting to be put to some good use. She pulled it out from where she had pushed it out of sight one day and took a good look at it. To her eyes, it still was a work of art imbued with exquisite beauty. She could think of nothing better than this to give to her dear friend. Yes, she would give this painting to Bill. A stash of gift-wrapping paper and all its accoutrements, she knew, was kept in a cupboard in the basement. So finding a swath or two posed no problem. And now wrapped and readied, with a ribbon running around its midriff, the present waited alongside the picnic hamper as she went up to dress for the day.

Trying to balance the hamper and the framed painting just up to the door, and out of the flat opened Nandita's eyes to her foolishness. Why had she refused to accept Bill's offer to come and pick her up? Would she have to call a cab, she was wondering when she had heard a familiar voice ask, 'Planning to haul that lot without any help, Mrs Roy?'

Startled, she looked up and found him standing alongside a tall tree a little to her right. 'You frightened me, Bill. You really did.'

'Sorry!' But he did not sound in the least bit contrite. 'Now if you'll let stronger arms than yours to do the heaving and hauling—'

'Oh, Bill, am I glad you came. I was wondering how I'd—'

'You should've known I'd come,' he chided. 'And what is this?' he asked, his curiosity aroused by the bulk of the wrapped-up item.

'A little gift for you.'

'That. And little?' And he laughed as he picked up the lot and walked off towards his parked car.

When the framed print had come out of its shiny wrapping, the look of joy upon Bill's face, in turn, filled up her heart with joy. 'How did you, how could you possibly . . . I mean, how did you come to know that Van Gogh is one of my favourite painters?' he asked in wonderment.

'You really like it?' And then wanting no share of pretence, she confessed, 'I liked it so much that I bought it at a garage sale. I hope you don't mind . . .'

'Mind? Mind receiving a gift as lovely as this?'

'I was afraid that—'

'That I would not like it? No, Nan, you couldn't have chosen better.'

'I wasn't sure at all!'

'He's so good I like the entire range of his work, Nan.' And then a sweep of sunshine came filtering in through the foliage and fell upon the print and lit it up as if from inside. And excited, he said, 'Look, Nan, look! Look at how beautiful this painting is, look at the pure bright colours . . .' His excitement was infectious and she smiled along with him in agreement. 'This painting must have been produced after Van Gogh went to live in France. One can see that he has left behind the sombre aspect of his pre-France period here.'

'You know so much about art, Bill, and I know really nothing . . . but . . . when I saw this painting, the colours and the strange brushstrokes just . . .'

'You sure do have an eye for beauty, Nan. These unique brushstrokes reflect something of the joyous perception of life that he had while he was immersed in creating these masterpieces. Incredible though it may sound, a man who could depict his inner joy so tellingly eventually committed suicide to escape from his own tormented self.'

'Human beings have so many layers hidden away from sight within them, Bill. So many selves within that solitary self that is visible to the world.'

'So they do, Nan, there you have an art critic and an amateur psychologist hidden away within you that you knew nothing of.'

'I hope you're not making fun of me.'

'No, I'm not. And thank you very much, Nan, for giving me a gift that's so close to my heart.' He was sipping slowly from a can of beer and had offered it to her; after receiving such a resounding compliment, what could she do but take a sip from the proffered can? She didn't like the taste but was too polite to show her distaste. But being a woman, her mind, however preoccupied it may have been with art and the strangeness of the taste of beer, did not stray once from the primary aim of this picnic. 'You shouldn't have, you shouldn't have worked so hard, Nan. Goodness, what a feast you've knocked up for me. And I can see you haven't forgotten the cake you had promised to bake for me.' And overcome by nostalgia for the joyous moments that he had left behind in time, he had to work very hard not to let his emotions take over. He smiled so hard to cover up his weepy feelings that his heartache had soon been converted into a mouthache!

'The mix is out of a packet,' she confessed.

And he burst out laughing on hearing her timid words of confession. 'You really are such a darling, Nan, how on earth have you managed to remain so innocent through the years?'

'Let me serve you,' she said gruffly, hiding her embarrassment as best as she could. She had taken two plates, and on one of them, she served portions of all the items she had cooked for him that day. On her own plate, she placed only those items that were totally vegetarian! Handing him his plate, she urged, 'Come on, eat.'

'Is that all . . . all . . . that you're going to eat?' he said, pointing to her plate.

'You see, Bill . . .'

'If you don't join me, I'll also eat exactly the same . . .'

'Please, Bill,' she pleaded. But he was unwilling to listen to any of her arguments. Slowly whittling away at her reserves, he managed at last to persuade her to eat one of the chops and to eat a slice of the cake. Little by little, the barriers she had built around her persona were coming down.

The party was soon over! It had been a comfortable, relaxed, and companionable day. And as a final token of his appreciation, Bill leaned across and brushed his lips across her sun-warmed cheeks; and her cheeks had gone warmer still with all the mixed feelings it brought forth within her.

She belonged to another civilisation with its roots planted in another age and time, where each touch between a man and a woman was weighed and measured and placed on a scale of values. Where did it at all have a listing within its lexicon for such behaviour, where a tall blonde giant with blue eyes could lean over and kiss a woman upon her cheeks in broad daylight? A woman who was no more than an acquaintance, and who was a widow of a Bangali Brahmon family, no less? Her upbringing had its feet so firmly planted in orthodoxy and in the deep-seated precepts of prudery that this commonplace, humdrum, oft-repeated gesture left her totally shaken. Her mouth gone dry, her heart beating a tattoo, she had wondered whether she should lodge a protest or not.

Having helped put everything together, Bill stretched out a hand to help pull her to her feet but she avoided his touch. Carrying the picnic basket to the car, he opened the door and ushered her in. The memory of his lips upon her cheeks had rendered Nandita speechless. Having stopped in front of the house, he got out and, hauling the basket out from the back, took it up the four or five steps that led to the entrance of her home. And he then waited for Nandita to join him there.

And recalcitrant, finding her lost tongue, she said, 'Happy birthday to you, Bill! I think I forgot to greet you properly earlier.'

Facing her upon the doorstep, he looked her in the eye. 'Proper enough, dear Nan, for you sure have made this day a very memorable one for me.'

'I'm glad that—'

'I want to thank you but you know, Nan, the trouble with that phrase *thank you* is that it is used so often that it has become like an over-circulated coin that has lost the entire imprint that had once been put upon it. It has rubbed so thin that it no longer has any real value left with it. To just say *thank you* to you, for all that you have done for me today, I know, would be quite inadequate.' He fell silent and Nandita, embarrassed by his search for a means to thank her when she wanted no words of thanks from him, took the key from her purse and put it into the keyhole. Having turned the key in the lock, she was on the verge of dragging the basket in, when bending low, he muttered, 'There are better ways of expressing one's thanks,' and softly caressed her lips with his own. 'There, that's a much better way of letting you know how I feel.' And with this cryptic summation, he turned around, walked down the steps, got into his car, and drove away well before Nandita could recover from her shock.

Slamming the door shut behind her, she stood as if struck by lightning, throat parched, ears aflame, perspiration beading her brow, panting for breath. So utterly confused and confounded was she that she stood on, rooted to the spot, and then the chimes of the wall clock in the living room penetrated through her paralysed senses and brought her back to the reality of the moment. Her wristwatch said that it would not be long before the children would be back home from school. She would have to pull herself together if she did not want the grandchildren to arrive to find her, picnic basket in hand.

She entered her bathroom and threw off the sari she had been wearing since morning; the pristine unblemished whiteness of the fabric had been stained by the lush young green of the grass. She looked into the mirror and barely recognised her own self. A pair of bright and luminous eyes looked back at her, and the escaped tendrils of her tresses tossed around in the playful breeze of the lakefront had fallen across her forehead, and then gone tumbling across her cheeks and created a strange foil to those eyes. Where had this woman come from? And what was she doing in her room? There was something wanton about this woman that she would have to eradicate! Lathering some soap upon her palms, she began vigorously washing her face and particularly her lips over and over again. It was as if she feared that some signs of the misadventure would remain adhering to her lips if she were not to scrub it off with care. She splashed some water onto her hair and ruthlessly set about the task of tutoring her locks into a more respectable state of sobriety. A more recognisable, more acceptable image of Nandita was soon reflected in the mirror she was facing. Having draped a fresh sari upon her slender form, she went down just in time to let the children in. She gave them something to eat and fell silent, and the sounds of the children running around on heavy feet barely fell upon her ears. Meeta returned home a while later, and none too confident about what her face would give away under closer scrutiny, Nandita had left the room and gone up to her room.

She came down only when the voices in the TV set had come alive, signalling the end of dinner and the beginning of leisure time for the young couple. As she was going past the family room on the way to the kitchen, Meeta spotted her. 'That was a lovely feast, Ma. What was the occasion, have we forgotten someone's birthday?' Meeta asked.

It was fortunate that Nandita's face was in darkness, otherwise the rising colour and the look upon her face might have invited a few conjectures from the questioner. With an embarrassed laugh covering her confusion, she mumbled, 'The prawns should be cooked while fresh, so I thought . . .'

She played around with the food on her plate for a while; eventually accepting defeat, she swept the residue upon her plate into the maw of the bin and went upstairs. Her eyes swept across the range of books given to her by her tutors two, to familiarise her with the life and letters of the US. She picked a book at random and tried to force her mind into reading it. But not a single line registered itself upon her brain. She had no option left with her but to retire for the night; but sleep evaded her eyes for several hours. Sheer fatigue at last came to her rescue and swept aside all the wild thoughts that had been rioting around in her head and keeping her awake.

And she had no idea when she had fallen asleep!

13 SEARING, SCORCHING GUILT

B ut soon the dreams came: beautiful and serene in the beginning, and then turning troublesome, tumultuous, and terrifying!

She was up there on the terrace at that ancestral home of her forefathers; it was a bright and beautiful day, the sky speckled with a host of colourful kites. She sat with her back resting upon a wall of the water storage tank, a book of poems held open in her hands, watching the movement of the clouds and wondering why Wordsworth thought clouds were lonely. There they were up there, having a wonderful time freely travelling along in fluffy flocks: how she wished that she herself had been born a cloud! And then all of a sudden, the brightness of the day changed to darkness, the playful clouds and the dancing kites all went away, and the empty rooftop had suddenly been peopled with myriad new faces! She stood up with a start and looked around and became terrified beyond terror.

To her left stood Thakuma regal as ever with all her battle colours on show, with her entourage of Ma and Daminidi in tow. Thakuma looked thunderous, Ma looked bland and impassive, while Daminidi looked worried and ready to burst into tears. To her right sat Bill facing Sue at a cafeteria table with her bared bronze legs angled and on show. Suddenly, Sue looked up and turned her head and saw her and threw 'Hi, Mrs Roy!' her way; Bill, on the other hand, had eyes for Sue's leg show alone and did not notice that she was standing there right next to the water-storage tank that dominated the terrace. And on the roof just across from her grandfather's stood a vaguely familiar figure, pole in hand, totally unaware that Nandita was not alone on that darkened terrace. She tried to call out and warn him but fear had congealed her voice and left her dumb.

And then she heard his happy laughter-filled voice proclaiming, 'Watch out, Nondu, I am coming,' and he was sailing across the yawning chasm that lay as a divide between the two homes. He had landed up with a clatter of the pole falling to the ground. And taking her into his embrace, he planted a resounding kiss upon her lips; immediately after, she heard Thakuma thundering a command that she go from the roof and, that too, immediately. The sternness of her grandmother's voice, sterner than it ever had been, sent a cold shiver down her spine as she moved towards the stairwell. And in her ears had rung the words 'How could you, how could you, how could you, the daughter of a saint, do what you have done?'

A little noise permeating into the fear-filled landscape of Nandita's mind shook the hold of that awesome nightmare that had taken over control of her subconscious self. Words of recrimination ringing in her ears, she abruptly came awake with the chimes of the clock downstairs marking out the passage of the hours. She looked around for all the people with whom she had been in communion moments ago, fearing to see their accusative stance, to hear their clamouring voices demanding retribution of her in recompense for trespasses that she had committed. But the room lay empty around her, for the striking of the clock had fortuitously dragged her out of the terrifying, tormenting impasse she had dreamt herself into.

Those awesome figures of Thakuma and her entourage made up of Ma and Daminidi, those accusing voices, those raised fingers, those contorted faces steeped in disgust and disbelief, and those nonchalant figures seated on the sideline had all melted away into the darkness. And along with them, the laughing, teasing, loving persona of Prodipto had also faded away, leaving her bereft and desolated. She was relieved, overwhelmingly relieved to find that it was but a dream that had been haunting her sleep, but it was a relief that was tinged, alas, with a shade of sorrow.

She was surprised to find her forehead cold and clammy to the touch as she passed her fingers impatiently across her brow to brush aside the tendrils of hair clinging there. The volatile, ever-on-the-move numbers on the digital timepiece seated upon her bedside table were stating five minutes past four as her eyes flitted across its illuminated face. How long had she slept? Not for very long, she knew, for had she not heard the selfsame clock that had woken her chime two o'clock into the night?

She rose, went into the bathroom and washed her face and then, coming back into the room, took a sip from a glass of water. She looked towards her bed, shrugged, and then, in search of some answers, began pacing around the room, mulling over the nebulous form and content of the vision she had just had. And the more she dwelt upon it, the more she felt that the dream had to be something more tangible than just a fanciful figment of her overworked imagination.

Though *she* knew that the kiss was no more than a gesture of gratitude shown to her by a lonely soul, how was she to explain that to her forebears? He was but a bird of passage that had alighted upon a branch to heal his broken wings, and by some quirk of providence, she had been there. Now that he had healed, he would take to flight and would be on his way to a new life and new relationships.

She would not be totally forgotten by Bill perhaps, but she was a realist and knew that with his moving away, she herself would soon become no more than a memory for him. She would have liked to ask him why then had he taken the liberty of kissing her as he had done; but she knew that would have been akin to asking an Eskimo why they rubbed noses. The terrain of their backgrounds were as different from one to the other as were the landscapes of the planet Mars and the moon. So how was he to know how she would react to such a simple matter-of-fact friendly gesture on his part? Bill knew nothing of the strictly regimented tenets under which she had been brought up, with their myriad demarcating lines. How could he perceive an existence where the mere shadow of a male who was not a relation by blood or by marriage falling perchance upon you would be frowned upon? How her Dipto had managed to slip in past all those barricades put up by those who controlled the very breath of her life, and then contrived to take her away without raising the least suspicion, had put her forever in his thrall.

How flippant Dipto could be about matters that were so very terrifying to her. He just could not comprehend why she should be so bogged down by the fear of what he liked to call the 'what will people say' syndrome. What to speak of Bill Brady, even Prodipto Roy had never really understood the constraints that an orthodox upbringing placed upon a person's every action. Had he but had an iota of the fettering inputs of her upbringing, he could never have courted her as he had done! But he was a free bird and found her fears of being found out, being caught in the act eminently amusing.

Though it was but a dream that she had just passed through, it had power enough to make her regress to the days of her young womanhood filled with all manner of fears and inhibitions. And shaking her up as if by her tightly plaited braids, all the dos and don'ts that had been dinned into her during her growing years came to the fore. Horror-struck, she asked of herself, *What am I doing with my life?*

'*Yes, what exactly am I doing with my life?*' she choked out into the darkness.

So sheltered and controlled was that environment where she had been born and brought up that it had automatically bred a certain vulnerability within her that had forced her to ask that of herself. A vulnerability that she had never been able to shake off, leave aside, wipe out, though it was more than three decades since she had set it aside. First by falling in love with Prodipto in an environment where falling in love was taboo, she had broken its norms, and then by walking out in protest and choosing to lead an independent life of her own, as a single mother, she had further reinforced it. But what had come to pass the previous day had been too daring by far, even for the newly reinvented Nandita to handle with composure.

What her ancestors would think of her getting herself into a situation where a near stranger had felt free to place a kiss upon her lips was beyond imagining to her. And a widow who made fractious forays into nibbling forbidden food such as prawn cutlets and taking sips out of cans of beer with the selfsame man, she knew for a surety, would have spelt a crime to their eyes that went way beyond redemption. How could she explain to them that none of these acts were of any real significance within the time and space and dimension in which she now lived! But why was she forever in need to explain every action of hers to her predecessors?

And then the laughing questioning eyes of Prodipto had been in her mind's eye as if asking her, 'Still allowing that gaggle of women to control your life, Nondu?' And as a corollary to it, she had found herself wondering what he would have thought of Bill, whether he would have liked him as much as she did. Most probably he would have, but chances were that he would have found that kiss Bill planted upon her lips as a token of his thanks unbearably familiar!

Her present life and its demands, and the pulls and pressures of her past were forever at loggerheads, and she who stood between the two was getting tugged this way then that and being torn apart in the process. The future—did she have a future? She could see the imminent departure of Bill from Saisborough, and her life, looming large, and her endless trudges to the Home in search of companionship also coming to a halt as soon as the clement weather would pass away. Would she ever cab herself there? And her past, though it was already in the past, she knew, with its compelling, controlling voice, would never ever be over and done with. So what was she to do? Perhaps cling to the present and let the past and the future take care of itself? No. No. No. No. The present was getting to be too complicated, fraught with too many dangers; prudence demanded that she stop seeing Bill. But how was she to do that? What would she tell him? What excuse would she give him? What if he asked for an explanation? Stop seeing Bill when he was on the verge of leaving for New York in a few weeks from now? What if he reminded her that he was going away in any case? Stop seeing Bill even though she knew it would hurt him?

How embarrassing it would be to let him get an inkling of the importance she was attaching to a mere gesture of thanks. Her ears had gone burning hot at the very thought of the look of disdain that would flit across his face when he would work out that it was that kiss placed upon an elderly woman's lips that was coming in the way of their meeting one another.

She was a sensitive woman and knew that if her sheltered existence had created a certain kind of fragility in her mental make-up, it had also endowed her with the strength to face up to disappointment, while the overt freedom of Bill's upbringing devoid of negation, deprivation, and censor had made him vulnerable in other ways.

To visualise a situation where she would be bringing about that separation even before his departure was beyond anguish for her. No, she could not bring herself to hurt him. And so she argued on with herself in search of a way out of the predicament she was now facing. Apart from the pain and hurt inherent to parting from someone you cared for, what other danger was there in this relationship? At the end of a lengthy debate she had asked of herself.

But the enraged vision of Thakuma whom she had seen just now definitely thought otherwise. Cutting across the dimensions of life and death, she had come along with her entourage to admonish her, had she not? They had got wind of Bill's overtures of affection towards her and had come post haste to remind her of who she was, what she was, and from where she had come. They had come to remind her of the bounding parameters of her background and the norms by which a woman was expected to live out her life within that framework. That she was a widow was not to be forgotten by her or by anyone else, and so her growing friendship with a man, any man, was not acceptable to them. And faced by their accusative stance, she had been compelled to recognise that her actions were taking her way beyond and away from the Lakshman Rekha that had been drawn at birth around her life by the society from which she had sprung.

A daughter born into the Ganguly family was well tutored to stay within her stays, and yet here she was, a grandmother no less, allowing herself to stray into a mine-strewn terrain. It would be better perhaps to retract from the dangerous grounds upon which she had strayed and go back to living a life as had been ordained by her birth for her.

She had risen a while later, heavy lidded and heavy of heart, and dragged herself through the routine activities that made up the early hours of the day. Even if she were not to meet Bill, she knew there was no way in which she could avoid going to visit the elderly people who so looked forward to seeing her. Come what may, she would have to wear a mask and face the lot for they had sharp eyes, sharper than those that hawks had!

The mail had arrived as she was having her Spartan breakfast. It drew her to its bulk by sheer force of habit. She lifted the lot off the floor and placed it on a table. And then from a corner she saw the edge of a blue letter-cover peeping out. It was addressed to her but not in a very familiar hand. The address at the rear spurred her on. It was from her home at Bhabanipore. Jhontu, the second of her Kakima's three sons, had written at the behest of his mother to inform Nandita that her Kakima, his mother, was not doing any too well. Could Nandita not come to Kolkata to meet her once?

Sturdy, strong, and yet gentle Kakima, the bulwark of her young days, was fading away in distant Kolkata. 'Could Nandita not come to meet her once?' she had wanted to know. Nandita had asked the same question of her own self. She could perhaps, and perhaps she would. The administrators at the Home had one day insisted that she draw a stipend for all the services she rendered to the inmates.

'What service do I render?' she had asked.

'That of companionship, Mrs Roy.'

'How can I accept money for that?'

'What we are offering is but a salutary amount. Something to allay our conscience. We know you walk here everyday. What if the weather turns foul or you don't feel like walking, should you not be able to cab down then?'

'I don't know, I have not thought so far, but even so, I don't feel like taking the money.' But on the first of the month, an envelope had been handed to her. In a few months, she would have money enough to buy a return ticket to Kolkata and back. She would go then to look up Kakima. She needed to get away from this place.

Key in hand, on the verge of stepping out, the telephone had trilled; she had halted in mid stride and picked up the phone wondering who it could be. Her habitual 'Hello,' in a questioning tone of voice was met with a 'Hi, Nan!' It was Bill and he was there on the other end of the line. What was she to do, bang down the phone? And he had gone on: 'Just wanted to find out how you're doin' after yesterday's long slog. You didn't get too tired, I hope?'

'I . . . I'm . . . quite all right,' she stammered in response as a part of her brain had observed that there was not a trace of self-consciousness in his caring voice as he asked her about her welfare. Was it possible that she had imagined that kiss? No, that had been as real as the man who was speaking to her, and as real as the fact that at this moment in time, they were both connected each to the other's voice by an invisible link that had been sketched by science across a void!

'You're sure you're OK?'

'I'm fine,' she lied, clearing her voice of all the cobwebs of emotion that were making it impossible for her to speak up and give a reply.

'Good. Something has come up so I won't be around for a few days. I'll call you when I get back. I'm in a bit of a rush, take care.' The very ordinariness of his words, the total lack of any contravening embarrassment in his words had made her feel very hysterical and foolish in contrast. Placing the telephone back on its cradle, she murmured, 'I mustn't let him know how . . . no, never!'

The barrage of questions all centred on the picnic was no less than an ordeal for her that day. The cake and Bill's reaction to it was central to the discussion, particularly so among the women! And then the Colonel trundled in and, parking himself at a distance, pretended not to notice Nandita's return to the fold.

'Good morning, Colonel.' Extending a hand, she beamed down at him, attempting to break through the iceberg-like stance he had adopted towards her.

Looking up at her with a squint as if hard-pressed to recognise her, he brought out 'Ah! So you are back,' with some reluctance. That he was none too pleased with her truant ways was on display to one and all.

'What's bitin' ya, Colonel?' Grace wanted to know. 'Gettin' jealous or what?'

'Jealous! Hah! Why should I be jealous?'

This is really getting out of hand, agonised Nandita. First, Thakuma, Ma, and Daminidi had all shown their disapproval to her, and now the Colonel was getting peeved all because of her friendship with Bill.

'I . . . I . . . I . . .' was as far as she had got in search of words when David Whitfield walked in.

'So you are back. Good!'

Nandita looked towards him enquiringly and the Colonel grunted, 'Yeah, she is back!'

'And she baked a terrific cake for that boyfriend of hers,' chuckled Helen. 'I told you, didn't I, Nan, that those cake mixes out of packets are just the thing for amateurs.'

'He's just a friend, not a boyfriend.' Nandita chose to clarify.

'Then why all this fuss? Bake this, cook that—goodness, one would think he was some kind of royalty.'

'There he goes again,' said Grace to the entire congregation and, turning to the Colonel, asked, 'What's biting you? Can't the poor kid make a young friend or two of her own without you getting all miffed up?'

'I . . . am . . . not miffed, why should I be? And why should it matter to me that she is making no progress in her study of American history?'

'Yeah! Why indeed?' challenged a protective Grace.

'Please, please, Colonel, please don't be so annoyed with me,' Nandita wheedled, placing a hand upon his knee and smiling into his eyes. 'Test me tomorrow if you like, and you'll find I've not been neglecting my studies.'

The Colonel was hogging all the attention and so her other tutor nipped in with 'And, Nan, I have been wanting to introduce you to Emily . . .'

'Which Emily? Emily Bronte? But I . . .'

And the subject thankfully veered away from cake and cold war onto American poetry. The Colonel, unwilling to cede ground as premier teacher to Nandita, dropped his mantle of indifference immediately and joined the discussion in order to keep his competitor from believing that he was the prime educator of their favourite pupil. Poetry, as far as he was concerned, was written and read by people who had little else to do. But if poetry was the weapon he would have to wield to hold on to the position that he had so far been in command of, then poetry it would certainly be that he would use.

'No, Nan, I think David is speaking of our very own Emily, right, David?'

'Yeah, it's Emily Dickinson I was speaking of.'

'Have you heard of her?' asked the Colonel as knowledgeably as he could.

'I think I have, but I haven't read any of her work.'

'Then you must,' broke in the retired schoolmaster. 'She was preoccupied with death as no one else ever has been. Death and the life after death obsessed her: the theme held a never-ending interest for her. I find that very intriguing.'

'One more word out of you on death, David, and I'll come and gag you,' Grace threatened. 'Haven't we all faced the awful reality of death once too often, so why would we want to read poetry about it, tell me?'

'Gracie, I knew you were a gem; but I had no idee you were a reg'lar Ko-hee-noor.'

'Thanks, Colonel, though it sounds mighty exotic, tell me what this Kohee . . . something is.'

David Whitfield had outmanoeuvred the Colonel and once again come to the fore and with a little bit of specialist help from Nandita the schoolteacher from Calcutta, the Koh-i-noor had emerged as a jewel in the crown of the British monarch.

Her visits to the Home continued and one happy day of companionship piled up on another. However, over the course of the days the troublesome topic of the birthday party and Bill her 'boyfriend' continued to come up at regular intervals. And with each new reminder, all the fears and doubts that she had so carefully swept together, bundled up, and put away out of sight would came tumbling out to confront her. With no escape route in sight, she had to face up to their playful banter. And slowly with continuous exposure, that which had appeared to be an incident of immense magnitude, an incident that had rocked the very foundation of her life became more manageable for her to handle. And soon she ceased to feel little or no embarrassment while discussing the party that was. It was but a simple matter that was between two friends, what did the world have to do with it?

This was not the voice of Nandita speaking but the voice she had picked up by induction. It was a perspective that she had no idea that she had picked up at all. The hours she spent among people who thought and behaved so differently from her had crept into her psyche and brought about a sea change in her very way of thinking on all things big and small. And with it, her own reactions towards the whole affair began to take on a very different colour from the one she had dipped it in when it had first come to pass. She saw no reason why she should not continue to see him when it was but a matter of no more than a few weeks at most!

But once she got back home, forces other than the ones that controlled her life while among her elderly friends at the Home would immediately take over and her head would once again fill up with troublesome thoughts. This dichotomy in her emotions, with its highs and lows, was out to tear her apart. Which way should she move, with the voices that spoke to her out of her past or with the voices of the elderly friends who peopled her present? And in the meanwhile, time having moved on, the generator of the troublesome thoughts was due back. What was she to do then? Banish him from her existence? Or sail along with the tide? In any case, the tide was to turn very soon now, and once it turned, it would carry him away from her shore. But what was she to do in the meanwhile? Sagacity demanded that she avoid him for now and forever!

As she ate her single-toast breakfast, the telephone summoned her with its shrill and compelling voice. She picked it up fearing it would be Bill's voice that would be at the other end, yet contrarily hoping that it would be Bill's voice that she would hear. And it was Bill's warm and exuberant voice that fell upon her ears. He was letting her know that he was back! Why did it make her so happy to learn of the return of Bill, when it was the one voice that she had been fearing to hear the most, the one voice that she had decided to avoid? He would be awaiting her downtown later that day, he informed her and put down the phone even before she could pick one out of the several excuses she had thought up to tell him that she would not be joining him.

How was he to know that to meet or not to meet was the big question that had completely held sway over her mind since the day they had so happily partied upon the lawns along the shores of the larger-than-life Lake Michigan? Pushing the dilemma into a secluded recess in her brain, she went on to meet her elderly friends. She knew an abundant supply of smiles, cookies, and large aromatic mugs of coffee would be awaiting her there to take care of her cares!

The coffee was hot, aromatic, and bracing. She took a long satisfying sip, then with mug in hand, circulated among her friends chatting happily about all manner of things. Someone suggested they play rummy and she was drawn in to form a foursome. She was not born to be a card sharper and lost so heavily that she took fright and withdrew from the table with the handy excuse that Charlie, and the letters she had to write for her, were awaiting her urgently. And once with Charlie and her companions, there were letters aplenty to be written and other chores besides that they wanted her to perform for them. She had nowhere to go but back to her home, so where was the need to hurry?

The afternoon meal had been announced and the senior citizenry all melted away! Emerging from the gate of the Home, she was hard-pressed to decide which way to face: on one end of the road lay the safe harbour of her home, while on the other end waited Bill. Her hesitant self, torn in two, had no ready answer. Her reasoning self wanted to withdraw and move away from the magnetic draw of Bill's charm, but that other less-responsible part of her always found a hundred reasons why she should not do so. Then Nandita's volition exerted itself and asked of her why the mere act of going to meet Bill should frighten her.

Because, she reminded herself, *a woman once married remained faithful to a man whether he was dead or alive.* Had she not led her entire life following the dictates of convention? She dressed as ordained, ate as ordained, and never once strayed from the norms laid down by the Brahminical society from which she hailed. *And even now, where was the question of straying coming up at all? What was she but an elderly widow to Bill's eyes? Where was the danger in this relationship? When in America, you have to do as the Americans do or stay at home for ever,* she informed herself as she took a hesitant step forward.

Little by little in imperceptible droplets, the thought processes of the people with whom she spent so many companionable hours had, unbeknown to her, begun to trickle in and form a pool under the crust of her hardened-by-centuries way of looking upon human relationships. And the pressure exerted by this slow and insidious percolation brought about a shift in the tectonic plate of the collective consciousness that governed her psyche. She would let things drift along as they had done so far. And then inevitably with the inexorable movement of time, Bill would pack his bags and move on, and her ancestors would have nothing to complain about then! And so the ancestral voices, though she had not been able to quell them completely, were satisfactorily mollified for the moment.

Two plus two always made four, therefore where was the question of its being five? She was a widow, and older than he was besides, therefore she was safely out of being attractive to him. A very cool and comfort-giving equation had been worked out by her regarding the emotions of Bill; but she had skirted the issue of asking her own self whether there was any possibility of her finding Bill attractive. What was she fighting shy of, what was the answer that she feared to face that she was not willing to turn around the coin and take a look at its face on that side?

A friend deserved better treatment than to be left stranded on a roadside! Falling back upon some of the lessons she had learnt from her elderly friends, she decided that she too must urge her friend Bill to return to a normal life. Her life was that of an upper-caste Hindu woman that was battened down by strictures that kept a woman at an immovable point from where there was no moving away. But there were no such strictures controlling Bill's life! But facing up to the prospect of a remarried Bill had left her inexplicably saddened. And she had felt as if someone had come and gouged out her heart and left behind an empty hole there.

Stilling the disquiet in her heart and squaring her shoulders, she marched on towards the centre of the town of Saisborough. And as she got nearer, she saw him in conversation with a little mite. What were they talking about? Evidently undone shoelaces, for when she reached close to him, he did not see her because he was crouching, head down, to help the little fellow do up his laces. It was a tender sight, this duo made up of a very large man and a very little boy intent on performing this simple task together. And then the mother arrived, red-faced at having put an unknown man to trouble, thanked him and fled with her child, and Bill looked up from his squatting position and saw her standing there. And he looked up and into Nandita's eyes and smiled!

And her heart filled up with light and the hollowed-out place within her filled up and became one again. She stretched out her hand, and taking it, he urged, 'Come on, Nan, let's see how strong you are, come on, haul me up.' And pretending it was her help that brought him to his feet, he rose in one fluid movement and stood before her and, still holding on to her hand, enquired, 'Why so late?'

'Sorry, but some of my babies at the Home were fretting today . . .'

'Why don't you take me along to meet your babies one day?'

'You don't know how naughty they are. They will just jump to . . .'

'Jump to what?'

'Oh, nothing, nothing at all.'

'You don't want them to arrive at all kinds of conclusions, isn't that it? Why don't you introduce me as your brother? No conjecture can attach to that relationship, can it?'

He was laughing at her, she knew. 'You are incorrigible, Bill, with your white skin, blue eyes, and blonde hair, you very well know that you can never be acceptable as my brother to anyone's eyes.'

'Thank God!'

'What do you mean?'

'Nothing, dear Nan, nothing at all. But all the same, let me take you for a proper meal today, at a proper restaurant, with proper seating.'

'Why?'

'Because I want to, does one need a better reason?'

They had settled down to their meal when Nandita remembered her earlier resolve. But how was she to bring it up? These Americans were such strange people. At one level of participation with human beings, there was nothing that was taboo to be spoken of between them, while on the other hand, there were those private preserves where no one could dare tread.

And then she found herself an opening! Bill was speaking of his dread of going back to New York at the end of the six months that he had given himself to normalise.

'You are young, Bill, why don't you get married again?'

He laughed and then placed a counter-question upon her platter. 'And you? Why don't you get married yourself?'

Her hands flew to her mouth and her face wore a look of 'My God, what are you saying?'

'Come on, girl, tell me.'

'The question doesn't arise!'

'Doesn't arise?'

'Not for me! Besides women age much faster than men do.'

'Sez who?'

'Come on, Bill, you very well know what I mean.'

'No, I don't,' he teased. 'But Meg had a theory or two on the subject to put all the male chauvinists of the world into a tizzy, Nan,' he informed her, his eyes dancing brightly in his unlined face. 'You should have heard Meg on the subject, you really should have.'

Nandita, smiling broadly, demanded, 'Tell me.'

'That girl of mine had strong opinions of her own and no way could you budge her from the position she had taken.' His eyes had fallen upon her plate, and realising that his guest had hardly eaten, he urged, 'Come on, Nan, eat up; cold pasta is terrible to eat, and you know that.'

'And cold steak is perfect?' she retorted. 'Look at your own plate.'

'You are getting to be as pesky as Meg, Nan, being in the company of us Americans is spoiling you rapidly, as I can see.' Today, Bill was sounding happy while speaking of the beloved wife he had lost. The gaping wounds were closing up; the process of healing had begun! His need for her would soon be over as well.

'I'm too old to get spoilt, Bill.' A tinge of sorrow coloured the edges of her words.

'There you go again, Nan, accepting all the misconceptions that the world has heaped upon women all through the ages. Wasn't I telling you something before your cooling pasta came in the way?'

'Something about Meg, you were telling me something about—'

'Yeah, I was telling you about Meg's mindset. Want some mustard, shall I pass it?'

'Thanks! And then?'

'There we were in a group, discussing one of these winter/summer weddings that had just taken place at our university. One of our colleagues, a male professor pretty advanced in years had married one of his students, a girl no more than nineteen or twenty.' *A stupid thing to do*, thought Nandita. And having eaten a mouthful, Bill went on, 'The male component in the gathering wanted to cite this as an example to prove that men remained forever young and could therefore marry women far younger than they themselves were.'

'Perhaps it's true.'

'No. It isn't,' he said, giving a big shake to his head. 'They argued that as women aged faster, they would catch up with their older male counterpart sooner rather than later.'

'And what did Meg have to say?'

'Plenty! She was not willing to accept their thesis and jumped right into the fray, saying, "No way can I agree with you guys about this business of ageing faster, unless the proof of youth lies in the continuing ability to increase the population of this already overpopulated world.""

'She said *that*, right to their faces?'

'Yeah, so she did, and some of the guys, caught on the wrong foot, stammered something like "We didn't mean that."

'Meg had her arguments well worked out and out she came with "You guys only have *that plus point*, which in reality is a *negative point*. What else should one call *the ability to impregnate a woman when a man is into his dotage, but a negative ability* in this world bursting at its seams?"' Nandita, squirming with embarrassment in her seat, heard. '"Resting your case on *that* point is all baloney. On all other counts, thanks to a little bit of help from medical research, women march one step ahead of you. They don't go on producing kids but they are just as active sexually, just as active mentally, somewhat better to look at physically, do you want me to go on?" The guys were all floored, and Meg and the other girls in that get-together walked out triumphant.'

'Please, Bill, lower your voice, what will people think?'

'People? What people? It is a fact, isn't it, that the birth control pill has freed women from the fear of unwanted pregnancies, and lifestyle changes and HRT have taken a great deal away from the fear of menopause? HRT has unfortunately come under fire of late, but at that point of time, it was not so and all Meg was doing was to remind the guys in the congregation of these facts.'

'Didn't she feel shy speaking of all this in mixed company?' she asked shyly.

'Should she have? It affects both sexes, doesn't it?'

The topic was getting too embarrassing to be dwelt upon further, and she changed tracks by paying a compliment to Meg's power of reasoning. 'What a fantastic woman your Meg was; she should have been a lawyer, Bill.'

He nodded agreement to both the compliments that had been paid his late wife but had persisted with 'So now tell me, dear Nan, does your argument that women age faster still hold?'

'May not be for an American woman, but for a woman like me it still does.'

'You are hard to convince, but one day I'm sure I'll be able to make you think differently.'

'Not likely, Bill, but I still think you should get married.'

'I see. Here, add a splash of beer to your lemonade and see if you like it?' He poured some beer into her glass, looked up, and asked, 'And may I ask why are you so intent today, to get me married?'

'Because you'll be so lonely when you go back. All right, at least get yourself a girlfriend.'

'Wow! Now she wants me to get myself a girlfriend, what's with you today, Nan? Shall I give you a little surprise?'

'Surprise?'

'What if I were to tell you that I already have one?'

'No, you don't. Do you really?' She had no idea how lost she looked as she asked this question of Bill. 'Is she nice, Bill?'

'Very nice, and surprisingly inexperienced and innocent.'

'She must be very young then. Men do like to be in the company of young women. I am very happy for you, Bill,' she ended, sounding extremely unhappy and downcast.

'Thanks! Now tell me when are you going to invite me home?'

'Home?'

'Yeah, the place where you normally live. I'd like to meet your family.'

'You want to meet them? What if they ask me who you are?'

'Tell them I am a guy called William Brady, whom you rescued when he was going to pieces.'

'What if they don't understand?'

'Come on, Nan, stop sounding like a teenager who is scared to introduce her first ever boyfriend to her parents.'

'Neither are you my boyfriend nor are they my parents, so please stop troubling me, Bill,' she said, rising from her chair. 'I will introduce you to them one day.'

Having settled the bill, he joined her at the entrance where she was waiting for him. And together they strolled down the road towards his parked car. 'Good. But make it soon, Nan, I'd like to meet those kids of yours.'

The car was parked across the street, the lights at the pedestrian crossing were on the verge of turning to red from green, so he grabbed her arm, tucked it safely under his own, and took her across at a near sprint across the road. Still holding on to her arm, smiling down upon her, he said, 'Now let me see, you were asking me why I've been—'

And then he was cut off mid-sentence by a not-too-familiar yet somewhat familiar voice that chortled, 'Hello, Mrs Roy, hi, Mr Brady, we meet again.' Taller than Nandita, shorter than Bill, long-legged and windblown stood Sujata, known as Sue, close to their entwined arms.

All colour instantly fled from Nandita's face, and she wanted the earth to open up and to swallow her. But to make that possible, she would have to first remove herself from Bill's strong grasp. She tried once, tried twice, and tried for a third time again; but he seemed not to notice and held on. Having failed on all three counts, she wished that she had some magical powers by which she could make herself disappear totally from the face of the earth.

The other two members that made up the roadside triumvirate had in the meanwhile got into a very healthy social exchange. Bill, though he had not once loosened his hold upon her, seemed to have become all eyes for the young female standing before them.

And then with a 'Bye-eee', the young woman in her micro-mini shorts sped on to whatever errand she was chasing at that moment.

Nandita, none too pleased, with a pronounced degree of petulance, demanded, 'Why didn't you let go of my arm?'

'You wanted me to let go of your arm?' he asked, all innocence.

'I tried to take my arm away so many times but you just would not take a hint and let go.'

'Why didn't you tell me?'

'And draw attention to the fact that you were just not letting go of me.'

'Oh, was that what I was doing?' He said, suppressing a smile, 'I should have understood but you see, Nan, I had become quite helpless.'

'Helpless?'

'Those long and tanned legs had completely mesmerised me, otherwise tell me why should I miss out on your wanting to get rid of me? You were perfectly right, Nan; we older men do have a terrible weakness for younger women. And particularly so if they have such long and bronzed legs.' His lips twitched with suppressed laughter as he finished with his confession.

'Do please be serious, Bill, that girl is my son's friend's wife, and who knows what she will go and say to them,' she added with a worried look on her face.

He unlocked the car and ushered Nandita in, checked her seat belt, and got in himself. 'I'm going to drop you home, it's much too hot to walk around after a meal. And don't you tell me that the neighbours as well will have something to report back to your guardians. What exactly are you afraid of, Nan? Don't tell me two adults can't spend a few hours together without setting the neighbourhood ablaze with gossip?'

'You won't understand Bill, you are an American, you will not understand!'

'But you live in the United States of America.'

'But that still does not make me an American, does it?'

14 WHY DON'T YOU TAKE ME HOME?

'I am a presentable enough guy, why don't you take me to meet your family?'
Bill had demanded of her once again just the other day. A very simple
request indeed, but how on earth was she going to fulfil it?

'I will, I will,' she had assured him, wondering when and how she was
going to fulfil this promise. It was a mind-boggling situation, and she had
no idea where she was going to garner courage enough to bring about such a
meeting. No, she just could not do it. Oh, the orthodoxy of her upbringing,
how it raised its head and stayed her every action! The tectonic plates of her
collective consciousness had gone crashing together and fallen back in place!

Did meeting a man almost a decade ago at an *annoprashon* ceremony in
New Jersey place him in any way within the framework of her own existence?
That she could just take him over and spring him upon the unsuspecting
members of her family as a blue-eyed, blonde, white male friend of her own?
It did smack of the incongruous! She had never weighed herself in terms of
courage and cowardice, but encountering her own trepidation in the face of so
simple a matter as taking home a friend, she had begun to doubt the quality of
the mettle of which she was made. How she wished she was not such a coward.
All she wanted to do was to present a friend and here she was getting all tied
up in knots.

Starting from New Jersey, she would have to do some bridge-building
that would smoothly connect Bill to herself and to this town in Illinois where
they lived. The Duttas had gone overboard while making out their invitation
list for their baby's *annoprashon*, so there was a distinct possibility that Tukun
might not have met the professor at all. She had mulled over all the factors
and had prepared a speech of sorts. As speeches went, it was not a bad speech
at all. But putting it across was quite another matter. After a handful of failed
attempts that constituted of no more than some humming and hawing that

no one had even noticed, she at last sought and found what she considered was a propitious slot to bring up the topic. The others had left and clearing her throat, she addressed her son softly, 'Tukun.'

'Yes, Ma?' Bowl of muesli before him, he looked up from his newspaper, spoon in hand.

'I've been wanting to tell you, I've been thinking of telling you . . .'

'What?'

'Never mind, it's nothing important.'

'Sure?' he quizzed.

'We can talk about it later.' The mother retreated in haste.

'Suit yourself.' And with a shrug, the son went back to his muesli and his newspaper.

And with one more failure notched up to her account, she had found excuses for herself. The poor boy was on the verge of leaving for work, how could she start off a long conversation with him at such a juncture? The lines were ready, waiting to be delivered, so where was the problem? However, the delivery of those lines never came to pass and her neatly laid-out plans fell by the wayside. And faced by her timorous self, she asked of herself, *Do I in truth need to present Bill to them at all?* In a week or so, the young people would be off on a vacation, and soon after their return, Bill's time in Saisborough would also be up! So where was the need? However, she did not know then, how this little act of prevarication and cowardice would come down one day as a landfall upon her.

Bill had wanted to visit her friends at the Home as well, why not take him there? When next Bill had asked, she was prepared with an answer.

'The family is leaving for a vacation by the sea . . .'

'When?'

'Soon after the children's school closes for summer; and as soon as the holiday is over, I'll—'

Alarmed he asked, 'How long will you be away?'

'I'm not going with them.'

'Am I pleased, I was wondering what I'd do with myself.'

She laughed, 'you have a girlfriend tucked away somewhere and you want me to believe that you'll miss me. Why, Bill, why are you making fun of me?'

'I'd have to be mighty courageous to make fun of you. So no visiting as of now for me as I can see.'

'What would you say if I were to ask you to come with me tomorrow, to visit my friends at the Home?'

'I'd say, at long last she finds me good enough to present to the world.'

'You know it's not that, Bill.'

'What is it then?'

'You Americans have such a terrible sense of humour, what if they were to tease me, Bill?'

'Tease you? Why? Is there anything to tease you about?' he teased.

'No, nothing.'

'Then you can take me along without any furrows creasing your beautiful brow.'

'Beautiful brow indeed! Stop flattering me, Bill.'

The Colonel was seated quietly in his wheelchair just outside the main entrance when Nandita and Bill arrived at the Home. They were hijacked promptly and taken to a secluded corner by him just to the right of the entry door. Nandita introduced Bill to the Colonel and told a little bit about him to the older man.

'May I leave out all that Dr William Brady bit and call you Bill?'

'Sure.'

'Come pull up a couple of chairs. Put Nan into one of them and take the other,' commanded the Colonel. Giving precise instructions was so deeply ingrained in him that he quite often forgot whom he was directing them to.

'Thanks.'

'I like this girlfriend of yours,' he told Bill with a smile, as he seated himself on one of the chairs he had placed beside the Colonel's wheelchair.

'So do I.'

'Excuse me, Bill, I am your friend, not your girlfriend,' Nandita corrected, bristling at the suggestion being made.

Bill grinned, looked at her then at the Colonel, and said, 'There she goes splitting hairs.'

'I'm doing nothing of the sort, Colonel.'

'Uh-huh!' The colonel was ostensibly clearing his throat.

'Bill is not my boyfriend. I know that he already has a very young and innocent girlfriend . . .'

'Is that so?' the Colonel asked and then went on, 'There's no shortage of old fools in this world,' in an undertone that was yet loud enough to be heard.

'Did you say something, Colonel?' Bill Brady asked in a voice replete with innocence, amusement glinting from his deep blue eyes.

'Did I say something? Perhaps I did; at my age one tends to forget, you know.' The Colonel, having made his point, smartly took refuge in his supposed state of acute dotage.

No wonder Grace called him an old fox, Nandita thought. How neatly he had commented upon Bill's very young girlfriend and then had smartly slithered out of it, pretending age-related amnesia! A barely concealed smile hovering at the corners of her lips, she felt the time had come for her to give a little nudge to the conversation to make it move a safer way. 'You know, Bill—'

'Yes?' He looked at her.

'The Colonel has been asking me to bring you over for a while now.'

'Yeah, because I wanted to check out what kind of a guy she was going around with.' The professor burst out laughing, and the Colonel threw him a questioning look!

And, 'Really, Colonel, you seem to forget at times that I am a grandmother,' Nandita remonstrated.

'I sure do.'

'But it makes me feel good . . .' she said, smiling into his eyes and taking his hand into her own. The Colonel chuckled and looked with affection towards her.

'I'd love to date her, but she isn't willing; so I have to be satisfied just being her teacher.'

'Teacher? I didn't know Nan was your student; that's a revelation!'

'The Colonel has been telling me about Vietnam and other—'

'Yeah! There have been too many wars in which we went and got ourselves mixed up. I can do without wars . . .'

'Yeah, the entire human race can do without wars,' the professor acquiesced.

Brooking no interruption, the Colonel declaimed, 'But warriors . . . that's quite another matter. A trained man in uniform is a cut above other men,' verging on the pompous. Bill smiled and let it ride.

And it was then that Bill told the Colonel how close he had been to being shipped off to Vietnam himself.

'You don't say, you don't look old enough to have been . . .'

'Perhaps not quite old enough, sir, but had the war lasted a bit longer I might have well been enlisted.' The Colonel chose to keep his silence and the professor, changing the topic, asked, 'So what have you been teaching her, Colonel?' The Colonel smiled and looked towards Nandita, urging her to speak.

'The Colonel has been most kind in letting me take a peep at the history of the United States. And Mr Whitfield—'

'Ah, speak of the devil; there's David. David, come and meet Nan's friend,' the Colonel called out. Stopping in his tracks, the elderly schoolmaster looked around, spotted the Colonel holding court in the alcove, and came forward.

'Yeah?' he asked.

And Nandita, taking the lead, turning to the professor, said, 'Bill, meet my other teacher, Mr David Whitfield, and David, this is my friend Dr William Brady.'

'Bill to my friends,' the professor said, rising and shaking hands with the retired schoolmaster.

'Watch out, Bill,' warned the Colonel, 'my friend David loves to teach . . .'

'And our Nan's a fast learner: watch out, she may spring a surprise or two on you one of these days,' concluded David Whitfield.

'Thanks for the warning. I'll guard my flanks from now on.'

'There's no need for anxiety, Bill, my tutors are just being very, very kind.'

'Yeah! David has been stuffing her head with—'

'I don't know that I've done anything more than the Colonel,' the rivalry, though well cloaked, was on show for the discerning to see, 'but between the two of us, poor Nan hasn't had much respite.'

'She makes a good pupil, Bill, and the two of us are slave drivers of a variety that has gone totally out of style these days. She wanted to know something about Mark Twain, since then, I have put her on to Thoreau and Emerson. I introduced her to our very own Emily the other day.' And turning to Nandita, back to being a schoolmaster, he demanded without any preamble, 'So, Nan, did you find any time to read any of Emily Dickinson's work?'

'Yes, a little bit, but even so, I find she touches a resonant chord within me that no one else ever has. Though I've been stirred deeply by Whitman and Thoreau, I've felt a special affinity for Emily Dickinson.'

'Becoming her fan?' demanded the Colonel with a sardonic glance. He had little or no patience with poets or with poetic outbursts.

'Perhaps a bit! I find her fascinating, for the way she looks upon death has made me feel very close to her.' She paused, took a breath to compose herself and went on, 'Even though I have had my share of deaths and disappearances in my life, I could never have said anything like this:

> The sweeping up the heart,
> And putting love away
> We shall not want to use again
> Until eternity.'

'Nan!' all three men exclaimed.

And softly she added, with sadness, 'Oh, the finality of separation that death inflicts upon us . . .'

Bill stretched out a comforting hand towards her and went on, 'Yeah, death is so final, and the poet minces no words to tell us that,' and his eyes had moistened as he said the words. The Colonel had turned his face away and the good schoolmaster mumbled something about something having gotten into his eyes.

'There's a great deal of power in her words,' Bill stated.

'So true, words are not inanimate or lifeless in her masterful hands, Bill.'

And then in a deep and sonorous voice, he began reciting:

> A word is dead
> When it is said,
> Some say,

Nandita had picked up from there and concluded:

> I say it just
> Begins to live
> That day.

There was a moment's silence and then a voice spoke up, 'Remarkable, you have not just been reading your Emily Dickinson, you've been studying her, as I can see, Nan.' There was a sparkle in the retired schoolmaster's eyes as he stretched out a hand to take hold of Nandita's hand.

'You are much too kind, David.'

'By God, Nan, at this rate you'll put us guys born in the United States to shame.' This had come from the Colonel, who was usually very chary with praise. 'But watch out, Nan, too much poetry can—'

'Addle the brains?' challenged the schoolmaster.

And Bill, unwilling to be diverted by either of them, looking admiringly at Nandita, huskily said, 'I had no idea that you've been making such good use of your time, Nan.' Turning to her duo of tutors, he added, 'But I think you two gentlemen do deserve a special mention in despatches. Yes, sir, you really do.'

'Thanks, Bill,' they said in tandem. And, 'We have a very receptive student in Nan,' the Colonel concluded.

'Thank you, gentlemen, for being so kind, thank you for introducing me to the real United States, that US which lies beyond discount coupons and tempting offers of two cans of soup for the price of one, and of burgers and Cokes and daytime soaps.'

'Bravo, Nan, "two cans of soup for the price of one"—that was a real good one! Our bluster and our crassly commercial exterior does manage rather too well to hide our inner more subtle and soulful core from the world. I'm so pleased that you have taken pains to discover it.'

'It's really not I, Bill, but all of you and the wonderful books to which I have been introduced that have made the difference. That has given me a glimpse of that which lies at the core of this nation.'

'Am I glad I came with you today; you have never once let it slip out of you that you are such a serious student of our country. Had I known, I'd have passed on a book or two myself.'

'Not of poetry, I hope,' warned the Colonel. And both Bill and Nandita chuckled at his obsessive dislike of poetry.

And David, just to spite the Colonel, or so it seemed to Bill, pulled out a few lines of Robert Frost and brought them out bright and shining from the coffers of his memory and placed them with a flourish before his captive audience. At the end of it, he asked, 'Heard of Robert Frost?'

'"The woods are lovely dark and deep . . ."'

'So you do know who Frost is. Good!'

'How could I help but know him, David? I was a schoolteacher back in India, as you know.'

'So?'

'We taught Nehru, and when we taught Nehru, we automatically included some Frost.'

'How's that?' the other schoolteacher wanted to know.

'You may not believe me, but these lines have been made famous in India by Jawaharlal Nehru. Not too many know that the creator of these lines is Robert Frost, not Nehru.'

'Really?'

'Faced with the reality of the ebbing away of his life force, faced with the fact that there was still so much to do before he could fall into his final sleep, he scribbled some lines from Frost to express his helplessness.'

'Poets do have their use, I suppose,' acknowledged the Colonel somewhat grudgingly. David frowned but let it pass.

'And what about your writers and poets, Nan?' asked the schoolmaster, and then exclaimed, 'Oh! Yeah, I know of Tagore if not of anyone else.'

Before Nandita could give a reply, the Colonel cut in with a near command, 'Come, let's go in, it's coffee time.' For a single day, he had had quite enough of this poetry business. From Dickinson, he had seen how they had veered off to Frost, and any moment now, they would be spewing Tagore as well! He had made an about-turn in his wheelchair and went off towards the foyer and the rest of the poetic society fell meekly in place and followed after.

Grace was sitting facing the entrance and spotted the foursome as soon as the door was opened to let the Colonel's wheelchair in. A frown creased her brow, and none too pleased, she looked towards Helen with a questioning look. *What was her Nan doing among these aliens?* She was *her friend*, so what were those two old gizzards doing with her? And who was that handsome young man who was trooping in beside them? Highly offended, she lowered her eyes onto her lap and pretended not to have seen them at all.

The welcoming aroma of coffee and cookies accompanied by the friendly clinking of cutlery against crockery stretched out a welcoming hand to the new entrants arriving upon the scene. It was a very large and spread-out area and groups of the inmates sat together in clusters. Grace, almost back to her earlier form, sat surrounded by half a dozen of her most intimate cronies. If Grace had chosen to sit with her head down, Helen and Kate were all eyes for the tall, blonde, blue-eyed man beside Nan. 'Must be the guy for whom Nan baked a cake.' Cocking her head to a side, Helen looked at Kate and Kate looked at Helen, questioning each other with their eyes. Was there perhaps a romance brewing here? And Ted oblivious to all this conjecturing, sat examining the cookie in his hand while sipping the scalding hot brew in his cup. Helen, trying to catch his eyes, wondered why men were so bereft of romance. Was this the moment to scrutinise a cookie?

'Hi, Grace, hi, everyone, see who I've brought to meet you.'

A very offended Grace turned a deaf ear to the greeting and continued to steadily look down at her lap. The floral print of her dress had never been as well examined ever before and revealed many nuances of shades and colours that she did not know even existed. She had always thought that a spread of pink roses was all this dress had to it, and all of a sudden today, she had spotted an abundance of little pale-green leaves peeping from behind all those pink roses.

'Gra-ace,' cajoled Nandita, 'see who I've brought to meet you.'

'Meet me? Or the Colonel?' she mumbled and, studiedly looking away from Nandita, went back to studying the print upon her dress.

Oh! My God! Thanks to the forced stopover with the Colonel, I've gone and incurred Grace's wrath, agonised Nandita.

Discomfited Nandita may have been, but the Colonel was certainly not. He was quite enjoying the outcome of having pipped Grace at the post. He had no patience with Grace's proprietary 'hands off, she's my property' stance. Starting with a throaty chuckle, he burst out into a teasing laughter-overlaid rejoinder, 'It goes without saying that she has come to meet me, Gracie. I'm a handsome, charming, and personable guy, so what else can you expect?'

Provoked by the Colonel, Grace abandoned the scrutiny of the floral print and went in to give battle. 'Huh! Handsome, charming, personable! No mirrors in your room or what, Colonel?'

The first volleys had been fired; before the skirmish turned into a full-fledged battle, Nandita moved into the brewing war zone to try and put an end to the hostilities. Stepping forward with Bill beside her, she dropped a kiss upon a wizened cheek and softly said, 'Grace, this is Bill.' Then looking up, 'Bill, this is Grace.'

Reverting to being the gracious dignified lady that she normally was, Grace straightened her back, arranged her dress upon her knees, looked up (but not at Nandita, she was still not forgiven), and stretched out a hand towards Bill.

Bill had gauged from the many conversations about the people who lived there with her that his dear Nan was popular with the residents of the Home.

But he had no idea that she was as popular and sought after as this! He remembered the timid friendless woman he had met one day seated alone upon a cold and lonely bench downtown and marvelled at the journey she had since undertaken. It was an eye-opening experience for him to see how central she had become to their lives. These little wars that were being waged over how much attention she paid to whom were quite mind-boggling. He could never ever have imagined that she could have so speedily moved on to such a position of pre-eminence among a bunch of people with whom till just the other day she must have had so little in common. And a strange sense of disquietude coursed through his heart: could it possibly be a twinge of jealousy? Fortunately for him, the extended hand of a very gracious Grace saved him from further introspection. With a warm and charming smile, he got down to charming a thoroughly out-of-humour Grace.

He was a charmer; having smiled into her eyes and shaken hands with Grace, he had stood a moment beside her, still holding on to her hand. The rest of the group was getting fidgety, he could see. How did Nan manage to balance her books with this gang, he wondered! Gently releasing his hand, he went around introducing himself with a smile here, a word there to the rest of the company. It was quite obvious that poor Nan was still not forgiven; taking pity on her, he decided to do some repair-work on her behalf. The poor girl had created a life for herself among these people; one visit from him should not disturb the well-being of these newly created bonds he acknowledged.

Professors do not become famous on acquiring and stashing away funds of knowledge and information alone. Like actors and orators and politicians, they too have to have the art of connectivity. That very special ability to make each person who looks upon them believe that the words they are uttering, the gestures they are making are being directed towards his or her individual self, and to his or her individual self alone, perhaps to be shared peripherally by the others who also make up the congregation but never going beyond that! And their visitor this morning was none other than the very famous Professor William Brady, who was well renowned the world over for his electrifying classroom presence. Mesmerising the entire group with an all-encompassing smile, he pulled up a chair and positioned himself beside Grace.

He began by giving Grace his undivided attention and had very soon brought back the smile upon her lips. And so a very bone-chilling cold war directed towards the person of Nandita was cleverly averted. Even while he was worming his way into Grace's heart, he engaged himself with eye contact here, a gesture or a smile there with the entire group as well. Nandita had looked on wonder, struck for she had never seen Bill in action prior to this. By the end of the performance, Bill had managed to become quite a favourite with one and all! And they soon got down to ferreting out some information from him.

Ted said he had once met a Brady back in Milwaukee, 'Did you have a relation who was an ornithologist?' he asked.

'Not that I know of.'

'You're not from Milwaukee, are you?' Grace wanted to know.

'No, I am from Illinois.'

'From Illinois, you don't say!' a very pleased Helen, for whom the boundary lines of the world began and ended with the state of Illinois, exclaimed.

'Was your dad a doc, you know, the real kind who treat sick people?' demanded Grace.

'Yeah! He was the "real kind",' he replied with a carefully suppressed smile.

'Gracie!' the Colonel and David chorused a warning her way.

But who was listening? And she went on as blithe as ever, 'Was his name the same as yours?'

'Is this an inquisition?' the Colonel demanded of her.

Throwing a smile denoting *I don't mind* the Colonel's way, Bill replied, 'Yes I have inherited my dad's name.'

And Grace, very pleased with herself, conjured up the fact that she had been acquainted with his father at one time. Triumphantly she had declared, 'Then I have met your dad. That was, way, way back though. He was a handsome guy, believe me, and a bachelor to boot, and so the girls just . . .' She ended with a chuckle.

'How wonderful that you'd met my dad.'

'Is he still around?'

'It's been two years since he passed away.'

'I'm sorry. But then . . . I suppose . . . the odds were stacked against getting any other but this reply.'

And from there, the topic moved on to his family and the whole lot of them had wept silent tears on learning that he had so recently lost his wife. Nandita, sensitive to Bill's pain, knew she would have to rescue him immediately from the surge of suffocating sympathy that was flowing over his head like a huge tidal wave. And then she thankfully remembered Charlie and her compatriots.

'Please don't mind, folks, but if I don't take Bill in to meet Charlie and co., I'll never be forgiven.' What better excuse could she have found to drag Bill away from the smothering morass of sentimentality into which the friendly banter of a few minutes ago was descending!

And the Colonel, gauging the reason, twinkled, 'You're a lucky guy, Bill.'

And Nandita went on as if the Colonel had not interrupted her at all. 'You can well imagine what Charlie would have to say if Bill came and went away. I shudder at the mere thought of . . .'

The heads nodding in agreement made it quite clear that they understood where exactly she would stand if such a faux pas were to come to pass.

'If you know what's good for you, better take this guy here to meet that lot, my dear girl,' David advised, then mulling further upon the matter, ended with an ominous 'They might even, as a group, apply some sanctions upon you if you leave them out.'

And with a loud chuckle, the Colonel added, 'And we Americans, as everyone knows, love applying sanctions on just anyone we can get hold of!' And the tension in the air melted away.

'Who knows, they may even stop talking to you,' a gloomy voice added.

'Now that wouldn't do, would it? Come, Nan, let us go forth to save you from social ostracism of the worst kind. The wrath of Uncle Sam must not be allowed to fall upon you, believe me.' And with a general farewell to the gathering, Bill took hold of Nandita's hand and urged her out of the foyer.

'Come again, Bill,' a chorus of voices sang out.

And the Colonel peppered the farewell with 'Coming under the pressure of my upright military ways . . . though mark you, I am jealous . . . I will admit though grudgingly . . . that you're an OK guy!'

'Thanks! That's fulsome . . .'

'And will just about do, as a boyfriend for Nan. Provided of course . . . you don't mind . . . sharing this here gal with me.'

Nandita frowned, Bill burst out laughing, the rest of them smiled indulgently, and the Colonel looked on, well pleased with himself.

The nurse on duty was a sweet young thing who ran off obligingly to take a look at whether or not her patients were in a position to receive guests. Visitors worked like a charm, like an elixir of vitality upon the bedridden; they were never sent away unless it was with a good reason.

And when presented to Charlie and her compatriots, Bill was an instant hit. Yes, to her joy, he was a hit with one and all. There was that touch of compassion without condescension in his conduct that endeared him to these not-so-fortunate people.

'Hope you'll keep visitin' us regl'ar-like from now on, Bill,' Charlie implored.

'While I'm here in Saisborough, I sure will, ma'am.'

'Where you goin'?' she demanded, none too pleased to hear that he would be leaving Saisborough sometime in the near future. And then she asked, 'Must you go away?' And Charlie's query had found an echo within Nandita's heart.

Though 'His work is there, Charlie, so he must leave,' was what she said, covering her ache with a smile.

Later when they were alone, she smiled up at him and said, 'I had no idea that you were such a manipulator, Bill.'

'Manipulator?'

'What else, you made the lot fall in love with you.'

'What an unfair assessment, my girl, here I was fighting to save your skin and you go and call me a manipulator. I am indeed hurt at being accused of being the kind of guy who makes a room full of innocents fall in love with him.'

'Hurt indeed! You had them eating out of your hand. They had eyes for you alone.'

'Jealousy will get you nowhere, Nan.'

'I'm not jealous, I was only commenting upon what I saw.'

'I see, is that what it is? But I fear I see the green-eyed monster there?'

'Really, Bill, you are incorrigible.'

'You say I was manipulative and I say I was not. Shall I tell you in truth what really happened?'

'Tell me.'

'Not that I'm saying that you are not easy on the eye, but even so in all humility, I must submit that it must have been my extreme good looks that hit them like a ten-tonne truck.' He had a mischievous glint to his eyes.

'Fortunately, I happen to be somewhat taller than your friends, so none of their adulating eyes was able to spot my thinning hair.'

'You are hopeless, Bill.' And they laughed together and moved on.

The house would be hers alone, for the next week. The family had taken off for the seaside without her, for she had opted out of the offer they had made that she join them.

The previous evening, Tukun had asked, 'Are you sure you'll be all right, Ma? We'll be away for more than a week, you know.' And Meeta going past, overhearing his words, had echoed his concern as she rushed in and out of the room. But Nandita had not budged from her position. She knew this offer made to join them had been made in the line of duty. And she also knew that being constantly on duty was a very wearing occupation! They deserved a break and so did she.

'I promise I'll take very good care of myself while you are away. But, Tukun, I have been feeling somewhat guilty about Mahadevan's mother.'

'Guilty?'

'We haven't asked her over.'

'I have sounded Mahadevan on a likely visit by her . . .'

'You did? So what did he say?' Nandita asked, as she measured out some flour out of a container.

'He asked her, but she refused. I believe she said, "If I'm not there, how will your father manage? Who will give him his lunch? Tell me who will make his evening tiffin?" Is he really that helpless, Ma?'

'All men are,' she had generalised with a smile. 'So what do we do?' Sprinkling a pinch of salt over the flour she asked.

'She has asked you to come over, if not now, then during Diwali.'

'That's a long way off. You come back from your vacation then I shall make some *roshogollas* that you can hand over to Mahadevan. Or shall I make some *shandesh*?'

'No, *roshogollas* will be better. Somehow the rest of India thinks in terms of *roshogollas* when they think of Bengal and us Bangalis.' And both mother and son had smiled.

'The cow's milk we get is good, so that should pose no problem.'

'That, I think, should do as a stopgap till Diwali,' he had acquiesced, 'but as of now I am a bit worried about leaving you alone here.'

Putting the partly kneaded dough aside, she had gone on to reassure him that she would see to it that no crisis would come to take place in her life during his absence. 'Don't worry, I'll be just fine.'

Surprised by her air of assurance, he looked upon her with new-found respect. The unspoken words *You really sound in control, Ma, just like the mother I have long since left behind in my youth*, had echoed around in his brain. But 'All the same, please be careful,' was all he had said, while placing a wad of notes and a loose sheet of paper in her hand.

'I've plenty of money, Tukun. There's no need to—'

'Please keep it, Ma,' he had coerced as he used to while asking for a favour while still a boy, 'it will make me feel more comfortable if you do.'

'All right, give it to me; I'll keep the money if it makes you feel better.' Then she looked down upon the scrap of paper. 'What are these numbers?'

'Numbers that will get you some help in case of an emergency. I'll fix it on to the fridge: here under this magnet. And you have my cell number, don't you?'

'Of course I do.' Going up to her concerned son, she had placed a solicitous hand upon his back and reassured him, 'And stop worrying. I promise not to get into any trouble.' And he had laughed, for he just could not imagine a scenario where his staid stay-at-home mother could get herself into trouble. What kind of trouble was she likely to get into?

'Take care you don't fall ill. It's getting very hot these days and you are—'

'Yes, I do go for walks, but because of the big trees, the roads are well shaded.'

'Sure you won't get bored? We leave early tomorrow; you can still change your mind, you know.'

'I know I can, Khoka,' he had not missed the appellation, 'but I really am not feeling like going on such a long drive. Have a good holiday and come back refreshed.'

'I'm looking forward to this break but . . .'

'Leave me out of this trip, please. You need to spend some time alone with your family; you really do.' The words were said in absolute sincerity for she recognised with a rediscovered perspicacity that it couldn't be much fun having a mother always tagging along with you like an albatross around your neck when you wanted to take a little vacation with your wife and your children. 'And believe me, I'll be fine.' She had reassured him once again.

'Look after yourself while we are away.'

'I will. And now I must get along with the making of some *loochie* and *aloo phool kopeer chenchki* for your journey. As you can see, even the dough is still to be done.'

'That'll be lovely, Ma! I remember we never went anywhere without a hamper full of these two favourites of mine when I was in school.' And steeped in nostalgia, he murmured, 'Somehow, rolled-up cold *loochies* with a cold *aloo phoolkopir torkari* filling spells the joy of holiday-time journeying for me, even now.'

She had smiled a happy smile. 'The children love sweet crisp *gojas* so I made some for them yesterday. I better go and complete the frying of the *loochies*; they have to be cooled before packing.'

And in the background could be heard the voices of another mother and son bargaining over what could be construed as essential to be to be taken along in an already overcrowded car while going on a holiday by the sea.

'You want to take along your skateboard with you? What will you do with a skateboard on sand?' The answer was not audible to Nandita as, head bent, she kept rolling out the *loochies*.

But later the same morning, she spotted a corner of the skateboard peeping out from under a pile of other 'essential' items that were going along with them on this vacation!

The house was empty, but not empty at all. The excited, happy voices of the foursome as they loaded and unloaded the car to get a perfect fit. The rushing up and down the stairs in search of items that had that moment struck them as indispensable towards making this holiday that little bit more commendable. The final bickering over which of the two children would sit directly behind their father and the final embraces before they set off had all left an indelible mark of happiness and filled up all the empty spaces within the house and in her heart!

The exuberance of the very young was so wearing. She would miss her son and his young family; even so, she was glad she had stood firm and not gone along with them! She had sighed out a breath of relief as they had driven off and gone in to make a decent cup of tea. Seated upon her favourite bench in the yard, she sat on, lost in rumination as she sipped the strong and scalding brew.

She could now understand what exactly it meant to be *a square*. On a beach, juxtaposed with the rest of the throng, she could be classified without exaggeration as a square peg that was attempting to fit itself into a world that was, had been, and always would be spherical. No wonder she had not once been able to adjust and enjoy a single one of these periodic jaunts that the family made to the seashore! Her very first experience should have been an eye-opener. The *sari* for Nandita was a symbol: an identification mark of her origins, the outward stamp of her individuality, a mark of her national pride. And so even after coming to the United States, she had never worn anything but a *sari*, an attire that she held was among the best in the entire gamut of dresses worn the world over by women. However, her personal experience upon the seaboard of the US had opened her eyes to the impracticality of the dress she wore so proudly everywhere. For she had immediately recognised the fact that there could be nothing more ludicrous on a beach than such an overt state of overdress as she was to be found in!

The sight of a woman draped in a six-yard-wide *sari* trailing around behind a group clad in an appropriate state of 'undress', both parties making the other uncomfortable, was a sight to be seen to be believed. She had hated every moment of it; the soggy lower reaches of her *sari* weighed down by sand, flapping around her ankles, had tried to trip her up with every painful step that she took. It must have surely made the others in the party equally uncomfortable?

And as for Meeta, with a mother-in-law draped in six yards of prudery, what must she have endured while making her attempts at blending in with the populace? Though the poor girl had donned a swimming costume, she must never have done so without vast amounts of self-consciousness. Nandita had just been able to decipher how her daughter-in-law had attempted to cover up her embarrassment with some bluster, and some studied looks of nonchalance! And had ended up appearing to be deliberately rude and insolent to Nandita's eyes. Poor girl, it must have been quite wearisome for her trying to balance the books between respectability and acceptability, and keeping her cool at one and the same time.

She must have left the transistor on, and a tune from it trickled out from the kitchen and reached her. Giving herself a feline stretch, she thought, what luxury, what bounty. She would have ten days all to her own self! She would make some excuse and stay away from all her usual haunts, and wander around alone instead, within her own consciousness! She had need today to get reacquainted with her own self, know who she was, and understand for herself where she was going. How long could this strange dichotomy in her existence continue to exist? Those chance meetings with that young woman named Sujata, who called herself Sue, had filled her heart with a sense of insecurity. She knew that all she had to do was to introduce her friends to her family to secure herself from any chance confrontation, and yet, what was it that made her so jealously guard these relationships close to just her own self? Did she fear that with sharing would come some depletion?

And had she not overheard the other day that Vivek had taken up a new assignment at Los Angeles and that Sue, succumbing to the lure of warmer climes, had agreed to make the move. And one day when the dust of Bill's presence in Saisborough had settled, she would take her son and his family to visit the folks who lived in the Home. Would they like them? Of course they would, how could they help but love her two grandchildren, and their more-than-personable parents? Once she had put all her problems into neat dockets, it had all appeared to be so simple.

But deep down within her, she knew that coming to terms with life and its realities was not an easy matter. She needed time and space, within which she must search out some answers about her own self. The house was all her own for the next ten days, and by staying away from all her other newly wrought relationships, she would create an oasis of her very own where none else could venture. And peering into her heart, she would take a close look at what went on within her own consciousness!

Bill was away to Toronto, so avoiding him posed no problems, and a white lie about the state of her health had raised a few anxious enquiries from the Home but had raised no eyebrows at her absence. And so it was that Nandita had provided herself with the perfect milieu for conducting an exercise at storming the bastions of both her head and her heart. But pinning down thoughts that were as recalcitrant as hers were was no easy matter. Each time she tried to get a hold on them, they would slip through her fingers and bound away like a fistful of live fish attempting to save their lives. So how was she to examine them and come to terms with them?

After three days of self-imposed seclusion, she had been driven out of her home with the need to take in a lungful of fresh air, if nothing else! The three days of hibernation that she had imposed upon herself had opened her eyes to the fact that the Nandita of today was no longer the same person. This Nandita would not be able to go back to the life she had led prior to that walk downtown in search of a post office one day. Deep down within her, a voice was also reminding her that time was fast running out for her. And though she was not willing to bring it up to her own self, Bill was to have returned this morning. And had she not told him something about meeting him downtown? In haste, she went up to her room and pulled out a freshly ironed *sari*. She looked into the mirror above her dresser and was surprised to look into a pair of eyes a-sparkle with life. Once dressed, she tugged a comb through her hair more as a salutary gesture than because she felt it would bring about any long-term improvement! She knew from experience that come what may, her tutored locks would come loose sooner rather than later and fall across her forehead once again.

Not a soul was to be seen walking on the somnolent heat-drugged street as she pulled the door shut and let herself out onto the street. The sidewalks bereft of humanity looked lost and lonesome. Could keeping away from the streets for just three days make such a difference? A sweltering, tar-melting heat had come and taken hold of the Chicago region, yet she loved the cloying, clinging feel of the breeze upon her already warmed-by-excitement cheeks! She felt as free as one of her Dipto's high-flying kites as she lent her eyes and her ears to the sights and the sounds around her.

A lovely somnolent song of the season had fallen with a friendly lilting cadence upon her ears. She breathed in the sweet, honeyed scent of freedom in the air perfumed by her favourite scent, that of mown grass. How did one describe the perfume of mown grass? By its colour perhaps. For it filled the air with a tangy-as-mint, fresh-as-lime, perky-as-a-grasshopper, crisp and cool-as-a-cucumber presence! It came wafting like an allure, to entice her on. A far-off hum of a lawnmower hung in the air like the summertime song of the bumblebees that she had grown up with, in far-off Calcutta. *These are the soothing, comforting, lulling sounds of summertime that make the discomforts of the season so much more bearable*, she thought as she began walking down the street.

But within moments, she was on the verge of thinking otherwise, for a cloying, damp, and muggy heat had seeped into all the folds of her clothing and wrapped itself around her within minutes. Her bathed and cool body had gone clammy and her blouse and her undergarments, having gone damp with perspiration, had taken a tight hold of her. The pleats of her crisp white sari had got entangled in the dampness of her petticoat and the ensemble of these two garments had erotically clung to her sweaty legs as she began walking down the street. It was such a long time since she had felt or recognised any such sensations related to her own body! She pulled at her wayward clothing, wanting to push aside the discomfiting sensations that they were arousing within her.

And then a snapshot frozen in time, pulled out of the album of her memory, had popped out right in front of her eyes. It belonged to a period of time when Nandita must have been barely ten or eleven years old, no more! Having awoken earlier than usual, she had risen quietly and tiptoed out of the room in which she slept beside her mother. The toilets and the rooms for bathing were placed away from the main dwelling areas at the other end of the courtyard. The sun was yet to emerge but it was not so dark as to make her feel really afraid, for a hint of brightness had already touched the sky in readiness for its advent.

The early morning air had a nip to it. Holding her arms across her chest to ward off the chill, she had crossed the courtyard and gone into the bathing area. She had emerged after a few minutes, to see Daminidi rise from under the tap tucked away under an awning near the kitchen. Damini draped in a length of semi-transparent cloth, her par-white coarse cotton *sari*, stood silhouetted against the lightening sky. Her sopping wet sari barely covering her generous curves, her hair streaming droplets down her back, she had stood transformed as a beautiful and exotic creature in the eyes of the little girl standing a short distance away. Nandita, standing engulfed by the shadowy sanctuary of the veranda, must not have been visible to Damini though. She was about to call out to Damini when the ring attached to the door leading from outside to the courtyard had been brought down gently once, twice, thrice upon the wood. Damini had picked up a shining brass vessel and moved towards the door swiftly and thrown the door open. It had surprised the little girl standing on the sidelines and watching this tableau that Damini had not cared to even cover her near-bare body.

Panchu Goyla, the milkman, was at the door with his large can of milk. The sky had got just a wee shade lighter, and with the help of that faint light, Nandita could see the tall and strapping youth look down upon the crouching figure of Damini as she held out the vessel to him. The task of pouring out milk from one container to another had taken a great deal of time. Muted whispers and suppressed laughter had reached her ears. And from where she stood, she had been witness to Panchu's wandering fingers lingering upon the person of Damini. She had known somehow that this was a matter that would best lie buried within her heart. She had not spoken of it to anyone. But for days, a compelling force had drawn her to the courtyard in those early hours of the morning to witness the selfsame tableau!

Then abruptly one day, the early morning drama had been brought to a close, Panchu's services had been terminated, and an elderly milkman who called only when the sun was really and truly up was given the vacated position. Not a word had crossed anyone's lips, no one had berated Damini, not a scorching reprimand had been hurled Damini's way, yet her reddened eyes were witness to the tears she must have shed each day. Too young to understand fully the drama that had been played out before her eyes, she had set it aside and put it away somewhere deep down in the inner recesses of her mind. It was much, much later that she realised that Damini had tried to stretch out and pluck some forbidden fruit for herself. She had been granted a reprieve because of all the services that she rendered expecting no payment in return. She was the one who had been loaded with the burden of gratitude. Had she not been given food and shelter for a lifetime? Should she perhaps have plucked that fruit and tasted some sweetness instead of opting for the dull stretch of security that she had held on to for the rest of her eventless life?

Why had this little tableau tucked away deep down within her head and her heart suddenly emerged from its hiding place and put itself before her on show now? Was it an omen? Was it a warning? Or was it but a chance occurrence that had caused a memory buried deep down within her consciousness to come to the surface and stand before her today upon this alien soil?

And then a stick came sailing through the air and a dog went bounding past her in its pursuit and broke her chain of thoughts. And it was then that she saw Bill; a spurt of happiness surged through her heart and pushed out all the other concerns that had been trying to crowd in there. He looked so cool and collected in his cool and comfortable car. Leaning across, he opened the door.

'Hop in,' he said, 'I knew you'd be crazy enough to have headed out my way, heat or no heat. So I came as soon as I could.'

'How did you know I'd come?'

'Because I know you're kinda crazy.'

'I promised I would come, so I had to come, didn't I.'

'Aw! Come on, you sure did have to come. I was just kidding!'

'But I won't be staying for long.'

'Why? Where's the rush? The kids are away, aren't they?' he enquired, turning towards her.

'Yes. But I have many things to do,' she lied. What exactly it was that she was afraid of she did not know, but she felt that gradually distancing herself from Bill would be the most judicious thing to do.

'So do I, but I don't intend going back to work this afternoon.'

'Not go back to work? But why?'

'Because, Nan, I have better things to do.'

'Such as?'

'Spending more time with you.'

'Telling lies at your age, honestly, Bill, this just won't do. But I really do have to go home.'

'Not now, not yet. And I was telling no lies, believe you me. Let's get ourselves some interesting stuff to eat and some really chilled beer to go with it, and then we can find ourselves a shady spot at the Lake Shore.'

'But . . . but . . . Bill.'

'Please, Nan . . .'

'All right, if you insist.'

15 WINE AND JAZZ DOWNTOWN

There was sand everywhere! They had returned from their seaside sojourn the previous evening, and no sooner than the young family had walked in, the house had instantly filled up with life and a little more than that. The luggage, the swimwear, and their footwear were witness to the fact that they had denuded the beaches of large quantities of its golden splendour.

With eyes on a voyage of rediscovery, the children had checked out every nook and cranny of their home and, with the sheer joy of reunion with a favoured friend, had run helter-skelter all over the place, spreading laughter, sand, and sunshine wherever they went! By late evening, even Nandita's slippers had acquired a grainy feel to them, making her feel that it was she who had walked upon the sandy stretches of Florida.

Though she had not gone to the beach, the beach itself had come home to her!

When Nandita took the steps to come downstairs the next morning, the scene of disarray laid out down below halted her steps midway. Some part of the baggage that had come back with the holidaymakers, she could see, was still slothfully lying around at the foot of the stairs. With rising irritation, she stood a moment where she was and contemplated the sight. One of the tote bags dragged in from the car lay on its side, languidly spilling over comic books, chewing gum, gummy bears, and game gear. A short distance away from it, a backpack lay, mouth agape, disgorging sundry unrelated items such as teabags and toilet paper, tampons and tomato ketchup, a watch, a wallet, a Walkman, and a water bottle, the last item dripping water. The lid had come off a canister of Pringles, and a clutch of its perfectly shaped, perfectly matched potato wafers had fanned out onto the floor like a pack of cards ready to be dealt out. On the other hand, a pack of playing cards having escaped its housing had spread itself out like a sheaf of handbills all over the place.

And then a swath of sunlight came in through a window and fell across this strange collection of disparate items and imbued the whole with an aura that had left her wonderstruck! What lay before Nandita was no longer a jumble of commonplace items of everyday use, but a vast still-life depicting a slice of modern-day life. The canvas was large; the artist was gifted, and had made good use of the sharply contrasting light and shade that the sweep of sunshine had splashed across the middle of the muddle spread out upon the floor. A little bit of illumination from within or without made such a difference! Nandita descended the remaining steps and picked her way across the mad melee in a thoughtful frame of mind.

A mellowed Nandita went across the length of the kitchen and from there out into the yard and made her way to her favourite bench. And there she sat on, lost in reverie as a pair of squirrels lending her company gambolled playfully under an apple tree that had but two apples to its name. The fat cat was not to be seen, no wonder the squirrels were so carefree today! In truth, she had not seen the fat cat for a while. She hoped he was doing well wherever he was! Yes, that was the moot point! Who cared about a little bit of sand underfoot, or for that matter, a little bit of untidiness; what mattered was that they were all back home safe and sound. It really felt good to have the family back!

The first cup of wake-up tea forgotten, Nandita sat on. It was the feel of the sand underfoot that had diverted Nandita's attention away from a lifetime's habit of tea drinking this morning. It was time she went in and made a cup of tea for herself. But as she rose to go in, the grainy feel of the sand that had got trapped between her toes had sent her mind wandering backward into another day and age.

Since coming to the US, she had been to the beach on more than one occasion, but the overwhelming otherness of the images of this world where she now lived had intervened and kept her memories of that other world, that other seashore at bay. The feel of sand underfoot was the same everywhere, with no obfuscating inputs coming in between her and that sensation; her thoughts had, as if skittering upon a grain of sand, taken a roller-coaster ride backward in time. Overcome by nostalgia, she sat on, remembering her first ever visit to the seaside.

The old couple, her grandparents, were going on a pilgrimage. And as they were preparing to leave, taking everyone by surprise, she had burst into a most unusual spate of tears. And once the dam had burst, there was no stopping the uncharacteristic deluge that she perpetrated! And with a gentle smile flitting across her lips, Nandita recollected how she had strategically taken sanctuary within the folds of Dadu's clothing and thereby put herself out of bounds to her mother. She could almost get the feel of the cloth that had been within her fist that day as she had held fast to Dadu's *panjabi* and cried her heart out.

And finally succumbing to the pressure of that outburst Dadu—dear, dear, Dadu—had pleaded long and hard with Thakuma till she had agreed, though reluctantly, to take her along with them on their voyage of piety. Thakuma had frowned, Ma had looked discomfited, Daminidi had looked concerned, but Dadu's will and her wailing had prevailed and she had tagged along with them on that *teerth yatra*. And even today, an aeon away from that era, positioned in another continent, she, a grandmother twice over, wondered from where she had dredged up courage enough to put up such a show of effrontery to that pillar of authority, her grandmother.

Was it perhaps that somewhere deep down within her, a hope had been kindled that she would find her father during the course of that journeying? By applying a simple formula, she had connected two sets of events and put them on a single plane: that of her own petulant retreats under the staircase-well of their home, from where she would emerge only when wheedled out by Kakima or Daminidi, and her father's withdrawal from their lives from where apparently no one had gone in search and brought him back home again. This simple little bit of logic that showed the exact path of cause and effect had given her something to hold on to as she waited for his return. The Nandita of today looked back in compassion upon the little girl Nandita who had lost her father and never found him ever again.

And so, as soon as they had reached Puri, she had started looking around for him. But her Thakuma had not approved of her restless ways: 'A girl must be decorous. I know she is very young, even so . . .'

'Let her be, what harm can a little looking around do?'

'What harm indeed!'

'Come here, Nandita,' Dadu had called out, 'come and take a look at these seashells,' and removed her from under Thakuma's watchful gaze.

But Nandita right then was looking for something other than seashells. She was but a child then, so inveigled by the sun, the sand, and the sea, she had soon forgotten the quest upon which she had come, and that had been the beginning of her first ever holiday.

That was to Puri that they had gone. Puri with its golden beaches was the favourite haunt of the Bengali gentry of that era who needed to put a bit of *punya* into their account while having a change of air. Puri was the abode of Lord Jagganath, as Lord Krishna was called in those hallowed precincts. He ruled supreme upon this temple town and along with him reigned his brother Balaram and his sister Subhadra standing shoulder to shoulder to him.

A dip in the sea at Puri was a must for a pilgrim and so they had all gone trooping to the shores of the sea in search of its cleansing waves. You bathed fully clothed in the sea to wash away your sins and only then paid your respects to Lord Jagganath and his siblings. The untainted soul of Nandita had had no need of cleansing but Thakuma had made it clear to her that she would not be taken along to the temple if she were not to take a dip in the sea. What could she do but take a tentative step forward towards where the sea and the sand met. It was a line that was ever on the move, now rolling forward towards you, now moving away out of your reach. She had touched the frothy white left behind by the receding waters. And then someone had given her a push and she was neck deep in the salty water; the skirt of her frock had filled with water had billowed up around her face. She was more afraid than she had ever been, and then the fear had vanished, leaving her with nothing but the joy of bathing in the sea.

She could hear Thakuma admonishing Dadu, her granddaughter's bare chest was on show for the entire world to see, and that she would not permit! And so she had been hauled out of the water, the wonderful playful fun-filled water. And as she had been dragged along, the sand had squelched under her feet, her hair had streamed water, and the deflated skirt of her frock had flopped down and clung to her legs. The sea as she had looked back upon it on her way to the temple was ever so beautiful, but with a touch of the forbidding. For it was creaming at the edges like the overhang of white lace that adorned the bottom of the sleeves of the fancy jackets that Thakuma wore on special occasions along with her Benarasi saris. It was beckoning and repelling and yet again beckoning, and she had wanted to go back to it but had not been able to!

That had been her very first encounter with a beach and its golden spread filled with excitement. Even today she could clearly remember how she had loved the feel of the inanimate grains of sand that came alive and behaved as if they had a life and a will of their own when you tried to contain a fistful of them within your grasp. The sea and how she attired herself on board the sea had always managed to come in between her and her communion with it. Since forever, she had been the cause of embarrassment for those with whom she went on these sojourns.

She was feeling mellow and happy this morning. The simple meal she had cooked for their return home had brought such glowing accolades her way that it had left her with a delicious sense of well-being. Being away from home-cooked fare did wonders, she could see. Tukun, who rarely commented upon what he ate, looked up from his plate and said, 'Ma, you always were a superb cook, and you still haven't lost your touch. May I have some more of that *macher kalia*, please?'

Meeta joined in with 'Towards the end of the holiday, we were dying to get back to the lovely food you cook for us.'

'I was really quite fed up eating burgers, pizzas, hotdogs and sandwiches big and small, with sundry salads.'

'Dad, you were not the only one,' remonstrated Tomal.

'Yes, the kids,' added Meeta, 'though they are normally willing to give their right arm for pizzas and burgers, were turning their noses up at . . .'

'I love pizza, but . . .'

'But what, Tam?' asked her mother, breaking into laughter. 'Shall we order some?'

'No, please!' wailed the little girl, and then turning to Nandita, 'Thamma, may I have some dal and rice, please.'

'See, Ma, we were all missing your cooking. Have you ever seen your granddaughter ask for more dal and rice?'

And then Nandita, smiling at Meeta, softly said, 'What all of you were really missing was your home.'

'It feels good to be back at home again,' said Meeta.

And Tukun asked, 'Hope you were not too lonely, Ma? You should have come along with us, you really should have.'

And Nandita, basking in the sunshine of their attention, acknowledged that both Tukun and Meeta were caring and good children and that it felt good to have them back.

She opened her mouth to confess to all her recent adventures and shut it again. Here was her son so concerned about her loneliness while she had been out in the city of Chicago, taking in its best! And coughing softly to cover up her confusion, she just stated, 'I've made a few friends during my walks, I kept meeting them, so I . . . I . . . was not so lonely.'

'Really? How wonderful! Isn't it a good thing that you started going out on those walks, Ma?'

'You are looking really good, regular exercise has brought the glow back on your face,' Meeta complimented her. 'I told you that you need to drink more milk, you are drinking milk regularly, aren't you?'

'Yes, I am. I'm glad I listened to both of you.'

Lost in thought, she sat on in the yard, and then the perfume of freshly brewed coffee wafted along upon a gently blowing breeze reached out alluringly to her nostrils. Someone was up and about! The aroma had drawn her to the kitchen, but when she reached the kitchen, that someone, whoever it was, was not there! The coffee sat perking in its usual corner, filling the air with its presence; she contemplated it a moment and then, pouring herself a mugful of the dark-as-the-heart-of-a-garnet brew, had gone out once again. When she returned from the kitchen, the fat cat, now no longer fat, was seated as usual under its preferred tree, but today it was not contemplating the possibility of a savoury snack that a squirrel or two might have presented. Seated on the rise at the foot of the tree, it was busy contemplating the reflection of its handsome self in the water brimming over in the inflated pool. Nandita watched contemplatively, wondering why its presence in their garden did not irritate her as much as it once did. By default, it was fast becoming the household pet of the Roys.

A line at one end of the yard was festooned with scraps of colourful swimwear that looked inadequate by far to have served as clothing for four human beings, of whom two were full-grown adults! She could see Meeta had been experimenting with a bikini this time round: what better opportunity than this, when mother-in-law dear had herself volunteered to stay away from the outing! A bikini top was peeping out from under a towel that had been drawn across it, but not too carefully. Looking to this side and that, she went surreptitiously up to the swimsuits and swiftly pulled the towel over Meeta's little bit of indulgence. She tried to visualise Meeta in a bikini; her initial plumpness had blossomed and grown over the years, what of that? If a woman felt like sporting a bikini, then she should certainly do so. What difference would it make to the world at large whether you wore a little shred of cloth as swimwear, or you wore a one-piece outfit? If you were willing to air your bulges, then that was your personal choice and your option.

The radio was on somewhere within the house. The coffee had worked its magic; the household was slowly coming awake. A beautiful piece of jazz was softly filling the air with its hauntingly beautiful strains. And she relived those beautiful magical hours she had spent with Bill.

All her saintly resolves towards self-introspection during the absence of the family, she remembered with a wry smile, had been brushed aside sooner than she had thought possible and she had found herself doing exactly what she had been doing for the last clutch of months. Up in the morning, a little bit of housework, and then a walk up to the Home, and if Bill was in town, she would join him downtown for a while and then go back home. He had been away quite a bit to Dallas to visit his daughter. She was into her second pregnancy and the concerned father was keeping as close a watch as possible on her.

'What do you do in the evenings, Nan?' he had asked her a few days after Tukun and his family had left for the sea.

'I read, I watch television, and read some more and go to bed early.'

'And listen to some music?'

'Yes, I do listen to music as well.'

'I do more or less the same; it is a lonely person's perfect recipe for killing time.'

'But believe me, Bill, even though I'm alone, now that I have all of you, I do not feel lonely at all.'

'But I do, Nan.' He had fallen silent for a brief moment. 'Tell me, do you listen to music because you have nothing else to do, or do you love music?'

'I like to listen to good music.'

'Then we'll go out to town and sit us down together and listen to some of the most heart-warming notes of music that man has ever made.'

'Where? What? How? How could I possibly?'

'The heart of the world of jazz is located here in Chicago. I shall take you where the best of musicians are playing these days. And as for that "how", I shall come and pick you up around seven in the evening tomorrow.'

'Tomorrow?'

'Yes, tomorrow!'

'I couldn't possibly . . .'

'But before we move on to taking in the joys of listening to the best of jazz, we shall dine at my favourite place. They serve the most delicious Midwestern fare that you can find anywhere in this big, bad, sometimes brutal, yet beautiful city of ours.'

'I told you I couldn't possibly . . .'

'The champagne chilled to perfection will be Dom Perignon, and—'

'I told you, Bill, I couldn't possibly come with you.'

'Why not? Why ever not?'

'My Khoka may call.'

'Who?'

'My son Tukun. He may call.'

'When he calls later this evening, tell him you're going out in the evening tomorrow and . . .'

'He called this morning. In truth, he calls every morning before they go to the beach.'

'Then, where's the problem? Just put on one out of your endless collection of white saris and, looking your usual lovely self, wait for me till I arrive.'

'You make everything sound so simple.'

'And you manage to make all things simple sound so complex,' he said, wearing a crooked smile.

'I don't think . . .'

'What's with you, Nan?'

'You won't understand, Bill, you are an American, you will not understand!'

'But you live in the United States of America.'

'But that still does not make me an American, does it?'

'We seem to have tread upon the same path during an earlier altercation.'

'Yes. So we have.' And then the humour of the situation had come home to them and they had begun to laugh together as only the best of friends can do.

And though she had told Bill that she would positively not be going out with him, she ironed and put aside an elegant ivory crepe silk with just a dash of gold on its borders. The blouse that went with it had longer sleeves than she normally wore. Who had given it to her, she wondered! Because of the touch of gold, she had never worn this particular sari ever before and, by default, the blouse as well. She pulled out an exquisitely beautiful box made of marble inlaid with flowers made of multihued stones that she kept with utmost care within the folds of her clothing—a birthday gift to her from her Dipto. Within the box, on a bed of cotton lay those few trinkets that she had not given away to her son's wife. Each piece had a little bit of her life attached to it, and so, even though she had eschewed all jewellery since the passing away of Prodipto, she had not been able to part with them. She picked up a single string of perfectly matched pearls from among the other little pieces that lay there and fingered them with a sudden surge of nostalgia. Lying there over the years, the pristine white of the pearls had become tinged with time and turned to a dull ivory lustre.

She remembered Prodipto's return from a temporary duty to Hyderabad. Around midnight he had walked in, carrying his usual Gladstone bag. Removing the leather fastening, he had whipped out a long and elegant jewellery box dressed in blue velvet. Giving her a big hug and handing her the box, with a wry smile, he had said, 'Now don't go jumping to conclusions, Nondu, it had to be done so I did it.'

'Did it?'

'Don't let it even cross your mind that this is a penitent's payoff to his conscience.' He had put on such a funny expression that it had brought a smile to her face.

'Really, Dipto! Must you crack strange jokes at this time of the night? What had to be done?'

'Pearls had to be bought, or that's what I learnt from my superior officers.'

'Pearls had to be bought? But why?'

'Because they have put it down somewhere in the Air Force orders that an officer and a gentleman, when he touches down at Hyderabad, must never return back home without pearls for his love.'

'What strange rules this Air Force of yours has.'

'And what a strange and lovely girl you are, believing every yarn I spin,' he had said with a laugh, and stretching out and taking hold of her hand, drawn her close to him. 'Come here, let me put them on and see how you look wearing them.' She could remember the touch of his starched and scratchy uniform caressing her cheeks, the familiar well-loved perfume of him that had reached her nostrils as he had bent across with his arms around her, to fasten the string of pearls around her throat.

'They are lovely.'

'And eminently suitable for your middle years. You may have seen Mummy wears them all the time: put them away in cotton wool, sweetheart, they will come in handy later.'

'Not now?'

'Not yet!'

A couple of tears escaped from her eyes and slowly made their way down her cheeks.

The occasion to wear them was staring her in the face; should she wear them, she asked herself. An adornment anticipating her middle years bought by a young husband for his still younger wife put away in cotton wool, awaiting what? Was she really going out with Bill? What would her son and his wife say if they knew that she had gone out on a date with a man almost unknown to them? Yes, the relevant word within the context of the geographical location where she now lived would make it a 'date'.

But time was percolating out of her hands and flowing away faster than she knew it could. Bill's six months were almost over, and never again would she have this opportunity of having an evening that was engineered with affection just for her. Perhaps this would be Bill's farewell present to her for all the companionable hours that they had spent together. What was it that was holding her back at home? There were no babies crying for her attention here. Then why should she not go and listen to some music with a friend?

Yes. She would go, she told herself.

And so, when Bill had called to remind her that he would be there to pick her up later, she had certainly not said *no* to him.

Where was that reflection in the mirror today that till so recently had made her avert her eyes and look away? The person she saw imprinted there was not the person who had been living in this home for so many years now. Beautiful garments, a hint of an adornment, a little bit of excitement had brought about a magical change in the persona of Nandita. Rediscovering her own beautiful self had caused a certain degree of embarrassment to her and had instantly heightened the colour upon her cheeks. She had wanted to tear the pearls off, had wanted to throw off her raiment of ivory and gold, but the look upon Prodipto's face had stayed her hands. As she looked into the mirror she was facing, she had seen the smiling face of her Dipto peeping over her shoulder. It was an eerie feeling, for Prodipto's photograph was seated on the dresser where she stood! That his reflection had bounced off the mirror placed upon the opposite wall to come and stand besides her had appeared to her to be some kind of an omen. There was a look of approval upon his face, so it must be a happy one, she concluded!

Passing her fingers over the smoothness of the pearls, she said, 'I'm glad you've seen me wearing these pearls, Dipto. You asked me to put them away, remember? For a suitable time and occasion, you said, so I have taken them out to wear today.' Turning her head this way and that to take in the grandeur of the pearls, looking into those eyes that were looking back at her she had gone on, 'I told you then that they are beautiful, see how lovely they still are.' And then wheedling, she had asked the smiling reflection, 'They do look good around my throat, don't they?'

'I hope you don't mind my going out with Bill, he is a sad and lonely man. You don't mind, do you?' And she was sure that he had sought to give her a reply. For she had seen that very instant, the reflection of Prodipto's photograph wink back conspiratorially at her. She had averted her eyes then, for it had seemed to her that he was saying that she was not going out with Bill because he was 'a sad and lonely man', but because he was a very nice man and because she liked to be with him!

'Yes, I do like to be in his company,' she had murmured, and the front doorbell had rung across the house and reached her. Placing a dab of perfume upon her wrists, she had moved to answer the summons of the call-bell.

The look upon Bill's face as she opened the door and stood before him had been one of awestruck wonder. For before him stood a perfectly groomed woman with a touch of class, dressed to perfection for an evening out in town.

That she was an attractive woman he had always been aware of, but that she was so beautiful and poised, he had not really known. And *let's forget all that jazz about jazz and stay at home*, he had wanted to say. Instead, handing her the bunch of red roses he had brought along, he had smiled and dropped a kiss upon her cheek and said, 'You look lovely, Nan.'

Being kissed by Bill was becoming quite a habit with her, but being complimented so blatantly when she herself knew how good she was looking was quite another matter. Going gruff, she said, 'Come in,' and it was then that Bill had crossed the threshold of Nandita's home for the first time since he had known her.

The look of admiration upon his face as he faced her had disconcerted her, and quite out of context, she told him, 'Dipto gave me these pearls.'

'He had very good taste.' She had looked up at him and nodded her agreement. 'But not only in his choice of jewellery, if I may say so.'

Shying away from acknowledging the compliment, she had centred her thoughts upon the bouquet she had in hand. 'The roses, yes, the roses . . . they need to be put into water. I must get a vase.' And then remembering that she had forgotten her duties towards a guest. still with the roses in her hand, she had asked, 'Would you care to have some tea or coffee?'

'No, we better get cracking, our table's been booked and these nose-in-the-air restaurateurs look most displeased if you keep them waiting. Don't forget your key . . .'

'No, I won't.'

'Otherwise, those alert neighbours of yours might send out an alert when later we try to break in.'

'Really, Bill . . .'

It was not as if she had never seen downtown Chicago by night. Driving into town from a visit out of the city, tired after a long drive, wedged in between two cantankerous children tied down to their respective car-seats, she had looked upon it as another stretch that would have to be endured before getting home. And that had not made for the beginning of a romance between her and this city striding like a colossus along the shores of Lake Michigan. An occasional celebratory dinner had also taken them to town, but the choice of the restaurant they went to had been limited by the need to have a place that would accept children as well. For Nandita, Chicago had been but a big city dotted with a plethora of tall and big buildings. For the first time that night, she had looked upon this majestic city, with some of the most magnificent buildings in the world, with something akin to a strange amalgam of love, respect, and awe! For never before this had she looked upon the city of Chicago with her own eyes and not the eyes of an entourage!

The elegant restaurant with its understated opulence had a mood-elevating air about it, and Nandita feeling desired and desirable for the first time in years, feeling expansive, had stated, 'No wonder you keep coming back to this city, Bill; this city is really and truly beyond compare.'

'Thank you, Nan. I'm glad you can see why I love this city so well.'

'I'm truly happy that I've made the decision to come out with you today. One day, before I know what is happening, you'll be gone. And then, this will be a memory that I will truly cherish.'

'Will you miss me?' he had asked with an intensity that had come as a surprise to her and, perhaps, even to his own self.

And to her surprise, she had replied, 'I most certainly will,' without a thought, and without the least bit of hesitation on her part.

'Time to order the champagne, what do you say?' he had asked, looking unduly pleased.

'No, Bill, no champagne for me, please, it wouldn't do to have me tottering in at this place where you are taking me to listen to some beautiful music.'

'All the training I have been giving you . . .'

'Those occasional sips of beer that you've made me have, haven't turned me into a hardened drinker yet,' she had countered, laughing softly.

'I certainly hope not!'

'Please, Bill, let's put the champagne aside for another day.'

'Fine, then that's a done deal; we shall find ourselves another occasion to split a bottle of champagne between us.'

And she had murmured, 'I doubt there will be another occasion like this one.'

'Did you say something?'

'No. I did not. But an occasion is coming up shortly, isn't it? We can always celebrate the arrival of your second grandchild.'

'There's still a while for that. My Irene is only into her eighth month.'

'And you'll be in New York by the time the baby arrives.'

'But I can always fly down from New York to open a bottle of champagne with you, can't I?'

'You make everything sound so simple, Bill.'

'Do I? Shall we order the food now?'

Nandita, who had been a vegetarian for years, knew that she would have to pick and choose with care to make it possible for her to eat at all. An occasional shrimp wending its way into her mouth was quite a different matter from handling chunks of recognisable meat and fish!

Her taste buds had led a strangely insulated life. Even here in the United States, what did she eat but the usual fare that was cooked in a Bengali's home? There was that fleeting moment of time when she as a serviceman's wife had touched the fringes of other kinds of food that were cooked in India. But that too had been predominantly Punjabi, for the cooks in the officers' mess had designated the food of Punjab as the standard for the whole of India's palate. As such, apart from what she had encountered in the officer's mess parties, she had not known food other than the kind that came out of a Bengali kitchen. And of course there were those days when she had learnt to eat the creations of Khansamaji when she had first got married. But then, that was but an interlude!

'Though I'm not as strict a vegetarian as I was when I met you, Bill, I still . . .'

'Leave that to me, I'll take care.'

And he had!

The maitre d'hotel had been summoned, a little conference had been gone into, and that had led to a bigger conference behind the scenes between the maitre d'hotel and the master craftsman whose wizardry kept the reputation of the place alive. And in a little while, the chef had emerged with a flourish and some fanfare, with a platter in hand, upon which reposed the dish that had been engineered by him for the very specific needs of Nandita's palate. She had thanked the chef for his pains, and not without reason, for the meal she had eaten that evening had been a culinary delight beyond compare; so delicately flavoured and novel on the tongue was it!

'Thank you, Bill, thank you very much for giving me this gift of a wonderful evening with you.'

'The evening is not yet over. The food we ate was just a preamble to what lies ahead. We came to listen to some soul-searching jazz, didn't we? Come. Let's get a move on.'

Ushering Nandita in, Bill had got into the driver's seat and eased out of the hotel parking lot. 'The jazz joint we're going to is not a pretentious place but the best of musicians play there. Hope you'll like the music you'll be hearing this evening there.'

'I know I will. I was introduced to some beautiful jazz pieces by Dipto very early in my life.'

'That's interesting. Real pleased that you're not totally unfamiliar with the music I love so well.'

'I can't claim to know very much about jazz, even so, I don't know why, but jazz does something to me.'

'I feel the soul-searching notes of jazz do not stand for ceremony, they rise and spread out and invade and fill all the empty spaces within a person. Yes, there is a soul-pervading quality to jazz.'

'Its origins lie . . .'

'In American ragtime and blues, and as it is played over a strong dance rhythm, it can be sad and it can be frolicsome by turns. It has a chameleon-like changeability that can make it possible for it to make your feet and your heart dance, or then, fill it with an all-pervading languorous melancholia.'

'No wonder its notes are so compelling to the listener.' And then moving for a moment away from jazz, she had asked, 'Have you ever heard the *shahnai* being played, Bill?'

'I'm afraid not.'

'I feel that it has a very similar quality to jazz, though perhaps in a very limited way. As your mood demands, you can ride along with the notes of the *shahnai* as well.'

'I'd sure like to hear some of that and to get to know what that music is like.'

'You should hear Bismillah Khan play the *shahnai* to truly appreciate the instrument. Without any doubt, he is the best. I have some cassettes at home with me, in case you'd like to listen to . . .'

'Bring them along, please, but as of now I better start keeping a close watch for a paid parking place that has not put up a board. They are all tucked away in the lanes around here. You'll have to walk a short distance; you don't mind, do you?'

'What have I done but walk since the coming of spring?'

'You sure do walk a great deal, Nan, but walking in those delicate sandals may be quite another matter.'

'I'll manage,' she had reassured him as she tried to assess the strength of the borrowed pair of delicate footwear that she was wearing.

They had found a parking lot that did not have a neon sign stating that it had no vacancy, parked, and then walked companionably together to the little place that they were going to.

'Where would you like to sit? Right in the front or somewhere a little distance away?'

'You decide.'

He had looked around, found what he was looking for, and indicated, 'Come, let's settle down; shall I get you something to drink?'

'Thanks! An orange juice would do fine.'

He had gone away to the bar and she had looked around to take in the atmosphere of the place. It was a simple, subdued, and very intimate place. It had no intentions of catering to a crowd and thus kept its clientele down to only those who really came in to listen to the music. He had come back with two tall glasses of chilled orange juice. And once he was seated, she had turned to him and said, 'I love the style but know so little about jazz and its exponents, could you help me out, please?'

And he had certainly helped. The piece playing upon the transistor that had transported her back to the evening she had spent with Bill now had a name to it. And wonder of wonders, she had even been able to identify some of the musical instruments that were being played. And then suddenly someone switched off the music and broke the thread of her meandering thoughts. And jolted back to her own backyard, she looked around as if trying to adjust to the changed scenario that lay around her.

Feeling as if a number of eyes were upon her, she looked towards the eerie feeling that had come her way. And there was the answer: the fat cat, who now was no longer fat, was looking at her with an unblinking gaze. And then she spied a number of little balls of fur that were there right around him. As she looked closer, she was astonished to see that seated where he was, he was suckling those balls of fur. *He was suckling his kittens? What a ridiculous assumption! How could a male cat possibly be doing that?* And only then had it dawned upon her that the visitor from the neighbourhood was no gentleman at all. The tawny visitor was a lady, and a lady who had become a mother but recently! No wonder he had lost weight. She corrected herself and said, 'No wonder *she* has lost weight,' to herself. She was still chuckling to herself when a ball landed from a window above; a host of other items joined the ball and then Tom came hurtling down and threw himself into the pool. The tawny lady, none too pleased with the confusion that had risen, gave a shake to herself, gave a shove or two to her kittens, and marched off with them in tow.

Boredom was the cornerstone of the lives of the young. The excitement of the holiday by the sea was already palling though only two solitary days had gone past since their return from the vacation.

'Aw, Mom! Mommy . . . Mom.'

'Yes?'

'I'm bored.' Voice gone nasal, Tammy trailing around behind her mother, whined.

'Me too,' her brother joined in.

Clearing the breakfast table, Meeta brushed it off with an offhand 'Go and play in the pool.'

'You call that a pool? That's not a reg'lar pool,' the son pointed out.

'It was fine for you till yesterday.'

'Susan and Jane and Vivian all have lovely humungous pools, heated and all, and they have lovely poolside parties there. And then they even get to sleep over at each other's places. And we can't even have a pool party.' Pouting, the daughter had refined, 'I'm so, so terribly bored.'

'Bored, bored, bored is all that they keep chanting all day long; I've told Tukun to pack these kids off to summer camp, but does he ever listen to me? No. He wanted his beloved kids at home.'

'We're not going to summer camp?' an agitated Tom wanted to know.

'Yes, but not immediately.'

'Aw, Mom, please, let's do something.'

'Like what, Tom?'

'I don't know.'

'Can I go and stay with Jane for a few days?' Tammy wanted to know.

'And can I go to David's place?' asked Tom, brightening up. They've just got themselves a pair of lovely Irish setters?'

'No, you can't.'

'Why?' asked the daughter.

'Why?' demanded the son.

'Because I said so,' she replied, putting down a foursome of mugs with a thump into the sink.

'That's not a reason.'

'Stop arguing, Tammy.

'That's not fair,' flared the son.

'Tom.' The boy refused to look her way. 'Tom,' she screamed, 'did you hear me?' The boy looked towards her. 'Good, that's better, no more of this backchat, do you understand?'

The victory had been achieved at a price; the pool had lay unused and the children, sulking openly, had withdrawn each to their own den. And a much-wiser Nandita sagaciously stayed away from the combat zone.

But two days from that date, an olive branch had been acquired and waved around with aplomb. The cold war had worn down the mother to the extent of her going in search of some remedial measures. Moreover, the party-giving roster which regulated their social life was clearly showing a large number of debit entries in their disfavour.

Something was surely cooking, and that it was a barbecue Nandita guessed soon enough when all the paraphernalia that went with this particular form of entertaining had begun to emerge from storage to be given a once-over before the big day. And the uncared-for yard, as if by magic, had become spotlessly clean all of a sudden.

Nandita breathed a sigh of deepest relief that long-legged Sue with her outrageously American ways and her husband Vivek would not be figuring in the guest list, for she had not forgotten that reassuring conversation where Meeta had let fall that they had moved to the West Coast. That mischievous look in Sujata's eyes whenever she had found her in Bill's company had been most unnerving.

How she wished she had introduced Bill to the family and got over this constant sense of impending doom that she carried around with her. Now that Sue had left and Bill was on the verge of leaving for New York, it was just not worth bringing up the matter at all. Perhaps it still was; she would have to make up her mind soon and do something about it. And then mind made up, she called out, 'Tukun.'

'I'm here.'

'You won't believe whom I met.'

16 SUE OPENS A CAN OF WORMS

The lawnmower had hummed its summer song, the pruning shears had done their bit, and the random flowers growing in the just-turned flower beds that fringed the yard looked smarter by far than they had in a while. The entire place in readiness for the forthcoming do had a spruced-up sprightly look about it.

Nandita looked down from her favourite vantage-point at her window, upon the well-groomed open space down below and thought that somehow, most gardens that she had seen here in the United States never quite came up to the multihued splendour of the wintertime garden, that the Major General and his wife had nurtured and grown in their home in New Delhi. But then, perhaps she had seen that garden through the eyes of a girl in love.

Just after her wedding, she had gone to Delhi with Prodipto. That was in the month of November; a month later, the entire look that Delhi wore had changed, for it had burst out in a plethora of multicoloured blooms. And Mummy's little acre certainly stood shoulder to shoulder with the best! Never in her life had Nandita seen such a garden, nor had she ever seen such a variety of flowers! She had been completely dazed by the brilliance that had erupted right before her eyes. Her concept of a garden till then had been comprised of a flowerless oleander tree, a venerated *tulsi* plant, a banana palm or two that grew aslant alongside the tap where the vessels were scrubbed and cleaned, and a solitary hibiscus shrub. This hibiscus with its abundant crop of brilliant red flowers formed the mainstay of the floral requirements for the prayers that were performed each morning in their *thakurghor* at Bhabanipore.

But so many different flowers with so many fashionably foreign names, wrought in the colours stolen from a rainbow, standing to attention like well-trained soldiers had come as a complete surprise to her. It was fortunate that Prodipto was beside her to introduce her to each one of them as they came to bloom. The hollyhocks stood like sentinels at the rear, lending colour to the multiple shades of green of the herbaceous border that flourished alongside the brick-red compound wall of her father-in-law's home. And then from the dominating height of the hollyhock, the floral plants kept coming down in serried ranks to take up their places according to the heights to which they grew. The zinnia and the aster, the larkspur and the cornflower, the salvia and the carnation, the poppy and the snapdragon, the funny-faced pansies and the trumpet-like nasturtiums among so many others made up the collection. And of course in this medley there always was a very special place for the many-coloured, many-splendoured phlox that lay spread out like a gorgeous border right at the foot of this lovely phalanx of flowers.

And then there were the roses, soft scented and perfectly formed! Too nose-in-the-air by far, to lead such a heterogeneous and cheek-by-jowl existence as the seasonal flowers led, and had therefore made sure that they had a stretch of loamy earth assigned just to themselves! The chrysanthemum, the dahlia, and the gladioli with their larger-than-life blooms lived a life of isolation in brick-red earthen pots that lined the entire periphery of the bungalow.

Nandita had gone nowhere near England; the closest she had come to experiencing a whiff of the British way of life was at the home of her parents-in-law. As such, the British and their Britain, as she imagined it to be, had been revealed to her only through the prescribed textbooks that she had had to gorge and to disgorge during the examinations that she had to each year take. Daffodils and poppies she had met during these sojourns but the flowers that set ablaze Mummy's wintertime garden were entities that were totally new to her. She had gazed upon the lookalikes of these flowers somewhat later while flipping through the pages of the collection of British women's magazines that always graced the magazine racks in the ladies' room in the officers' mess at the air force station where her Dipto was posted. These magazines had opened her eyes to the multihued wonders of the British garden, and only then had she recognised that the winter adornment of New Delhi was but a mock-up of the summers of England, a slice of England that had crossed the seven seas and made a place for itself in the wintery gardens of North India!

Then why not here? How lovely it would look if they too could grow a bank of flowers along the hedges on either side of the yard right here in their home in Saisborough; Mummy used to get some special seeds from Poona. Yes, the little packets out of which those special seeds she used, had something like 'Pocha's Seeds' written upon them. What colourful pictures of the promised blooms used to adorn the front facing of those little envelopes! She was wondering how to bridge the gap between her dream and its fruition when the telephone rang, cutting across her thoughts!

All thoughts of Poona and Mr Pocha's famous seeds driven from her mind, she went out of her room and onto the landing to pick up the instrument stridently calling out for attention to her. Bill was on the other end.

'What were you doing?' he asked.

'Daydreaming.'

'Daydreaming? About what?'

'Flowers that my mother-in-law grew in her garden at Delhi.'

'That's interesting. What brought it on?'

'One has these bouts, you know, when one just takes off and travels back in time.'

'I know how it is, there are those moments when the past grabs hold of you and carries you off on a journey back in time. And by the way, talking of journeying, I am off to Dallas today, so I won't be able to come over this evening. I was really looking forward to meeting your son and his family. But my daughter Irene—'

'What's happened to her?' she asked, the alarm showing in her voice.

'She's all right but . . .'

'You're hiding something from me.'

'Honest, she's all right, but I feel I should go. Her last pregnancy was a difficult one, but her mother was with her then.' Bill's voice had gone gruff.

'Yes, of course you must,' Nandita had soothed. 'But wasn't the baby due next month?'

'You know how it is with the kids of today, always in a hurry!' The words were light and frivolous but the tone of voice was a total giveaway.

'Not a caesarean, I hope.'

'Some complications have cropped up, so perhaps the baby'll have to be pulled out earlier.'

'Oh, no!'

'Am afraid my poor Irene might have to go in for surgery.' He sounded worried.

'I wish I could have been of some help to you.'

'I wish you could have. Something will have to be done about that . . .'

'What do you mean?'

'I'll be back as soon as I can, because I have some unfinished work here that I have to take care of before I move off New Yorkwards.' Ignoring her question, he had gone on.

'Important work?'

'Yes, very important, I'll tell you about it when next we meet, and I'm truly sorry that I won't be coming over this evening. Please make my excuses to the young couple, tell them I'll meet up with them as soon as I can.'

'When you return, you must visit us then.'

'Will do.'

'But will you have time, Bill, don't you have to go to New York in a few weeks from now?'

'Yes, that I do, but I'll find time, Nan. I certainly will.'

'How kind of you.'

'There's no kindness involved in my wanting to meet you, believe you me.'

'Please take care, there are more important things in hand for you at present, Bill, go and look after your daughter; she needs you. Believe me, all will go well. I shall pray for your Irene and her baby's safety every day.'

'How good of you, Nan. Do please pray for her. The strongest become weak when it comes to their kids.' And with a gruff 'Thank you,' he rang off.

For a few moments, Nandita stood beside the just-stilled instrument. 'Poor Bill,' she thought, 'trying to cope with a father and a mother's responsibilities all alone.' He had gone, for his heart said he had to go; what else could he have done? What else can one do but fulfil one's obligations towards life and its responsibilities, she told herself. But deep down, she knew that it was not thoughts of obligations and written-down responsibilities that had drawn him to the side of his daughter. That he was a famous professor she had heard, but that he was a wonderful and caring father she knew without any reservations now. And with these thoughts in her heart, she went back into her room to go and stand before her little niche where she performed her daily prayers. Eyes squeezed tight, she prayed long and hard and sent off a fervent prayer for the well-being of Bill's daughter and her yet-to-be born child to the all-powerful Ma Kali of Kalighat, who reigned supreme in Kolkata.

Having placed her cares into the more competent hands of the Mother Goddess, she moved across to her favourite chair, and there, hands crossed upon her lap, she sat thinking about the vagaries of fate. At long last, after much deliberation, she had decided that presenting Bill to the family would be the right thing to do; but fate had gone and intervened! It was true that Sue had gone away; even so, a random phone call from Bill, from New York, would not be very easy to explain away! And now, putting paid to her plans, he had flown off to Dallas. She mused; perhaps it was destined that her son, his family, and he should never meet. And the words 'never meet, never meet, never meet,' echoing within her head brought forward a further painful corollary to the same stream of thought.

With a tremendous surge of pain, she had had to acknowledge that in the true sense of the word, she too might never meet Bill again in the manner in which she had done during the last few months. With his sudden departure, the lazy days of meandering that they had spent together as he healed had come to a sudden close. It was not only that he had flown off to Dallas; in truth, he had flown more or less completely out of her life itself! Nandita had known all along that her companionable days with Bill were fast drawing to a close, but that it would come to pass so suddenly had never crossed her mind. Just a handful of precious days was all that had been left with her before his final departure back to his university and his work and his home. And holding them close to herself, she had looked forward to savouring these last few days that she had left with him before bidding him farewell forever. Was it necessary for the powers that be to have snatched them away from her so precipitately?

When he returned, if at all he did, he would be embroiled in the winding-up process. And then he would be gone. Once he was back to his responsibilities, a woman called Nan would slowly fade away out of his mind. And then there was his innocent and inexperienced girlfriend awaiting him there. Why it should make her so sad to think that there was someone there waiting to take care of him was beyond fathoming for her.

The barbecue was just two days away; there was a great deal to be done. She rose, picked up sundry mugs that lay strewn across the bedrooms, and made her way downstairs. Shaking off her sense of despondency, she opened the cupboard within which a huge stack of plates were stored for all such informal large-scale entertaining. They would need to be rinsed and dried, as would all the glasses that would be put to use for the party upon the lawn. With a dozen or so plates in hand as she had looked out of the mesh door, she saw her friend the cat; placing the plates upon the counter, she poured out a saucer of milk and took it out with her. After positioning it at a strategic point, she went in again. She wanted *her* fat cat to become a fat cat again. Motherhood had robbed her favourite neighbour of her distinctive layer of padding. That look of opulent corpulence had given a certain distinctive edge to her personality. Something certainly would have to be done to bring back that look again.

The sun completely off any restraining leash was reigning supreme. The days were getting to be hot rather than just warm. And the trees few and far in between were hardly up to the task of providing some reprieve from its rays. Keeping the sun out while out in the open on a clear and sunny day, as the next day was sure to be, was the challenge of the moment. Tukun had gone into the basement in search of the two garden umbrellas that the family had acquired somewhere along the way. He had brought them out, unfurled and vacuumed them and then positioned them strategically. They had each a circular table attached to its pole, and each table cum umbrella had four chairs to its name. Done with the job, he looked upon the completed task with some satisfaction. 'Doesn't it look good, Ma?' Nandita smiled her approval. 'Look, Meeta, how festive the place looks.'

And then, Tom asked of no one in particular, 'Who gets to sit under the umbrella?'

'We can draw lots,' Tammy suggested.

'Only a girl could think up such a stupid idea. Ever heard of guests drawing lots to . . .' And the rest of his sentence got lost in a splutter of derisive laughter.

'Just because you didn't think of it yourself, you're calling it a stupid idea.' And her little tongue came snaking out. Running up to her father, the little girl asked, 'Dad, don't you think having a lucky draw would be a cool idea?'

'For what?'

'To decide who gets to sit in the shade.'

'Yeah, quite a cool idea but . . .' Turning towards his wife, Tukun called out, 'Have we any more garden umbrellas, Meetu?'

'You know very well we don't.'

'We don't, aw sh—' he cut himself short. 'Come on, guys, let's go to Sears, we need some gardening gear to liven up the place.'

'And to save face,' the wife completed for him.

When later Nandita looked down from her lookout up above, she found the most exotic of possible gardens had come to life there. Magnificent flowers had sprouted and dotted the place with the brightest of colours, where there had been but a bare stretch of green just a little while back. Giant versions of Mummy's prize-winning dahlias and chrysanthemums had come to life upon the newly mowed stretch of green. It was a happy and hospitable sight. The trip to Sears had produced a rich harvest of blooms! No one would have to draw lots now to get into the shade!

The telephone trilled. She picked it up.

'Hi, Nan! You can congratulate me.' He sounded so very happy.

'How's Irene?' she asked.

'A little uncomfortable but otherwise fine. I'm afraid it had to be a caesarean.'

'A pity, but what can one do? All the same, let us thank God that all has gone off well. Is it a boy or a girl, Bill?'

'A lovely little granddaughter has just arrived in my life. The little lady is the spitting image of my Meg.'

'Isn't that just wonderful.'

'*You won't believe this, Nan*, but she winked at me when I picked her up.'

'She must have,' she responded with a little bit of laughter spicing up her voice.

'I must be off now, grandfatherly duties are hollering for my attention.' Nandita could hear a child crying loudly somewhere in the background as she heard him hang up.

Relieved she had moved towards her *puja*-room designate and bowed her head in a prayer of thanks.

The next day dawned crisp and clear, and warm as warm can be. Tukun had got into a pair of shorts, a faded T-shirt, and a pair of raggedy sandals, the trademark leisure attire of the United States. Meeta had shed some weight and a great deal of her inhibitions during their trip to the sea and had wormed her way into a pair of shorts that had been waiting in line in her wardrobe for a variety of reasons. A halter top in cobalt blue with 'Nirvana' written in green across her ample bosom completed her attire. Tammy appeared in a transistorised pair of shorts with a bikini top with little French knots embroidered over its smocked front. Tom was dressed in a pair of jeans that had been sawed off just above the knees. The jaggedly cut-off edges had a feathery fringe to it. And to cover his torso, he wore a singlet that put on view the areas where he would be cultivating muscles someday if he were but to pump iron when the time for pumping iron came.

The dress code for the day was casual. And it was amply clear that minimality of attire was the norm. It was in no way as abbreviated as beachwear had to be, yet that its objectives were upon the same lines was amply clear.

With a wry smile hovering across her lips, Nandita looked awhile upon the contents of her wardrobe. A sea of white met her eyes. She had nothing in the same league! She would be the odd one out as usual! A *sari* it would have to be, but which one? And then a *sari* gifted to her by a friend of Tukun's, a Swede who had come for but a handful of days but had generously left a gift for one and all, fell to her eyes. He was an observant young man. And had gone in search of a white *sari* for her and returned with one. It was a white *sari* but a white *sari* that according to the strict norms she had set herself was not quite white enough. A delicate sprinkling of palest of green leaves had invaded its pristine purity and rendered it out of bounds to her. It was a *sari* that had been leading a life of cloistered boredom in her wardrobe for a very long time now. She had taken it out and taken a close look at it. It was a beautiful *sari*, a *sari* that deserved to be worn outdoors; a *sari* that deserved to be worn under those beautiful colourful umbrellas that her son had put up with such care. Like Meeta, Nandita had also shed some weight and a great deal of her inhibitions in recent times. She took the *sari* and a matching blouse down to the basement, ironed them, and brought them back.

She draped the *sari* with care, pinned it in place, and converted it into a very beautiful fitting garment with a few deft movements of her fingers. That hint of colour spread across the field of her garment touched her attire with magic. Nandita looked and felt fresh and young and daring all at once. For much more than thirty years, she had never allowed colour to touch her personal attire. But today she felt there was something in the air that urged a person to boldness. Had Meeta not dressed as she pleased? Would Tukun and

Meeta be shocked to see the change, she wondered as she combed her hair back and knotted it into a low-slung bun at the nape of her neck. A tendril from her just-combed hair sprang out of its bondage and came and fell across her forehead. Paying no heed to it, she stepped out of her room, a very beautiful and elegant woman, and took the flight of stairs to go down.

The kitchen platforms had batches upon batches of marinated meat waiting to be broiled. Bottles of empty, near-empty, and yet-to-be-opened containers of barbecue sauce lay alongside. A breakaway lot of chicken breasts had chosen to be doused in fiery red *tandoori masala* and yoghurt. When all your guests were of Indian origin, you could smother everything in barbecue sauce and get away with it, but with a more variegated guest list, you had to make a statement of ethnicity by varying your choice of sauces. A platter full of salmon steaks in what looked like a mustard dressing with a few green chillies perched atop them clearly showed the host and the hostess had gone a step further. No Indian was just an Indian and this was a dish that pointed clearly towards the Roy family's Bangali origin. Nandita had wondered if there were no vegetarians at all in today's guest list, and then she had spotted the most colourful of all the arrangements she had so far seen sitting at one end of the platform. Sliced bell peppers red, yellow, green, and purple; succulent morsels of pineapple and avocado; and luscious pieces of *paneer* with a light and aromatic sauce had been put together, she knew, not just for any chance vegetarian, but specially for her. Meeta should not have gone to so much trouble, she thought, there was so much food in the refrigerator, she could have pulled out anything from there and eaten it. But it was so very thoughtful of her to have taken such pains just for her.

There was food aplenty but everything was in a frighteningly uncooked state as far as she could see. Thank goodness for the gallons and gallons of ice cream in the deep freezer; that would be something to fall back upon. The overwhelming smell of the lighting fluid spoke volumes. The charcoal was yet to take hold of!

A buzz of voices met her ears; the guests had begun to arrive.

She stood at the rear door of the family room that had been thrown open today. It led onto the garden, as did the door of the kitchen. The scene laid out before her had the air of a carnival. A music system just behind her was filling the air with the strains of a very popular number. *Sholay* had been shelved; the Latinos were in charge of music for the festivities that were underway out there in the yard. Jennifer Lopez had taken up from where Ricky Martin had left off as Nandita stood at the door. There were many unknown faces here today. The children's friends and their parents, she could see, were among those who had been invited. It was a gathering of many-hued individuals under the shade of a collection of many-hued umbrellas.

The children were busy filling the much-maligned pool that they had dragged and placed at the far end of the yard. She remembered Tammy fretting over the lack of a regular pool in their home. But today, heated pools, Olympic-sized pools, flashy and fashionable pools had been given the go-by, and a regular poolside party was underway around the little inflatable tub that had been filled with a few gallons of water!

She could see Tukun bending over the broiler. The coals had stopped smoking and were turning red at long last. The first lot of marinated chicken breasts, she could see, had been put atop the glowing embers; the food was on the way to being cooked. Slowly the smell of burning flesh filled the air. There was something primeval about the cooking of raw flesh upon an open flame in the outdoors.

A barbecue seemed to hold all men under its thrall. It was as if, as they handled the pieces of raw meat and put them to cook on an open flame, they moved back in time, to those days when they hunted for their own needs and that of their dependants and celebrated the return from a successful hunt with festivities out in the open with their entire tribe congregated admiringly around them. Today the supermarkets provided what the skill of the hunter had at one time brought in. But, one could always pretend that the drive down to the mega store and the choosing of the desired packets of food followed by the paying for them somehow stood in for the rigours of the hunt! Even so, so as to concretise these make-believe hunts, men donned aprons instead of shields and held spatulas where once they had held spears. The hunter, converted to chef, stood proudly cooking the meal for the throng.

Nandita could see the hunter for the day, Tukun, was busy getting things going. She would talk to him later. She threaded her way through the throng of guests and went up to Meeta. She was shovelling more ice into a huge receptacle that contained cans of beer and aerated drinks. 'Need any help?' she asked.

Meeta shook her head. 'Your son is in charge. You and I are on leave today.'

'For how long?' And they laughed together.

'Till the microwave and the oven have to be pressed into service.'

'Is he planning to cook and feed all these people on that little open fire?'

'He has two more of those contraptions, see, there they are, behind him to his right. Dinesh and Milind are soon going to find themselves wearing aprons and dishing out burnt meat as well.'

'Did I hear you mention my name?' And Dinesh was looming large over their shoulders.

'I was telling Ma that you are shortly to be inducted as an assistant cook.'

'I'm going home,' he said, pretending a hasty retreat.

'Shall I inform Tukun of your intentions?'

'Please don't,' he croaked. And then looking closely at Nandita and turning to Meeta, he asked, 'Same mother-in-law?' and then after a short pause, 'Or is she the younger sibling of your mum-in-law? Let me see.' And bending across, he rubbed his none-too-smooth cheek across Nandita's. 'Feels the same,' he declared ponderously.

'Stop flattering me, Danny.' Nandita's cheeks had gone warm. 'How can you possibly tell apart through that beard of yours?'

He looked startled for a moment, for never before had she addressed him as anything but Dinesh. 'No flattery involved. I have a sensitive beard, so I can tell.' And smiling down upon her, he seriously asked, 'What have you been doing to yourself?' Then as if assessing what he saw before him, 'You look gorgeous,' he stated with absolute sincerity. And it was then that Meeta looked at her mother-in-law closely. 'Must get myself something to drink and then, if I've still not been caught by Tukun, I'll be back.' And he was gone, showering kisses as he went along, upon all the females he could safely lay his hands upon.

'I've never seen you wear anything but pure white, Ma. What made you change your mind today?'

Nandita could have said, 'Just as you took courage in your hands to dress differently, so did I,' but smiled a gentle smile instead.

'But you are looking really lovely today. You really are, Ma.'

'So are you, my dear child.' Meeta flushed as her mother-in-law had caressed her cheeks with a fleeting passage of her fingers. 'I saw the spread of colour from up above,' she said, 'and thought it was time I too brought in some colour into my life.'

'Good thinking, Ma,' and then with 'I think Tukun is calling, the he-man needs some help, I think!' she was gone.

Just then, a young man with aquiline features and feathery blonde hair framing his face poked out a hand at her and introduced himself: 'Jason's my name.' He was an outstandingly good-looking man, almost Nordic in his build and colouring. Who was he? Nandita wondered as she offered, 'I am Nandita Roy.'

'Real pleased to meet you, ma'am, related to the Roys?'

'Yes. I am Tom and Tammy's grandmother.'

'You don't say! But you make a really lovely grandma, if I may take the liberty to say so.'

'Thank you. Are your chil—your kids here?'

'Those two kids making the most noise are mine.'

'Like all parents, you find your own kids the most noisy of all.'

He laughed and said, 'Perhaps!' And then taking a look around, 'I don't know too many people here. What about you?' he asked.

'I know only a few.'

'Then your score is sure better than mine. That pretty girl in blue there is my wife,' he said, pointing to a cluster of young women. 'I brought some beer for her, but she has found some company and something to drink, as I can see.'

'That blonde girl?' she said, pointing towards a cluster of heads.

'Yep!'

'Yes. She is lovely.'

'Thanks! And smart besides,' he said, as proud as proud could be. 'She is an investment banker. She rakes in the bread while I go chasing my dreams.'

'She doesn't mind? I mean doing all the hard work while you . . .'

'Go chasing my dreams? I don't earn all the time, but when I do, it's not so bad. But she doesn't mind. She married me with her eyes open, she says.'

'You seem to have married a very unique person.'

'That she definitely is. Hey, this beer is going warm, care to have it?' And he handed her the can. She stood clutching the frosted-over can of beer as he rambled on. 'Care to sit down?' he asked, pointing towards a couple of chairs lying carelessly at one end. 'Or were you off somewhere when I hijacked you?'

Looking around to see if she was needed, Nandita said, 'I don't have to run anywhere immediately, so I think I'll sit a little while with you.'

'Come,' he said, dragging the chairs to a shady spot under a tree with a trestle table within easy reach. 'Let me open your can before the beer turns warm.' And taking the can from Nandita, he ripped open the tab and handed it back to her. She took a very small sip and put it down before her; the beer went down her throat in a luxurious cooling trickle. 'Lots of interesting characters to study out here, in my line of work, one looks out for interesting persons, interesting faces, interesting expressions.'

'What's your line of work?'

'Didn't I tell you?'

'Not that I remember.'

'I'm an actor.'

'Really? How interesting!' Brushing off an ant that had ventured onto her sari, she smiled at him. 'You may not believe this but I've never met a professional actor ever before.'

'You don't say?' Then cultivating a put-on starry look, 'I could give you an autograph if you like.' And he had laughed. 'We guys who do our bit on the stage believe we are the true thespians,' and he shrugged, 'but even so we don't get asked for autographs as often as, say, Tom Cruise, Michael Douglas, or Nicholas Cage do.' And he laughed uproariously at the comparison he had drawn. Sobering up, he asked, 'Where are you from? Not too difficult to guess; from India, I presume?'

'Yes. I am from India, from Calcutta to be more exact.'

'From Calcutta? No way! Never! Jacqueline won't believe this.'

'Why not? Lots and lots of people live in Calcutta. Actually too many!'

'I began my acting career with *Oh Calcutta*! You must have heard of the play?'

To buy time, Nandita took another small sip of beer. Had she ever heard of this play, she wondered. Yes, perhaps she had, but in what context she just could not remember. She had seen the film that had been made of the book *City of Joy*. Not a particularly joyous movie on the city of Calcutta, she thought. With the despairing 'Oh!' tagged onto it, this was perhaps a far happier rendition of the city of Calcutta. What should she say, she was trying to decide, when Jason spoke up!

'That's where Jacqueline and I first met. She came to meet the cast backstage, a very courageous act, I tell you, with all those guys milling around, but we had already covered up our onstage costumes by then.' And he began laughing, remembering that encounter. 'We got talking and from the next day on we began dating.'

'She must have liked you then and there.'

'Yeah! I guess she must have. But it was my onstage costume that had got to her, I think.'

'I see, the costume . . .' *What were they wearing, dhotis?* she wondered.

'She told me later that a girl is usually not as lucky as she was' and grinning widely, he went on, 'to have seen the man she was to marry . . . in the raw, the very first time she clapped eyes on him.' A bewildered Nandita, looking puzzled, held on to her can of beer and wondered which way this conversation was going. 'It helped her assess my naked worth, I believe. She really has some sense of humour,' he ended with a chuckle.

'The whole man in the raw'? 'Naked worth'? *Whatever did he mean by that?* She had to say something, she felt, so she asked, 'Are you still acting in *Oh Calcutta*?'

'Oh! No! That was over and done with a long time ago. Soon after we married, Jackie said she was afraid I'd catch a terrible chill one day, and made me move on to more staid stuff.' And he chuckled remembering that episode.

He knows nothing about the weather in Calcutta, and nor does that wife of his, Nandita thought. *Imagine a man who lived in Illinois, catching a chill because he was acting in a play about Calcutta? It was really strange, even if he were to act a scene said to be located in Iceland, would he catch a cold?* Then Nandita caught herself short. *How did the weather in Calcutta, or for that matter Iceland, come into the picture because a man was acting in a play about that place? This man who claimed to be an actor was surely a little mad,* thought Nandita, planning to make good her escape.

But just then the hordes descended. And contrary to what he had told her, there were a number of autograph seekers in that group. She sat on, wondering how famous he really was. The crowds around Jason had waxed and waned, then waxed again and then faded away. At a distance, she could see that both Milind and Dinesh had been conscripted and put in charge of the back-up broilers. Where was Tukun, she wondered?

He was standing right behind her with his wife beside him when she looked up. 'Sorry, Jason,' he said, grasping his outstretched hand, 'I couldn't take better care of you. I don't cook normally, so I tend to become all thumbs.'

'I've been having a great time with your mom. We have been chatting most merrily over a couple of beers.' And three pairs of eyes were riveted onto the can of beer that Nandita was holding on to.

And it was then that Nandita realised that she was sitting there holding on to an alcoholic beverage as if it was the most natural thing for her to do! Where on earth had it come from?

And it was then that the son realised that his mother was sitting there holding on to an alcoholic beverage as if it was the most natural thing for her to do. *I hope Ma knows what she's drinking,* he thought as he looked upon her. And then, *She looks comfortable enough.*

And it was then that the daughter-in-law realised that her mother-in-law was sitting there holding on to an alcoholic beverage as if it was the most natural thing for her to do! And she thought, *So, ma-in-law dear, you have started at last to let your hair down. Not bad, not bad at all.* And looking towards Jason, she said something to him about his children.

Nandita, caught with incriminating evidence, said nothing. Instead, bending forward, she placed the offending can of beer out of sight under the table as if to obliterate its very existence. As if to expunge it from all records!

The son also said not a word; a slight tightening of his lips was the only giveaway signal that he had observed anything unusual at all. But his mind had gone racing off, wondering why and how his mother had begun to change. Though not unduly alarmed, he was not amused. That she looked young, fresh, and energetic he had attributed to the daily walks she took. But to what could he attribute this particular change in her? Or perhaps there was no change at all! Jason must have handed her a drink, and out of politeness, she had not let go of it. Mind in a whirl, he argued back and forth. And all the while, using another layer of his consciousness, he kept up a conversation centred on plays and playwrights with his guest.

The daughter-in-law, remembering the looks of disapproval that had crept onto Nandita's face whenever some hint of an alcoholic beverage had strayed into her own hands, smirked. But she too had not said a single word. It was time her mother-in-law began to accept life as it really was. Maybe she already had, Meeta reasoned, eyes narrowing. Had not the chill winds stopped blowing her way for a while now? That a thaw had come about she was willing to accept, but from which end the warm winds had blown in to bring about the change, she had no idea. Even so, that particular drink in Nandita's hand had come as a complete surprise to her. Such a dramatic turnabout certainly needed to be investigated. And that printed silk she was wearing and that comment about bringing some colour into her life, what was going on? A cool mother-in-law would be far easier to live with than a frosted-over one. Even so, the change would have to be researched. She was amused but far from alarmed. And having urged Jason to come and sample Tukun's cooking, she fled, with a show of legs and bouncing breasts, on to another group of guests.

And Tukun dragged Jason towards the barbecue. 'You must try the salmon in mustard sauce, my wife's speciality. Coming, Ma?' he asked, turning to Nandita. She made her excuses and moved away. She watched the suave host gathering other guests along the way as he went along. And in the charming host Sudipto Roy, she caught a glimpse of the charmer, Flying Officer Prodipto Kumar Roy, peeping out.

Nandita, lost in thought, wandered off, not quite sure what next to do. Avoiding the other guests, she walked along the periphery of the yard. She needed some solitude to sort herself out. She said, 'Tell me, Dipto, why do I feel so guilty, when I've done no wrong?' She got no reply but the voice of Dipto's grandson cut across her thoughts.

'Hi, Thamma,' he was calling out, standing by the pool, dripping water. What had befallen her grandson today? He normally avoided her when in the company of his peers. 'Come and meet my friends.'

'And if my *sari* gets wet.'

'I promise it won't. Guys, meet my grandmom, she's real cool.'

'She is my grandma as well.' Tammy laid claim.

'Hi, Mrs Roy,' a chorus of young voices chirped in unison as a whole lot of wet hands were stretched out towards her.

'Hi!' Forgetting her *sari*, she stretched out both her hands to shake hands with them.

'She knows lots and lots about our country.' The use of the definition 'our country' while speaking of the United States caused Nandita a brief moment's concern. But it was but an amorphous feeling that drifted away no sooner than it had taken a step across the threshold of her mind. And her grandson had gone on: 'About Mark Twain and George Washington and national parks and the first American on the moon and stuff. If you need any help, just ask her.' Tom, in good form, was showing off his unique grandmother to his friends.

'She dresses funny,' chirped up a little voice. The much-mortified elder sister, classmate to Tammy, tried to hush her. But the child had no desire to be quietened. 'But I like her,' said the honest little mite.

'Thank you for liking me. I like you too. What's your name?'

'Miranda.'

'That's a pretty name. But tell me, Miranda, have you eaten?'

'No. And I'm hungry.' She pouted.

'Why don't you kids go and eat?'

'Who'll guard our pool? There's lots of sunken treasure down there,' said a handsome little lad with a thatch of curly black hair that sat like a crown upon his head.

'An imaginative young man,' thought Nandita. But in all seriousness, she offered, 'Let's make a deal. I guard your pool while you go and eat.'

'Yeah! The Martians are all over, they could take over the place,' said another knowledgeable youth.

'More the reason why I should guard the place while you go and eat, and remember there's plenty of ice cream in all kinds of lovely flavours in the freezer. Leave some for me, *please*,' she coaxed. 'I love chocolate,' she added conspiratorially, and the children left giggling in a flurry of wet arms and legs and dripping clothes.

But little Miranda, halfway down the yard, stopped in her tracks and, turning round, loudly lisped, 'I'll save lots and lots of choklit ice cream for you, Mrs Roy.'

Nandita ran up to the little girl and, taking her into her arms, gave her a big hug. Her sari had gone damp, and the well-informed mite warned, 'Your pretty dress has gone all wet, your mommy will be real mad at you.' And freeing herself from Nandita's embrace, she ran off behind her elder sister.

'Quite likely she and many more besides will,' she murmured, more for her own benefit than Miranda's. There were more reasons than a mere damp *sari* to answer for, she knew. *Yes, her mommy and many others besides would be mad at her.*

She could imagine the star-cast for this terrible showdown! Her Thakuma, looking forbidding with her Ma in tow and her Dadu, wearing a non-committal 'what can I possibly do' look would be leading the entourage. Her mother-in-law wearing a frozen deadpan expression, her father-in-law the major general robbed of words but looking apologetic would be hovering in the background. And a tearful Daminidi, looking woebegone and confused, would be all over the place. She had transgressed beyond redemption; that can of beer clutched in her own hand in the presence of her son and his wife had brought it forward and placed the fact before her eyes! Unfortunately life and its living was not a simple matter. Like that polluting grain of rice in her Boroma's life, this innocuous drink would be her undoing. She had been perched, bored perhaps but without drawing attention for ever so long, upon the periphery of other people's concerns. Why then had she chosen to deviate and move away from its safety to create a life of her own?

Life for the Nanditas of this world was not that simple! The veil of modernism that they occasionally drew across their face was but a mere cover-up to delude the world into thinking that they had moved out of the bondage of their orthodox and restricting backgrounds. Any deviation, any disappointment engineered by you yourself, or even by fate, and you were pulled up short. The fact that Nandita's father, an only son, had fled from life itself, leaving her, a female child, as his descendent, bringing to a close Dadu's line, had been cause enough to have earned her disapprobation. The fact that her husband had carelessly killed himself and left her a widow had earned her a life sentence of leading the life of an ascetic. And finally the one act of defiance, the fact that she had chosen to walk out of the folds of both the Roy and the Ganguly families to lead a life of her own, had brought down a wall of silence upon her. No strictures had been passed, but that she had turned herself into an outsider by her own actions was evident to her at every turn. Knowing as she did how little it took to fall from grace, how then had she allowed herself to risk her all in search of a little bit of companionship? Those friendships that had urged her on to so many daring acts were but transient relationships; her real life lay here with Tukun, his wife, and their children.

And as she sat thinking, the chairs around her had emptied out; hunger had drawn almost one and all where the hot and sizzling food and the freezing cold dessert were being served. She moved to one of the seats under one of the umbrellas and sat down. An empty can of beer coming in contact with her foot rolled away and came to rest a short distance away. She looked long and hard at that harmless piece of moulded aluminium and remembered that day when a teasing Bill had urged her to take a sip from his own can. 'See what you have done, Bill, did you have to teach me to drink beer with you?' But it was more than beer that she was, in truth, talking of. The inflated pool lay to her right. It was full of water, but without the children, it looked absolutely empty and lifeless. Without Bill, what would life be like? Empty as the filled-up pool was?

And then little Miranda was clambering onto the chair beside her. 'See my tummy,' she said, pointing to her taut and stretched-out belly.

'I think it's nice and full,' Nandita said admiringly. 'Did you get to eat any ice cream?'

'Yes. Lots and lots! I even saved some for you.'

'Thank you.'

And then all the other children returned in a rush, and drawn to them as if by a magnet, Miranda ran off behind them.

'Hope she's not been bugging you?' asked a pretty voice, and Nandita looked up into the face of a more grown-up version of little Miranda.

'Not at all, she's a lovely child, and as I can see, she looks just like her mother.'

'So you guessed, not so difficult to place us together, what do you say? Most folks say she looks a lot like me. But behaves just like her father.'

'That should be a compliment to the father.'

'I didn't intend it as a compliment.' The young woman smiled.

'She is such a well-behaved and friendly little girl. We took an instant liking for one another. I am Mrs Roy, Tom and Tammy's grandmother.'

And thrusting forward her hand, 'I guessed as much. I'm Valerie, Miranda and Victoria's ma; we have to rush off. I've still to pick up the week's groceries, do the laundry, and a million other things besides. See you, and thank you for saying all those nice things about my baby.' And she moved away towards the little pool. 'Come on, kids, let's get going,' she could be heard calling out to her children.

Nandita rose and slowly walked up to the centre of festivities: the food. The children and their parents were about to leave, she could see. Jason, holding the hand of his wife, came up to her. 'Mrs Roy, meet Jacqueline. Jacquie, this is Tom's grandma, Mrs Roy.'

'Hello, Jacqueline, your husband had much to tell me about . . .'

'What rumours have you been spreading behind my back, sweetheart?'

'Rumours, honey, are better left unheard,' he said, bending over and planting a kiss upon her lips. 'What do you say, Mrs Roy?' he said, squinting up and smiling into her eyes.

Nandita smiled in response. 'Come again, please. It was nice getting to know you, and I have still to get acquainted with Jacqueline, as you know, Jason.'

'Will do—come, honey, let's round up the boys and get going. See you.' And with a wave of their hands, they moved off.

Spotting her, Suhasini asked, 'Where have you been?'

'At a safe distance making sure I don't have to work.'

'Not you.' She said, 'Milind has been cooking and I've been keeping an eye on him. I caught glimpses of you but couldn't come over.'

'Yes, he could burn his hands.'

'No. He could eat up *all the mustard fish all by himself.*' And a number of persons within earshot had laughed.

'Kakima, I am indeed a wronged man. Would I? Tell me would I ever eat up my undue share of anything?' he coaxed, coming up from behind, pretending to be hurt.

'Yes. Of fish you would,' said the unrelenting wife.

'Ah! There you are, Ma. Where have you been?' asked Meeta on her way to fulfil some errands.

'Guarding the pool.'

'Did I hear you say you were guarding the pool?' asked Danny.

'Yes, you did.'

'From?'

'The Martians.'

'You don't say,' chortled one of the dads in waiting, who was standing just beside Danny. He was a big man with the most tantalising of smiles that she had ever seen. His teeth flashed white, and his skin gleamed ebony black. 'Did they really ask you to guard their pool for them, ma'am?'

'There is sunken treasure in that pool, and the Martians are all over the place, I've been told.' It was a matter-of-fact statement, with not a hint of condescension coming in the way of its importance.

'I see, the Martians are all over the place,' grinned the man with the tantalising smile.

'Imagination running riot,' said Tukun, joining them. He had a platter full of just-barbecued breasts of chicken in his hand. 'These are fresh from the coals; could I tempt anyone?'

Danny took a piece and the rest shied off.

Meeta called, 'Tukun, the Johnsons and the Nordstroms are leaving.'

Handing the plate of barbecued chicken to Danny, he replied, 'I'll be with you in a moment.'

And one by one, all the guests who could truly be designated as guests left, leaving behind a close circle of intimate friends who would be leaving later.

'Hands up, all those who are starving,' Tukun called out as he placed some items to cook onto the open flame on his way back. 'Ma, both your hands should've shot right up. You should be starving. Just give me five minutes and I'll have something for you.' Nandita let out a long breath of relief; her Tukun, after that momentary sign of disapproval, or would it be better to call it surprise, had gone back to being his normal self.

'I can wait, I think Milind, Dinesh, and you should—'

Interrupting Nandita, Dinesh declared, 'We are the chefs today, so we get to eat right at the end,' even as he bit into a succulent piece of chicken.

'This spirit of service is most touching, my friend.' Putting his arms across Danny's back, Tukun asked, 'More beer?'

'Sure. Beer is nothing but water.'

'Water?'

'OK, firewater if you like. More one has of it, the better it is for one's health.'

'Sez who?' asked his wife.

'Stop quibbling, darling,' cajoled the husband, passing a set of caressing fingers across her cheek.

'Wish Vivek and Sue were here,' said someone. However, Nandita thought otherwise!

'We are missing them, aren't we?' questioned Meeta. And Nandita thought, *True perhaps, even so . . .*

'I don't know why Vivek had to move west,' Suhasini complained. 'Sue called the other evening and when I told her about the barbecue, she said how she wished she could join us here.'

'Catch that *kanjoos*, I mean, that fellow Vivek, fly across the US for a barbecue,' declared Dinesh.

'Catch anyone,' replied his wife in a tone as dry as dry could be. 'Hey, where are the Kidwais?'

'They've gone for a wedding to India.'

'Where?'

'To Lucknow.'

'Ugh! Can you imagine how hot it must be there?'

And the barbecued *paneer*, hotter still than summertime Lucknow, with its colourful attendants, arrived just then spluttering before Nandita. 'So much?' she said with a shake of her head. 'Get me a plate, please, Meeta, I can't possibly eat so much.'

'I fixed it, Ma, I know it's really not that much.'

'Please.'

A plate was produced and placed before Nandita; the first morsel had been forked, and it was at that precise moment that they heard the front doorbell peal.

'Who could it be, shall I go and take a look?'

'Don't worry, Tukun, the kids will take care of the door.'

There was some commotion from within the house. And all eyes had turned that way. Then, a very excited troop of children came spilling out of the house, shouting, 'Look who's here, look who's here . . .' and before their eyes, framed in the door that led out of the family room onto the yard, stood Vivek and Sue.

Long-legged and bronzed, dressed in a minuscule top and what appeared to Nandita's eyes to be the shortest pair of shorts that God or man had ever created, stood Sue. The husband, dressed in a pair of shorts that went past his knees, and a roomy bush shirt with flapping sleeves that was a burst of psychedelic colours, stood like a dwarfed peacock beside her.

Nandita's loaded fork, having gone up to her mouth, came back to rest on her plate again. Throat gone dry, she took a long sip from the glass of orange juice that was lying in wait before her.

Meeta rushed forward and took Sue into her embrace. Vivek leant over and brushed his cheek across Meeta's.

An avalanche of words spilled over from all corners. When, where, how had they managed to be in Saisborough today, everyone together wanted to know. And Nandita, nibbling at her food, sat on as the babble of voices kept washing over her.

'We were really missing you. I'm so very happy you could join us today.'

'Viv was to come to Michigan midweek, so I said, why don't you bring it forward by a few days, darling, then we can pop in at the Roys' and have some fun. His firm was paying his fare.' And mimicking her husband, she continued,

'What about you? Do you know how much it costs to fly to the East Coast from here?' he asked me.

'I was just being practical,' mumbled Vivek in reply to the spate of laughter his wife's mimicry had evoked.

'Or a regular *kanjoos yaar*,' Dinesh, surfacing from a bracing gin and tonic, commented. 'Your wife's wish should always be your command.'

'I've taken note of that, Dan,' said his wife.

'Well, here we are, aren't we?' Vivek defended himself.

'Yeah, only because I went out and got hold of a ticket that said, "Buy one ticket and your partner flies free."'

'That was very clever of you, Sue,' Tukun lauded her.

'Not so difficult to get hold of one of these. If only you want to get hold of one of them of course.' A telling look was beamed Vivek's way. 'The one we are flying on is one of those convenient tickets for executives to fly around all over the world with their girlfriends without having to pay for the pleasure or the privilege. I'm sure, all you guys know about them.' She studied each male face in the circle with an amused assessing look. 'I wonder how many of you guys have quietly made use of them.' The final conjecture drew a lot of flak and a skirmish of sorts broke out. Arguments and counter-arguments had flown thick and fast till the host had thought fit to pour oil on troubled waters.

'Come on, Sue,' he pleaded, 'you didn't come all the way to sow seeds of dissension in our lives, now did you? Come and sample some of the burnt offerings I've been dishing up with the help of Dan and Milind. If it tastes good, you can praise me, otherwise you can apportion blame you know where.'

'Where's your mom? Haven't seen her,' Sue said, helping herself to the so-called burnt offerings. 'We used to keep bumping into each other in downtown Saisborough, she's kinda cute, you know.' The use of the adjective 'cute' in connection with his mother came as a surprise to Tukun.

'There she is, right in the centre of the storm you just kicked up.'

'Yeah! There she is, how did I ever miss her?' And waving out to Nandita, she said, 'I really miss Saisborough, and all you guys out here,' scooping up a can of diet Pepsi. 'I think I'll go and say hi to her.'

'Wait a moment, I'll get something to eat and come along with you. Hey, Vivek, have you tried the fish, there was a rumour afloat that it's pretty good. Helped yourself? Good, let's go and sit down.'

'Hello, Mrs Roy, sure glad to meet you.' Placing her plate upon the table, she bent across and kissed Nandita upon her cheek. 'You know, don't you, that we have moved away from here?'

'I told you, Ma. Didn't I?'

Nandita replied with a quiet 'Yes.'

'We bumped into one another ever so often.'

'Really? Ma, you never said anything about meeting Sue.'

'I must have.'

'How's your pup doing, Danny?' asked Vivek.

'Grown any bigger?'

'Longer, not taller, Sue.'

She laughed, 'Oh, these dachshunds are so funny.'

'Does she still piddle all over the place?' Milind wanted to know. 'You didn't bring her along today?'

'She is a big girl now and can take care of herself. Any day now she'll be acquiring a boyfriend for herself.'

'That's cool. You can start a sausage factory and get rich, what say you?' Milind suggested. There was a ripple of laughter, and Nandita laughed along with the others.

Looking upon Nandita's laughing face, Sue softly said, 'You look quite different from when first I met you, Mrs Roy.'

'Different? How can that be? I am the same person.'

'No, you aren't. You are far more beautiful, more composed, more in control than ever you were before.' And then suddenly as if, in a moment of sudden perspicacity, having discovered the source of that which brought about this unique change, she opened her mouth to speak. And at that precise moment, the masking burst of laughter that had so far been covering her speech completely died down. And into that well of silence, she dropped, 'Where is your handsome boyfriend today? Or has he already come and gone?'

'Sue,' scolded Vivek, aghast at the behaviour of his wife. Had he but kept quiet, the question would have passed off as a joke.

What are they speaking of? thought Tukun. *My orthodox mother and a boyfriend, why, why, why?* His lips pinched and compressed, he sat on and not a word had crossed his lips.

What does Sue mean? thought Meeta. *My staid mother-in-law and a boyfriend?* A little smile flitted across her lips; well, why not, she thought.

And the rest of the persons collected around that table just sat conjecturing at this strange turn of events. Sue should not have spoken as she had done, they all felt, but there never was any smoke without fire, as the proverb said. But an Indian woman of her age, from her background, how could that be?

That which Nandita feared had come to pass! Cold anger swept through her head and crept into her heart. What right had this woman to question her about her friends? Pulling herself together, with her newly acquired self-assurance, she turned to Sue and with dignity said, 'Dr William Brady is my good friend. He has been close to our family for many years now. Had he not gone to Dallas, he would have been with us here today.'

But her son did not break his silence. Not a word crossed his lips. But Meeta quickly stepped into the breach: 'We have known Dr Brady for ever so long. My Tammy must have been just a few months old when first we met.' She turned to her husband. 'You remember, Tukun, how tiny Tammy was when we went to New Jersey with Ma?'

Caught in the vortex of such a frontal attack, he was forced to nod his head in agreement. But the way he sat with his body turned at an angle to shut out his mother from his view spoke volumes to her. *So, Dr William Brady and his mother had been going around together for a long time now,* he thought. He was intensely hurt and embarrassed. *Why then had she given him the impression that she had bumped into him just the other day?* He felt completely let down. *Why this subterfuge, why this shade of a lie? What exactly was going on? It was not as if his mother was a teenage daughter whom he had to guard. Why had she suddenly moved away from the fixed norms by which she had lived for ever so long? Why? Why? Why? What would all these people think?* And aloud he said, 'More beer, guys, or a vodka tonic perhaps?'

Nandita rose and bid farewell to all those who were seated around the table and went up slowly, but her son Tukun's self-conscious laughter, louder than ever it was, followed her all the way up to her room.

17 NANDITA FALLS FROM GRACE

O nce she was alone, the enormity of that which had come to pass took hold of her and made her wince. If only she had not been such a coward and introduced Bill to the family while there was time. But what was done, was done. That she had shocked her son, she knew; but was that not to be expected? Had she not imposed the harshest of rules that governed a Bangali Brahmon widow's life upon herself and lived out her life adhering to them? Since gaining consciousness, what had Tukun seen but a woman in nunlike habit, who lived the life of a penitent?

And she remembered a dialogue from very long ago: 'Ma, why do you always wear white?' And then a complaining, 'I don't like it.'

'Why don't you like it?'

'Because it makes you different from the mothers of my friends, and I don't like my ma looking different.'

She had tried to explain why she lived a life that was different from others, but her son hadn't been willing to accept those explanations. Not then, but later, bit by bit, it had become a part of him. One day, a few years later, someone had offered mutton chops, among other things, to her at a get-together, and an observant Tukun had removed the plate from her hand with a curt 'My mother doesn't eat all such things!'

And then she looked down upon her *sari* and wondered what he must have thought of this garment. With an impatient gesture, she removed the *sari* with its offending adornment in green and threw it without care across her bed and went into the bathroom. She washed her overheated face with the refreshingly cool water. Thankfully the lakes of Chicago always delivered ice-cold water in its taps come summer, come winter. Face tingling, she came back to the room, made a tight ball of the offending six yards lying upon her bed, and opening her wardrobe, threw it into a corner. She searched and found the most desolate among her collection of six-yard lengths of white and took out the one that had lost all its allure with years of use.

She went down again only when all the guests had left. While putting away sundry items lying on the kitchen counter, she looked out of the door and saw the neighbourhood cat come in through the hedge that divided their property from the one next to theirs. She was the last guest to call, and she had not come alone; she had brought along her brood. There was still fish aplenty, and just stepping out, Nandita offered some. Having feasted, the family of four soon left.

And as she went about her tasks, she watched the winding down of a busy and colourful day taking place out there in the garden! There were rivulets of water flowing past the kitchen; the children, she could see, had let the water out of the pool. She watched as, leaving a trail of destruction in its path, its emptied-out carcass was dragged along behind the children and put away out of sight into the garage. Tukun had been hard at work. The instant garden that had bloomed for but a while, with its array of larger-than-life flowers now lay uprooted! Felled, the umbrellas lay, eyes shut, with folded petals upon the ground, waiting to be taken away. The mussed-up yard, bereft of all embellishment, wore the look of a deflated balloon, flat, colourless, and tired. She felt a resonant chord of kinship for the emptied-out space that lay before her eyes!

The aftermath of a day's unmitigated entertaining spelled out a great deal of work. Stacking soiled plates and glasses, separating spoons, forks, and knives, she wondered whether it was fatigue that had sealed Tukun's lips. He had been busy outdoors, she had seen, but he had also made several entries into the kitchen on some errand or the other, and gone out again. She had made several attempts to speak to him, but he had always appeared to be too busy to take in what she was saying to him.

Tukun came in, climbed onto a little stepladder, and started putting away the appendages that went with barbecuing. She herself was busy sorting out and putting away the leftover food into the refrigerator, and attempted to exchange a few words with him. But except for an occasional yes or no that had been wrung out of him, he remained silent. He was there in the same room with her yet not quite there. Was he being rude, she asked herself. *No, just too tired and preoccupied!* Nandita had told herself, in trying to justify her son's strange behaviour.

But from that evening, onto the next day, and into the next, nothing changed. Her son asked her for no explanations, nor gave her any opportunity to give any! And Tukun with his tightened lips and unsmiling face had emerged to her eyes as the symbol of all the imposing presences that had so often dominated her life. She knew from experience that men had a way of conveying their disapproval without making use of any mundane tool such as words! Their silences, she had learnt from experience, spoke volumes.

And little by little, her son's disapproval began to anger her. What business had he to disapprove of that which he knew nothing? And her anger spilled over and brought to mind many others against whom she had harboured a passive sense of grievance for ever so long.

What right did her father have, to abandon her after having brought her into this life? Leaving her holding on to a void where he should himself have been. What right did Dadu have to hold his council when wars of succession had been fought over her head by Thakuma and by Mejo Thakuma? What right did the Major General have to stand mute when he should have spoken up? Generations of men had let her down. Why then was she hurt when her son had chosen to keep quiet? What else should she have expected of him?

Should she have remained in her shell and not ventured out?

But why should she not have?

Perhaps she had done some wrong!

No. What wrong had she done?

Then, why the disapproval?

She did not know. But this she did know: that she just could not live out her life carrying along the burden of her son's disapproval.

Or could she?

The dialogue within her had gone on till fatigued, she came to a decision of sorts. She would eschew all her new bonds and shame her son into understanding how unreasonable his behaviour was. But life could never be, would never ever be the same again.

A leopard, they say, never changes its spots: Nandita had in haste decided to revert to form. She would withdraw from the world and go back into the shell from which she had emerged so timorously. In trying to bring the world down on its knees, she had decided to KO her own self once again.

A long time ago she had told her Kakima that she would protest as the Japanese workers did. 'Kakima,' she had told her, 'you must have read about how the Japanese workforce protests? They don't down their tools; they voice their displeasure by silently putting in some extra amount of work.' Her aunt's words of caution had gone unheeded then as now. And she decided upon a course of action that would eventually hurt her and no one else. But while remembering her aunt, she decided that a visit to Kolkata to see her pain-wracked, arthritis-crippled Kakima had become long overdue. She felt that moment a sudden yearning to go back to her roots and to visit her beloved aunt. Yes, she would have to make some arrangements to go and visit her and, that too, very soon.

That her husband was a disturbed man had become amply clear to Meeta. Harking back to the day of the barbecue, she remembered how he had mechanically gone about the task of putting away all the heavy items that had been brought out for the outdoor festivities. Under normal circumstances, he would not have bothered to immediately give the yard a once-over. She had said, 'Come on, Tukun, you can do that later.' But he had paid no heed to her suggestion.

He had eaten in silence and gone up directly. Meeta could hardly remember a day when Tukun would go without his daily dose of the day's news.

A day or two later, when she saw no change, she asked, 'Something troubling you?' following him upstairs.

'No, nothing,' he responded in a flat toneless voice.

'You haven't been behaving normally,' he gave her a short belligerent glance, 'since the day we had that barbecue.'

'What do you mean? Not normal—what an idea. Huh!'

'It is what Sue said, isn't it?'

'Oh! Sue!'

'Yes. Sue! She passes a comment about your mother having a boyfriend and you go into a huge sulk. Don't be so medieval, darling.'

'I'm not being medieval.'

'Yes, you are! But I find the whole thing very amusing.'

'You have a strange sense of humour.'

'Honestly, tell me, at her age is your mother in any danger of getting into any serious trouble? Particularly *your mother*, perpetually in white.' And she gave a long peal of laughter.

'I suppose not,' he agreed grudgingly as he removed his trousers, threw his underwear into the laundry basket, and stepped into his pyjamas.

'Are you afraid that a torrid love affair is taking place behind your back?'

'Don't be silly,' he growled.

'Then?'

'I don't know.'

'Stop being ridiculous, Tukun. I mean, be realistic! She is a grandmother twice over. Just think . . .' And this time, the paroxysm of laughter brought tears to her eyes.

'So?'

'So you think there was some truth in what Sue had to say.'

'No. I didn't say that,' he responded, very irritated. And turning onto to his side, he shut his eyes and pretended to go to sleep.

And then the telephone call came! And Tukun, breaking his vow of silence, had to go and hand the instrument to his mother. He knocked and entered her room and, putting a comforting hand upon her back, handed the cordless to her. She looked up with surprise and found nothing but compassion there. Who was calling, she wondered, that it should have softened her son's stance towards her?

It was, alas, a long-distance call that had come from Calcutta. Nandita's cousin Jhontu had called to inform her that his mother had died of heart failure the previous evening.

Tukun, seeing the pain in her eyes, asked, 'Do you want to go to Kolkata?' He knew how strong his mother's bonds were with this aunt of hers and wanted to alleviate her suffering as well he could.

With a slow to-and-fro sideways movement of her head, Nandita indicated that she did not wish to go anywhere. 'It's no use going now; I should have gone much earlier.' And her eyes filled up with unshed tears as she stretched out a hand to her son to convey the sense of gratitude she felt at his thoughtfulness.

Taking the outstretched hand in his own, he lowered himself onto the bed beside her. 'Shall I get you a cup of tea or something?' he asked, spying the unshed tears in her eyes and the ashen look upon her face. How vulnerable his mother looked, he thought as he rose and poured a glass of water for her and handed it to her!

'Go back to bed, I am all right.' He looked closely at her. 'I really am,' she reassured him.

Shutting the door, her son let himself out of the room and then she rose and went and stood by the window. Not a single ghost out of her past was calling out to her today! She slumped into a chair and broke into tears, recognising that she had put off her visit to Kolkata till it was too late to do so.

And while she had dawdled, a generation had passed away!

The voice that had cautioned her that the ways of India were not those of Japan had been stilled.

Nandita wept for the woman she had loved so well, and along with that, for the sad woman who lived within her own self, before falling into a disturbed sleep late that night.

The crisp and cool early dawn air, cutting through the thin material of her dress, had sent a shiver down Nandita's spine! She had pulled her clothes together closer and crossed her arms tightly across her bony breast to ward off the cold. Sensing a movement, the little girl Nandita had stood a hesitant moment in the secluded corner where the toilets lay, and then she had seen Damini emerge from the shadows, a sensuous and shapely silhouette draped in nothing but a wet and clinging sari.

But Daminidi was dead; she knew Daminidi was dead!

But even so, before her stood Damini: a compelling sight, a riveting sight that allowed no turning away from her magnetic voluptuary! Someone was at the door. A tentative knock and Daminidi, a picture of vibrant beauty and youth, had gone flying to throw open the door that led from the road onto the courtyard. Panchu *goyla* was there. She could clearly see his towering form, his rippling muscles. Daminidi had stretched out her hands to touch that strong-as-steel body of the milkman, and he had folded her into his embrace. But then some unknown force had come into play and had wrenched her out of his embrace! And Panchu had retreated away, away, away, and then gone completely out of sight. And Nandita had felt as if someone very important to her very own life was slipping away from her, as she had watched Damini shed those silent tears.

And someone was saying, 'Damini has run away.' Then another: 'No, she is still just where she was; she did not have courage enough.' And still another: 'With that Panchu, but where?' The first voice, weighed down by wisdom, had declared, 'The world would have caught up with her and brought her back anyway, so why try?'

But Daminidi was dead; she knew Daminidi was dead.

Then how, then how was she standing in the courtyard crying? Why was she crying? Was it because Panchu *goyla* had gone away from her reach and out of her life? Why had she not held on to him if she loved him so desperately? 'Damini should have run away,' Nandita's inner voice had prompted. Yet another voice from within her had demanded, 'To live out the rest of her life in the shadow of rejection and shame?' And while this debate raged around her head, a lonely, broken Damini had shed silent tears.

But Daminidi was dead; she knew Daminidi was dead! And death was final and absolute!

The sun, harsh and searing, came through the window and fell across her face. Painfully, hesitantly, she wrenched herself out of her dream-drugged sleep to look around to see if there was anyone besides her. As she opened her eyes, a terrible shooting pain coursed through her head and made her wince. She shut them tight once again, shying away from whatever reality she would have to face if she were to open them wide to look around.

A leaden weight seemed to have settled down around the region of her heart. Her limbs, heavy and tired, were unwilling to respond to her brain's commands. She tried to rise but fell back on her pillow once again. Why did she feel this way? She was sick, with a soaring fever. Yes, that was the reason. What else could it be? She felt her own forehead; no, she did not have any fever. Why then did she feel so sick and downhearted?

And then she remembered all that had come to pass on that fun-filled yet fateful Sunday: the surreal drama that had been played out in the garden behind their home, and the cold war that had waged since then within the four walls of this home. And then the final assault on her sensibility: that call from Kolkata, with a weepy voice on the other end.

And then with total recall, she remembered with agony that her beloved Kakima was no more. That heaviness sitting around her heart flowered and became one palpable burst of grief. A spurt of tears welled up and, overflowing out of her eyes, coursed along the sides of her eyes and onto the pillow. With effort, she urged herself out of her prone position. Head between her hands, she sat on, bleary-eyed. Why had she dreamt of Damini and the lost cause of her futile love?

Moving away from her dream, she asked of herself, 'Why did I not go and visit her while there still was time?' There was nothing but regret writ large in that question! There were excuses aplenty. But could they not have been overcome? Since Meeta's parents had moved to Vancouver, where two of her siblings lived, both Meeta and Tukun had lost all motivation to go rushing back home to India. But could she not have gone? The enormity of her loss was compounded by her sense of guilt. She should have gone back to visit this woman who had loved her with such an unselfish and undemanding love. Did a woman called Nandita need to hold anyone's hand to travel back to the home of her childhood, to look up the sheet anchor of her life? Not one person remained today who had walked alongside her in her journey of growing up. Today of all days, she wanted to lay her head upon a caring shoulder and to cry. But no shoulders, alas, now remained to shed one's tears upon.

Slowly, insidiously, the fact that with this passing away she had bid her final adieu to her childhood and her young days was coming home to her. With a sense of intense loss, she recognised that this aunt, a fragment of the adult world that had nurtured her in her growing years, just being there, somewhere in the background, had in truth been a warm and reassuring fixture for her. The fact that they never met, nor exchanged letters was somehow different from the fact that they could now never meet, nor exchange another word ever. Death was final and immutable and absolute.

Late last night when she had heard of Kakima's passing away, later still into the night she had sat up and written a few lines. Never before had she attempted to write anything in rhyme but her pen steeped in grief had carried her along. The piece of paper lay alongside her spectacles on her bedside table. She picked it up and read the lines, wondering what had made her write as she had.

She was no poet, and she never would be. There was nothing diffuse about what she had written. The words held no pretensions at being anything other than what their face value denoted. She had written of an escape from a disease-wracked body, of the forlorn hankering of those who were left behind, and the total lack of concern on the part of the just departed. Though she had herself written the last lines, they had hurt! Something had told her that even if she were to call, Kakima would not look back!

For she was out there
Playing, with a bunch of kids yet to be born!

Looking out sightlessly through the open window, she thought on. The image of a careworn Kakima freed from the travails of this care-filled world left her with a receptacle full of mixed feelings. But why should her beloved aunt look back when she had transcended into freedom and joy, when she had moved on to a plane that was out of reach of the trials and tribulations of this troublesome world? The writing of those few lines had been cathartic and had brought a modicum of relief to her grieving heart. That she, her beloved aunt, had returned to a state of innocence had been painful to accept, for she would now, never ever be available to her again. The truth was that death was tragic for those who remained behind to grieve.

For the one who died, death was an escape, a return to innocence, and an entry into a beautiful untrammelled zone. Had not her Dipto looked upon early death as a recipe for eternal youth? Maybe it was all for the good that Kakima had at last been granted reprieve from constant pain. Even so, she hankered for a last look, for a last word, a last touch that had now all gone out of her reach! She wished she had plucked up courage and made some travel plans on her own while there still was time. But that would have been a departure from the normal. That would have compelled her to ask Tukun for a ticket. And that she had never been able to do!

Of late she did have the money, but the will to act on her own was still missing. Having handed over charge of her life to others, she seemed to have forgotten the very art of decision-making. And she had prevaricated and let the opportunity go by till it was too late to do anything at all. How she wished Bill was here, she needed so desperately to share the turmoil of her heart with him. He would have understood how she felt about the passing away of her beloved aunt. He would have understood the amalgam of pain and regret that came in the wake of all such departures in a human being's life! But in truth, she knew she could not have shared that which really troubled her with him at all. For Sue's question, her own response, and Tukun's reaction to both the question and the answer were centred on him and his presence in her life. And his presence in her life had all but come to a close! How strange were the ways of life that now, when she stood at the threshold of a final farewell with him,

Bill's presence should have come knocking at her family's door! And that she should herself have started to feel his absence so acutely.

It was time she got over the need to share all her troublesome thoughts with Bill. That which was out of reach was best put aside. A human being had to look ahead. But at what: an empty lifeless void? A sense of desolation flooded her heart as she faced up to this grim reality. This was the other reality that was compounding the sense of total loss into which she had been steeped since hearing of the passing away of her Kakima.

A few days later, Bill returned, but only to pack his bags and leave again, this time round for his place of work at New York. Too many persons were going out of her life at one and the same time. And though he had called and promised to return, she was not too sure that this was not a final parting of ways for them.

'I have some unfinished work with you, and besides, I've still to meet your family. My Irene has sent her love to you. She says she wants to meet you.' He had chuckled, 'Take care.' And he was gone. He had had no time to spare, so they had not met. So much the better, Nandita thought as she put down the telephone, back onto its hook, and positioned herself back into her chosen life of seclusion.

Kakima's sudden passing away had provided the required catalyst to restore a modicum of normality between her and her son. The channels of communication that had come to a near close had to an extent opened up. Tukun's grunts and monosyllabic responses had now been replaced by short sentences. The subject of Bill had not been brought up again. And Nandita, having moved back to the position where she had been before she set out on that walk on that very chill springtime day, gave her son no cause for further concern.

Meeta had already left for work and Tukun was letting himself out when Nandita went downstairs.

Though not quite looking directly towards his mother, he said, 'I'll be playing a set of tennis with Mahadevan after work, Ma. I forgot to tell Meeta, would you tell her, please?'

'I'll let her know when she gets back home.'

'Thank you.'

'How are Mahadevan's parents doing? I must visit them one day.'

'I'll talk it over with Mahadevan.' Polite civilities over, he had left.

The last two days had been hectic; the children were being packed off for their respective summer camps. What a relief it must be for the parents, thought Nandita, to have the organising of their empty hours out of the way. And vacation time always managed to throw up too many empty hours! And her own vacation was just beginning! There were no summer camps awaiting her, to fill up her empty hours!

To give a plausible reason for her absence, she had called and told them at the Home that she was not well. But how long could she continue to pretend ill health? She would have to find a more permanent excuse to ensconce herself at home henceforth. More angry with her own self than with Tukun, she had decided to punish herself. Stubborn as she was, she was bent on carrying out her meaningless resolve. But her heart had quivered at the prospect of abandoning all her elderly friends. But what was she to do? Which way was she to move? Who was she to please?

But all such trivia was driven from her mind when Tukun came home in the middle of the day. It was such an unusual experience that it caused her to wonder what it was that had brought him home. 'Are you unwell?' she asked.

'I have bad news . . .'

Rendered apprehensive after the recent passing away of her dear aunt, she asked, alarmed, 'What kind of bad news?'

'Mahadevan's mother passed away early this morning.'

'Oh, no!'

'I have to go there,' he informed her, taking off the jacket of his suit and removing his tie.

Once again I have put it off till too late. I should have visited her while there was still time. While mentally accusing herself of tardiness, she asked, 'What happened?'

'I don't know exactly.' And under his breath while searching for some suitable attire, 'I thought his father was the one with health problems.' He turned to his mother, shirt in hand. 'Would you like to come along?'

'Yes, I think I should, and Meeta?'

'We can leave a note for her.'

And seated beside her son speeding on towards that home where an elderly woman called Parvathi lay dead, she remembered that little walk she had taken outside that home as the elderly couple had rested. She had gone silently into the kitchen that day and let herself out from the rear screen door onto the yard and looked out upon its vastness.

There were no clear demarcations of 'your yard begins here and ends there', in that luxurious home that Mahadevan had acquired. The green of the surrounding rolled up to the doors of that home, she remembered, and rolled away to the far distance once again. The garden furniture had beckoned to her but she had chosen to go past and wander down an uncertain path that went into an uncertain distance. Not a soul had she sighted anywhere. That there were other living beings somewhere in the vicinity could only be assumed from the hum of a distant lawnmower going about its task somewhere at an uncertain distance. The scent of mowed grass had hung enticingly in the air. It was an idyllic place, beautiful and serene and set apart. So serene and set apart was it that a person could well feel lost in its abundant aloneness, she had recognised. And then she had remembered that booming bark of a large dog that had led her on and brought her in sight of another house. That home standing there cloistered in a knoll had given lie to her assumption that the Mahadevans had no neighbours at all. But the fact that one would have to journey out of one's home to even get a glimpse of that neighbouring homestead was also a fact.

She remembered thinking, what will happen when one out of these two persons dies? How will the other live on alone in this desert island? A tremor had passed through her heart at the very thought of such a situation coming to pass. And today that which she had feared had come to be. The inevitable had arrived at Mr Neelakanthan's door.

It was as if her wish had been transformed into reality, for Parvathi had quietly slipped away, leaving her old husband clutching on to his remote. She remembered her own incongruous murmuring, 'I hope Mr Neelakanthan will outlive his wife. He at least has his television set,' as turning back, she had walked back into the house that day.

And as she ruminated, the car had come to a standstill. A number of other cars stood crowding the drive fronting Mahadevan's home. The news was out that Parvathi was no more!

When Tukun and she had parked and gone in, they were not met by any overt show of grief. A dry-eyed Mahadevan met them at the door.

'How is your father doing?' was the first question Tukun asked!

'He seems to be all right.'

'And how are you?' he said, placing a commiserating arm around Mahadevan's shoulders.

'I'm all right.' He sounded distracted. 'But a very important board meeting is coming up . . . and there is so much to do. The timing is most inconvenient, most inconvenient . . .' He had trailed off.

Sumathi, dressed today in traditional attire, came bustling into the living room, a look of irritation creasing her countenance. 'I don't know where Amma keeps the *kumkum*, the *karpooram*, or the wicks for the *deepam*. And that woman . . .' she complained as she went to attend the summons of an elderly Tamilian lady who seemed to have assumed charge of the proceedings. She could be heard querulously calling out, 'Sumathi, Sumathi, Sumathi,' in tremulous tones. So harassed was Sumathi that she had not spared so much as a glance at the duo that was standing to one side with her husband.

So sudden had been Parvathi's passing away that it had taken her son and his wife quite by surprise. The fact that she had slipped away forever out of their hands had not as yet quite sunk into their consciousness. In their peeved stance, there was a petulance that went with a sense of having been let down by someone who was known to stay the course! It was as if the goalkeeper, no less, had deserted his post, in the middle of an important football match, leaving the team to fend goalkeeper-less for the duration of the tourney.

An apparently calm Mr Neelakanthan, seated on the sidelines, looked incomplete without his remote control. His detached demeanour further cemented Nandita's earlier belief that the old gentleman would get by better on his own than would have his wife, had she been positioned where he was today.

Then Mahadevan, remembering his social responsibilities, went up to his father and said, 'Appa, see who has come.'

A pair of lacklustre eyes looked towards Nandita. Not a flicker of recognition came into those eyes!

'She is Sudipto Roy's mother; remember she came to visit Amma sometime back?' He gave a very slow nod of assent, as his arms lay slack upon his lap. And then losing interest, he looked away. And it was then that Nandita felt a tremor of concern pass through her heart as she looked upon his passive countenance. He had not recognised her, she knew, though he had implied that he had. What was he thinking of, she wondered!

Some days later when they went for the *shraddha* ceremony, Nandita observed that a marked change had come about in the personality of Mr Neelakanthan. The sprightly cockiness that had marked the demeanour of the elderly gentleman as he had bickered and argued with his wife Parvathi was completely missing from his persona now! A shrivelled-up old man sat before her. He looked so much like an orphan that Nandita wanted desperately to console him. She wondered now why she had thought that he would get along fine in life without his wife by his side!

The rituals of the *shraddha* ceremony over, Mahadevan came across to Tukun to exchange a few words with him. 'Thank you for coming and standing beside us, it really helps . . .'

'The least we could do,' Sudipto murmured.

'The house has fallen so silent since Amma went away. And yet, she spoke so seldom.'

'I can well imagine,' Tukun soothed.

'I never realised how much of the burden of this household was being borne by her, and as for Appa . . .'

And it was then that Nandita remembered the reason that Mrs Parvathi Neelakanthan had given her son for not being able to accept her invitation to visit them at home. 'If I am not there how will your father manage? Who will give him his lunch? Who will make his evening tiffin?' she had asked of him.

Yes, how will he manage, she pondered as Tukun asked, 'Is he unwell?'

'I don't know. But he has changed. He and the TV set were almost integral to one another and yet he hasn't switched on the TV even once since Amma passed away.'

'Can he stay alone? Will you be able to leave him at home and go to work?' Sudipto enquired.

'That's another hurdle I will have to confront very soon. Amma shouldn't have died so soon.' It appeared from his words that Parvathi had shown a marked lack of thoughtfulness by choosing to die when she had! Evidently her absence was becoming palpable to one and all!

And then Mahadevan was called away and the Roys took their leave soon after and left for home.

On the drive back, Tukun asked, 'How did you find the old gentleman, Ma?'

'I don't know. I had expected to see him in a better condition than I did.' And once back at home, Nandita mulled over that question her son had asked of her. The hunched-up figure of Mr Neelakanthan, lost to the world, haunted her waking hours.

They were in the kitchen together, Nandita cooking some fish and Meeta baking a cake, when Nandita suddenly spoke up, 'You know, Meeta, I was really quite unhappy to see the condition of Mr Neelakanthan.'

'I'd never met him before, so I wouldn't know. Did he look unwell or something to you?'

'No. Not sick, but somehow terribly disconnected and lost,' she said as she dunked the fried pieces of fish in the gravy simmering upon the stove.

'Not very surprising if he feels lost. They must have been married for simply ages.'

'I suppose you are right. He appeared to be independent enough but she was always there, so perhaps he was more dependent upon her than anyone realised.'

'Yes, being married is very habit-forming.' And then she bit her tongue for she had seen Nandita wince. 'Sorry, Ma, just forget what I said.' A whistle had blown, and a beautifully browned cake emerged from the oven.

'Lovely cake!' Nandita said.

'Thanks! We'll eat it tonight all the way feeling sorry that the kids are not getting a slice.'

'Missing the children?' Nandita asked. 'So am I!'

'The rogues—when they're around, I hate them.'

'Hate them?'

'Not quite. But . . .' She grimaced and fell silent.

And then the hunched-up figure of old Mr Neelakanthan swam before her eyes. He was showing no outward signs of missing his wife, yet the last time Nandita had seen him, he had had such a stunned and beaten look about him that she had come away with the impression that he was totally lost without his Parvathi by his side. How wrong had been her assumption that Mahadevan's father would get along just fine as long as he had someone to serve him his meals on time and had the company of his television set to while away the rest of his available hours! That she did not have a better understanding of the workings of the human mind had come as a surprise to her. An elderly widower was vulnerable by far, she could see, than a widow of similar vintage ever could be. But then, her life had been sprinkled by a plethora of widows, so how could she have gauged that? And then she remembered Bill as she had first seen him, a broken rudderless soul! And she sighed!

Hearing the little sigh escape from her, Meeta asked, 'Burnt your fingers or something, Ma?' but got no reply.

The next morning was as bright and clear as only a summer's day can be. She would go today to the Home and visit everyone, she had decided. Moving towards the stairs to go to her room, she caught her foot on a loose end of the rug and stumbled, and the telephone shrilled; the Colonel was on the line.

'Nan?' the voice, brusque and gruff, asked.

'Yes, speaking!'

'Are you well enough to come over today? Charlie has taken a bad turn so . . .'

Fearing to hear the worst, she gasped out, 'Is she very unwell, Colonel?'

'Yes. Very! If you want to see her, then . . .' And unable to complete the sentence, he rang off. Heart constricting, she recalled a popular belief that mishaps always came in threesomes. She had lost Kakima, then Parvathi, and now . . . No, she just could not face another death.

Life and its vagaries just could not be trusted, so she knew she had to be there and, that too, very soon. All senseless resolves forgotten, Nandita rushed to the Home, to find to her despair that the essence of Charlie had already fled.

Among her close friends, the first person she chanced upon was Grace. 'She was asking for you,' she said, in a sharp accusing tone, wiping off a tear. 'Where were you?'

Yes, where was she? She could not repeat the lie of ill health, so she bowed her head and kept quiet. Once again she had erred. Missing out on opportunities was becoming her forte. In trying to battle with circumstances and her conflicting emotions, she had frittered those precious moments away when she could have been near those who loved and needed her. She seemed forever to be out of reach of the people who reached out towards her. Kakima had called out to her and so had Charlie, but she had not heard one or the other, and she had lost three good friends within the span of a few days.

The cortege was soon to leave for Charlie's final resting-place. This was one funeral she would have to attend however late it got for her to get back home.

She went to the telephone and called up her son's office number. She never called; he was alarmed at first to hear her voice. Slowly the astonishing story of her forays into the real-life world of the United States had unfolded to his ears. But if he was astonished to hear of her bonds with the people at the Home, he did not reveal it in his exchanges with her.

Gently, like a parent caressing his wounded child, he wanted to know, 'What time is the funeral, Ma?

'You must of course attend. I shall inform Meeta that you will be coming home later.'

'Thank you, Tukun.'

'You sound very sad.' And as if as an afterthought: 'Was she very close to you, Ma?'

'Yes. She loved me as if I was her daughter.' And a little sob escaped from her. 'I wrote all her letters for her. She was asking for me, they said. If only I had gone.'

'Why didn't you?'

'What with Kakima passing away and all the activities at home, I did not go to see them for the last few days,' she lied.

'I'm truly sorry, Ma, that you have lost such a good friend. Had I only known.'

'I should have told you.' *But then you and I have stopped communicating with one another for such a long time now.* She sighed the unsaid words to herself.

Charlie belonged to a very large family with its feet very firmly rooted in the soil of Illinois. So in death, Charlie had a very large number of blood relations calling upon her. Nandita had not seen a single one of them while she was alive. People have their preoccupations, and lost in those preoccupations, they forget the ageing and the old.

Nandita stood out, in her regulation dress of white, in a sea of black clothing beside the freshly dug up grave. To her left was Grace and to her right the Colonel in his wheelchair. Grace was holding on tightly to her hand. And Nandita allowed a comforting hand to stray across the sagging shoulders of the Colonel. And then Nandita sensed someone come up and stand behind her. A hand came gently to rest upon her trembling back. She looked over her shoulder with tear-filled eyes to see who it was and gave a start. Correctly attired in a dark suit and dark tie, giving her support, stood her son right behind her; never had she felt so beholden to her son as she did that moment. And a fleeting thought crossed her mind: *He has missed his game of tennis to be with me.* And turning back, she softly mouthed, 'Charlie, meet my son,' to the coffin waiting to be lowered into its readied receptacle of earth. 'I wish I had brought him with me earlier,' she added, in a strain of regret.

And the son thought, *I really don't know my mother at all. At one time I did, or so I thought.* When he had reached the Home, almost everyone had left for Charlie's funeral. The few who were holding the fort while the rest were away had wanted to know who he was. Nandita Roy was an almost unknown entity, but then someone had worked it out that their beloved Nan must have another, more fussy name. 'What did ya say, Mrs Nandita Roy? Oh yeah! Our Nan is a Mrs Roy, I think.'

'Are you related to her?'

'I'm her son. Could you please tell me where I could find her?'

'So, our Nan's your mother!' The tone was incredulous.

'Our Nan!' So his mother, who had such an aversion to the Americanisation of names, had herself become Nan to all these people.

'My mother? Oh . . . yes . . . she is . . . my mother!' Sudipto covered up manfully. He had no idea that his mother's name, having come in direct contact with the United States of America, had shed some weight along the way and become Nan! But wasn't she totally against the Americanisation of Indian names?

However, it had taken him very little while to realise how well loved and well admired was this woman called Nandita Roy. And his eyes had very soon been opened to the fact that he was related to a heroine, no less! How could he be her son, they asked one another; she was not old enough to have a son as grown-up as this, was the final assessment.

But once he had been able to persuade that he was in truth her son, their curiosity had known no bounds. 'Come on here, let's take a look at you,' a wheezy old lady had commanded. 'He is a good looker all right; not surprising, our Nan's a regular beauty herself,' said another. It had come as a complete surprise to Tukun that in the eyes of this segment of the universe, his mother was not just his mother but a fairly young and a rather interesting individual.

Clearing his throat, he had ventured to ask again, 'Where can I find my mother?'

'At the cemetery—they just left.'

'You can make it there before our Charlie is buried.'

No apparent show of grief could be detected in the words. There was a matter-of-fact, everyday-occurrence air about the matter of a funeral among these people, he could see. Funerals came up in a place like this with such monotonous regularity that they had learnt to live with it. A placard stating 'We will miss you, Charlie' had been placed alongside a photograph. And a couple of vases spilling over with white flowers had been placed on either end. A friend had left on a journey and they were wishing her well!

'But how do I get there?' And a long spiel of instructions had followed. And with a word of thanks, he had moved on in search of Nan, the friend of so many. Spotting her had not been difficult, for she had stood out in her pristine white in that ocean of black! And now here he was, standing beside a woman who had created a niche for herself in the community. And he had not so much as had had an inkling of it.

The very old woman to her left and the elderly gentleman in the wheelchair, he could see, were both seeking sustenance from her! And looking upon the tableau, he remembered that day when she had refused to go to the post office. 'Why don't you post it yourself?' he'd asked, looking down at the letter she had just handed him. And her reply as unyielding as a slab of granite: 'I'll go for a walk, *but . . . you* get the stamps for me,' he remembered, had left him confused and bruised. During the course of that exchange over the posting of a letter, his eyes had been opened to some of the perceptions his mother held about her life here in this land where she now lived. She had claimed that day, that even after ten long years of stay in the United States, the people and the tongue of that nation had remained outside the periphery of her existence! And today looking upon her, he marvelled at the change that had come about in the selfsame person.

Vignettes of the person his mother at one time was, flashed across his mind's eye. There she was, the stern and caring deputy headmistress of his school who had at one and the same time also been his gentle and loving mother. There she was, the shoulder upon which so many of their neighbours had placed their concerns and their anxiety-filled loads. And just out of nowhere, he remembered those cakes she baked for all and sundry in her little round oven. She was the baker for all seasons, the baker for all, for all kinds of reasons. He was too young to have realised how difficult it must have been for her, to have stepped out of her totally protected environment, to carve out a career and to bring him up all on her own. Was it a wonder, then, that once she had stepped out of home here in Saisborough, she should have found ways and means to conquer the world?

Sensing a change in the tempo, Nandita thought, *the speeches are getting over, the time for the burial is drawing close.* Charlie's relations seemed to have a lot of nice things to say about her. Memories of happier days, when she had reigned supreme within the folds of her family, had been dredged up and placed before a congregation that had been acquainted with the old and ailing Charlie, and none other. *Where were these people all this while, but for that matter, where was I when she needed me the most?* she asked of herself. And with moistened eyes, she watched as the coffin was readied for its final place of rest. And Nandita, weighed down by the two other deaths that had visited her own life in such quick succession, thought on.

Kakima had been consigned to flames, but the soul, they said, remained untouched by fire. *Her soul must be waiting in line somewhere now,* thought Nandita, *to take up her karmic journey once again.* The coffin, in the meanwhile, had been lowered into the grave and was being covered up with the loose earth that lay heaped alongside. Nandita stepped forward and trickled in a handful of the soil onto the coffin, while bidding her friend a fond farewell for the last time. 'Charlie has been consigned to her grave,' she said softly to herself, 'may her soul rest in peace.' The thought of the maggots getting to Charlie made her shudder, *but they will not be able to touch her soul,* she consoled herself. There was no rebirth on the agenda for Charlie! So Charlie's soul would be looking forward to a long wait.

Seeing her tremble, Tukun asked, 'Are you cold, Ma?'

'No, just very sad.' *And very guilty,* she added for her own benefit.

The Colonel, wheeling around, faced Tukun. 'Thank you for joining us.' And then he commanded, 'Join us at the Home, a little prayer meeting and a glass of wine has been organised for our just-departed friend there,' and then looking towards Nandita, 'Bring your son along, Nan.'

The speeches were over sooner than Tukun anticipated. Having exerted beyond their capacity, the speech-makers had little or no energy to lengthen the proceedings. The wine was passed around and a toast was proposed to the memory of Charlie.

Bidding a tearful farewell to her friends, Nandita had moved towards the exit, Tukun beside her, when the Colonel spoke up from somewhere behind her. 'Where is that boyfriend of yours, Nan? I had expected to see him here today.'

Pretending to not have heard him, she hurried out of the door, but not before she saw the expression change upon her son's face! The cold front had moved in and wiped out the warmth from the atmosphere!

18 OUT OF THE BLUE

An instant change had come about in Tukun's demeanour as the elderly veteran had called out and asked why Bill her 'boyfriend' was absent from the funeral. Like a tree uprooted by a gale, the word 'boyfriend' had come crashing down and lain obstructively between Nandita and her son. She had seen him recoil and seen his back go rigid and his face freeze into a mask of immobility as he kept on walking out of the Home alongside her! The lines of communication so recently restored had shown painful signs of getting snarled up once again!

Having to contend with violent mood swings always left her with a sour aftertaste in the mouth. The lurching feeling within her bowels as she observed Tukun react to the Colonel's words brought to mind the mixed memories of a stolen ride she had once had upon a hurdy-gurdy. She was just a little girl and had run off with her male cousins to the fair that had pitched camp near their home. She had gone there but once, because girls of 'good' families did not run around wild among all and sundry!

The whirling contraption that had been put up as an attraction was the greatest draw of all for the young ones. The sensation she had of the world going round and round around her as she went whirling around in an up-and-down circular motion was exhilarating while it lasted. But she had come to abhor the aftermath of that ride! The feeling of nausea and giddiness that Nandita had carried with her had come as a bonus to the scolding she had had to face when she got home that day.

Light as a feather, the word 'boyfriend' was blowing around in the wind! Sujata, Sue, or whatever one liked to call her, had thrown it around with a certain piquant relish leaving behind a number of unasked questions in its wake. But there was some room for manoeuvre there, for Sue and her risqué jokes were well known to one and all. But where was the room for manoeuvre here, when the Colonel had in complete seriousness wanted to know of Nandita why *her boyfriend* was not to be seen on a day such as this?

Tukun, who had with difficulty come to accept (with a little bit of nudging on from his wife, of course) that Sue had blown a chance encounter with a little-known acquaintance out of proportion, was now confronted with a situation that was far more difficult to wish away. Till a few hours earlier on, he had had no inkling of the friendships his mother had formed with the folks at the Home. But it had pleased him to observe how well received she was among these elderly people. And having accepted these new dimensions in his mother's life, he had stood with pride beside her at Charlie's funeral, but this?

The Colonel's question directed towards Nandita had shown the fact that Bill Brady was no casual acquaintance of his mother's. That she could in some way be held accountable for Dr William Brady's whereabouts and his actions smacked of an intimacy between his mother and the esteemed professor that was way beyond what his sensibilities could cope with. Marching ahead, he unlocked the car, waited for his mother to be seated, got in, and drove off. Having dropped her at the door to their home, he drove off to garage the car.

Letting herself in, she looked around; no one was in sight. Usage demanded that, having come from a funeral, she have a bath and get into fresh clothes. While removing her shoes, Nandita pondered upon the word 'boyfriend', a word that had of late been cropping up like a recurrent theme in the conversations flowing around her. Sue had used it and now the Colonel but alas, in both instances the word had been put to use in a context where she was the protagonist of the tale that was being told, leading to a great deal of misunderstanding and turmoil in her life.

She heard footfalls from above and then the sound of someone coming down the steps leading down. The doorbell pealed, and she saw Meeta go across and open the front door. 'Where were you? What happened?' she wanted to know. 'Where's Ma?'

'She came in ahead of me, haven't you seen her?'

'No. But I was upstairs. Ah, there she is,' she said as Nandita emerged from the closet, handbag in hand. 'You left a mysterious note that I could make neither head nor tail of. So, tell me, where were you?'

'Ask Ma.' And Tukun went inside, tugging so violently at his tie that it turned into a knot and set about the task of choking him.

'Where were Tukun and you?'

'Attending a friend's funeral,' the answer was as cryptic as it possibly could be.

'Which friend?'

'A friend called Charlie. She died early this morning.'

'How sad, but I had no idea you had a friend by that name. Where did you meet this Charlie?'

'At the old folks' home that's not so far from here.'

'Really, Ma, you do get around.' There was a sly twinkle in her eyes and something besides in the tone of voice. And that irked Nandita. She could sense that Meeta was harking back to Sue's jocular questioning about Bill.

'I must go and bathe. Tell Tukun to take a bath.' And she moved on to go up to her room.

While plodding up the stairs, she thought that misinterpreting innocent relationships was not just the prerogative of countries such as the one she came from! A man and a woman had to be seen together but a couple of times and all kinds of inferences would be arrived at! The geographical location made some difference but not all that much. Bill was certainly a friend, then why attribute a bond that went beyond that?

And on the tail of these random thoughts, the image of Bill swam before her eyes, and she smiled, thinking how incongruous it was to append the word 'boy' while referring to a man of Bill's stature, size, and vintage. Only the people of the United States, she thought with some amusement, could append words as innocent as 'boy' or 'girl' to bring about such a major change in the quality of the friendship that had been built up between a man and a woman. What exactly did this word 'boyfriend' connote that it instantly brought a mischievous look upon Sue's face, a touch of languid romance upon the ageing faces at the Home, and a frown upon her son's countenance?

Meeta had left for work and the children for school. Head down, she sighed softly as she heard the front door shut as her son, the last to leave, let himself out. She and this house, her companion, were back together again in their aloneness.

Why did she feel so alone when in truth nothing much had changed? The Home had pulled her back into its vortex. The death of Charlie had made it impossible for her to continue with her childish resolve to stay away from any human encounters outside home. While at home, she still went about her everyday activities as she had done for the last so-many years! The grandchildren still came to their newly found teacher for an occasional bit of help! Tukun had thawed to an extent. And Meeta, having discovered a chink in her mother-in-law's armour, had adopted a more benign stance towards her. She was more a friend today than she had been for years. Even so, Nandita felt dreadfully alone and bereft at times. Nothing really had changed and yet the flavour and flamboyance of life seemed to have drifted away and gone out of her grasp. She sighed and looked out of the window. Everything appeared to be the same, but she knew nothing was the same. For even the wind blew differently, now that the month of August was here.

The summer had worn itself out and was making way for more clement days. An occasional puff of cool air had started blowing through its overheated tresses. The colour of the leaves had begun to change. An occasional leaf, wanting to be ahead of the crowd, could be seen detaching itself from the branches to come drifting down to earth. The trees would soon be a blaze of colour. She went out into the yard and sat there a while. The cat and her kittens were nowhere to be seen, and the squirrels too had decided to stay out of sight. Not a leaf stirred; life appeared to have come to a standstill.

She rose and went in and, putting on a recorded piece by Bismillah Khan, sat back. The *shahnai* lent itself to your mood. You could choose to waft yourself along upon its notes and feel blissfully happy, or you could plunge down along with it into a state of abject gloom. Today, Nandita's heart was not willing to soar. She picked up a book of history, about the Civil War, that the Colonel had recently handed and found nothing there to lighten her frame of mind! Too many wars had been fought by mankind, leaving behind nothing but wounds gaping wide open upon the face of the earth! And yet, no one learnt anything from these exercises in futility. No one did, and chances were they never would!

Earlier the same day, she had gone and sat with many of her friends at the rose garden; though decay was round the corner, the garden was as yet in bloom and looked delightfully fresh and cared for. The elderly ladies in their regulation make-up and formal attire looked every bit a part of the scene. Grace had come and so had Kate. But Kate had to leave; after all, her favourite soap could not possibly be missed.

'Must you go, Katie?' Nandita had looked from one to the other. *Yes, letting go of a friend was such a painful task!*

'Yeah, I must. Never know what them there dudes would be up to if you turned your back on them.' *She watches Ninja Turtles, like the kids do,* thought Nandita, setting off a little chuckle within her heart.

'What happens when you pop it?' *Was that a politically correct question to ask,* wondered Nandita, mulling over the baldness of Grace's question.

'I don't know. I don't really know. In truth, Gracie, the only reason I don't want to die is coz if I do, I'll have to leave behind the morning soaps.' Sitting on the sidelines and listening to them, Nandita asked herself, *Will I also become as dependent on television as they are?*

Checking on the angle of her hat, and repositioning it by a millimetre, Grace exclaimed. 'You're crazy.' The lipstick had run and had spread out along the crevices fanning out from the corners of her lips and had become scarlet rivulets.

'No. I'm not. A lot of guys feel the same way as I do.' *I'm learning all the time,* thought Nandita as the debate continued.

'Maybe the good Lord has a TV channel for guys like you up there.'

'Singing hosannas more likely than not.'

'You're hard to please, Kate.'

'Nah, not hard to please, only summat particular! But I'll hobble off now. Nan is here to keep you company, and I can see Ted coming from that end.' She turned to Nandita. 'Why are you so quiet, my girl?'

Nandita mulled over that conversation as she walked back home. It was so hard to break away from a habit. The weekend was upon them, so there would be no visit to the park and the Home for the next two days. These visits she paid to her friends were as addictive as the daily soaps were for Kate!

To fill up time, she usually cooked something special for the family on the weekend. It had been a while since she had made any *motor shuteer kochuri* for the children. They loved the delicious pea-filled savouries accompanied by an *alur dom.*

Having fried the last of the *kochuris* and having scraped the unctuous *alur dom* into a bowl, she set about the task of making herself a cup of tea. The aroma of the just-fried *kochuris* hung invitingly in the air. And then she remembered Bill's reaction to the *kochuri* and *alur dom* she had carried downtown for him on a couple of occasions, gone cold and limp in transit; even so, he had proclaimed, on taking a bite, that the little savouries she had cooked up were really delicious, as were the potatoes accompanying them! Was it kindness, she wondered, or did he really appreciate her cooking? She sighed, recognising the fact that never again would she have occasion to carry home-made food for him again. Those happy days were all in the past now.

The doorbell pealed. Looking out from the kitchen towards the entrance, she saw Tukun go, newspaper in hand, towards the door.

And in front of Tukun's eyes stood a very large man wearing a splendid all-encompassing smile.

'Hi! I'm Bill.' Extending his hand, the man said, 'You may've forgotten, but we met years ago at New Jersey.' Nandita heard the familiar voice, and her hand flew up to her mouth, for she had known immediately who it was. *So Bill was back and he had come straight home without informing her. Why? Why? Why had he done that?* Feeling unprepared and confused, she fumbled on with the simple task of pouring herself the cup of tea that she had just brewed. When she turned back to the cup, she found tea everywhere. Having mopped the spillage off the kitchen counter, she went out of the kitchen and took a peep towards the open door, and framed within the frame of the opened door, looking larger than life, stood Bill.

'How could I possibly forget, sir? Sorry you couldn't drop by the other evening.' She could see Bill enter and Tukun shut the door. Was Tukun being sarcastic, she wondered.

'I had to go to Dallas; my daughter lives there. She just had a new baby and had a few problems.'

'Congratulations on your becoming a grandfather, sir! I am sorry though, to hear that your daughter wasn't too well. How's she doing?'

'She's doing fine now.'

'That's good.'

'And I'd like to tell you that this is not the first but the second time round that I've become a grandpa.'

'Pleased to meet a veteran, sir.' And Nandita heard them laugh together. Then she heard her son ask, 'You've just arrived from Dallas?'

'No. As a matter of fact, I left Dallas almost a fortnight ago and went on to New York. I came into Chicago just yesterday and had called.'

'Was no one here?'

'I got no response.'

'I'm sorry, we must have all been out, and as usual, not one of us remembered to switch on the answering machine.'

'That happens to me all the time. It is on when I'm at home and off when I am out.' There was a small ripple of laughter that capped the sentence, and then sounding contrite, he continued, 'Sorry to have come in unannounced, but as I was going past, I thought I'd . . .'

'That's perfectly all right, sir. Please do take a seat.'

'Thank you.'

'No, not this one.' Guiding the professor away from the chair he was about to occupy, he said, 'It looks good but isn't very comfortable.' The apologetic laugh explained all. 'But my wife insists it stays.'

'Yes, looks can be deceptive, and women can be adamant.' And he gave a short laugh before settling into the proffered chair.

'Are you going to be in town a while?'

'Hasn't Nan told you?'

'Who?'

'Nan, your mother.'

'My mother? Oh . . . yes . . . of course!' History was repeating itself, and once again, Tukun covered up manfully. He would have to get used to this new name his mother had acquired!

Though he was aware of the fact that his mother's name, having come in direct contact with United States of America, had shrunk for all time, he had to put up some struggle with himself to come to terms with this new name. For as far back as he could remember, she had always proclaimed to be totally against the Americanisation of Indian names! And today she was Nan to almost everyone under the sun!

But the familiarity with which Dr William Brady took his mother's newly acquired name made him wonder, for it indicated a far greater intimacy between the two of them than he could have ever imagined. He had no idea what exactly had been going on in his mother's life, but whatever it was, it was certainly most perturbing!

'She must've told you that I am leaving Saisborough for New York.'

'You are leaving?' The surprise was genuine. And the secondary thought coming in its wake was one of relief.

'As a matter of fact, I've already left. I work there.'

'But rumours were rife, sir . . .'

'Rumours?'

'I have friends in the university circles and they were saying . . .'

A quizzical look on his face, he asked, 'What were they saying?'

'They felt, considering your standing in the field, that you had been invited to take a look at the CU, the haven of all great economists.'

'I don't know that I'm all that great. Just an ordinary guy, with a theory or two to his name—that's all.' Then changing track: 'There were other reasons that brought me here.' A little bit of silence stretched out between them, then clearing his throat, the professor asked, 'Isn't Nan at home?'

'She should be around.'

'I'm afraid I don't have much time. I'm leaving for New York in a few hours from now.'

'I'll get her, sir.' He didn't have to go far, for Tukun found his mother coming out of the kitchen and stopped her. Very matter of fact, very cut and dried, he informed her, 'Dr Brady has come to see you. He's waiting for you in the living room.' The scrutinising look he had given her as he spoke made her narrow her eyes and look closely at him. None too pleased with the expression upon his face, she wondered what was going on in his mind. That he was displeased she could clearly discern. Why should a man who had adopted the United States of America as his motherland be so prehistoric in his reactions, she asked herself. Could not a woman of her age have a friend or two to her name?

She was the one who had put those blinkers upon her son's eyes and today she resented the fact that he should have such a narrow world-view! 'I'm coming,' she said.

The image she had imprinted upon his subconscious of the ideal mother figure was that of a puritan who never wavered from any laid-down norms that had been set down for her by the Brahminical society to which she belonged. And the person who stood before him at this moment did not quite match with that image that lay so deeply etched in his mind. But, 'He's in a hurry,' was all he said.

How rigid and stern he looks, thought Nandita as she moved towards the entrance to the living room. She had somehow forgotten to account for the fact that the precepts she had adhered to as he grew up under her sole sheltering wings had robbed him of all flexibility when it came to matters pertaining to her. The look that had flashed across his face when he had caught her, beer can in hand, should have opened her eyes to this side of his personality. She had shown no desire for change and, as such, she had never had any need to confront the orthodox Indian gentleman who lived within her own son!

Ma has changed, he thought, *she has not offered a single word of explanation for all that has been going on in her life.* As far as he was concerned, change was acceptable in all else, in every other person but not in his mother! The rest of the world could do as it wished but not she! The upbringing that she herself had endowed him with was so rigid that it allowed for no leeway for any deviations within its framework. Trying to get a hold on his emotions, he turned his back to her; he stood facing the door to the kitchen.

She had wanted him to ask, and she had wanted to explain that there was nothing amiss. Bill was just a friend she had made along the way, but confronted by a rigid back, she turned away from him and moved forward. Bill was leaving and had come to bid farewell to her, and with his departure, the warm and lively relationship that she had built up with him would automatically come to a close. A savoury chapter that had been inserted by mistake into the bland story of her life would be shelved and set aside forever. And life gone drab once again, she would move back into her shell and comply with the dictates of the civilisation from which she hailed. Her son was her guardian now, and she would abide by the wishes of her guardian!

On entering the living room, she formally stretched out a hand, softly saying, 'How are you, Bill?' The hand was but a device to measure out a distance between this man and herself. She knew that if the distance were to be closed, he would surely kiss her, and that she could not possibly allow him to do, not today, nor ever again from now onwards. The reaction of her son to Sue's flippant words had showed her that in going ahead with her friendship with Bill, she had literally been playing with fire. He wrapped his large hand over hers. It felt so good to feel the warm touch of his palm upon her own;

even so, withdrawal would be the better part of valour. And she extracted her hand from his as soon as she could.

'I had to stay rather longer at Dallas than I'd thought I would. I've just a few hours before I leave for New York, but I told you, Nan, that I wouldn't leave without seeing you,' he smiled down into her eyes, 'so here I am.'

She felt the entire breath of her body being sucked away from her. Gasping for the very breath of her life, she murmured, 'Thank you. And do please look after yourself.'

'Where's that son of yours?'

'Tukun,' she called out.

'Yes?' And he came in. Evidently he had not been too far away.

'I hope you don't mind my taking your mother out for a bite. We have a great deal of catching up to do before I leave.'

Nandita gave a start. What was Bill doing? Why could he not understand her compulsions? She had but opened her mouth to tell him that she could not, that she would not go with him, when her son spoke up before she could.

'No, why should I? My mother does as she wishes. Who am I to tell her what she should do?'

The words replete with irony had fallen harsh and condemning upon Nandita's ears. But Bill had noticed nothing amiss. 'There you are then, let's get going, I have a flight to catch in a few hours from now.' He extended his hand to Tukun. 'Nice meeting you Roy, when next I'm in town, I promise to buy you a drink. I have to get to know you.'

Tukun wanted to ask why but, too polite to really do so, kept quiet.

'Come on, Nan,' the professor repeated.

'I can't come.'

'Why ever not—a headache?'

Taking refuge in the ready-made excuse handed to her, she nodded her head in agreement.

'I'll buy you a Tylenol or something; come on, Nan, I really don't have much time and—'

The tone of informality adopted by this near stranger while speaking to his mother dressed as usual in her carapace of conventionality had jarred. Tukun, standing on the sidelines, looked from the professor's face to his mother's and back to the professor's face again. And then he remembered Meeta asking him in jest, 'Are you fearing that a torrid love affair is taking place behind your back?'

Afraid of what Bill Brady might next choose to say, Nandita cut into his sentence. 'Wait for me, I'll be back in a moment, and then we can leave.'

The cab Bill had taken to come over was still waiting for him; as he opened the door of the vehicle to usher her in, Nandita's eyes strayed towards the living room window. A pair of eyes was trained steadily upon her. Tukun was watching her every move. From there, her eyes travelled upwards to find yet another pair of eyes boring down at her. Meeta was at her bedroom window, looking down upon the scene of her mother-in-law leaving *on a date!* And then the door was shut, and her son and his wife were shut off from her view.

Bill, coming around, seated himself. 'Bloomingdale's, please,' he directed the cab driver. Turning to Nandita, he asked, 'How've you been, Nan? You don't look too bright?'

'I'm all right but . . .'

'Honestly?'

'But I wish you'd called. Your sudden arrival came as such a surprise.'

'Oh, I'm sorry. Perhaps I shouldn't have come as I did,' he said, going frigid.

'No, Bill, it's not that,' she pleaded.

'Then what?' he asked, unable to understand her argument.

'I could have come to see you.'

'I know, you could have but I came. What difference does it make, which one of us comes to meet the other?'

'How can I explain? You'll never understand my limitations.'

'Perhaps I never will. Perhaps that is what makes for the piquancy of our relationship. No open books here, to be read and to be understood immediately!' He looked closely at her. 'Tell me, why are you looking so thin and drawn? Have you been ill?'

'No, but a lot of things have been happening and I thought I'd never see you again. But you came and, that too, to my home.'

'Had I not promised I'd come?'

'Yes, that you had . . . but . . .'

'But what? Did you think I would not come?'

'I was very confused for while you were away, I have lost many friends. My aunt in Kolkata passed away, and the—'

'I'm sorrowed to hear of this. You were very close to her, weren't you?' Nandita nodded in response. Taking Nandita's hand in his own, he commiserated, 'On top of that, you had to face Charlie's passing away as well. She was very dear to you, wasn't she?'

'Yes, we did get very close. She was a very courageous person and inspired me in many ways. I do miss her a great deal, Bill.'

'I met her just that one time. Even so, she did leave a mark upon my mind.'

'The permanent parting of ways is so difficult to face.'

'I should know!' he murmured.

'Who told you about her?' she asked.

'My colleague Mike Cheyney, I met him this morning in connection with a research paper we are working on. He said that he'd seen you at Charlie's funeral with a young man.'

'My son was with me. But what was your colleague doing there?'

'He was distantly related to Charlie, I understand.' Nandita frowned while trying to place the person in question. And in trying to give a nudge to her memory, he filled in, 'You know that plump guy we bumped into, a couple of times, around downtown Saisborough?' He looked closely at her. 'Can't place him? Nev'mind.'

And then a flicker of a remembrance of a plumpish person creased Nandita's mind and her brow, and quite out of context, she remarked, 'But he doesn't look like a professor.'

'What do professors look like, Nan?' the professor asked with a little laugh.

'I don't know, but he certainly doesn't look like one.'

Looking quite like a naughty boy, he asked, 'Shall I tell him?'

'No. Please don't,' she warned, looking horrified.

'How are the rest of the folks doing at the Home?'

'They are used to facing the reality of death, even so . . .' And she sighed. 'The Colonel wanted to know why you were not there,' she said, wanting to move away from her painful thoughts.

'I hope you explained.'

Fortunately for Nandita, the cab came to a stop in front of the imposing façade of the Bloomingdale's building in downtown Chicago. She looked towards and then up and up at the magnificent building that sprang from the pavement and went right up into the sky. 'You intend shopping, Bill?'

Having paid the cabby he had responded with a cryptic 'No.'

'Then?'

'There's a salad joint, somewhere towards the top of the building that I really like. I've been waiting to show it off to you for a while. Let's go and check it out, shall we?'

The salads had been chosen, and when he was ordering the white wine, she protested, 'No, Bill, no wine for me, please.'

'This is a celebratory lunch, honey. Won't you please join me in celebrating the arrival of my little Meg with a sip of wine?'

'Honey'? He had never called her *honey* ever before. She shrugged and moved on. 'You have named her Meg? How wonderful!'

'Neither Irene nor I, but that wonderful son-in-law of mine; he suggested we name her after her grandma.'

'Bring on the wine, Bill, today we shall take a sip of wine in the name of both the Megs.'

Looking her straight in the eye, he asked, 'And why not to you and to me as well, while we are at it?' And unable, or rather unwilling, to read the message there, she looked away.

The carafes of ice-cold water gently flavoured with the scent of the sliced lemons floating atop and the chilled wine made excellent companions to the cool and crisp salads they had eaten. But the meal was soon over.

Carefully positioning his fork upon his plate and taking up his wineglass, Bill asked, 'Are you done, Nan? A fruit salad perhaps?'

'No. Nothing else, please; this in itself was too much.'

'Then shall we talk of more serious things, I have a plane to catch.'

'I won't keep you, Bill. You can drop me off and move on.'

'That is the point, how can I move on when . . .'

'What you are trying to say, Bill?'

Going suddenly serious, he said in a cut-and-dried tone, 'Enough of this pretence, you very well know what I'm speaking of.'

And she looked sharply up at him. 'Pretence'? What kind of pretence, she wondered. And what did she know that she was not willing to acknowledge?

'Let's get married, Nan,' he suggested, cutting short the preamble of finding out whether or not she was willing to do so. And with those few words, the entire mystery had been solved and laid bare before her.

So unexpected was the matter-of-fact suggestion that it had come and hit her like a bolt of lightning out of a clear and cloudless sky. Mouth agape, she kept looking at him, wondering whether she was suffering from some kind of delusion. But when she looked closer, she found that in truth it was Bill himself who was seated before her. Somehow pulling herself together, she said, 'You are mad, Bill. Must you joke even as you are leaving?' But her voice had tended to wobble as she spoke. She poured herself a glass of cold water and took down half a glass without taking a single breath.

'Did that sound like a joke to you? I . . . am . . . asking you to marry me, Nan.' The pitch of his voice had risen considerably. She looked around fearfully, wondering if anyone else had heard. All softness wiped off his face, he went on in a taut and tense voice, 'The only other woman whom I asked to marry me was Meg . . .'

'I am honoured Bill, but . . .'

'And she married me and we were very happy together.'

'I know,' she mumbled as she scrutinised the expression upon his face. She was surprised to find that there was no levity there. He was absolutely serious. How was she to explain to him that she just could not do what he was asking of her? She was Nandita Roy, born in the orthodox, steeped-in-tradition home of the Gangulys of Bhabanipore. Married for a dizzy moment to a fey creature called Prodipto, she had but begun to take on some of his frothy ways when he had been whisked away from her by fate. Had he not died so soon, things might have been different, but he had, alas, died too soon—so soon that his vision, broad as the very horizons, had not been able to bring about any real change in her. The safety and security of a known set of rules had provided her with a framework within which she could chalk out her existence. And so, wearing the 'keep off the grass' badge of widowhood, she had gone through the years that had lain stretched out empty before her with the passing away of her beloved husband. Her entire existence had been measured out and placed within the parameters of that state of being a widow that forbade the rest of the world to look her way. And in a fell sweep rapidly ceding ground, she had regressed to accepting, and adhering, to the indoctrination of her roots.

Her voice sounded strange even to her own ears as she said, 'I can't possibly marry you. It won't be acceptable to anyone.'

'To anyone, who are these so-called anyone?' Silenced by the fury hidden within those words, she did not speak another word. 'Who really cares what you do? Who are these people who rule your existence?' he asked, throwing his hands out. He was angry, she could see. She was surprised because she had no idea that he could be angry!

'A widow from a family such as ours never remarries,' she justified softly. And then, head bowed, worrying a shred of lettuce with her fork, she questioned herself, who were these people whom she feared? Most of them were gone anyway. Even so, she just could not deviate to this extent and move away from the tenets that ruled her life. And then, had she not seen her own ancestors through the eyes of her very own son for the last few days? She rose abruptly and, grabbing her purse, half ran, half stumbled out of the restaurant. Tears had blurred her vision and she hesitated a moment, wondering which way lay her route of escape.

She felt fingers close over her upper arm and then she felt herself being moved like a puppet on a string towards a bench tucked away within a mass of potted blooms. 'Sit down,' said a voice and she obeyed. And the same voice went on, 'Give me a good reason why you can't marry me. Unless of course it's because you don't like me quite enough.'

'You know, Bill, that I like you very much. You could even say—' And she cut herself short. She brushed back a recalcitrant lock of hair with a worried hand from across her brow. Endowed with a will of its own, the strand of hair came back to rest at its original location.

'You were going to say something. Why did you stop? You do love me, don't you?'

'Please, Bill, let us not talk of all that,' she pleaded. 'I just can't go into all that. If nothing else, I am much older than you are.'

'So?'

'Please, Bill, I can't marry you.'

'I agree you are a bit older than I am, but I was not planning on starting a new family.'

She felt heat rise and suffuse her entire face. Her ears burnt as if they were on fire. Suddenly sex had come and positioned itself between them. That marriage implied a degree of intimacy that went beyond just saying hello or shaking hands had been pointed out by him to her with those words and it had embarrassed her beyond measure. She just could not carry on with this conversation with Bill. It shocked and worried her that she had allowed herself to get into a position where such a discussion could at all take place.

'There are countless reasons why we should not marry. You should marry a much younger woman than I am.'

'It is perfectly all right that you don't wish to marry, but I would be very obliged if you would stop giving me advice as to whom I should marry.'

'But I am your friend and I—'

'No. You are not my friend.'

'But I really am. What happened to that lovely young girlfriend you told me about?'

'I said nothing about a young girlfriend, only about an innocent and inexperienced one.'

'I never realised you were playing with words, Bill, otherwise . . .'

'Otherwise what? Would you have run away earlier?'

'Please, Bill, let us not part in bitterness. I do need you . . . I do need you . . . ever so badly . . . as a friend.'

'I don't want you as just a friend but as my wife as well.'

'As your wife?'

'Yes, as my wife, to love and to cherish till death do us part.'

'But I really and truly cannot marry you.'

'Even if I tell you that I need you.'

'How can I? I just can't.' Torn in two by the pull of tradition, she sadly gave her verdict.

He rose and kissed her on both cheeks and said, 'If that is your wish, then so be it. I'll reach you home and go on to the airport.'

'Will you write to me?' she asked.

'Why, whatever for? What is the use of keeping up a pretence of friendship, when our relationship has gone way beyond that?'

Having got into the cab, she said. 'Please drop me off near the rose garden, I'll walk home from there.'

'Just as you wish, Nan.'

What had come to pass during that meal of salad and chilled white wine was beyond anything that Nandita could have imagined would happen even in the widest meandering of her imagination! Whatever else she might have expected as the culmination of her relationship with Bill, this ending as a possibility had never crossed her mind. A wayward scriptwriter had been at work and written in the most incongruous of lines that could possibly be thought up!

On the verge of alighting from the cab, she turned towards Bill and, for the first time ever, leaned across and kissed him on his cheek. And there were tears in her eyes as she said, 'Thank you for everything, Bill, bye-bye, and may God be with you.'

'Goodbye, Nan.'

Rising precipitately, she choked out yet another 'Goodbye,' and fled without looking back.

And the cab had swept out of sight, carrying Bill away from her forever.

She plodded back home and, later that evening, went to great pains to let her son and his wife know that Dr William Brady had left Saisborough, perhaps to never return ever again.

And a few hours later, Dr William Brady took a flight from O'Hare and went away to New York.

19 PERSPECTIVES CHANGE

To fold herself up and put the essence of herself out of reach was but an old habit with Nandita. Whenever hurt, had she not as a child hidden herself away under the cavernous staircase-well in that ancient mansion of her ancestors? Though she lived within the little group that made up her family and visited the Home, where she interacted with so many different persons, she in truth remained inviolate and alone! Life coursed along around Nandita, yet nothing really touched her. She had sealed herself away in a vacuum so that the world around, even if it ventured to, could not stretch out its fingers and touch her! She would allow no one to peer into her heart to try and take a look at what was going on there. A 'no entry' sign had been placed there, and Nandita allowed no inquisitive, invasive thoughts of enquiry to stray there, even if those recalcitrant thoughts had emanated from within her own self!

She laughed and she smiled; in truth she smiled a great deal more these days than she had ever before. And Helen even went so far as to say, 'That girl is happier than I've ever seen her before.' And of course Nandita, overhearing these words, had smiled wider still!

Grace had observed Nandita from a distance and seen the smiles come and go like the moon does in a clouded-over sky and had remarked, 'There's more to it than meets the eye.' And Nandita had laughed loud and clear. Could there be a better cover-up for a court of enquiry?

'What a wonderful change of personality this girl has had,' remarked the old schoolmaster one day. 'Has anyone ever heard her laugh so loud before?' And a number of heads had nodded in agreement.

The Colonel, with his eyes of experience, was not that easily fooled but said nothing. Instead he called out to Nandita and warned, 'Watch out, Nan, you don't lose any more weight. Skinny women I can do without.' And Nandita had chuckled in response.

Grace had given a derisive snort and said something rude about how he was an old fuddy-duddy who knew nothing about modern trends. And the Colonel, not to be outdone, had given a fitting reply. And Nandita, smiling benignly on the sidelines, had sat through these exchanges. There was a smile for all reasons; there was a smile for all seasons in her repertoire these days!

With her honed-to-perfection skills at projecting the face she wanted the world to see, Nandita had managed to an extent to fool the world! And by stolidly keeping up the pretence that she was happier by far than she had ever before been, she had almost succeeded in fooling herself as well! But hidden behind that ever-present, ever-pleasant smile was hidden away a woman whose life, like a can of beer left open to the atmosphere, had gone completely sour and flat. And that woman did keep looking over her shoulder to make her presence felt more often than she really liked!

When you have read the last chapter and put down an absorbing book, a vacuum of sorts is created in your psyche. Each day as you progressed with the characters that peopled that book, you became a part of them and they a part of you! It is possible that you might have even singled out one among the so-many characters, with whom you had felt a very special affinity and created a bond! But you very soon picked up another book and got involved in the protagonists who peopled the pages of that book. Bill had left, and getting back to the humdrum reality of everyday existence was proving to be more painful than the putting down of an interesting saga in print ever could be. Life would have been far easier had Bill been a character out of a novel; then she could have picked up another book and moved on from there.

He had asked her to marry him, and she had refused. For how could she possibly take such a major step away from the laid-down norms of her life? Remarriage even in those early days when her Dipto had passed away had not been an option with her, so how could it possibly be considered an option now? Now, when she was getting to be an old woman with grandchildren growing up fast around her? She knew she could not possibly marry him but that did not change the fact that she hankered after his company, his friendship, his warming presence. He wanted all of that, but much more besides! And she found it difficult to even accommodate a mere friendship without embarrassment, so where was the meeting point? None! A clean break was the only way out of this predicament and Bill in his wisdom had chosen to make a clean and complete break from her. It was better that way, she knew. Even so!

She had walked away from an offer to taste the joys of life and living once again, but what else could she have done? That which belonged to the realms of fantasy was best allowed to remain where it belonged. That which was impossible to achieve was best left untouched. She had hurt Bill, she knew, but what was she to do? He understood nothing of her compulsions, how could he? Belonging as he did to a civilisation that was so set apart and different from her own, he had misunderstood her and gone away if not in anger then certainly in disappointment.

Making a final attempt to hold on to a friendship that she did not wish to lose, she remembered timorously asking him, 'Will you write to me?' But to her utter disappointment, he had refused without let or hinder, with a terse set of questions instead that had left her wounded. 'Why, whatever for? What is the use of keeping up a pretence of friendship when our relationship has gone way beyond that?' he had demanded of her, his voice gone harsh. And with his refusal to comply, all the links that had been wrought, all the pathways that could have been kept open between them had broken down and fallen by the way! This abrupt delinking of their two lives had catapulted her with a wrenching force up, up and away, into a dark and yawning void. And from within that intense darkness, she had looked down with despair towards the arid and parched-for-companionship future that now lay ahead of her. It had shaken her up completely that they had parted if not as enemies, then certainly not as friends! For Bill had become a habit with her, his presence and his responses an unacknowledged need with her! She missed him so badly that it caused her a near-tangible pain in the pit of her stomach!

And so to cover up her wounds she smiled more and more each day.

The grandchildren, untouched by all the undercurrents that had flown through the lives of the adults, remained much the same. Totally detached and self-absorbed one moment, they could, when the need arose, become the best of companions to their grandmother. When you had such an all-purpose grandmother waiting on the sidelines, how long could you ignore her presence?

'Thamma,' Tom had called out just the previous morning and, coming up, had given Nandita a big bear hug.

Knowing that most hugs were entailed, she had asked him, 'What do you want?' with a knowing smile.

He was big enough to know that he had to placate if he wanted his ends met. 'No, nothing, Thamma. I just wanted to give you a big hug.' Then sheepishly he had added, 'Could you please take a look at my math problems.'

'Come let me see what's troubling you,' she said as she put on her glasses and stretched out her hand. And Tammy, who always kept a close watch on how close her brother was getting to all those upon whom she believed she had a first claim, had immediately sidled up to Nandita and tried to wedge herself in between her grandmother and her overreaching brother. And this sibling rivalry in search of her favours had helped restore some of Nandita's lost self-esteem.

But as for her son, Nandita really had no idea what exactly went on within his head. Feeling saddened by the subtle change that had come about in their relationship, she had wondered at times what misconceptions he held about her. Sue's words had sown the fractious seed and the Colonel's comment had brought that seed to life, and Bill's arrival at their home had watered that seed and brought it to full bloom. And the garden of distrust and discontent had begun to grow and to flourish!

Tukun's brows had furrowed in disbelief for after all it was not every day that a man of his ilk found out that his staid-as-a-*sadhvi* mother had a man friend tucked away somewhere out of sight! This was a parameter that just did not fit in with the equations that made up the sum total of his life! When Meeta had wanted to know what was troubling him, he had wanted to tell her that it was the fearsome face of change in the one constant factor in his life that was troubling him. For him, the entire world could change but no, not his mother. But he had said nothing at all to Meeta!

But he just could not put his mind to rest. He was seated in a secluded corner, book in hand; his mind had wandered off in a trail of remembrance! Since his coming to consciousness, he could not recollect having seen any obvious changes take place in this woman who was his mother. She had dressed and eaten and behaved in much the same way all through the years he had known her. And even today, all these had remained much the same. And yet, he could sense rather than see that in several subtle ways, she was a different person from the one he had known through the years. Till the very recent past, he had never once seen her deviate from her chosen path of rigid observance of the dictates of orthodoxy! And things had been so comfortably the same. Moreover, she seemed to have been happy enough ensconced in that little niche where she had positioned herself! Or had that been but an illusion?

In truth apart from the changes that had inevitably come about in her positioning within the family, her hierarchy in the school, and her standing in society with the slow but steady process of ageing, there had been no other obvious changes in his mother that he could think of. Changes must have slowly and insidiously come about in her appearance as well, but he did not remember having consciously taken note of that! But today, some change seemed to have come about within her, making her an altogether different person from the person he was familiar with. The mother who had guided his destiny, the mother who had been a senior teacher of his school had been an interesting person. Somewhere along the way, that little bit of zing that set her apart from the herd had been frittered away and she had become a flat and unidimensional individual with little or no sum or substance to her personality. In a corner of his heart, he had to admit that she was emerging as an interesting person, as once she had been, all over again! He could have admired such a woman, made such a woman his friend, if only this woman were not his own mother!

They were lying in bed together, Meeta with a colourful magazine in hand, a leg thrown across his belly, when, removing the draped leg and turning towards her, Tukun asked, 'Have you noticed how Ma has changed?'

'Yeah! But for the better, I think.'

'For the better? You must be crazy.'

'You're jealous.'

'What a stupid conclusion, tell me why should *I* be jealous?'

'But you are. And there's reason enough.'

'Bah!'

'She's been your monopoly for ever and ever, so you just can't adjust to any change in her, that's all.'

'Where was the need for her to change so late in life?' he had muttered, getting ready to turn over onto his side.

His wife held on to him and did not let him move, '"So late" indeed. I went to the Home with her a couple of times and realised that she isn't really all that old.'

He frowned, 'I hope you're not changing as well?' And he squirmed out of her embrace and turned onto his side and pretended to go to sleep.

'Stop behaving like a child, Tukun,' she scolded. But he gave no reply.

The last thoughts to flit across his mind as he drifted off into sleep were 'Why did this have to happen to me?' and then, 'Oh! How I wish this whole business was not revolving around my own mother!' But she was his mother, and he her son; there was no wishing that relationship away. Tukun was a man who had been taught to hold his emotions in check; bred to politeness, he had crossed no limits. Though he was punctilious in his conduct towards his mother, his formal 'Ma' remained but a formal appellation wherein no lilt was ever allowed to stray, and even that lifeless version of that most important of all two-letter words he used with absolute parsimony. Nandita felt as if she was being punished for some unmentionable trespass.

And though perhaps there was nothing deliberate in her actions, in an unconsciously generated retaliatory move, Nandita on the rare occasion when she did call out to her son, always addressed him with a crisp and cold 'Tukun'. She used neither the punishing 'Sudipto', nor the caressing 'Khoka' while speaking to him these days. And watching the twosome, Meeta wondered at times what exactly was wrong with them for she had seen that the newly regenerated warmth that had developed between them was nowhere to be seen. She should have recognised that both mother and son were but birds of a feather, one a Ganguly of Bhabanipore and the other a part-Ganguly!

Meeta quite liked the changes that had come about in her mother-in-law since she had ventured out into the big bad world and come back with a trophy or two of human relationships that were her very own. She had mellowed and become far more loveable than she had ever been before. In truth there was a vulnerability about her that strangely enough was rather endearing. She did not wish to go back to living with the tight-lipped and disapproving woman that Nandita had become during the last few years. Fearing a return to the cold ages, Meeta thought, *They and their spats,* as she went about the task of putting together a meal for the children! Nothing had quite been the same between mother and son since the day of the barbecue; she thought on, while slapping slices of cheese onto the sandwiches she was building for the lunch box. Stretching her hand out for some ketchup, she muttered, 'Sue and her big mouth and Tukun and his old-fashioned ways!'

And in order to compensate for her husband's cool behaviour towards his mother, she had made a special effort to be nice to her mother-in-law. But it was not just that; she could not help but feel a certain niggling admiration for this woman with whom she had spent so many years of her life, and yet had not come to know at all! She wondered how she had got so close to the real heartbeat of America in so short a while, while the rest of them were still floundering around, trying to work out what made these Americans tick. Setting the sandwiches aside, she fished around for some ziplock bags in a drawer. Out of the blue, cocking her head to a side, she asked herself, *'Does she really have a boyfriend? If so, good for her.'* And then with a self-conscious giggle, she told herself, *'Not likely.'*

On the other hand, being totally unaware of what went on within Meeta's head, Nandita had been surprised by the attitude she had adopted towards the whole episode of Bill that had been brought forth and placed before them with that brash comment passed by Sue. Her daughter-in-law, who had been her friend and her ally for but a very short while, seemed to have suddenly turned protective towards her. Nandita was touched to see that there was a touch of solicitude towards her these days that she had never before displayed.

'You are losing weight, Ma,' she observed, looking at Nandita closely one day and then falling silent for a while. She suddenly asked, 'Any news of Dr Brady?' as if connecting the weight loss to his going away. Before her lay a magazine opened at a page displaying curvaceous females in minimal swimwear.

'He's a busy man, he mustn't have found time.'

'So typical, isn't it, Ma? How much time does it take for a man to pick up the phone and say hello?'

'Why should he, Meeta? We were but chance acquaintances.' The sceptical look upon Meeta's face made her avert her face and change the topic. And like a 76-rpm record with its playing needle stuck in a groove, the words 'Let's get married, let's get married, let's get married,' had repeatedly gone on and on and on inside her head. Pulling herself out of its hypnotic hold, she asked totally out of context, 'Shall I cook some *malai kari*?' with a beguiling smile. There was a smile for all reasons, there was a smile for all seasons in her repertoire these days!

And surprisingly, Meeta, veering away from scepticism and curried tiger prawns, inspired by the illustrations in the magazine said, 'You know, Ma,' then she hesitated. Then plucking up courage once again, she added, 'When I went to the beach this time . . .'

'What happened?' encouraged Nandita.

'I wore a bikini.'

'You did?' There was approval rather than censure in that question.

And a smiling Meeta pointed to the open page of the magazine. 'Have a look at these, they cost so much, but need so little cloth to make up.'

'A good business to be in.' And they laughed together. Nandita was surprised to see that her supposed lapses had brought her daughter-in-law much closer to her than she had ever before been. In truth, she was treating her more as a friend than as an elder relative!

Meeta pointed to a set of the skimpiest. 'Mine was nowhere as daring as these are.' And she giggled, recollecting her great adventure.

'I know,' Nandita said with a soft and mischievous smile.

'How could you?' she asked, aghast.

'You had put them out to dry.'

'And you said nothing!' she exclaimed, full of awe.

'I thought everyone should do a little bit of what they want.'

'But your son does not think the same way.' She pouted. 'You should have seen his face.' And attempting to imitate the face her husband had made, she giggled. 'But it was fun!'

'I can imagine the look of disapproval he must have worn,' she said, smiling, and then in more subdued tones, she added, 'Experience has taught me that men don't take kindly to change, particularly when it is in connection with their own womenfolk!'

'But shouldn't men of this modern age be different?'

'What they should be and what they claim to be and what they really are, all quite different, one from the other,' she said, going to the deep freezer and searching for a packet of tiger prawns. 'Ah, here they are.' And she brought out a packet.

'In what way?'

'Men have made the rules that govern society and like to abide by them. They quite often take the useful shield provided to them by the other women in the family group, so that they can continue to maintain the status quo of the equations that have come down to them.'

'Down to them?'

'Through their collective unconscious!'

'Even if it is illogical?'

'But they don't think they are being illogical.' Nandita moved to the microwave and placed the packet to defrost and went on, 'They seem to deem these tenets endowed upon them as immutable legacies that they must retain in as unbesmirched and unchanged a condition as possible.'

'How strange!'

'Tukun's great-great-grandfather, mind you, was a lawyer, and yet he allowed himself to be coerced into marriage by his mother. His upbringing said that he had to obey his mother, and so against his will, he dressed up as a bridegroom and went and got married, and then of course, you know what happened! Tukun's great-grandfather, the patriarch, my Dadu, allowed Thakuma and Mejo Thakuma to wage a war of succession over my head, pretending all the while that he was but a mere bystander. Deep down, he must have believed that he deserved a male heir. And Tukun's grandfather the major general, modern on the surface, allowed his wife's will to prevail.'

'I had no idea you were so angry inside you. I always thought . . .'

'That I was cool and composed. Now that I have thought the whole chain of cause and effect out, I really am cool and composed.' And after a short pause, as if having come to some further assumptions, she went on. 'What the women voiced was but an echo of what the men wanted voiced. But while confronting this so-called will of their women, the men pretended a helplessness that I am not sure, Meeta, was helplessness at all. For the sake of maintaining familial harmony, this charade had been repeated time and again, through an endless string of years, and will continue to be repeated till some cataclysmic occurrence will come about to bring a change.'

'How does that connect with Tukun's grumpy behaviour?'

'Tukun, when he saw you in a bikini, was behaving in much the same way as his male forbears have done through the ages.'

'Only in the matter of my bikini?' she asked, beaming a mischief-filled look her mother-in-law's way.

'I don't know,' Nandita lied with a short laugh. 'And if I don't start on the *malai kari*, you will not get to eat it tonight.' The topic was moving dangerously towards the topic of Bill, and the curried tiger prawns were a useful ploy to change the topic.

And she remembered Bill had asked, 'Who really cares what you do? Who are these people who rule your existence?' *Yes, who were these people she was so afraid of? Or was it something that went way beyond that?*

And out of the blue, Meeta asked, 'Tell me, Ma . . . yes, tell me, who is serving as a front now?' Nandita frowned, not quite sure which way the question was veering.

'As a front?'

'You said women served as a front to men's wish fulfilment. You have not objected to my bikini and I've not objected to your having a friend who is a man. In fact I quite liked the fact that you've had the courage to go ahead and make friends with Dr Brady! So why should I object and become a front?'

Nandita had no answers, and if at all she did, she had no desire to voice them. For a niggling voice inside her was saying that the woman who was serving as a front to Tukun's obtuseness was she herself. 'Enough of this fruitless discussion,' she said as she burrowed into the freezer in search of some coconut milk. 'If this curry is to be eaten tonight, I better get on.' When she emerged from the entrails of the deep freezer, carton in hand, Meeta and her magazine had disappeared from the kitchen. But the thoughts of Bill brought forward by Meeta's questions lingered on with her.

Late that night, as she was undressing for bed, she remembered that memorable luncheon date she had had with Bill when he had not asked, but stated that they get married. She had refused just as precipitately, giving myriad reasons, and she once again remembered Bill had asked, 'Who really cares what you do? Who are these people who rule your existence?' Yes, who were these people she was so afraid of? Or was it something that went way beyond that?

Throwing the clothes she had just taken off into the laundry basket, she stretched out to reach the nightdress hanging on a hook beside the door. The full-length mirror reflected and placed her entire naked form before her. She had seen her own unclothed form over and over, time and again, yet today, with her thoughts linked as they were to Bill and his proposal of marriage, she turned her eyes away. But with so many confusing, contradictory thoughts regarding her body and her bodily needs coursing through her brain, she was compelled to stand awhile before the mirror and take a closer look at herself once again. The austere and regimented lifestyle coupled with the amount she walked each day had left her with a body that had been barely touched by time. It was as if she was discovering her own body for the first time in her life.

She did not know if it was beautiful, but it certainly was not repelling! Since she had grown into young girlhood, no eyes apart from her own had seen her unclothed. And then Prodipto, drifting upon a kite, had landed himself into her life.

And it was in his expert hands that she had learnt that a body was beautiful and a source of joy and wonder, an instrument upon which a tune of love could be invented, reinvented, and played in variegated cadences over and over again! And with his death, her body had returned to her and gone into her sole care.

In truth, it was earlier than that when she had last been with him. He had written, *Stop being such a perfect daughter-in-law, disobey them and bundle up that little bundle and come home to me. Come back to me, I need you desperately.* And then petulantly he had added: *Tell me, don't you need me?*

And she had replied: *How can I displease them and come away, tell me? Both Mummy and Daddy feel that we'll not be able to manage little Tukun.*

And to that he had replied, *I promise to wipe his bottom and change his nappies, and prepare his feeds and stay awake at night. I am willing to go bleary-eyed to work, but I can't live without you. Don't you know that it is more than three months since I held you in my arms?* And then he had asked, *Don't you understand what kind of agony it is for me to be alone?*

That was the last letter she had received from him. He had asked her to come but she had not gone. As was her wont, she was not there where she had been needed the most. And before she knew what was happening, he had gone away forever. And he had bequeathed the agony of not being held in a loving embrace, of living on alone, to her, for the rest of her life!

Since those distant far-off days in the past, no eyes other than her own had ever fallen upon this body of hers. And Bill had asked her to marry him!

The month of August had slowly but surely percolated away and the month of September had come in with its occasional gusts of cool breeze and its ever more misty mornings. And life had gone on almost just as it had been before. Nandita could see that the neighbourhood cat was getting all fat and sleek all over again. The kittens were no longer to be seen trotting along behind her. Seeing her alone, with a touch of melancholy tingeing her heart, Nandita had wondered whether they had been given away.

She visited the Home on all her assigned days. And at the end of each visit, she would steal away downtown, as if to meet the pigeons who always flocked there in search of tasty titbits! Where once she had shared endless al fresco meals with Bill, she now handed out fistfuls of wholesome treats to the birds milling around, but each day as she fed the ever-hungry host of birds, her eyes would go darting around as if in search of something or someone. Having come to the end of the exercise of feeding the pigeons, she would give one last look around, then with a shrug of resignation would rise and slowly begin to walk back home. The exercise was repeated with regular monotony each day. And then one day, on the verge of giving up hope, she came upon the single ray of hope that she had been in search of! How many pigeons had she fed in the hope of sighting this one man?

On the verge of dipping her hand into the bag of corn, she looked up, and her hand was stayed and her eyes lit up as they had fallen upon the tubby figure of a man she had met but a couple of times. Today, the none-too-alluring figure of Professor Mike Cheyney, colleague and compatriot to Bill Bradley, looked a picture of perfection to her eyes! Gathering together the open mouth of the satchel and snatching up her handbag, Nandita moved swiftly in the direction where she had seen him; she just could not let him go out of sight! But before she could reach the portly figure, she saw him get swallowed up by the shining glass portals of the bank that lay just ahead of her. Finding herself a bench facing the entrance to the imposing edifice, she sat down to wait for his return. But the reason she gave herself for making the sudden move was the lack of sunshine at the other end of the quadrangle. 'It's nice to be in the sun,' she told herself as her back began to prickle under the onslaught of its penetrating rays.

That Mike Cheyney, a man whom she had been so hard-pressed to even recollect, could bring about such a strange transformation in the persona of Nandita was impossible to believe. But then, stranger things are known to have happened to humankind!

Somewhat later when the professor (who, according to Nandita, did not at all look professor-like) emerged from the bank, he was both pleased and surprised to find Bill's friend Nan seated right in front of him. So preoccupied was she in feeding the pigeons that she appeared not to have seen him. He was wondering whether to disturb her or not and had taken a tentative step forward to move away when as if by chance, she looked up. As a matter of fact, she looked up and smiled at him. He was rather pleased that she had recognised him, and smiled back warmly at her and walked up.

'Hello, Mrs Roy, how're you doing?'

She had risen and they shook hands. 'I'm fine. I hope all's well with you.'

'Not bad. Somewhat busier than usual, that's all.'

'Don't push yourself too hard.'

'It's Bill who does the pushing. Heard from him?'

'You just said, didn't you, that he's very busy.' The answer was evasive and the smile as non-committal as it possibly could be. There was a smile for all reasons, there was a smile for all seasons in her repertoire these days!

'I don't know what's troubling him. But he's working much too hard. So hard that he hardly finds time to go out and eat. When I was last with him, he was making do with a slab of chocolate.' Nandita paled on hearing these words. 'I asked him why, and he said something about its being high in calories and low in volume. It had sounded funny enough but . . .' After a very minuscule pause, he capped it with 'In fact it's getting to be pretty hard for a mere mortal like me to keep pace with him.' And making a funny face, he looked down at his watch. 'I didn't realise it was this late; I must rush.' Rising, he said, 'I'll be with Bill this evening, any message for him?'

'Just tell him please,' she fell quiet for a moment, 'to take care.'

'I sure will. See you.' And he was gone.

She had sat on, head down, as a horde of thwarted pigeons milled around expectantly at her feet. She was none too happy to hear that Bill was working harder than he ought to and that he had gone back to snacking on chocolates. Why was he being so foolish, she wondered, anxiety taking hold of her and pervading her brain. What was he trying to do, ruin his health? Did he not remember what had happened to him when he had driven himself to a near breakdown? How she wished that he was close at hand so that she could din some sense into him. But he was in New York and she in Saisborough. But it was not just a matter of location, she knew, for how do you speak to a man who has shown no desire to keep in touch with you? Otherwise she could have picked up a telephone and spoken to him, could she not have? She knew his address, but how could she write to him when he did not wish to hear from her?

Along the path of life's long journey, she had, somewhere along the way, taken yet another turn and come back full circle to a familiar and well-known spot, a site where she stood hovering unnoticed upon the periphery of other people's preoccupations. She had been born by circumstances into that niche and would die in that selfsame slot one day, she knew. She stood at her bedroom window and looked out upon the deserted yard. The days were getting shorter and shorter, and with the advent of fall, the skies were getting darker each day. The trees, barely visible, stood silhouetted like a blur against the fast-fading light of the day that was on its way out. There was a hankering in her soul that she could not account for; the sad and despondent colour that lay outside the window matched perfectly with the hue that had spread, like a bottle of spilt ink, through her heart and soul. And even so, on the surface she smiled on!

She was never alone, nor was the house ever empty, for as always, no sooner than everyone had left, that all-too-familiar swath of all-enveloping silence that had been on leave for a while had moved in and filled every nook and cranny with its well-known, ever-present presence. She and the silences within and without her had started taking over her life once again.

Tukun and Meeta had left for work and the children had left for school. The all-pervading silence was getting to her; she had walked across the length of the family room and switched on the TV set and news had spewed out. Inconsequential happenings dressed up to look important were being aired as important events. Tukun must have been the last to have watched a programme. He was the one who watched news all the time! A cup of coffee in hand, she slumped into a chair and absent-mindedly allowed the news to pour out and cover up the silence spread out like a rug around her. Her eyes were not on the screen nor were her ears bent upon the words that emanated from the TV set, when a sudden change of tempo in the delivery of the news had fallen upon her ears. She had heard something about breaking news and then something about a plane crashing somewhere! Her heart missed a beat, fluttered around, and brought itself back upon its feet again!

Human beings being the selfish creatures they are—any disaster that can touch their own lives fills their hearts with dread and immediately holds them spellbound. Like hunted animals caught in the beam of some headlight, they are mesmerised and riveted to the news that dwells upon such happenings. And Nandita was no different from the majority of the human race. A boat capsizing with five hundred human beings upon some turbulent river in Bangladesh merits but a moment's attention from the inattentive people of this world, because both that boat and Bangladesh are so far away from the reality of their own existence. A cyclone that hits the Orissa and Andhra Pradesh coasts and wipes out entire villages causes a frown to crease across a brow perhaps. An earthquake that devastates Gujrat does send a quiver of fear to course through the selfsame hearts, because an earthquake has this bad habit of visiting people and places unannounced and, who knows, could come home one day! But a plane crash is something else altogether. There is a whole slab of humanity for whom flying has become as natural as walking. If you don't have legs, how do you walk? If you don't ride planes, how do you get anywhere?

Setting the empty coffee cup upon a table, Nandita turned her full attention towards the television screen. A clip from a movie was showing there. A plane, a high-pitched voice was saying, had crashed into the building. And what she saw before her was the most prestigious of all buildings in the United States, standing there, apparently billowing smoke. The sight of the devastation was too awful to behold! Thank God it was only a movie!

A niggling doubt crossed her mind. *Was this real? This can't be real, no, this can't be real; this must be from a movie as I had immediately thought,* she reassured herself. And then angrily she asked herself, *Why do they make movies like these? It could give all sorts of wrong ideas to the imbalanced and the immature.* She thought on, and then a second plane came shooting out as if from nowhere and crashed into the second tower rising into the sky. There was fire and smoke, still more fire and smoke, and human beings no larger than tiny puppets were hurling themselves to their doom out of windows. With their penchant for drama, the newscaster was making it all sound like it was a slice of reality. Was viewership rating so important that they had to do that?

Unable to take her eyes off the screen, she sat on, for how long she did not know. And then before her very eyes, the towers began to come down like a loosely but laboriously put-up house of cards. It was only then that the near-hysterical voice of the newsreader managed to penetrate her senses and make her look upon what she was viewing. This was for real; how terribly, terribly horrible it was that, that which was being unfolded before her very eyes, was for real!

Both her hands had flown up to cover her mouth, from where a scream was all set to emanate. Fear stalked her heart as she realised that this was fact, not fiction, that was unfolding right there upon that little screen. What was right there before her eyes was happening just this moment in New York, in

Manhattan, to the World Trade Center and its famous sky-searching twin towers. One plane you could believe had flown accidentally into a tower, but two in a row was not credible. And then images of a battered and bruised Pentagon flashed on and off the lit-up screen before her. Was this an invasion? Was this the beginning of World War III? Was this the beginning of the end of this civilisation that had been built up with so much of care and cruelty over the last several centuries?

And then from her macro anxieties about the continuing existence of this world, her brain crashed gears and came plummeting down to a micro but very pertinent reality. Bill lived in New York, in truth in Manhattan, how was he? Her concern for the future state of the world, her concern for the future of the United States, her concern for the city of New York, her concern for the millions who inhabited that city became distilled and became a pinpoint that was centred into her concern for a single individual who was called Dr William Brady.

That morning, Bill Brady rose later than he normally did. He had not slept any too well. He should have already been on his way to work, but then he had worked well beyond midnight the previous evening. Mike, who was with him, had pointed out that the world had no intentions whatsoever of coming to a screeching halt if this research paper of theirs did not see the light of day immediately. But who was listening? Certainly not he! When Mike had repeated himself, he had shut down work but had said nothing, but the expression in his eyes had been thoughtful as he had let Cheyney out.

He would take it easy today; the hamburger he had eaten somewhere towards midnight was sitting like a stone in his stomach. The afternoon meal of a slab of chocolate washed down by a polystyrene cup of scalding hot coffee helped, along with the build-up of this Rock of Gibraltar that was now playing merry hell with his innards. He went to the bathroom, opened the medicine cabinet, searched around, and found some Alka-Seltzers. He grimaced as he had felt a bubble of gas rise and then go careering painfully around in his abdomen. Shaking out a few Alkas, he dunked them in a glass of tepid water and gulped down the fizzy content in one long breath. And then burping loudly, he went and stood at the window of his thirty-fifth-floor apartment.

Meg had dared, and he had reluctantly gone along with her; otherwise, he could not possibly have been sitting on such a prime piece of property as this. It was no bigger than a postage stamp; even so, paying off the mortgage had been a long and painful haul. But the view was spectacular and worth every bit of the hardship they had endured along the way. Right before his eyes, the East River arced like a ribbon of silver by the Brooklyn and Williamsburg bridges, and the twin towers stood proudly to the right, the Hudson like a backdrop behind them. The traffic down below looked like a lazy noiseless serpent crawling along on its belly. He looked up from the street down below and looked up and to his right, towards the reassuring twin presence of the towers that dominated the city.

And then he saw an aeroplane come out as if from nowhere and head towards one of the towers. Leaning out of the window, flailing his arms irrationally, he began to scream at whoever was piloting the plane, 'Watch out! Watch out! What are you doing, where are you going? Dammit, veer, veer or you'll—' And the aircraft had hit the tower. 'Oh my God! The pilot has had a heart attack. This couldn't have happened otherwise.' He looked down at the watch strapped onto his wrist and grimaced. 'A lot of people must already be in there,' he agonised.

He wanted to move into the room, to go and change, to see what he could do, but he stood mesmerised on the spot, unable to move. He had no idea for how long he stood there, watching the horrific sight of destruction that lay just ahead of him. The measurement of time by a watch rendered meaningless for the moment, he looked upon the heartbreaking sight of a mauled World Trade Center billowing smoke! And then he saw something that looked like a smudge on the horizon that grew bigger in a moment and became identifiable as an aeroplane. This plane was also zeroing in on the already mutilated edifice. And his unbelieving eyes saw the second tower also being hit.

What was going on? What was happening? 'This is a body blow on the pride and prestige of the United States. Who has done this, and why?' he asked, anger surging through him, as he grabbed up some clothes and rushed towards the bathroom. Splashing some water onto his face, he the guru of centralisation and compacting remembered Grandma Brady telling a clutch of her grandchildren that they should never put all their eggs in one basket: 'What if something happens to that basket? What if it slips out of your hands?' she had asked with a gentle smile of enquiry. 'We should have listened to the wisdom of our elders. We have gone and put too many eggs into that one basket that has just gone up in smoke.' Passing a comb through his thinning hair, he fretted, 'Oh my God, why did we not think of that before?' Because what he was seeing before him was not the mere bringing down of a building, but the economic strength of the United States of America being challenged! When he emerged dressed, the telephone was ringing. He scooped it up and, out of sheer practice, mouthed, 'Brady speaking.' He had met with silence. 'Hello, hello, hello.' And he heard a telephone on the other end being put down. The connection had been cut and then there was the burr of the dial tone!

Nandita sagged with relief on hearing Bill's voice. As of now, he was safe! She had wanted to speak to him, but a wayward, disobedient hand had let her down. It had gone and put the telephone back on its cradle. Sometime later when she dialled his number again, she was not able to reconnect. A lifeless line lay between them now!

And then the telephone started ringing: Meeta, somewhat breathless, somewhat hysterical, her words chasing one another and tripping over the tail of the last one, sounding both excited and scared, wanted her 'to take care'. Take care of what? Nandita had wanted to ask. She rang off abruptly, saying she was off to the children's school. And then immediately after, Tukun called to ask if Nandita knew what was happening in America. That she had been sitting right in front of the television set and had, from the very beginning, seen what was happening out there in New York and Washington seemed to come as somewhat of a surprise to him. He was in a discursive mood; the upheaval of the moment seemed to have jarred him back to a notch above normalcy. Normally given to very few words, he seemed unable to get off the line today. The constraint that had lain between them for the last so-many weeks seemed to have vanished without leaving a trace upon his tongue. It was as if he wanted to feel the security of his mother's womb once again today.

Though he was not apparently showing it, there was an undertone of concern and anxiety in his voice. When examined more closely, his runaway tongue revealed an undercurrent of fear. 'Don't worry, Ma,' he inserted after almost each sentence he spoke; evidently he was asking her not to worry because he himself was a very worried man. The sense of security that this country of his adoption had given him seemed all of sudden to have been taken away from him.

He sounded somewhat like Linus would sound if his security blanket were to be suddenly yanked away from him!

Rekha was on the line soon after. 'Oh, Nandita*di*,' she wailed, 'I am so frightened, my Arnab goes to the World Trade Center so often, what if he had gone there this morning?'

'Just thank God that he was not there,' Nandita soothed.

'I will tell that son of mine that we should go back to Calcutta. Tell me, how much do we need for the four of us to live on?'

'It is not so easy to move back,' Nandita said introspectively, as much to Rekha as to her own self.

'Why don't you visit us, please?' The little girl Rekha had re-emerged in that tremulous voice today. She was reaching out to grasp a finger that she could hold on to as she walked on the terrain of uncertainty that her environment had suddenly become.

As if considering the possibility, Nandita replied, 'Maybe I will,' after a very short pause.

And, 'Please do come,' Rekha pleaded once again, just before ringing off.

And through the length of the day, the calls kept pouring in. But Bill had not called! Some had called to convey their joy at the near misses their near and dear ones had had, while others none too sure of the fate of their friends and relatives sounded a note of alarm. The Indian diaspora was buzzing with concern and anxiety. So many upwardly mobile persons of Indian origin worked in and around what had been that upward-surging, skyscraping building!

The days that followed were harrowing in their unmitigated sameness. There was a dirge in the air. And the felled building smouldered on! It appeared as if each home had lost a favourite relative, and in truth many, rather too many, had. A nation that had kept itself at arm's length from marauding invaders, a nation that had carefully fought its wars away from its own soil had suddenly come face to face with the trauma of being on the receiving end of an invasion. And yet, there was no invader in sight that one could lash out upon to assuage a nation's feelings of injury and insult. Totally unprepared for such an assault, it found itself hard-pressed to cope with that which had so suddenly come to pass.

It was truly shocking that such a cataclysmic event had come to pass and not a whisper of its advent had been found floating in the air: no sense of impending doom, no premonition of a lurking peril had touched the hearts of the millions who lived and worked there! Had a tremor of apprehension coursed through Nandita's heart as Flight Lieutenant Prodipto Kumar Roy had ridden headlong into the rear of a stationary truck to his death? But then, when does one ever get a warning of occurrences that bring about startling changes in one's personal life, or even that which comes about in the life of a nation? Would life in the United States ever be exactly the same again?

When a thief enters your home in stealth and leaves after ravishing it, then that home ceases to be the safe harbour it had been for you till then. Some constraints creep in where earlier there had been none. You look behind doors as you enter a room; you yank aside curtains to see that no one is hiding there. Your very own shadow begins to frighten you! That which had come to pass in New York and in Washington held similar undertones, for it had left an entire nation holding on to a feeling of having been violated. Was this how a victim of rape felt?

The recurring images of the wounded duo of buildings upon the television screen reminded Nandita of an early springtime evening when standing at the window of her bedroom, she had looked down upon the pristine beauty of their snow-clad yard. In the quiet of the night, a short and unannounced visit of a sudden squall had mauled the unblemished beauty of the picture-postcard-perfect terrain and left it lacerated. And on waking, she had found an unkempt and bedraggled garden lying before her eyes. No prior intimation of the dramatic changes so soon to be wrought had been sensed or had been felt by her as she had gazed out upon the moon-draped yard the night before. Her heart, she remembered, had been deluged by a sense of melancholy at the sight of that ravaged yard. Melancholy was the companion of loneliness. And all that was negative had flooded in and taken over all the lonely spaces within her heart. Steeped in pessimism, she had been unable to see a single ray of light or hope ahead of her. But those were the days before she had to pick up the broken pieces of her life and put them back together again!

And today, looking upon the images of the destruction that had been so swiftly wrought, that melancholic strain had come upon her again, and inexplicably this sense of melancholia had been further overlaid by an aching sense of sorrow, a sense of personal grief, a sense of personal bereavement as she had looked on. How she wished Bill had not gone away. But Bill had gone away and had not even called! Even so, though her heart was replete with sorrow, she had not allowed pessimism to take over her heart and rule it, for there were those who needed her. After one whole day of being chained to the TV, she took herself in hand and set out for the Home. How distraught must be those elderly people? How many hearts would be in need of unburdening their anxieties and concerns into her ears, how many letters would need to be written, how many telephone calls placed? She admonished herself, as she pulled the door shut and set off for her destination.

The roads were almost empty today, the rose garden devoid of a soul! And not a single person was in sight as she reached the outer gates of the Home. She entered and found that the foyer too was empty, though it was the mid-morning coffee hour. It was as if every one had removed themselves and life had been put on hold. And then she heard the reassuring sound of the raised voice of the large television set that sat squat and square in the lobby that came off the main foyer. She entered and stood quietly watching; a bank of grim faces was looking intently upon the grim images that were flashing on and off upon the face of the TV set.

'Some coffee?' she asked, and the spell was broken. Bleary-eyed, a number of faces turned towards her.

'Come here, my child,' Grace beckoned, her voice gone tremulous. She appeared to have further aged overnight. 'See what they've done.'

She comforted Grace as best as she could, and then moved on comforting, soothing with a word here, a touch there as she went along. The good schoolmaster David Whitfield, looking thoughtful, was sitting quietly to one side. Going up to him, Nandita asked, 'How are you, David?'

'I'm all right, I suppose; but what of the world, Nan?'

'Why do you think this happened,' asked someone, 'have we been riding roughshod or what?'

'What rubbish!' Helen, at her protective best, exclaimed. 'What harm could this beautiful, peace-loving country of ours ever have done that such a thought should have even crossed anyone's mind?'

David, clearing his throat in a manner which only schoolmasters can do, looked around. Helen had fallen quiet, and the rest of the class had received the signal as well, and he had their attention for the moment at least. 'It's possible we have. I had a cousin who was quite a puny lad in comparison to the rest of us when we were all growing up.'

'What does your cousin have to do with what happened yesterday?' the Colonel, at his caustic best, wanted to know.

'Nothing, I'm just using him as an illustration, that's all. Will you please pour me another cup, Nan?' And clearing his throat, he went on, 'So as I was saying, there he was, a little fellow one day, and next when we looked around, we found that he had suddenly shot up and gone way beyond all of us. He had taken to playing football and his shoulders had become broad, and his arms had become really strong.'

'It happens all the time,' added the normally laconic Ted, 'these transformations from tiny tykes to lumbering giants . . .'

David continued as if no interruption had taken place, 'He was a good-natured lad, but as he had grown so suddenly, he really had no idea of his strength. Sometimes a friendly nudge from him could send one of us less-endowed guys sprawling, and to . . .'

'I guess I know what you are getting at. My mama used to say, "Take care not to step on any toes, Nathaniel, who knows who will retaliate by treading on your corns?"' Ah, so the Colonel does have a name, thought Nandita as the words flew fast and fierce around her. And the veteran soldier continued, 'What are you hinting at, David, that we have grown so fast as a nation that we ourselves don't know our strength?'

'I think, like my cousin, we as a nation have not realised how fast we have grown, and how a little nudge from us can hurt. And advertently or inadvertently, knowingly or unknowingly, it's possible that we have hurt a whole lot of people along the way.'

'Tell me haven't we helped many as well?' Kate wanted to know.

'Who remembers when you stretched out a hand to give help, Katie, but a push by the same hand, everyone does.' And many heads nodded in acceptance of this very major truth related to human behaviour that had been placed before them by their friend the schoolmaster.

'But, David—' the Colonel had begun when he was cut off.

Tiring of all the ifs and buts of the hypothetical discussion raging between the soldier and the tutor, Grace pointedly changed the topic and asked, 'Heard from Bill, Nan? Isn't he in New York?'

To that, the Colonel, wheeling up closer, said, 'Bill called this morning, wanted to know how we were all doing. Wanted to know how you were doing, Nan.' And then looking directly at her, 'Said he called your home several times, but the line was always busy.'

'I'll call him tonight,' she lied. These were not happy days; even so, a surge of something akin to happiness had coursed through her heart. Bill had called and had asked how she was doing.

'He said he'd have come, but there are no flights going in or coming out from New York so . . .' And the Colonel lapsed into silence.

But Nandita knew that he would not come. He had told the Colonel he had called, but in truth had he really?

The days following the 11th of September went by in a painful blur for an entire nation. Like a bird with injured wings, grounded by circumstances, the people of America floundered around, wondering whether they would ever be able to take to their wings again! And when they had opened their eyes to look around and had tentatively tested their injured wings, had found that armed to the teeth in search of a culprit, the powers that be had rushed them off to Afghanistan in search of retribution.

Nandita had dialled Bill's number on two occasions and each time it was the answering machine that had spoken to her. Irrationally she had held it against him that it was not he but his recorded voice that was there at the other end. He should have been there to receive her call, where was he? She had fretted and had left no message and called off.

The month of October had slipped away in a blaze of colour. And it was in the month of November when she had given up all hopes of ever hearing from Bill that she received a letter from him.

Dear Nan, Bill had begun, *letters have gone out of fashion these days, even so I thought I'd try my hand at writing one. I've tried to call you on several occasions, but it was not destined that we speak, for whenever I tried to get through to you I found the line busy.*

And I, Nandita thought, *always got through but to your answering machine.*

And then he had rationalised. *Not surprising considering these are worrisome times.*

Yes, these are terrible times, she thought, as she read on.

Finding the world on the very brink of engineering its annihilation, I thought I should write and apologise to you for my boorish behaviour. What gave me the right to think that just because I'd asked you to marry me, you would have to say yes? I really and truly am sorry that I have behaved as I have done.

Nandita felt tears prickle behind her eyes.

I was at my window when the entire episode of the Twin Towers being hit came to pass. Since then the view from my window and my view upon life has changed forever. I wonder at times what the Statue of Liberty thinks of the skyline now. Does she also feel as downcast as I do? All the theorising upon compacting and centralisation that I did with so much certitude pervades my sensibility with a great big question mark today!

Nandita raised her eyes from the letter and gazed out of the living room window and out onto the road thinking, *I did not have a grandstand view as you had, Bill, but by some quirk of fate, I was seated right before a television set tuned on to a news channel, and so I was almost there standing beside you that day!* It was getting to be gusty, she could see, for a hoard of fallen leaves robbed of all will or volition was being driven along willy-nilly upon the surface of the sidewalk. Why did Bill sound so sad, she asked of herself as she turned her attention back to the letter in hand.

As you look upon the Coliseum, you can still imagine the place resounding with the roars of the lions, the grunts of the gladiators, and the hysterical screams of the spectators. The Great Wall of China meanders on, still etching a clear demarcating line, the pyramids still straddle the sandy stretches of the deserts of Egypt. The paintings in the caves at Ajanta in your own country are still there to be seen. We built ourselves a monument just the other day, and it has already fallen by the way. It is a very humbling feeling that I have today.

I think one should not put off doing all those things one wants to do, because it's quite possible that there may not be too many tomorrows left with this world of ours. Who knows when, where or at which turn, or by whom a nuclear holocaust may be set in motion. And then there will be no looking back. I for one intend clearing the decks in case that comes to pass. I want no concrete blocks weighing down upon my chest when I go up to meet my maker. I surprised both my children by writing and telling them how much I loved them. They promptly called to ask if I was sick. So much for my noble intentions! Both of them though, asked me to join them for Thanksgiving as well. It is incredible, but surprisingly Thanksgiving is round the corner, and I hadn't even realised.

Raising her eyes from the letter, Nandita thought, nor had I. Or not consciously at least: I know that Tukun and Meeta are going to Canada to visit her parents next week. But that it was in the Thanksgiving break had not come to my mind.

Lowering her eyes, she read on. *I have told them I am feeling too lazy to accept their invitations. I can only go to one of them; so to keep peace in the family, I intend staying put exactly where I am.*

He really is a kind and considerate father, mused Nandita, as her eyes moved further down the letter. *And now coming to the unsettled account between us, won't you please accept my apology and let me off the hook from which I find myself suspended?* That sounds more like Bill; let him off the hook indeed! Having enquired after her son and his family and about the residents of the Home, he had brought his letter to a close and scrawled 'Bill' in a lazy hand, across the bottom.

But there was more to the letter, for evidently he had had an afterthought. Going down a few spaces, he had placed a P and an S, and just below that had written: *In case the offer of friendship you had made that day is still open, I would like to have a slice of that, please. Love, Bill.*

And Nandita, clinging to that letter, with a smile upon her lips, sat on till hunger pangs managed to pry her away from its magical hold.

Late that night, she had a serious chat with her Dipto.

'He wants me to be his friend, Dipto,' she informed his photograph shyly. 'But you know how Tukun reacts at the very hint of this friendship. And all those people back in Kolkata and Rekha in New Jersey and Meeta's parents in Canada, and even Tukun and Meeta's friends. The list is endless. I can well imagine how they will react when they know that Bill is a very special friend of mine. It was different when I met him in downtown Saisborough. That is, of course, while no one knew about it.' And the snapshot of Flight Lieutenant Prodipto Kumar Roy caught by a camera lens, squinting into the sunshine, smiled on. 'I think I had better back out; what do you say?'

And then out of the recesses of her memory, she heard him ask, 'Why did she not rebel, Nondu?' This was in response to when she herself had complained one day about the life her Boroma had been made to lead because of the widowhood that had been forced upon her.

'How could she?' she had asked of him, reminding him that the rules had been laid down by men, and all in the favour of men, and that Boroma, a woman, would have to abide by them or face total social ostracism.

Suddenly becoming uncharacteristically serious, he had advised, 'Maybe *she* could not rebel but *you*, Nondu, can. If you want something, even if it is change, you will have to go after it yourself. No one will give you any space, no, not a single inch, without your fighting for it all the way.' She wondered why she had chosen to fight back at society by further reinforcing its unfair tenets! 'If one day the occasion does arise for you to stand up to the unjust laws of society, *please do put up a fight*,' he had pleaded. But she had not abided by his wishes.

'I wish I had listened to you, Dipto,' she told the silent, smiling photograph of her husband. 'I think I have put it off till too late in my life to start a revolution.' And he had still not broken his silence and had continued to smile back upon her! 'And in truth, I don't think I want Bill as a friend.'

They were leaving for Vancouver when she told them, 'I think I'll go and see Rekha.'

'I wish you'd told me earlier. What about tickets and things?' Tukun asked.

'Don't worry, I'll manage. You have a key to the house, don't you?'

'Go and meet your friend, Ma,' Meeta spoke up from behind. 'I have a key right here with me.'

'Sure you'll be able to manage.'

'Don't worry, I'll take care.'

The flight, thank God, was uneventful; taking to the air was no longer the matter-of-fact, run-of-the-mill affair it used to be! She had thought of calling up Rekha from the airport, had changed her mind, and had taken a cab. Handing the cab driver an address, she asked, 'Could you please take me to this place?'

'Sure.' And he took off.

Clutching the small suitcase she had brought along with her, tucking her handbag safely under her arm, she walked up to the entrance of the building where she had had herself dropped off. The elevator was right there as if waiting for her. She chose the floor indicated in the address and rode up.

Arriving at the door of the apartment, she stood a moment and collected her wits together. Feeling gauche and timorous, heart pounding against her ribcage, she put her finger down upon the doorbell, withdrew it, and then taking courage into her hands, pressed down upon it in a short and shaky spurt.

The door was thrown open almost immediately. And right before her stood Bill, dishcloth in hand. How wonderful it felt to look upon his face again! The look of surprise upon his face brought a nervous smile onto her lips. In a voice filled with wonder, he just said, 'Nan,' and a smile filled with joy spread across his face. She had not felt so safe and so good and so coveted for aeons as she did looking upon that joyous expression upon his face.

Realising that she was still hovering on his threshold, 'Come in,' he said, picking up her bag and taking her with his other hand, ushered her in, forgetting to shut the door. And the first thing that she saw was the Van Gogh print in all its splendid colours sitting centrally upon the far wall.

She wanted to say something to show him how touched she was that he had given her little gift such a position of importance in his home. But all words having dried up, she remained silent.

'What a totally unexpected delight this is, my darling Nan,' he said, as he gathered her up and held her close to him, and she, breaking all the boundaries placed around her by her upbringing, reached up and kissed him.

'So you have come,' he said, as if unable to believe that she was in truth right before him in his very own apartment.

'I had to. Didn't I? You wrote to say that all unfinished tasks must be taken care of.'

'Which unfinished task have you come to complete?' he asked, a trifle mischievously.

'I came to tell you that my offer of friendship is no longer open. So you can't have a slice of that.'

'That sounds grim.'

'But I have come to cook a Thanksgiving meal for you: turkey with a cranberry sauce, pumpkin pie, and all.'

'But you don't eat turkey.'

'But you do.'

'Will you stay a while?'

'I might,' she said and smiled a smile that spread out like a warming ray of sunshine on a biting cold early springtime day. There was a smile for all reasons, there was a smile for all seasons in her repertoire these days!

'Please do,' he said as he shut the forgotten door and embraced her again.

The End

Jharna Banerji